"*The Keeper*'s a smart, brand-new take on the haunted house story and it's a dilly—crammed with startling images and framed by a sense of overwhelming dread. It's really hard to believe this is a first novel. In vivid, compelling prose, which runs from the wry to the lyrical, Langan here gives us nothing less than a sharply realized portrait of an American town in the death throes of decay. Susan Marley is a subtle juggernaut of a character—and she inhabits the mind once you've finished like a dark, lingering smoke."

Jack Ketchum, author of *Offspring*

"*The Keeper* is a brilliant debut, heralding the arrival of a major talent. This disturbing, spooky novel is written by someone who knows about dread, and imagery, and fear, and who knows that a good ghost story needs soul."

Tim Lebbon, author of *Dusk* and *Berserk*

"Deft and disturbing, *The Keeper* twists expectations into surreal surprises. Sarah Langan's tale of haunted lives and landscapes is hypnotic reading—an assured and impressive debut."

Douglas E. Winter, author of *Run*

"A dark and bracingly bleak tale of supernatural terror. Its brooding atmosphere comes as much from the social and psychological as from the ghostly, and best of all, from the quality of the prose."

Ramsey Campbell, author of *Secret Story*

THE KEEPER

SARAH LANGAN

HarperTorch
An Imprint of HarperCollins*Publishers*

HARPERTORCH
An Imprint of HarperCollins*Publishers*
10 East 53rd Street
New York, New York 10022-5299

Copyright © 2006 by Sarah Langan
ISBN-13: 978-0-06-087290-8
ISBN-10: 0-06-087290-X

First HarperTorch paperback printing: September 2006
First HarperTorch special printing: April 2006

HarperCollins®, HarperTorch™, and ❦™ are trademarks of Harper-Collins Publishers Inc.

Printed in the United States of America

Visit HarperTorch on the World Wide Web at
www.harpercollins.com

10 9 8 7 6 5 4 3 2 1

For Carole, Chris, Michael, and Peter

Acknowledgments

More people than I can thank here offered their support in the creation of this book. I'm indebted to my tireless film agent, Sarah Self, for getting the ball rolling and keeping it that way; to my wise literary agent, Joe Veltre; and to my smart editor, Sarah Durand. A better bunch I couldn't wish for.

Thanks also to my writing group (Dan Braum, Nick Kaufmann, PZ Perry, Stefan Petrucha, and Lee Thomas); the poor suckers/good sports who read *Keeper* in its various stages of undress (Dallas Mayr, Peter Straub, Maribeth Batcha, Cathleen Bell, Meg Giles, Rob Sutter); the folks at Chizine, especially Trish Macomber and Brett Savory; the HWA; Nick Mamatas; and Susan Kenney, Richard Russo, and Debra Spark at Colby College.

Finally, for their general good-eggedness, lots of thanks to JT Petty, who makes things better; Tim Carroll; Milda Devoe; Jon Evans; Michelle and Erik Gustavson; Marybeth Magee; Maura Maloney; Debbie Marcus; Laura Masterson; Margaret McDermott; Marianna McGillicuddy; Lori and Ryan Stattenfield; and the Langan and Henrich clans, particularly Mom and Dad, who never winced, even though they wanted to.

The darkness of this house has got the best of us,
There's a darkness in this town that's got us too

—"Independence Day,"
BRUCE SPRINGSTEEN,
from *The River,* 1980

THE KEEPER

PROLOGUE

SUSAN

They knew Susan Marley. They saw her climbing to the top of Iroquois Hill at dawn, or dipping a stick tied with string into the polluted Messalonski River, waiting for fish that would never come. She was seen knocking on store windows after "Open" signs had been flipped to "Closed," and at the Clott Paper Mill in the dark twilight hours, where shifts of men had once departed into the night. She was even seen standing on the front stoop of her childhood home, her hand suspended over the bell, as if waiting for someone to open the door.

She was a beautiful woman in the most classical sense of the word; curly blond hair; blue eyes; a small, childlike body; and delicate features. So impossible to attain, it was not the kind of beauty that inspired envy. It was also not the kind of beauty that appealed. She was too empty to allure, too fragile to touch. Perhaps this was what made them especially aware of her, so that when they felt her presence on the street or outside their homes, they stopped for a moment and held their breaths like children passing through a graveyard.

By the time she was nineteen, Susan Marley stopped speaking. She did not thank the cashier at Puff-N-Stop when she bought her weekly supply of Marlboro Reds and Campbell's Tomato Soup. She did not offer the sign of peace to her neighbors when she sat in the last pew of Sunday morning services at the Catholic Church of Our Lady of Sorrow. She did not even wave hello when old family friends driving by in Chevys and Subarus honked their horns in greeting.

They discussed this silence over family dinners, and in the vestibule of the town hall after monthly meetings had ended. From her grammar school teachers and family friends, they gleaned the fragments of her sad history, and attempted in vain to decipher a language. They made a map of the houses she passed during her late-night walks, trying to divine a pattern, only to discover that she walked a wide circle around the town that closed smaller and smaller within itself.

They heard that she frequented Montie's Bar in the afternoons, drinking vodka gimlets like water. She often shared her bed with the men she met there; country men, lost tourists, and—God help us—Bedford boys thinking they'd discovered the world. The women near her apartment kept an eye on who came and went, and only rarely did rumors surface about married Dennis Murdock, sweet Jonathan Bagley, or drunken Paul Martin sneaking with hunched shoulders out the back door and walking to cars they'd parked a block away.

For a while, she was all they talked about. "Did you see Susan Marley last night?" they asked each other over the phone, or at Montie's Bar, or in the Shaws Supermarket. "I saw her lying on her back in the cemetery with a blade of grass sticking out of her mouth like it wasn't thirty degrees outside," one person might say, and another would answer: "Danny Willow told her she should check herself into a hospital but she wouldn't go. These days, you can't do anything for these people unless they slit their own wrists."

Beneath their curiosity was outrage. The town had its share of troubled souls who drank all day, and women who hid the bruises on their faces with thick layers of skin-colored makeup, but even these people knew the limits of their behavior. They did not stare, they did not wander the town, they did not display the scars of their lives for all to appraise and pity. *Doesn't everyone have scars?* was the unspoken question. *Haven't we all had to live through bad times, and come out the other side?* What made Susan Marley so special, when poor Margaret McDermott was raising three girls on her own, and Bernard McMullen had been born without the sense of a bird? These people did not complain: These people had the courage to face their lives and find happiness where they could. Their outrage drew full circle, and they were offended by Susan's circumstances, and offended again by her silent insistence on making those circumstances known.

After a few years, they became inured to her strange behavior. The Clott Paper Mill, in decline for years, was about to close. They had decisions to make and lives to attend. An implicit agreement was made, and in unison they let her recede. Slowly, the talk of her died down. If they saw her walking at night, they did not mention it the next day. They stopped studying her peripatetic wanderings, and they stopped caring whom she chose to bed. They decided that she was just another crazy, a drunk perhaps, who was broken beyond repair. Some girl, lost, who could not possibly be found. These things, never pretty, never nice to admit, do happen.

Eventually, she became a shadow to them in their thoughts, a hazy image without shape. When they saw her they did not remember how she looked, or what she wore, but only the feeling of something undone, something quite wrong, at the sight of her. They did not talk about this—they would never talk about this—but when they spied her in the woods, or near the paper mill, or in front of their homes at night, didn't she turn to them? Didn't she look them right in the eye? And did she smile? Was there the trace of a grin? Didn't it seem, in that instant before they turned away, thinking about the next big snow and whether their cars would make it through another winter without a tune-up at Ed's Domestic Auto, that she had stirred something inside them? Hadn't there been the faint sound of locks turning, doors opening, drapes drawn to reveal dusty attics that should never see the light of day?

Later, those who survived would say that they were not surprised by what happened. They knew Susan Marley, after all.

PART ONE

THE FALLS

ONE
Behind the Cemetery

Liz Marley was a pretty girl with brown eyes and brown hair. Her attractiveness came less from her looks than from a generosity of character. When people spoke, she listened. When they needed comfort, she overcame her natural shyness and offered words of consolation. These qualities, easy to overlook, can make a plain face beautiful. But underneath her eyes were chronic dark circles, the result of too little sleep and bad nutrition. Over the years she had tried the cabbage diet, the protein diet, and the toothpick diet, all supplemented by late-show nachos and Cheez Whiz. Throughout these diets, her body had remained an adamant fifteen pounds overweight. In bed at night she sometimes squeezed the extra inches of fat on her stomach, silently accusing her body of betrayal.

It was an early Thursday morning in March, and the sun would not rise over this stretch of northern Maine for several hours. Liz Marley was standing inside the wrought-iron gates of the Bedford Cemetery. She blew out a deep breath, and watched the cloud of it billow in the cold air, and then dissipate into nothing. Down the hill the town still slept, and in front of her the cemetery was veiled in a layer of the most recent snow. Though this visit was a somber occasion, she was giddy with courage. Being here was a brave secret that no one would ever know.

In the center of the cemetery, a large stone angel presided over William Prentice's body. One of its wings was missing, and over the years the features of its face had been ground smooth. William Prentice had invested heavily in the Clott Paper Mill, and for a long time, it was his vision that had allowed the town to prosper. But the mill closed last month, and "For Sale" signs now adorned the houses on Nudd, Chestnut, and Mayflower Streets like decoration. The stone angel reminded Liz of a poem she'd read in English class about a forgotten king in a wasteland, warning all to look on his works, ye mighty, and despair, in a place where lone and level sands stretched far away.

Liz walked to the back of the cemetery. At the far corner, she found what she was looking for. The stone was smaller than most, and there were fresh red roses, their petals clinging closely together, at the foot of the grave. The inscription might have read *husband* or *father* or *skinny asshole,* but it said none of those things. *Ted Marley (1963–2001),* it read, and that was the best way to remember him: a name.

"Hi Dad," she said. "It's me. Lizzie. The daughter who isn't crazy."

She waited, almost expecting him to say hello back. *Hi, princess!* he might say. In her most perfect fantasy, he would call her princess and look at her with eyes full of pride like those dads on the WB: *I'm not really dead. I was just sleeping. But now I'm back and I'm going to make everything right.*

She sat down on the wet ground, and snow seeped through the nylon of her jacket. In the months after his death, Liz's mother had quietly embarked on a mission to erase Ted Marley. She donated his clothes and Red Sox caps to the Goodwill in Corpus Christi, and took down the photos of him, even family photos, from the end table in the television room. The rest of his things she stuffed into boxes and abandoned at the public dump.

Despite her mother's best intentions, Liz remembered a lot of things about her father. He used to drink Rolling Rock because he said it was worth the extra fifty cents, rather than choking on a Bud. He'd smelled like skunk from working around hydrogen sulfide fumes all day at the mill. Each night he'd showered with Irish Spring soap, and then announced at the dinner table, "Fresh as a daisy, ladies and gents." On his days off he'd worked in his garden, planting beans and spinach and cucumbers that they had eaten all summer long. After dinner he used to have her sit on his lap. He'd say things like: "Don't worry Lizzie Pie, you're okay. And all those nasty girls who say you have cooties are gonna be toothless and pregnant by the time they're sixteen, so don't you worry."

Really, she liked almost everything about him. It was just the other things, the things he did to Susan. There had been a time when she wondered if it had happened to her as well. But eventually she had accepted that for some reason, she had always been safe. For some reason, she was the lucky one whose stomach he had not scored with bruises.

And maybe she had it all wrong. Maybe none of those bad memories were true. Just stuff you invent when you're feeling blue. Susan was not normal. Long before things with their father went wrong, Susan had been strange. *I can fly if I want,* she used to tell Liz. *I just have to move my arms really fast. I can make myself invisible. I can see things you can't.*

Years later, when Susan was in high school and the bruises stopped appearing, Susan was still strange. She moved down to the basement and only came up for meals, and she got mean. Like something rotting right in front of them at the dinner table, she got mean.

Susan dropped out of high school and moved to an apartment on the east side when she turned eighteen. Occasionally, Liz saw her taking one of her famous walks through town. Always, Susan would smile at her like they shared a dirty secret. And then she'd turn away, like she couldn't stand the sight of her own blood.

People in Bedford said Susan was a witch. They said she visited their dreams. They said she was the reason the mill had closed. They blamed her for the rain that came every year, and all the fish that had died in the river. They said she told them things about themselves that she had no business knowing. When Liz let herself think about Susan, which happened almost never, she knew that the people from town were right. Susan *was* a witch.

"You shouldn't have left us," Liz said to her father's stone. "Sometimes I pretend you didn't die. I pretend you made Susan come home and you fixed her." Liz sighed, "But then, I also pretend I have friends. . . . So maybe I'm the one who's crazy."

She waited, as if the man now made of dirt and ash would answer back. He didn't, and she continued. ". . . I'm not depressed anymore. I don't watch nine hours of infomercials on the weekends or anything. I met this guy. He's nice, you'd like him. Well, I don't know if you'd like him. I don't know you very well. . . . Anyway, I guess I was your favorite, but that doesn't mean I forgive you. I'm going to college soon and I'm never coming back to this stupid town. I came here to tell you that."

His stone answered her in silence.

"I mean it!" she said.

She waited, realizing now why she had come to the cemetery today. She had hoped he would send her a sign. Lightning would flash in the sky and sever a tree, and she would know that he was listening. She would know that he was sorry. If she heard that, she thought that maybe she could go on. She could leave for college and live a normal life, marry a nice boy, maybe even Bobby Fullbright, and trust what lay ahead of her.

But there was no bolt of lightning, no rose in bloom that fell from the sky. She traced the engraving on his headstone with her fingers and whispered, "I miss you, Daddy."

As she stood, she looked out onto the northern edge of the cemetery that led to overgrown woods. She spotted movement out there, the color blue. She squinted and saw that the blue was a dress. Beyond the wrought-iron fence a woman watched her. The woman was small with blond hair. Her dress fluttered in the wind to reveal a set of bony white legs, and her skin was as pale as the snow.

A bubble of dread inflated and then began to leak in Liz's stomach. It filled her arms and legs and chest until she was wet and heavy with it. She walked toward the woods. "Susan? What are you doing?" she asked.

Susan pressed her face between the thick black bars of the gate and smiled. Her teeth were small and white against bright red lips.

"It's freezing, Susan. Why aren't you wearing a coat?"

Susan didn't answer. Instead she pointed at the iron crossbar two feet off the ground, and motioned for Liz to mount it.

Liz shook her head. It was dark over there. Thick trees blocked the rising sun. "You come here, Susan. It's dead over there."

Susan continued to point, and Liz wanted very much to walk away. For years she had tried to forge some sort of peace with her sister. For years she had sent letters, and ridden her three-speed Schwinn by her apartment, and waved hello at her in town, only to be greeted by silence. It was because of Susan that people looked at her like she was Jeffrey Dahmer's drinking buddy. And now, at five in the morning in a cemetery on a cold winter day, Susan wanted her to climb a sharply spiked fence. Sounded about right.

Susan's small white teeth chattered. Her eyes were wet and dewy from the cold. Crocodile's tears, Liz thought. But still, this woman was her big sister. This woman was her blood. Against all her best instincts, she put her foot on the first crossbar and hoisted herself up. She didn't see Susan's gleeful smile as she jumped down and landed squarely in a snowdrift.

It was dark on the other side of the fence. Light did not penetrate the clouds or dense forest. The air was thick, and Liz's breath came heavy, as if trying to extract oxygen from water. Even her mind felt different, like someone had disturbed a snow globe full of buried things and shaken them to the surface. There was anger—no, not anger: rage. There was sorrow. There was happiness, a manic kind of joy, and if it had been a color, it would not have been green or blue, but red.

Liz stood. Though she didn't know it, she was crying.

Susan's irises danced, blue against black. The blue got big, and then small. It moved in waves, like the ocean tide. Liz knew suddenly that her sister was insane, and that the feelings she had inside her right now were somehow coming from Susan's mind.

"Stop," Liz mouthed, but her voice was trapped in her throat.

In a grotesque parody of a little girl's curtsy, Susan lifted her dress. She pulled the thin blue fabric over her knees, her hips, her white panties, all the way up to her gaunt waist. On her stomach was a sunset of bruises colored red and orange, black and blue. Some had faded over time while others looked fresh.

"Who did this to you?" Liz whispered. "Did *he* do this?"

Susan dropped the dress's hem and it fell back down over her knees. When Liz looked up again, she saw that Susan's face was bloody. A gash opened in the back of her scalp and blood dripped down her forehead and along either side of her neck. Her pretty blue dress became wet. Like menstrual fluid, it trickled between her legs and stained the white snow red.

Liz took a breath. Then another. Another. All in a row. Quick. Another. She grew dizzy, no longer breathing, simply hitching. In the sky, it was as if dawn had receded into night. And were they alone? No, she and Susan were not alone. She could feel eyes watching her from the woods, from the cemetery, from the town. If she looked hard enough, she thought she would see faces.

"What have you done?" Liz cried.

Susan smiled. Clots of blood as thick as phlegm clung to her front teeth. It was an angry smile, a mean smile. A smile Liz knew very well. A hungry smile. In the snow, the stain of blood grew larger.

Liz ran. Her feet sank below the drifts as she charged the fence. She slammed against the metal posts and hoisted herself up. But then, with a strength she would not have guessed possible, Susan yanked her by the back of the neck and hurled her into a snowbank. The wind rushed from her body in a whoosh as she lay dazed on the ground.

Suddenly, something heavy was on her chest. Something was squeezing her throat. She screamed, but all that came out was a muffled whimper. Her air was cut off. All gone. Her eyes felt tight and bulging, and the meat of her tongue flopped in her mouth. What was happening? She tried to breathe, but the air, where had it gone?

She lurched left and then right. Tried to roll. Balled her hands into fists and punched the thing on her chest, the weight. What was this? What was happening? A moment of clarity told her it was Susan. Susan was kneeling on her chest. Susan was strangling her, of course.

She punched harder, but she didn't have any leverage. Her lungs spasmed in silent screams. They hurt. Everything hurt suddenly. Everything was screaming. She needed to breathe!

She jammed her fists into Susan's back. Tried to

breathe again. Gasped, then sobbed, even though there was no sound. She punched again, but it wasn't easy. She could hardly make a fist. Her muscles were beginning to cramp. They curled up inside her like basement bugs playing dead in unison.

Overhead, all she could see was the dark sky and her bloody sister's dancing eyes. She swung her fists again, but this time only reached Susan's sides. Her eyes hurt so bad, she thought they might have popped out of their sockets. Her throat hurt, too. But she only vaguely knew that part. Only vaguely cared. All she wanted was a breath.

She punched again, more weakly. Again. Again. Still trying to breathe. She punched again. This time she missed completely, and swiped at air. Something thick and wet dribbled across her face and she knew dully that it was Susan's blood.

Please, God. Dear God. I'm only eighteen. Please, she thought.

Red and gray sparks filled the air, and her body stopped screaming. She sank deeper into the snow that crumbled around her. She thought about sleep, but she noticed the way the trees weren't moving. Birds weren't chirping. Even Susan's struggles above her were without sound. She kicked up her legs and tried to roll even though Susan had her pinned. It was the sound of silence she fought against. She knew it was the sound of her own death.

A warmth trickled between her legs as her bladder released. Her legs stopped wriggling. She felt herself go loose. Felt herself stop caring. Knew that she *should* care, but somehow, she didn't. The sparks faded into nothing, and her eyelids fluttered before they closed.

She drifted. Not a good kind of sleep. A terrible one. She didn't see a light waiting for her. The tunnel was shiny black, and inside of it was her daddy.

Daddy? Daddy, did you do this?

He was walking toward her, and he wasn't smiling.

But then the tunnel got farther away, and his body became a speck in the distance. Then the sparks returned. And the pain. Then she was on her side, gasping at air that tasted so sweet it might have been sugar. Just as quickly as it had happened, it was over. Susan had released her. Susan had let go.

Liz coughed. She looked up at her sister. The blood had matted Susan's blond hair into something dark and wet. Her face was bloody, too, so that she was unrecognizable, save for her wild, blue eyes.

Overhead, a breeze came and the trees shook in the wind. The snow they carried fell on the two girls, sprinkling their hair with white. If there were birds foolish enough to venture into these woods, they would have flown away. If Liz had not been prostrate where she lay, she would have run. It did not matter where.

Susan pointed at Liz, and though she did not speak, Liz knew what she was thinking. *You. It should have been you.*

"No," Liz rasped.

Susan nodded: *You.* And then she retreated, her bare feet treading soundlessly, deep into the woods.

TWO
Instruction

Paul Martin wondered if he might be suffocating. But that was life, you were always suffocating. The radiators at the Bedford High School were on overdrive today, and beads of sweat ran down his back and under his arms. He kept his elbows bent as he wrote on the board, but only a red-eyed albino wouldn't notice the crater-sized pit stains on his shirt.

He drew an isosceles triangle with a phallic-looking pipe at its apex and the words "Capital" and "Jobs" at either angle along the base. Couldn't make it much simpler. He looked down at their bent heads. He had asked them a question about the mill, and they were supposed to be reading about subsidies in the handout he had given them from the *Wall Street Journal* in order to answer it. Most were examining their fingernails or doodling on the white space of their Xeroxes. Even their doodles looked bored; little hearts, lyrics to songs. A few were looking out the window.

He followed their gaze and noticed that it had just begun to rain. Although he'd lived in Bedford for almost twenty years, he'd never gotten used to the rain.

Some people could predict when it was going to come or how bad a year it would be. They said they could feel it in their fingers, their knees, and their lungs, as if it came from something inside them.

Last year, the rain had flooded all of Main Street and filled up the valley like a bathtub. The water had mixed with the chemicals from the mill so that when it rolled down his nose and inside his lips, he'd tasted rotten eggs and acid rain, the stuff people used to breathe every day here, on his tongue.

The Clott Paper Mill had closed one month ago, but even now Paul could smell traces of the sulfur that had leached to the air and water. Vats of the volatile stuff were still sitting in the vacant mill, waiting for pickup by waste management vendors. If a few kids, or better yet, brain-damaged former employees, set off a couple of firecrackers in the old place, the town could go up in a puff of smoke.

Paul looked at his students. There had been no rebellion from them the day the mill had closed its doors for good. No indignant editorials in the student paper. No efforts from the town council to lure new industry. Just tight-lipped, New England resignation. And now the rain that came every year was falling, and none of his kids seemed surprised. They did not marvel at it or wonder why it happened only in Bedford. They were crazy, like everyone else in this town.

He sighed. "What's the news?" he asked the nineteen high school seniors in his American history class. He taught both history and math and tried, whenever possible, to combine the two into economics. It was one of the few perks about teaching in a low-paying district with a small population and only a handful of teachers. You could do whatever you wanted and no one gave a damn. That, and down here in the valley there wasn't any cell phone reception, so he didn't have to compete with phones chirping to the beat of Kelly Clarkson's latest crap anthem in the middle of his lectures.

His students stared off, watching the metal clock that hung behind him. It was three-fifty on a Thursday afternoon in March, five minutes before the bell rang and school let out for the day.

"It's raining," Carric Dubois said. She smiled an aren't-I-cute? sort of smile, but he did not smile back.

"Yeah. That happens. What do you think about what you read?" he asked, then pointed at the board. "I don't have to explain this, do I?"

No one volunteered a hand. He tried to think of something that would make them laugh. He could not. It made him feel old. It made him feel like he couldn't blame them.

He looked at them again. A showdown. Talk, people. Talk. Say anything. Jaine Hodkin, the self-declared trendsetter of the class because she visited New York during Christmas breaks and carried purses made out of junked seat belts, yawned. Paul glared at her. She directed her eyes at the window as if to say: *The rain. Sorry buddy, it's the rain.*

He cleared his throat and pointed at the triangle. "I'm assuming you know what this means. I won't insult your intelligence. What about subsidies? Do you think they could work?"

No one answered. He tried to lock Louise's eyes. Maybe even Craig's; he always had something to say. They stared down at their hands, which were folded over their notebooks, and he knew they were counting down the seconds until the bell rang.

He took a breath of wet air, opened a window, and considered running away. "You're right. It doesn't matter. Hey, it was just a mill. It smelled anyway. And look what the chemicals did to our water. So what if all the amphibians are dead, and we've got five times the pediatric asthma rate as the rest of the country? They don't owe us anything for all the years they've stolen, do they? What do you care that the company moved to Canada? No skin off your backs. It's not like your parents were canned, right?" he asked.

He caught the eye of Owen Read, whose long legs were wrapped around the seat of the girl in front of him like he was Christ's gift to anything in a skirt. Paul felt his control give way. In its place burgeoned a dull, impotent rage.

He knocked on Owen's desk until Owen reluctantly sat up straight. "This isn't study hall," he whispered, knowing as he said it that he sounded like an ass.

"Hey, it's not like I care. I'll keep my job for at least another year, until so many people move away that the school shuts down. And anyone who leaves here'll be fine, unless your parents stay, in which case you might have to support them. But that's okay, too. You'll just let 'em starve, right? Who the hell cares?" He raised his voice and noticed that most of the class was looking in his direction now, surprised expressions on their faces. "Who the hell gives a shit?"

Bobby Fullbright raised his hand. Paul nodded at him in a way that said: *Make it short*. Bobby was a basketball player. All those kids were pretty dumb. Hell, all the kids in Bedford were pretty dumb. Liz Marley had even written that the European Economic Community was comprised of "sugar, spice, and everything nice," on the last current events exam.

"I don't understand why we're talking about this. The mill's not gonna open again. Even if we'd gotten government subsidies, it was a losing business. There's no reason for a grant to reopen it or anything, it doesn't make sense. It'd be buying time." Bobby's voice was soft and croaking like a dying frog. Paul had to admit he respected the kid. But he always had the easy answer. He never thought things through. Or maybe he did. Maybe he was the heartless descendant of Adam Smith.

"Does anyone agree with Bobby?" Paul asked. No one raised a hand. Bobby blushed.

"Do you care at all?" he said, maybe to Bobby, maybe to all of them. "How can you people give up like this? How are you going to get through life if it's this easy for you to give up? There won't be another industry. We've gotta have subsidies unless we want to turn into a micro Worcester where everybody looks like they're two paychecks away from a park bench and their teeth are black because they can't afford a dentist. That's how the world works. It doesn't need to be efficient. It just needs to keep everybody with a job." Paul leaned over Bobby's desk. "Tell me this—who cares about economic sense when you're dealing with real people, real live people who have to stand in line for day old Dunkin' Donuts crullers in a church basement while some doctor who puts in four-hour days at his country club gets to send his kids to private college in the good old U. S. of A. Tell me, Bobby." Paul finished by waving his arms in a big, sweeping gesture.

Bobby opened his mouth. The bell rang. Students filed out.

"So read your texts tonight!" he called out to the second-semester seniors who had either been accepted at a college and didn't care, or weren't going to college and had stopped caring a long time ago. "Do some homework, for once," he said as the last student exited the class.

A half hour later, Paul was looking over some papers at his desk. The door to his classroom was closed, and he took a swig from his metal thermos. Absolut vodka and lime juice. His stomach gurgled queasily and he wished he'd brought something else, maybe a big ole martini. No, that wouldn't go down any better. His favorite was scotch and soda, a wee splash of soda. This morning, he'd found his liquor cabinet to be depleted of the scotch. He'd have to remember to drop by Don's Liquor Bonanza on his way home in case Cathy forgot.

Since Cathy had gotten better two years before, which, coincidentally or really not so coincidentally, coincided with Paul's affinity for morning nightcaps, she'd stopped buying booze. She said she didn't want to be a codependent. From her years of lying in bed and watching *Oprah* all day, she had learned words like "straight talk" and "tough love." She used them frequently, and it reminded Paul of that movie *The Stepford Wives*, where all the women turn into mechanical robots that repeat the same meaningless bullshit over and over again. If it weren't his life, it would be funny.

Unfortunately, it was his life.

Cathy liked a mix of lithium and Prozac. At first they put her on Xanax, but that just made her cry more. Then they tried pure lithium. That was around the time Paul would come home straight from work, dress her, plant her at the kitchen table, and cook dinner for the kids. When she'd start crying over her pasta, he'd say things like: *Mom's crying happy tears!* After that they tried straight Prozac and that was better, but not much. She'd get up at night and dig at the Saran Wrap–covered leftovers with her fingers. She gained thirty pounds and wouldn't go out in public because she said she looked pregnant. Finally, two years ago, they found a doctor who prescribed the perfect combination. It was like finding the right drink, really. Two parts scotch, one part soda, a little lithium with your gin? And she became cool and busy and never got sad and never got really happy, either.

Paul wanted to say he liked the change in her. But he couldn't help feeling that people don't miraculously get better in the same way that people don't just get sick. There is something inside them, some chemical imbalance, that makes them who they are. The pills might chain it down for a while, but any day now, it would surface. Funny or not so funny, he hadn't seen that sickness in her until after they were married.

Paul knew that he was a magnet for nuts. In the same way that they had something inside them that made them sick, he had something inside him, some special pheromone, that drew them to him.

He sipped his drink again, swallowing hard to keep it from coming back up. "Cheap shit," he muttered, because it sounded funny, like something a hard-core drinker would say. *But you are a hard-core drinker,* a familiar and unwelcome voice whispered in his ear. He ignored it.

He pulled out Bobby's paper, then put it away. The mood he was in, he'd probably give the kid a D. He pulled out Louise's paper. Now she was a lot like Susan Marley, at least in the looks department. Except Susan probably knew what the EEC stood for. That was one thing, he could never say Susan was stupid. A borderline schizophrenic with a mean streak the size of Texas, but not stupid.

And the nuts go marching on.

Paul took another drink. Louise had confused imports and exports. He drew a double-ended arrow between the two, then wrote: "Do they still teach English in English class? Look it up."

He was on his fifth paper when he heard a knock at his classroom door. He dropped his thermos into a drawer and called, "Yes." Kevin Brutton, the principal, walked in. Kevin was always wearing these cheap suits like he picked them out at the Salvation Army thrift store and threw a little starch on them. He also always smiled. No matter what he said, he was always smiling. It was the politician in him. "Heya, Kev."

"Hello, Paul." Kevin brushed his finger across the souvenir conch shell from Mississippi that Paul's elder son had given him five years before. "I always wondered how they did that," Kevin said.

"What?"

"Made these carvings—this picture of the water and the beach with the tree in it without cracking the shell."

"Tiny elves, Kev."

"Yeah." Kevin replaced the shell. "Sleep well last night?"

Paul shrugged.

Kevin rubbed his eyes. "Well I didn't. I had a nightmare about that friend of yours. Susan Marley. My wife, too."

Paul rolled his eyes. People around here were obsessed with Susan Marley. They thought they saw her behind their mirrors, outside their houses at night, and even in their dreams. Paul was safe from such things: Never once in his adult life had he been able to remember his dreams.

"Dreamed the mill was on fire," Kevin said.

Paul looked at him. This was what happened when you lived in the sticks. You turned into a half-wit. "Mmm, Kev. That's a real coincidence. Maybe you and Allie should be special guests for the Psychic Friends' Network."

Kevin's voice got far away. "There's something wrong with that girl, Paul. Anyone can see it."

Paul cleared his throat. "You stop by to say hi?"

"No," Kevin said.

Paul swallowed a burp, and the air got caught somewhere between his esophagus and stomach. "Then what is it?"

Kevin walked over to the open window, stuck his hand out, and felt the rain on his palm. They all liked to do that, the people of this town. They liked to touch the rain. Kevin spoke with his back to Paul. "I never said anything about the girls, although I didn't agree with it, you know that." He waited for Paul to offer some sort of confirmation, but Paul offered none. Kevin shrugged. "Forget the legal problems. It's just not smart."

Paul stood. "You've been listening to crap."

Kevin turned from the window. For the first time that Paul had known him, he wasn't smiling. He leaned over Paul's desk and they locked eyes. "Yeah, Paul. It doesn't matter. That's not why I'm here. I'm here because they used to like you. Not because you hung out at their little dive bars, but because you did your job. Now they're coming into my office asking for transfers because you're staggering around the classroom."

"What does staggering mean?"

"Drunk, Paul."

"Who said that?"

"I'm saying it."

"You're wrong."

"Enlighten me."

"I do my job. I grade the damn papers. I get up in front of four classes every day and I teach."

"You're drunk."

Paul looked down. His desk drawer was partially open, and his thermos peeked out at him. "They're just pissed because I don't pass 'em unless they deserve it," he said. "They think they can doodle their way through and I'm gonna be a nice guy because they're about to graduate."

Kevin leaned closer, so close that Paul could smell the tuna salad on his breath. "What, Paul? I just want to get this straight. I just want to know so I can write it down, Paul."

It surprised Paul, this petty bureaucrat who'd never taught a class in his life with his cheap suits and his doltish smile, talking to him like he was some bum off the street. It made him wonder at what point he had changed so much that someone like Brutton could do this. Whether it had happened slowly or if there had been a single, watershed event that he could have prevented. Paul said nothing.

"Consider this your warning, Paul. I don't like you so you'll get only one." Brutton shut the door behind him.

Paul fished his thermos from the drawer and emptied it in one gulp. Then he set the rest of his papers aside and closed his eyes. If he were to rate this day on a scale of one to ten, he would give it a three. A memorable tune, but the lyrics lacked soul.

He knew he should go home and get something to eat. He didn't feel like going home. He looked around his classroom, the same classroom he had been decorating for seventeen years. The same classroom he had come home every night to Cathy from: *Every night as it Was, Is, and Ever shall be, Amen.* The classroom with the copies of the *Wall Street Journal* that he paid for out of his own pocket and nobody ever bothered to take home. The classroom with its posters: "Remember to Register," and the one of Uncle Sam saying, *"I Want You,"* pointing at him like a menacing Mark Twain dressed up for a costume party. He went to Montie's Bar because he couldn't stand to be there any longer.

THREE
A Locked Door

It took eighteen years for Georgia O'Brian to grow into her teeth. They were big and sharp and when she was little she soaked her pillow with drool because she could not close her mouth around them. Paul Martin, back in the days of Paul Martin, had called them crocodile's teeth.

At twenty-seven, her choppers fit perfectly into an admittedly spacious mouth. She was a tall woman with long, red hair and an overripe body. At times she wondered if someone had sneaked human growth hormone into her now deceased mother's prenatal vitamins, because Georgia was six feet tall and she could never find shoes that fit. When she was at the Chop Mop Shop where she cut hair, and a new customer, a rarity in this town, sounded the jangling bells above the front door, he or she would often ask, "You Irish?" or better still, "You from the old country?" To which she would reply, "No, Borneo."

Georgia's son, Matthew, had curly brown hair like his father, the merchant marine. Well, not a merchant marine, but if she lived in a port city during the 1950s, that's what she would tell people. She'd tell them that Matthew's father had been lost at sea rather than admitting that he was a local man twenty years her senior. For a long time she hadn't even known his last name. He was just some guy she'd met, drunk at a bar, underage, the back of a pickup like a bad white trash movie. These things happen.

She acquired the marine's particulars during her sixth month of pregnancy, assuming that the existence of a child was something he'd want to know about, but when she called and he didn't remember who she was, she hung up. Not fair to him or her son maybe, but how fair was life anyway?

Right then, Matthew was trying to pump himself into the sky on a swing at the park five blocks from their house. When he came home from elementary school, she had asked him what they could do together on her day off. She'd suggested the Paris Theater, a misnomer at best, sarcasm at worst, that had been screening *Spider-Man 2* in second run for the last month. He'd said no, he wanted to go to the park, and she suspected he chose this location because none of his schoolmates would be there to identify him as the nine-year-old who still played with his mother.

And of course, no one else was at the park, because in addition to the drizzling rain that had been falling for hours and soaked her red hair into a clowny frizzle, the park was also covered in snow. Feet of snow were piled all over Bedford; on lawns, up high on the sides of driveways, and atop roofs where it fell to the ground in little increments, making thudding sounds all winter long. They found the swings because they had spotted the points of the ten-foot-tall supporting bars. With mittened hands, they had dug for an hour, interspersed with snow angel breaks, until they cleared a path for the arc of one of them. And now, victorious, Matthew pumped his feet with a look of grim determination on his little brow, under the apparent impression that if he swung high enough, he might actually get somewhere.

Cabin fever, she thought. *He's got cabin fever.* She felt the same way.

For most of the year in Bedford, you forgot that there were seasons, or that in other places, you did not need to warm up your car for a half hour every frigid January morning. But at the end of winter, when the sting of cold air lost its bite, you remembered. It happened not only in her own house, where Matthew and her father paced the rooms at night without the concentration to read or even watch television, but all over Bedford, and it felt like a bubble of latent energy, suppressed for half a year, about to burst.

This rain right now was a prelude, a warning like the dull mist over a humidifier. By tonight it would come down hard, flooding the banks of the Messalonski River, the streets, and the bridge to the highway, as it had done every year for as long as she could remember. And in seven days, after it was over, the world would fill with color and she'd trade her snow boots for a pair of flip-flops.

Georgia looked up into the sky. Dark clouds were not so much floating as swarming overhead, and she thought that the hard rain might be coming sooner than she'd expected. "Hey, Matt?" she called.

"Yeah?"

"Time to go home."

He whined and said he wanted to stay, couldn't they

stay for a half hour longer? Fifteen minutes? Five minutes? One minute?

"Fine," she said, looking at her watch, "One minute.
You have one minute."

"Let's just go, then," he grunted.

They lived five blocks south of Main Street, a safe
mile away from the Halcyon-Soma Tent and Trailer
Park. Things by the trailer park were strange. People
who had gotten funds from the Salvation Army had set
up camp there. Some of them owned scraggly dogs or
cats that roamed the streets, their fur clumpy. Georgia
did not touch those animals. They had a hungry look.
Occasionally, she saw Susan Marley down by the trailers. Susan lived in a rented apartment near there. Georgia never said hello. Susan had a hungry look as well.

Georgia had dreamed last night of Susan Marley. In
it, she'd been walking down Main Street on her way
home from the Chop Mop, when suddenly the sidewalk had turned soft and sticky. She'd tried to run, but
her feet sank into the ground. Around her, the trees
had turned black. She'd wanted to scream, she dis-
tinctly remembered wanting to scream, but when she
opened her mouth nothing came out. The rotting trees
surrounded her, and the ground sucked her deep inside. And then in the distance Susan Marley had
walked toward her, leaving a snaillike trail of blood in
her wake. She'd held her hands protectively over her
bloated stomach, and Georgia had understood that the
girl was pregnant. Understood that something terrible
was about to be born. She woke up with a start at six
this morning, just as the sky had opened up to rain.

Now, the rain really started falling. Little streams of
water slid down Matthew's face and dripped off his

nose. "It's only rain, we could have stayed," he said, kicking at newly formed puddles in the center of the street.

"It might make me melt," she said. She joined him in the street and grabbed his hand to hurry him along, but he pushed her away.

"Oh, I forgot, you don't hold hands anymore."

"Mo-om," he mumbled, his jaw sticking out.

"Okay, no hands. Look, no hands!" She pretended that they had disappeared underneath the sleeves of her jacket.

He rolled his eyes, but she knew that he was amused. She walked ahead in hopes of getting him to move faster, and then felt a splash of water across the backs of her legs. She turned to find Matthew wearing his trouble grin.

"Oh yeah?" she asked, splashing back but with longer legs so that he was soaked in cold, muddy water, head to toe. "Oops!" she said.

"Mom!" he cried, lunging at her. His hands were open rather than closed and he pushed lightly just above her waist. She was tempted to hold him there, and he lingered before letting go.

"You didn't think I'd do it, did you? You thought I was just your old mother, huh?" she asked softly.

He ran ahead to another puddle and waited for her to walk by. "I'm gonna get you so-o bad!" he shouted. But despite all earnest attempts, for the rest of the walk home she successfully dodged his splashes.

When they arrived at the small, neatly kept wooden house, she rang the bell and waited for her father to answer the door.

Matthew stood close behind her and shivered. "Don't you have keys?" he asked.

"No, I forgot them," she said.

"I always remember my keys when I come home from school and nobody's home."

"I know you do, you're very good about that."

"How come you don't remember your keys?"

"Because you're a freak accident of the gene pool, Matthew."

"What?"

"Nothing."

He sighed and began to play on the front steps. There were eight of them, all brick, leading to the porch. She banged on the door.

"He's not home, Mom."

"He might be." She banged again. Her knuckles started to hurt.

Matthew waited a few seconds, then reiterated. "He's not home. He left for those talks he has on Thursdays."

She remembered now. Her father had been kept on Clott's payroll to help the town through its transition. On Thursdays he went to his office at the mill and directed conference calls with management in Boston. "Yeah. I guess you're right," she said. "We'll have to go through a window. I think there's a good one around back."

"I can do it, I'm smaller."

"That's all right, Matt. You wait under the door and try to keep dry."

"But if the window isn't open, I can climb the trellis up to my bedroom. I've done it before. I'm really good at climbing."

"Don't tell me these things, Matt. You're not allowed to do that," she said with a look of anger that she did not really feel. He was always doing crazy things; scaling the house, climbing trees, bouncing around like he was made of India rubber.

"Okay," he told her in a way that said she was missing the point.

"And stop jumping down those steps, you're gonna slip and brain yourself," she hollered.

"Uh huh," he mumbled as she turned the corner of the house.

Around back, the first window she tried was open. She wormed her body through the opening, falling gracelessly to the floor of the living room. It reminded her of one of those old Abbott and Costello movies, the fat-guy-squeezing-through-the-small-space gag. "Very dainty," she muttered while walking to the front door.

"Matthew, stop messing around," Georgia called out as she turned the lock to find her son still playing on the icy steps, her irritation no longer just for show. "Come inside."

Just then, a woman appeared from behind the wall of snow piled against the front walk. It was Susan Marley, dressed as if about to attend a Fourth of July barbecue. She wore high-heeled sandals, a blue dress, and no coat. Her curly blond hair had been straightened by the gales of rain, and it spilled down her shoulders to her hips. Her head, weighed down by the water, was tilted back just a little so that Georgia could see the smooth underside of her chin and her long, graceful neck.

Susan turned. Her gaze settled on Matthew and she grinned in a way that made Georgia uncomfortable.

Then she walked on, heading south and out of view. A lump formed in Georgia's throat, and she thought she was going to cry. What a strange world in which to raise a child, where snow angels and monsters lived side by side.

"Mom?" Matthew asked, having missed Susan's appearance.

Georgia pretended to have some dust in her eyes. "Yeah honey?"

"Look what I can do!" He jumped down all the steps and landed gracefully on the ground. Then he took a bow and she clapped.

"Wow. That's something. Now come on inside. I'm freezing."

He looked up at her from the bottom of the steps. His lips spread into a small smile, the trouble smile. She realized what he was about to do. Things suddenly got very slow. She noticed the rain on his nose, his yellow jacket that seemed too bright, the six or so feet of air between her son and the top cement step. "Wait—" she started to say, but there wasn't time. He took a running leap.

She reached out to catch him as he propelled himself up over the icy steps. But her hand hit his shoulder in mid-air and knocked him off balance. She lunged again but her fingers only brushed the slick nylon of his jacket. He tumbled down. The back of his head pounded against the last step in a loud thwack.

The sound reverberated inside her, carving holes into her organs and making them hollow. She ran to the landing just as he sat up. He curled his lip at the offending step like it was his mortal enemy, and then slapped it. She let out a sigh of relief so forceful it sounded like a sob.

What was he thinking? Who jumps *up* icy steps? "Come here right now, Matthew O'Brian," she said. She was thinking about grounding him, spanking him, sending him to his room without television for the rest of his natural life.

He stood. His winter coat was browned by mud from the rain and puddles. "You pooshed me!" he slurred. His pupils were wide and out of focus.

The hollow feeling inside her returned: Something was very wrong. "Come here," she said.

He tried to walk but stumbled drunkenly. She caught him in her arms. There was something warm and wet on her fingers, and in her mind she said a silent prayer to the Virgin Mary that the obvious had not happened. But when she turned him around, she found a jagged cut along the back of his scalp. Three-inch-long flaps of hairy skin hung loose on either side of the wound, and she could see the white of what looked like his skull. Blood gushed down his back. The snow where he had fallen was diluted into red whirls like a cherry Italian ice.

She bit down on her lip and tried not to let him know from her expression how bad this was. Head wounds, they tended to bleed a lot, right? Buckets, even . . . That didn't mean he was going to slip into a coma or anything, right?

She pressed hard against the flaps of skin with both hands. "How do you feel?" she asked.

He didn't answer.

"Matthew, come on, I'm sorry. I did a stupid thing. How do you feel, are you dizzy?"

His eyes rolled upward like he was trying to see his own brows. "Huh?" he asked. He didn't look like her son right then. He looked empty. The little boy she loved, she realized to her horror, was pouring out all over her hands.

She took him inside, grabbed the set of keys she had left on the kitchen counter, and took off for the hospital in Corpus Christi, eight miles south of Bedford.

On the ride, she took off the turtleneck under her sweater and wrapped it around his head like a turban, continually shaking him, afraid he would fall asleep. Wasn't that what you were supposed to do? She wasn't sure. On the highway she made a conscious effort to drive slowly. The way the rain fell against the windshield was like standing underneath a waterfall.

She parked in the area designated for emergencies and carried him inside the sprawling building marked Mid-Maine Medical. A nurse hurried toward them and showed them the way to an examining room. Georgia laid him down on a long padded table, her hands still pressing hard against the wound.

"Can you hear me?" Georgia asked. There was too much of it to be sure, but it looked like the flow of blood was waning. "Matthew!" she shouted, unaware that she had become completely hysterical.

"Um," he muttered. His eyes were almost closed.

The doctor came in and pushed her aside, unwrapping the bloody turtleneck-shirt from his scalp. He was a short, stocky man with gray-yellow hair. "How'd this happen?" he asked.

"Well, actually," Georgia admitted, "he was jumping and I got in the way—"

Matthew rose from his stupor. "Fell, thassssall," he slurred with his eyes now completely closed. The doctor shrugged, turned back around, and began his examination.

* * *

"Just some coffee, thanks," Georgia told the woman behind the register at the hospital cafeteria. The woman was small and wore a blue smock that snapped at the sides as part of her uniform. She craned her neck to see into Georgia's face, then took in her bright red hair and massive body. Georgia realized she must look a sight with her wet, bloody clothes. Like a Viking come home from battle. Georgia pointed at the coffee on the counter.

The woman shrugged, then added up the sale. Georgia paid and found a seat.

The doctor had told her that Matthew was fine, possibly a mild concussion, the kind of thing that happens all the time. The bleeding wasn't out of the ordinary—in fact he'd lost only a pint or two. By the time they'd gotten to the hospital it had pretty much clotted. The confusion he'd had on the steps was just shock. Still, he would have to stay overnight as a precaution. Fortunately, he was insured by Clott through her father. "Don't worry," Dr. Conway had said, patting her on the back, "They're not made of bones, these kids. They're all cartilage."

Georgia had stayed for the stitches. He was too tired to cry, or even object when she held his hand. Afterward, the Demerol worked its magic and he fell asleep. She finished filling out insurance forms, then left a message for her father, telling him that Matthew was fine, nothing she couldn't handle; she'd see him tonight and explain.

Now, she sat in the cafeteria. She would drive home after the shaking in her body subsided. This was nothing new, just an inevitable progression. Last year, he broke his arm trying to climb through his bedroom window for no other reason than he'd wanted to see if he could do it. When he was three, he swallowed a bottle of his grandfather's digitalis because it was candy coated and that had been really fun: pouring ipecac down his throat and watching him throw up all night, hoping his heart wouldn't explode.

She sighed. It was probably something she should be used to by now. If he turned out anything like her, he'd be coming home drunk from junior high dances, or else he'd wander the Puff N Stop hours after curfew, so stoned he thought he saw God in the lines of his hand. Or maybe he'd even get a girl pregnant and decide to be a father in more than name. Now that would be cosmic justice.

Georgia finished her coffee, slurping up that last bit of sugar at the bottom, and thought about how much she'd like a merchant marine to help her out right around now.

FOUR

The Thing in the Woods

Earlier on that same Thursday in March, Liz Marley rubbed her eyes and rolled over in her bed. "I'm up," she called out to her mother, who had shouted her name from the floor below. For some reason her legs ached, and her head was pounding. She felt like the sandman had visited her during the night and slapped her with a twenty-pound bag of cement.

She buried her face beneath her red quilt, and wondered if her mother would believe that for the third time this month she was suffering from a mysterious twenty-four-hour flu and needed to stay home from school. Not likely.

She'd had a nightmare last night, a pretty bad one. But she couldn't remember it anymore. Something about her father, and Susan. Something so scary that she must have cried in her sleep, because her eyes were wet and her throat felt raw. She remembered snow, and blood, and the red roses on her father's grave. If she thought about it, she could probably remember the rest. But she didn't want to think about it. So instead she counted slowly: one Mississippi, two Mississippi, three Mississippi . . . twenty Mississippi until the veil of sleep lifted, and her thoughts returned to the day ahead of her.

The house was quiet and she could smell eggs frying in the kitchen. Her room remained as it had been before she fell asleep. Eels and White Stripes posters cluttered the walls. Jack White mugged at her from across the room. "Hi, stranger," she grumbled while looking at him with one eye still shut. On her desk was her trigonometry homework, which, damn, she hadn't started, and this would be the third time in two weeks that she got a zero. Yes, this was life as usual. High school still sucked, and so did Bedford. But at least there was Bobby, and maybe now that basketball championships were over, they could go to the Dugout and eat imitation neon cheese fries after school today.

She got out of bed and pulled on her robe. The rain had started today, which meant that spring was on its way. And after spring came summer, and after summer fall. Soon, she'd be in college. Soon, her bags would be packed. She'd hop the Greyhound to Orino, and never look back. Hooray! Feeling almost back to her good old self, she skipped her way into the bathroom, oblivious to the icy linoleum floor against her bare feet.

But then, in the mirror, she saw. What was this? She stood on tiptoe and leaned over the sink. She didn't want to look. A part of her knew already what this was. There was a giant red splotch across the center of her trachea. Fingerlike red tentacles spread out and around the sides of her neck. Hands. The splotches were shaped like hands.

She leaned against the cold glass and closed her eyes. One Mississippi, two Mississippi, three Mississippi. *Calm down,* she told herself. *Just calm down. There's enough bad stuff in the world, stop inventing more. You're going to fail home economics if you don't sew that retarded sweatshirt, you know. And even if it is a stupid class and you totally should have taken art instead, you'll still lose your scholarship to UMO and then you'll never see Bobby because he'll be in college and you'll be waiting tables. Stop making things up!*

"Liz? You're going to be late!"

"I'm coming!" Liz cheerfully answered in a voice not entirely her own. Six Mississippi. There were tears in the corners of her eyes, but she managed to stifle them. She had three options. She had gone crazy on the anniversary of her father's death, and was now imagining bloody sisters instead of little green men. She had dreamed this. It really had happened.

She chose the least frightening option. She had dreamed this. Right. It had all been a dream. But what about her throat? Maybe she was coming down with a cold. Had wrapped her fingers around her neck in her sleep because she'd been trying to scratch away the soreness. Or maybe she'd had an allergic reaction to the sheets. Or, well, who knew?

"Liz, do I have to come up there?"

"I'm awake, Mom!"

In the shower, she counted slowly. Fifty Mississippi. *A dream. Just a dream.* By the time she dressed, pulled a turtleneck over the bruises, and came down for breakfast, thanking her mother for such delicious eggs, the dream was forgotten. Only its feeling, the mood it had carried, remained. *Forget it. Let it go. Stop making things up!*

By the time she walked to school in the light morning rain, a tree could have fallen down in front of her, a bus could have careened off the road, and she would have looked at the sight with only a hint of surprise. She would have kept walking, repeating the same refrain over and over in her head. Tap your ruby slippers three times and say it with me: *It was only a dream. It was only a dream. It was only a dream.*

At lunch in the cafeteria at the Bedford High School, her boyfriend, Bobby, asked her if something was bothering her. "Nothing," she told him with a too wide grin.

"You sure? You look wiped out," he said.

"Next week on *The O.C.* Ryan's getting back together with Marissa and she's such an attention whore with all that closet drinking. I can't even deal with it."

"You're so weird," he told her.

By fifth period, while her teacher talked about the function of imaginary numbers when building bridges ("See, they do have a use!" Mrs. Adams chided the class. "Nothing is truly imaginary."), she found herself thinking about Susan. How long had it been since they'd seen each other? What if the dream was a portent? She remembered the blood in the snow, a circle growing larger, and her brow started sweating.

Before eighth period, she stopped Bobby in the hall and told him, "I need to visit my sister tonight. Could you drive me?"

Juggling his books in his hands (for efficiency's sake Bobby believed in visiting his locker only twice a day), he asked, "Seriously? I thought we were going to the Dugout. Is something wrong?"

She grinned at him, a pretend grin that worked on her mother, but never on Bobby. "Top secret. They'll boil me in oil if I tell you."

"Who?"

"The Mormons. They're very violent. It's all those wives. They don't know how to handle them."

He frowned. Equipped with Liz Marley radar, he always knew when she was hiding something because, truth be told, she was always hiding something. "You're weird, Liz."

"No, really. I want to visit my sister. Pick me up tonight. Around eight."

After school let out, and all the buses had left, and she told Bobby that she wanted to walk home in the rain instead of riding with him (No offense, Bobby. I just feel like walking. I know, it's raining really hard. If I get pneumonia it's all my fault. You're right, Mr. Martin totally sucks. You could light the guy on fire if you took a match to his breath. I'll see you tonight.), she found herself walking, not home, but to the cemetery.

Ridiculous, really. She knew it had all been a dream. A fevered nightmare caused by too many late-night Cheetos. But still, she walked. At her father's stone she saw no roses, just his small marker. Gales of rain flattened her hair and plastered her jeans to her body. She'd forgotten her mittens, and the bars along the metal fence were cold. She peered between them.

The woods were dark. The backs of the pine trees were bent like crippled old men by the weight of the snow. She wished that she'd asked Bobby to come with her, because these woods weren't normal. The dioxins that came from bleaching pulp had killed a lot of the river animals and even some of the birds, but that didn't explain the way these woods made her feel. There were rumors that something lived out here. Something that watched.

The rain made a plinking sound as it fell on her vinyl

hood. Her teeth chattered. She wanted to go home. But she had to know if there was any truth to her dream.

She scaled the fence. The posts at the top were sharp, and as she straddled them, she got the idea that if someone gave her a good hard tug, she would be impaled. Liz Marley, split in two, the *Corpus Christi Sentinel* would read: *She went mad, and was looking for a dream she'd misplaced. It's true she had a better half. It was her left. Less freckles.*

But she got to the other side without incident, jumping down off the high fence and landing squarely in a snowdrift. The thick trees overhead blocked much of the drizzle, and she could hear the soft patter of the rain as it plinked against wet leaves. It felt funny being in these woods. It felt like being inside an animal's mouth.

She turned in every direction, but there were no footprints, no signs of struggle. No blood. "Hello?" she called softly. "Susan? Is anyone here?" No one answered, and she grew bolder. "Hello?" she said. "HELLO?" she bellowed, because even though she was scared, bellowing is kind of fun. But still, there was nothing.

She smiled self-consciously. Nothing up her sleeves, kids. Nothing behind the trees. Had she really dreamed the whole thing? Maybe so. A relief on one hand, on the other hand, an indication that she needed some serious headshrinking. But this was good news. She could have found something a lot worse than proof of a restless night's sleep out here. This expedition could have been a disaster.

She took one last look between the trees. "Susan? Hello?" she called out once more, if only to reassure herself that she'd tried her best to solve this strange mystery. Nothing answered her. Only the patter of the rain. She let out a sigh of relief, and started for the fence.

Just then, out of the corner of her eye, something blurry whizzed between two trees. It was pale, and its body shined in the dark. She jumped, getting almost two feet of air between herself and the ground in a way that would have made her basketball-playing boyfriend proud. Then she backed up against the fence and faced the woods. "Who is that?" she called, then winced at the way her voice sliced through the silence.

She waited, watching between the trees, with her back pushed up against the fence. Her pulse pumped audibly in her ears. But she didn't see anything. After a while she laughed at herself, silly girl. Probably just a white fox, or maybe even a falling branch.

When she turned to climb the fence, she heard a branch break behind her in the direction of the trees. She swung around and listened. This time she didn't call out. This time, just in case there really was something out there, she didn't want to invite its attention.

The branches that bridged the gap between the two trees expanded and contracted in a quick burst. Her heart skipped a beat and then started playing the mambo. The trees were about fifty feet away from her, and she could tell they hadn't been blowing in the wind. Something had pushed them. Something big. A bear?

Oh, shit.

She backed further against the fence until the bars pressed through her coat and into her skin. She stood as still as she knew how, hoping that this thing would not see her. She slapped both hands over her mouth to muffle the sound of her breath.

"Huuuhh-huuhhh," she heard behind the trees. She listened closely and it came again: huuuuh-huuhhhhh. She did not want to believe what she was hearing. It wasn't the kind of sound a dog or even a bear would make. It was deep and rasping.

Okay kiddo, she thought. *Shake a leg.*

Just as she was about to turn around and climb the fence, the branches between the two trees opened up. The thing came out from between them—

"Huuuuhhhh-huuuhhhh."

—It was big, maybe six feet tall. It was still too dark to see clearly, but she saw glimpses of its pale body. It didn't have fur; it had skin. It looked human.

"Huuuuhhhh-huuuhhhh." Its breath was thick and wet. Its body was all out of proportion. Its knuckles almost reached the ground, and its massive chest was balanced over a pair of skinny legs. It lumbered, like it was sick or just too hulking to move quickly. It dragged itself toward her by its arms. She wanted to turn away but she couldn't. What had happened to this thing? What *was* this thing?

Its skin was white, like all the blood had been drained from its body. Something shined. Its eyes. They were intelligent. They were watching her. It pulled itself along by its arms, and when it met her eyes, it smacked its lips. Like it was hungry.

She spun around and lurched for the first crossbar, but her foot missed the mark. In a panic, she tried to squeeze herself through the fence. She pushed as far as her left knee, which got stuck so that her foot waved at her from the other side.

"Dammit!" she whispered. Its breath was getting closer. Its panting was more labored: huhh-huhh-huh. She wiggled, and her leg plunged deeper through the hole so that her entire thigh was stuck in the fence. The hairs on the back of her neck stood on end, and she could feel the thing closing in on her.

She tugged on her leg, but the intricate design of wrought iron held her as firmly as human teeth. "Huhh-huhh-huh." It was so close that she expected to feel hot air on the back of her neck. She tugged and tugged, but her leg was lodged between the bars.

"Huhh-huhh-huhh."

How far away now? Twenty feet? Fifteen? She could tell by the sounds of breaking branches that it was gaining speed. It was getting excited.

"Huhh-huhh-huhh!"

Her face crumpled and she started to cry. It was going to get her. She could smell its breath like paper mill smoke and rotten meat. Haunted place. Why had she come? Susan. Tricked by Susan. This was how her life was going to end. Stuck in a fence four months before leaving this stinking town.

"Help!" she screamed, but no one ever came into these woods. Not unless they were crazy. She stopped struggling and began to whimper. But then she smelled its body behind her, the smell of human sweat and river shit. Then she heard it smack its lips, the sound so wet and greasy. The sound so terrible she knew she'd rather chew off both her legs and hobble through the opening than let it touch her.

She took a deep breath, in and out. She let her muscles become loose even as she heard it grunt (how far away now? Ten feet? Five?). She made herself count to three Mississippi, even though she wasn't sure she had the time. One Mississippi. She swallowed and took a deep breath that she held before letting go. Two Mississippi.

"HUH-HUHH-HUHH!"

It was so close! She could see its long shadow on top of her! Pretend you're watching this from far away, she told herself. Pretend you're home in bed where nothing can ever touch you.

"HUHHH-HUHHH-HUHHH!" it screamed. In victory? Had it gotten her?

Three Mississippi. She eased her leg out from between the bars.

OUT! SHE WAS OUT!

She scrambled for the first crossbar and hoisted herself up. The thing was so close she could feel it blocking the wind. She could smell its scent of shit and sulfur water. As she straddled the bars, it took a swipe at her dangling leg. She kicked as hard as she could. Came into contact with something firm that grunted in either pain or surprise.

"HUUUUHHHH!" it shrieked.

She jumped to the other side of the fence. Rolled in the snow a few times. Then she got up and ran. She didn't stop until she reached the valley, and she never looked back.

FIVE
Mother, May I?

While Liz Marley fled the Bedford woods in terror that Thursday afternoon, three black cars sped out from Mary Marley's front curb. Mary waved as they pulled away. Their headlights shone against the rain, and she was suddenly reminded of a funeral procession. She experienced a kind of déjà vu, and she thought about her husband in the past, and her elder daughter in the future.

Susan?

In her mind's eye a little girl wearing black Mary Janes took a baby step toward her. She'd been thinking about Susan a lot lately. Every time her mind wandered or she closed her eyes at night, there was her daughter frozen forever as a six-year-old girl. A cheerful little girl with her whole life ahead of her. A life not yet formed or gone wrong. Mary blinked to dispel the image. Silly to think about the past. Like those people who worried about what lay inside the *Titanic*. They swam deep under water looking for jewels and instead they found corpses.

Mary was a tall, handsome woman with clean features and sharply tweezed brows. Her hair was still brown save for the shock of white that framed the side of her face and gave her the appearance of perpetual surprise. Now she looked around the house. Cookie crumbs were scattered across the table. The ladies had tracked mud through the kitchen. Little high-heeled footprints circled the room like dance-step stickers at an Arthur Murray dance studio. She filled a bucket with warm water and Top Job cleanser and began cleaning.

Today had been a pretty good day. It had been her turn to hostess the monthly bridge game she played with the girls, and she'd won every hand. It was easy. Over the years they'd been meeting, only Mary had had taught herself the nuances of bidding. She stayed up late at night with borrowed bridge manuals from the Corpus Christi Library. On yellow legal pads she wrote complicated notes like: "Clubs against diamonds means no hearts."

Out the window she saw that the rain had turned from a drizzle to a downpour. Work would be slow tonight. People didn't leave their houses in this weather. For a quick second she thought about Susan. If she went for one of her walks tonight without her coat, she'd be chilled to the bone. *A skinny thing, just like her father. A mean thing, just like her father.*

Mary blinked, and banished the image from her mind. Usually, she didn't think about her daughter. It was best that way. It was best, in fact, to pretend she'd never been born.

Bridge. Right, bridge.

Today, she and the girls had gossiped about former

classmates, divorces, and people who'd given up on being middle-aged and moved to Florida. The girls were old friends from Corpus Christi High School. All except Mary still lived there. They were housewives now, drinking mixed pink drinks with names like Loosey Lucy at the local golf club and complaining about their husbands who worked too hard. When it was their turn to hostess, Mary liked to go to their houses and touch the little ceramic figurines they all seemed to have, or smell the rose potpourri in their bathrooms. She did this when no one was looking, and it felt like stealing.

For a long time she had thought that she would move back to Corpus Christi, where the owners of things lived, but somehow that never happened. Ted didn't get the right promotions, and her father never forgave her for running off and getting married. If she hadn't eloped with Ted, her high school graduation present would have been a trip to Europe. She still thought about the places she would have gone: Madrid, Barcelona, Zurich, Florence, Rome.

There were a few leftovers in Bedford who still had money—the Martins and Fullbrights. Surprisingly, her girls had located both. But those families were different. Their presence was a reminder of poverty rather than a respite from it. The Martins had inherited their money from Cathy's great-grandfather William Prentice. The Fullbrights came by theirs by more honest means: Adam was a surgeon. Both lived in big, modern houses with central air conditioning and spanking new furnaces. They dropped money all over town, and told people they'd never leave; this place held their roots. Mary found this logic hard to swallow. Like being a millionaire who lives in the worst part of the

Bronx, not because you want to show things off, just because you like being shot at.

Mary sighed. After Ted died, she had thought that she and Liz would finally grow closer, now that reminders of another era were finally gone. Instead, Bobby Fullbright came along, and it was as if Mary had no family at all.

Like most of the houses in the area, hers came with high ceilings and a sparseness that could never be filled, not even with clutter. When she was alone, she thought she could hear history within its walls. Memories replaying. Her elder child bouncing a pink rubber ball, the thwack-thwack that was really the boiler in the basement, or she would forget for a moment that the radio was turned on and it was the sound of Liz and Ted laughing.

These were the things she always thought would happen to her when she was old. But they started after Ted died, maybe because that's what widows do, ruminate and grieve. Or maybe now that he was gone, she finally had the time to regret.

Mary looked out the window. Melting snow slid down the valley like a slow, liquid avalanche. In Corpus Christi they used to have jokes about people from Bedford. How many of them does it take to screw in a light bulb? What are you if your cousin is your brother is your uncle? What's the place that God forgot?

There were some who blamed her daughter for the darkness that had swallowed Bedford. They were right, of course. Right about the thing that for nine months had lived in her womb. And the terrible dreams, that with every night grew more vivid.

Last night Mary dreamed that she was standing in her basement. The floor had flooded with water as high as her knees. On the other side of the room, six-year-old Susan had held her arms open wide. The water level kept rising, and Mary had wanted to run to her daughter, but she'd been frightened. *Cruel girl. Angry girl. Heart full of ashes,* she had thought. The house began to settle, creaking and groaning, and then the ceiling came crashing down.

When she saw Susan on the street now, Mary turned and walked in the opposite direction. But that didn't stop the nightmares. Mary shut her eyes tight and tried to think of something else. Anything else. Rain. Spring days. Work tonight. In her mind's eye she saw her elder daughter, six years old. Pretty girl. Angry girl. You could see madness in her eyes.

The boiler kicked, and Mary cried out. In her mind, it was Susan in the basement. It was Susan, coming home.

Just then, the back door opened. The sound startled Mary and she jumped. Standing in the kitchen was Liz, looking wet and out of breath. She tracked mud on the freshly mopped linoleum as she walked toward Mary.

Though her children looked nothing alike, Mary became confused for a moment, lost in time. She thought this cherub before her was the other daughter. Instinctively, she stepped back. She pointed at the muddy floor, "Boots!" she screeched.

Liz halted. She must have run home from school, because she was panting so hard that her breath was wheezy. She unlaced her boots and held them by their heels with her index fingers. She started toward Mary again. "All of it," Mary said, still pointing, "Coat, too!"

"Mommy," Liz said, still panting, "Something ha-happened." Her still face crumpled into a look of pain, and she held her arms wide, as if for a hug.

"Coat, too!"

Liz took off her coat and rolled it into a ball. Then she looked down at her jeans, which dripped water onto the floor. She sniffled, her nose and eyes runny. She peeled her jeans off, too. Wearing only a red wool sweater and pale blue cotton panties, she stood in the center of the room. Her plump little legs were red and splotchy. Though Mary knew better, she recognized the daughter with whom she was now speaking, she could not help but keep her distance. "Go take a shower," she said, "I have to cover the night shift for Matt Ambrosia, so dinner's in half an hour." With slumped shoulders and still sniffling, Liz skulked out of the room.

A half hour later, Liz came down the stairs freshly showered, dressed in a light blue Champion sweat suit, and smelling of Ivory soap. "Just in time!" Mary said as she placed a pot of steamed rice and stir-fried vege-tables on the table. They sat and said their grace, Mary out loud, thanking God for their bountiful feast, and Liz silently with her head bent.

"Don't you like it?" Mary asked after she had por-tioned out heaping servings of wok-fried broccoli and carrots on each of their plates. "I thought you'd like it, what with your diet."

"I'm not on a diet. I'm not fat," Liz said.

Mary leaned back and sipped her glass of Gallo Zin-fandel. "Fine," Mary said. "You told me you were on a diet so I made this special for you. I never said you were fat. You're a very pretty girl." The wine quickly warmed her ears and cheeks, and she suddenly realized how tired she was. How much she wanted to stay home tonight and share a blanket with Liz in front of the television like normal people.

"Mo-om," Liz moaned.

"Li-iz," Mary moaned back. "You know, you didn't do any of that laundry like I asked. It took me at least an hour."

"Sorry," Liz said.

Mary softened. Liz seemed very sad just then, defeated in some way. This was not the kind of dinner scene she'd imagined when she married Ted. She'd expected a place full of laughter and gentle teasing. "Well, we know you won't make a good cleaning lady. Not the worst news in the world."

Liz smiled, and the two of them almost laughed. "I'm sorry, too. For being short with you before. I just get tired sometimes."

"It's okay," Liz said.

Mary leaned forward. "I know!" she said, clapping her hands together. "How 'bout Portland? It might be nice in another month. We could take a day trip to the art museum. I know someone who works there."

"Portland?"

"We could bring a picnic lunch and eat it at that park where the jazz musicians play. They do Charlie Parker. You'll love him."

"That sounds nice," Liz said.

"I'll need to take the Buick to the shop, of course. I think the fuel pump's on its way out."

"Right."

"But you'd like that, wouldn't you? A trip? I get so tired of this town. I just want to look at something pretty once in a while. It'll be nice when you go away to college. I'll have a new place to visit."

"I'd like that, Mom," Liz said. "We could—" Liz's voice broke, and she pushed her chair away from the table. Tears welled up in her eyes.

"What is it? What's wrong, honey?"

Liz buried her face in her hands.

"Come on, honey. Tell me."

"I—" Liz broke down sobbing. "It was . . . It wa-was awful."

Mary got up and held her daughter. At first, Mary said nothing. It had been a long time since they had been this close, and Mary savored it. She felt Liz's skin, so soft and full. Every once in a while she forgot the obvious: She loved this girl so much it hurt.

Finally, and with regret, Mary pulled away and asked, "What is it?"

"Susan," Liz whispered.

Mary tensed. She took a step back and left Liz to cradle herself. "Who?"

"She came to me. She tricked me into going behind the cemetery."

Mary's throat went dry. Panic set in, and it felt like a car alarm screeching in her ears. The basement. Was Susan in the basement? She walked toward the back door, and made sure that it was shut tight. Then she closed and locked the windows in the kitchen. "In this house? Did she come into this house?"

"I dreamed I went to visit Daddy, and she was waiting for me. I think she's mad because I still love him and I shouldn't."

Liz was rocking back and forth now, her eyes shut tight, and Mary wanted to hold her, to make everything right. But if she did that, she'd start crying. She'd start crying and she'd never stop. She owed it to Elizabeth to be strong. To protect her. She looked at her wide-knuckled hands, and the cracks in the ceiling shaped like spider's webs, and at the walls of this house that seemed to silently close in on her with each passing day. "Liz. I can't talk about this right now. I just can't."

Liz did not hear. "She wants to hurt me. She's so angry. Did you ever get the feeling she wanted to hurt you? Do you think maybe she can, because she's so different?" Liz pulled at the neck of her sweatshirt, and Mary saw red splotches all over her daughter's throat. That these splotches were shaped like human hands was undeniable. "In my dream she tried to strangle me. And when I woke up I found this."

Mary averted her gaze. She felt nothing. Not even numbness. She would never have guessed that the sight of her daughter's bruised throat bothered her in the least, if she had not gagged into her napkin.

Liz continued, oblivious. "Lots of people dream about her. Have you noticed that since the mill closed, the dreams have been worse? I'm afraid I'll go to sleep one night, and I won't wake up in the morning."

Mary squeezed her eyes closed. "Stop it, Liz."

"Have you dreamed about her lately?"

Mary took a deep breath. "I can't talk about this. You know I can't," she said.

Liz frowned. "I went to the woods today because I'd dreamed about them. Something was waiting for me there, Mom. I think Susan sent it. It . . . it was a bad thing." Liz broke down crying. Her voice became a whisper, and she leaned close to Mary, as if afraid that someone else might overhear. "It wanted to hurt me the way Daddy hurt Sus—"

"Stop," Mary said. "Stop right now."

Liz's face froze and she tried to control her tears, but

they kept falling. "It—" she started. She stopped when she saw her mother's expression.

Mary felt herself go cold, and her face became set like a plaster cast. She did not like the feeling. She tried to fight it. Tried to care that her child was hurting. Tried to say the things that needed to be said. The things that had been palpably silent for so long that over the years they had altered the terrain of the house, so that all the doors seemed slanted, and the hardwood floors seemed to buckle with warps in every direction. She tried, just as she'd tried long ago with the other child. But still, she went cold. Dramatic Liz, always making trouble. Liz with her crying over things long buried. Frightening herself with her own imagination. Liz and her nightmares, so inconsiderate that she shared them. Fat little Liz.

"Oh, Liz," she said, "Don't we have enough problems? I hate to see you do this to yourself. Have you noticed the basement? The basement's a mess. I really think you need to sweep down there."

Liz shook her head. "I asked Bobby to take me to her apartment tonight. I haven't seen her in a year. How long has it been since you've seen her?"

Mary leaned in close to Liz. So close that she could smell the Ivory soap on her skin. "Not another word, Elizabeth Rebecca Marley. Not one more word."

Liz's frown hardened, and Mary saw that she was angry. Furious, and for a moment, Mary was frightened. There was something inside this girl, something foreign. Something that surfaced when Mary least expected. A formidable thing, and Mary knew that one day, she would be outmatched. "Did you ever call her after Dad died? I'll bet you didn't. I'll bet you never asked her to come home. You let her live in that terrible place, just like you let her live in the basement. You never even tried to help her because you don't care."

Mary was tempted to strike her daughter. A quick slap to the cheek to bring her to her senses. To shut her up. "Not another word," Mary said. "You had a bad dream. It's over now."

"It's like she's dead to you. Maybe you should take all her stuff to the dump. Just like Dad. You can take my stuff, too."

Mary grabbed Liz's shoulder and held it firmly, too firmly. Liz winced. She didn't know she was lucky; Mary's first instinct had been to slap her.

Liz's face turned red. "Look at my neck, Mom!" she shouted. "Who did you think did this?"

Mary sank her fingers in more deeply. She pushed her thumb into the skin beneath her collarbone until Liz yelped. "You were thrashing in your sleep. You've always been strange that way."

"No, Mom."

"You were, Liz."

Liz didn't answer, but Mary knew she almost had her. "You need to be careful with that imagination," she said. "Crazy runs on your father's side of the family."

They locked eyes, and Mary could see Liz's resolve slip away. First Liz's shoulders fell. Then her eyes sank toward the floor. Then she sighed deeply, and it was all over. "Fine," Liz said.

"Fine what?"

"You're right."

"About what?"

Liz swallowed. "I had a bad dream. I'm not going to visit her."

"Did you tell Bobby?"

A silent communication passed between them, and Liz shook her head. "No. I never tell him anything."

Mary nodded. "Good. Because he seems like a nice boy, but you never know. He hears those kinds of things and maybe he'll change his mind about you. Maybe he'll decide he likes blonde better," she said. Then she sat back down and closed her eyes. She thought about the coming spring, bridge, the rain, new shoes. She thought about jazz musicians, Portland, her swollen knuckles that ached on wet days, the sofa that needed new fabric. She thought about these things until the flush left her cheeks, and the tenseness in her jaw slackened, and she was able to convince herself that she had done nothing wrong.

She smiled at Liz. "Eat something. You'll feel better," she said.

Liz blinked, and placed a forkful of rice in her mouth. She chewed mechanically. "You like it?" Mary asked. "I got it from the health food section. It's not bleached so it's supposed to have more vitamins."

Liz nodded and continued eating until her plate was scraped clean. Then she stood.

Mary said, "Why don't you stay home tonight? I'll call in sick. We can snuggle. Watch a movie like when you were little."

"Why?" Liz asked.

"Why not?"

"I don't want to," Liz answered.

"You don't want to what?"

"Be here," Liz said. Again, her look was stony, not like the daughter Mary had raised, and Mary thought about how quickly you can lose your children. You turn your back, and they become monsters who live under your roof. "Then go," she said.

Liz raced out of the room. A few seconds later, a door slammed.

Mary got up and poured herself another glass of Zinfandel. She knew she shouldn't. She had to leave for work in another fifteen minutes. She did it anyway. As she sipped from her glass, she thought about Liz. Smart Liz, who had always taken A's in her science courses. Angry Liz, who would go away to college and never come back. Probably not even for Christmas or her own wedding. In a way, the second daughter would follow the footsteps of the first.

Just then, in her mind's eye, Mary saw Susan as a little girl. Pigtails tied with yarn. Small, white teeth. A speck of blood rolling down her chin. She took a step toward Mary, and it reminded her of that children's game:

Mother, may I?

No, you may not.

Mary leaned against the counter. Up the stairs, Liz's stereo blared. Down below, the boiler kicked. In her mind, Susan Marley approached with an angry smile.

SIX
Screaming Trees

At six o'clock that Thursday evening, Georgia O'Brian finished what remained of her coffee and left the Mid-Maine Medical Center. Stuck to the vinyl of the passenger side of her white Honda, she found dried blood. She started to scrape it away with her fingernails, but then stopped, leaned back in her seat, and cried. She did so with her eyes fully open, looking out over a parking lot full of cars and falling rain. When she finished, salty tears dried to her cheeks, she was able to clean away the blood. She was able to start her car. She was able to turn on the radio, and drive along the highway through gales of rain that became thicker with each yard that she approached Bedford. The Moose 105.1 blared classic rock through the speakers of her radio, and though she did not feel ambitious enough to sing along to Meat Loaf's "Paradise by the Dashboard Lights," she hummed.

As she neared Bedford, the long pipe of the mill came into view. Until it closed last month, it was run by a corporation that had serviced the office paper industry. Clott's demise happened slowly, and at first hardly anyone had noticed. In the eighties Clott instituted a hiring freeze. In the mid-nineties the layoffs started in earnest. Each year before bonuses and raises at Christmastime, her father handed out pink slips to another ten percent of his staff. The men who stayed worked two and three jobs at once. They fixed machines, they sorted, and they worked the assembly line. Even her father moved out from his air-conditioned office and started working the floor.

They should have seen it coming. They should have noticed that the population of the town had dwindled from six to four thousand. Fewer people had gossiped over early-bird specials at Olsen's Diner, eating biscuits, pancakes, eggs, and heavy meat. Fewer people had shopped at the stores on Main Street. But they had expected things to come around. A down cycle, they had thought, which would invariably lead to an up cycle. No one truly became alarmed until Paul Martin wrote an article for the *Corpus Christi Sentinel* pointing out the obvious: Clott was preparing to close its Bedford mill. But by then it was too late.

Last December, Paul had spearheaded a protest rally against the Clott Corporation. In the *Sentinel* article he'd explained that if enough people showed up for his rally, the company might be shamed into keeping the mill open for another year or so. The extra time would allow Bedford to invest in and attract new industries like tourism.

Georgia's boss was sick on the day of the protest, so she had to work at the shop. But she watched what happened. The protest was to begin at noon along Main Street's center. From there, people would march the half mile down the road to the paper mill. The local television news had agreed to cover the story, and rumor had it that Paul had gotten the go-ahead from the *Boston Globe* to write a follow-up piece for the cover of its Sunday business section.

At noon, WABI set up their cameras outside the Chop Mop Shop. About three hundred townspeople attended, all dressed in their Sunday best. Most of them had called in sick to their shifts at the mill or the hospital in Corpus Christi. Even Georgia wore pressed slacks and a lace blouse, just in case things ran over, and she had time to close the shop and join the festivities. But Paul never showed up. Two hours later, only a handful of people remained. WABI packed up its van and got back on the highway. She'd been disappointed in Paul, but more than that, she'd been disappointed in Bedford. They should have done it without him. Instead people had tossed their "Save the Mill" signs into the trash cans and spent the afternoon watching TBS reruns like it was just another day off.

That's when Paul showed up. He pulled into the middle of the street, and stumbled out of his car. Then he started walking toward the mill, a one-man parade. She'd watched from her window as he'd looked from one corner to the next, searching for the people who had left hours before. Maybe he didn't know he was five hours late. Maybe he'd had a drink or two for courage, and two drinks had turned into a bottle, so even then he wasn't sure whether he was late, or early.

There was a handful of people sitting on benches or in the park. They watched, but nobody said anything. Then Bernard McMullen, whose family had worked at the mill for three generations, threw a rock. It sailed past the side of Paul's head. Paul turned slightly, like he thought somebody might have whispered in his ear. Bernard picked up another rock, and Georgia swung open the door to the Chop Mop and shouted: "Get out of here, Paul. Just go home. You missed it." The expression on his face when he recognized her had been terrible. She'd never seen a man so ashamed. She'd wanted to say something kind, but instead she'd shut the door.

Not long after that, Clott's management announced its plans to close the mill. Nobody bothered writing articles or staging another protest. They were embarrassed, mostly. They'd trusted Paul, and he'd made fools of them. WABI ran a clip of Bedford's empty Main Street in a sequence entitled, "What if you threw a rally, and nobody came?" But maybe they also knew, just as Paul must have known, that their protests wouldn't do any good.

And so, when Clott finally shut its doors last month, it came as no surprise to anyone. Despite this, they were all, somehow, surprised. Georgia's father and three other foremen had been kept on payroll at Clott for an indefinite amount of time. Two days a week they were supposed to administer severance, hire vendors to clean out the mill and the chemicals stored inside it, and sell off all the old machines to the highest bidders. In the mornings now her father watched game shows in his bathrobe. Though he was almost seventy years old, it was only this last month that he had started to look like an old man.

Georgia kept driving down I–95. She had once heard that when you cut a tree, you can hear it scream if you listen very closely. If you traveled ten miles north of Bedford, you might find strips of land cut away, fallen branches, rotting roots, and stumps of trees. You might imagine the historic echo of buzzsaws, or the groaning of the earth itself. A few years ago when she had been driving, just to drive, to get away from the colicky baby whose fretting never ceased, she had discovered the tree graveyard. She'd pulled over to the side of the road and touched the massive stumps. Her fingers had traced their ridges: countless years recorded by slim bands of wood. She listened for the screaming. She never heard it.

At her exit, Georgia turned off the highway. By the time she traversed the Messalonski River, she had managed to forget the trials of the day. She concentrated on the comfortable way the town made her feel. With the heat blasting through the vents and the rain falling hard outside, she felt like she was wrapped inside a warm cocoon.

At six P.M. that Thursday evening she pulled into the driveway of her childhood home, a half mile south of Main Street on a cul-de-sac that led to the parking lot of the Catholic Church of Our Lady of Sorrow.

"You home?" she heard her father call when she got into the house.

"Coming." She found him playing a hand of solitaire and smoking a cherry cigar behind the desk in his study.

Ed O'Brian was one of the few men she knew who was larger than she. Even now, as his bones shrank with age, when he stood next to her, she never wondered whose shadow was bigger. "Everything hunky-dory?" he asked very slowly and calmly. It was the only way he ever spoke.

Georgia sighed. "Fine. He's fine. Nine stitches, but he'll live."

Ed's shoulders drooped, and she knew he was relieved. "Good, he needed a whupping."

"Not funny."

"Georgie." He smiled at her. " 'Course it's not funny. You eat dinner?"

"Sort of."

"I've got some leftover garlic steak."

She pulled up a chair and sat next to him. "Burnt on the outside, bloody on the inside?"

"Yup. The way I like it. You tired?"

"Yeah. But I'm gonna go back and bring him some things."

"You need a nap," he said, grinning at her. "You've got that funny look in your eyes you get when you're tired."

"You think I'm cranky?"

His eyes widened in mock horror and he nodded.

She sighed. "I think I'm cranky, too."

"You been sleeping okay?"

"No. Nightmares."

"Marley, right? Me, too. Loony broad. Maybe she'll go for one of those walks and forget her way home. Corpus Christi can have her."

Georgia laughed. "You work on that. I don't know what time I'll be back so you don't have to wait up."

She made a move to stand but he held up his hand and she settled back into her chair. "I got some news," he said. "You'll hear about it anyway."

"What?"

"The conference call today. They said the transition's over. Two months severance for management, one month for everybody else," he said without emotion. If she were not his daughter, if she had not lived with him all her life, she would not have known that this information caused him considerable pain to relate.

She sighed heavily. "You're fired?" she asked.

He didn't answer, and she realized that she had

overstepped the boundary between daughter and father. She had admitted that he was fallible. She was
briefly irritated that she had a father like this, so lost
in time, so old when she had been born.

He shrugged. "Don't worry, Georgie, we'll get by.
Just tighten our belts a little. How was the park?" he
asked, changing the subject just like that, like their
lives would not be different after this. *Don't worry
your pretty little head about it, Georgie.* She wanted to
remind him she was no longer ten years old. He could
tell her that it wasn't about the mill, a job he didn't
even like. It was about having nothing to fight against,
wishing you did. Not even a reason to be angry, just
this biting in your stomach that you can never release.
No good reason to let it go, nothing to set it loose on.
*I get it, Dad. I sympathize, believe me. I cut hair for a
living.* But they could discuss this later, after things
had time to settle. For now, she could let it go. She
could give him that.

"I'm sorry, Dad," she said.

He shrugged and she knew he was embarrassed.
"Yeah."

She got up and he restacked the cards, shuffled.

"Sure you don't want to play a little pot poker? I'll
spot you."

She laughed. "Good night, Dad."

SEVEN

The Husband of the Woman Who
Jumped Out the Window (Fall from Grace)

It was six o'clock on that same Thursday in March, and if Danny Willow had to name the one place he did not want to be right now, it was at the police department. He hadn't slept well last night, and his eyes were narrow slits reading small words in blurry type. He sighed, pushed his six-inch-deep pile of paperwork aside, and looked out his window.

The rain was heavy now, and cold enough to cramp his fingers. Cars drove slowly down Main Street, and already runoff from the hill was collecting in the valley. He guessed that with record snowdrifts this year, the flooding would be severe. Maybe the worst in Bedford's history. Danny rubbed his eyes. He was sick of this. Sick of the whole damn thing.

When he was born fifty-six years ago, Bedford had already started its decline, but still, the town he'd grown up in was a different place than the one he was watching right now. In those days Clott had still been operational, and there had also been a pretty success-

ful textile mill on the other end of Main Street. People
who put in their time at factory jobs had raised kids
who wound up moving to Corpus Christi, or else to
the top of Iroquois Hill. In church and at town meetings those same people had all been on their best behavior because their reputations had mattered.

Even when he'd first started as sheriff fifteen years
ago, things had been quiet. He'd mostly kept his head
down, surfacing every once in a while to lock a rowdy
drunk overnight in the clink, or else to direct lost New
Yorkers driving BMWs to the nearest deer hunting re-
serve (and hope to God they didn't get drunk and shoot
each other within town limits). But now every day
seemed worse than the last. Kids didn't sneak their parents' whiskey or their big brothers' pot; they huffed
spray paint under the bridge. Gangs of them wandered
stoned through Main Street like zombies. And then
there were the twenty-year-olds who'd never left Bedford, but discovered crystal meth. Danny could spot
those poor slobs a mile away, because for some reason
half their teeth were always missing, and the other half
were broken and soft as rotten fruit.

He got a domestic abuse call at least once a week.
And he didn't break up benign lovers' spats, and take
husbands out for walks to cool down, reminding them
that raising a hand to a woman is probably the lowest
thing you can do. No, not so easy. Now he saw women
and even men with eyes swelled shut, and furniture
broken to bits, and no matter how many times he saw
these things they never ceased to shock him.

He sometimes wondered why this was happening to
Bedford. Why the people seemed to have soured right
along with the land. He couldn't say. He only knew it

made him tired. There were people who liked to blame Susan Marley. But he didn't hold to that kind of superstition. She was just a girl after all, and things had started getting bad long before she was born.

He would have quit this job long ago if there had been someone willing to take his place. But people were leaving Bedford in droves, especially now that the mill had closed, and he felt a little like the captain of a sinking ship. It was his duty to make sure that every last man safely reached dry land, which, given the circumstances, could be taken literally.

Danny sighed. At least summer was on its way. At least he and April would soon take a vacation. He liked Florida, because at night they could watch giant sea turtles lay their eggs in the sand. She liked Saratoga Springs, so she could see her sister's children. She went there at least once a year and when she got home she would tell him: *They're such trouble. Thank golly we never had kids.* In return he'd ask her, "Then why do you go?" *I like to see what I missed.*

April had a little problem. When she was a kid, around fifteen, she got put in the family way by a boy named Kevin Brutton. She'd been too young to know any better, and had waited until the thing was seven months along. She never got very big around the middle, which he guessed was how she'd been able to convince herself that she'd only gained a few pounds until pretty late in the game. And then one night, while her parents were at a recital of Handel's Messiah at Colby College, she stole a bottle of their Tennessee whiskey. She drank half of it, and she was a tiny thing back then. Then she jumped out her second-story bedroom window. She landed stomach first on the snow below. Somehow, she didn't wind up breaking a single bone.

Hardly any bruises. It must have been a terrible feeling. Thinking that one way or the other, her problem was going to be solved. And then, after all the courage it took; sitting on the sill of her bedroom window, wondering if she might die right along with the thing she carried, and finally jumping out, only to stand back up again, the lump in her stomach still present, ready to raise its hand and say, *Howdy.*

She got up off the ground and went back inside her parents' house. Ate a sandwich. Got hungry the way you sometimes do when you're drunk, only she didn't know she was drunk. She said she hadn't been sure which was scarier, that dizzy sick feeling in her head, or the other feeling in her stomach. She wound up throwing up right there in the kitchen, hunks of peanut butter and jelly on Wonder Bread. She got all kinds of upset when he asked her what bread and what jelly (grape), and did the peanut butter have chunks (nope, creamy), and what was she wearing (a blue pleated skirt and yellow blouse under her pea coat), and even what kind of day was it (a sunny winter day with birds chirping), but he couldn't help it. Told her it was the detective in him. Hated, actually, the idea that she had gone through it alone, and with those details he'd wanted to follow her there in his mind.

After she threw up, the pangs started. She called them pangs. Told him it came from the drinking. She tried to take a nap, sleep it off, but wound up sitting on the toilet for five hours, full of cramps that came in waves. Never labor pains, she never called them that. The thing came out and she told him it was too big to flush. What was it? He asked. *Nothing, it was just a lump,* she told him. No matter how many different ways he asked, she always said the same thing: *It was nothing.*

She put it in a Hefty bag and buried it in her back-yard. Managed, tiny as she was, to dig right through that frozen dirt behind her garage. She told him it was born dead. And he believed her. Well, why not believe her? What would have been the point in doubting?

He married her twenty years later. She was a gossipy town librarian who'd never been able to get past more than two months dating a man before her phone stopped ringing, or some fight brewed and she wound up saying the kinds of things that most people can never forgive. She had a habit of running off at the mouth and making comments, delivered innocently enough, that you could never quite shake off. "You really shouldn't eat so much," she told him on their first date at the Beefsteak Charlie's that was now a Weathervane in Corpus Christi, "You've got a belly as it is."

Never the most clever of men, a man who admit-tedly could not follow half of what Paul Martin was saying on any given day, Danny had still learned a few things by the time he took April out to dinner. He un-derstood that she did not mean to cut him down. It was how she made conversation. People who say the wrong kinds of things are not always bad people. Sometimes, and this was a feeling with which he could identify very well, they were just lonely, and so unac-customed to having people look them in the eye that they got overwhelmed. "Glad you noticed," he told her. "I was hoping you'd be looking at my belly." She blushed that day, and it had surprised him that, aside from when he spilled food on his shirt or licked his fingers in public, he could make any woman blush. They were married within the year.

Since she was in her mid-thirties and he in his late forties, they immediately tried to conceive a child.

When nothing happened, she told him the story of her pregnancy. He was the only person she'd ever told. Not even Kevin Brutton knew that buried behind her parents' old house was a child that with one spank might have cried.

After that, they just kind of gave up on kids. April never went to a gynecologist, and he never pushed her because he knew she didn't want to have to explain. She did not want to know for sure what had happened to her body that day she drank too much and hurled herself out a window.

So it made him feel pretty low when she got back every year from taking care of those spoiled kids in Saratoga Springs who complained about her cooking and laughed at her Maine accent. It made him feel pretty low. If they'd had kids of their own, April would never have let anyone treat her that way.

When she got back last night, April had been pretty upset. She'd talked about the kids, how they were growing up, how one day she expected they'd get married and have children of their own. He'd tried to keep the news from her but it had been impossible. "Where's Benji?" she'd asked.

"Taking a stroll," he'd told her.

"Where?"

"I don't know." Too tired to accompany the old mutt, he'd let it out the back door earlier in the day to conduct its business, and mysteriously, the damn thing never returned. Five minutes later they were wandering the streets searching for Benji. April shouted his name until her throat was hoarse. They didn't get home until after midnight. If he'd slept peacefully straight after that, he might not be feeling so badly today. But April had tossed uneasily next to him for a good couple of hours, and when he finally did fall asleep, he'd had a nightmare about Susan Marley. And now here he was, so sleepy he'd had to swallow five cups of coffee this afternoon just to keep from nodding off.

Just then the phone rang in Danny's office and he moaned. "Who is it, Val?" he called to his secretary. *Please,* he thought, *not an accident.*

"Your wife," Val answered.

He picked up the phone. April immediately began jabbering in a voice so shrill he thought maybe only harpies could understand it. She told him that Benji was nowhere to be found. She'd phoned all over, put notices up on the bulletin board of the church and some of the lampposts in town, but no one had any news. "You think he maybe got run over?" she asked. "Somebody ran him over and buried him?"

"Naw," Danny said, rubbing his temples, "Everybody knows Benji. He'll be back. Probably just met a pretty little she-dog."

"I think you should put out an APB," April said.

"Now, April. You know I can't do that."

She sighed for a moment, a funny sigh that sounded like a shriek. "You think maybe Susan Marley has him?"

"No," Danny said. "We'll find him. I know we will."

"You never know what people are like on the inside, Danny. You're too kind. You think everybody else is the same way. But that girl is different. And Paul Martin, too."

"They're just down on their luck, April."

There was silence on the other line. "I know it's crazy, Danny, but would you check for me? Would you see if Susan has my Benji? I heard she goes to Montie's Bar in the afternoons."

"April, this is daft."

Her breath hitched, and he felt himself melt. Foolishness, he knew. But she sounded so sad. And he really should have put the dog on a leash. Partly, this was his fault. "Well, I've been meaning to say hi to Paul, and he'll probably be at Montie's, too."

"Oh, please, Danny." She brightened.

"Yeah, after work I'll drop by."

"Ask about Benji," April whispered excitedly.

"Yes, dear," Danny had said before hanging up.

In a way it was a relief. He knew he wouldn't sleep tonight with this rain, and he'd rather worry about a mutt than the people who might get hurt this week, or the feeling in his gut that told him something bad was about to happen. He looked over a few more reports, gulped down two more bitter cups of coffee (his secretary brewed it like syrup, hoping that he would stop asking her to make it), and drove to Montie's Bar.

EIGHT
Guy Walks into a Bar

The windows at Montie's Bar were taped over with double-layered Hefty bags. The inside of the place was dark, as if no one's eyes could possibly adjust to the light emitted by a sixty-watt bulb. By the time Danny Willow got there, Paul Martin had been slugging scotch for the better part of two hours.

Danny grabbed a stool and parked himself next to Paul. They sat together in companionable silence, or what passed for it. Danny was a broad, soft man with tufts of white hair that sprouted in a circle around his head. He lit a cigarette, a Captain, the cheapo kind, and took a short, nervous drag. A layer of smoke drifted a few inches above eye level like visible ozone.

"I like the Dugout better," Danny said.

"Then why are you here?"

"Thought I'd stop by and say hi."

"Hi."

Danny grinned. "Howdy."

"Aloha. April's in Saratoga, huh?"

"Springs. No, she got back yesterday. Benji's missing. She's wound up tight as a clock."

"Your problems started when you named your dog Benji," Paul said.

"Started when I met you."

"Benji, come home," Paul whined in an uncanny impression of Danny's wife April. Danny grinned.

Montie, the bartender and owner, poured Paul a scotch and soda without having to be asked. Then he returned to his seat behind the bar to watch the local news.

"You sure you should drink that?" Danny asked after Montie was gone. "It gets Cathy all upset and then she goes to April and I have to hear about it for days."

Paul took a gulp. "So look. April send you to look?"

"Yeah, I got that much free time."

When Paul finished his drink, he clanked it against the bar and called over to Montie, "Honey, I'll take another."

"You shouldn't," Danny answered him.

With an old man's grunt, Montie got up and poured Paul another drink. Paul often thought Montie looked like an angry Buddha with his stocky body, round stomach, and small arms. He smelled like an alcoholic that stale, sour smell, but still, Paul liked him. Well, sort of liked him. The way smokers liked the friendly folks at R. J. Reynolds.

"Paul," Danny said, "slow down."

"Fucking inbreds," Paul mumbled.

What?"

"Cathy, she's inbred, ya'll are. Everybody's a cousin. That's why my kids can't pass their math midterms. Their parents are siblings. You and April are probably cousins."

"Something happen today, Paul?"

"Yeah. Something always happens. Something or nothing."

Danny sighed. "Fine."

"Pain in the ass," Paul mumbled at him.

Danny looked down at his beer. Paul looked straight ahead. A reporter on the local news announced that the rain over the next week would be relentless, and that Bedford would be hardest hit. Danny sighed. He seemed despondent and sad sitting there, and Paul wondered if this was his special gift to the world, making everyone (even his only friend, pitiful as that was) miserable.

"Hey, Danny," Paul said, clapping him lightly on the shoulder. "I'm sorry."

"You always are, aren't you?"

"Are you going to take my apology or not?"

"I'll take it."

"Buy me a drink?"

"No."

Paul smiled winningly at this expected reply. Danny, at first grudgingly, and then freely, smiled back with crooked yellow teeth. "It was worth a try," Paul told him.

Paul noticed that, after drinking two Miller Lites, Danny was on the road to joining him in the land of the inebriated. The three of them were talking about the 2004 Red Sox. Having been raised on Long Island, Paul was a Met fan to the bone. "What about eighty-six, Montie? Remember Buckner in eighty-six?"

Montie's eyes widened and he smashed his fist against the bar so hard it must have hurt his hand. Yes, Paul thought, people in Bedford were very stupid. Instead of telling Paul to get the hell out of his bar, Montie looked in the direction of the back of the room where a couple of underage kids were shooting pool. He smiled. Paul followed his gaze, and saw Susan Marley. She was leaning against the back door while some hick who looked like he was from one of those nontowns up north and thought of Bedford as a city fumbled through his pockets, searching for a light for her Marlboro Red.

Paul hadn't seen Susan in a while. Not that that was a bad thing. Ending it with her was the smartest thing he'd ever done in his not-so-smart life.

"Crazy bitch," Montie said, nodding at Susan. "Dreamed about her last night. Swear to God it felt like it was really happening. My wife thinks she's the devil."

Right now, Susan was swaying to Stevie Ray Vaughn's "I Like the Way You Walk." Her hands were clasped around the hick's shoulders. She wore a long, sopping wet spring dress that showed off her headlights. Paul made a motion to stand. Danny caught his wrist. "Leave it alone. You know she makes you nuts."

Paul ignored him and walked over to her. He glared at the hick until the hick, fists clenched, asked what he wanted. "Spend your money someplace else," Paul said.

The hick asked Paul if they could take their problem outside. He puffed out his chest like a rooster, and Paul knew that this hick could probably take him. These days a tough cheerleader could probably take him.

"Sure. See that guy over there?" Paul asked, pointing at Danny. "He's a cop. This is a bust. Go home before you get in trouble. We're not after you." Paul winked.

The hick took another look at Danny. Danny waved, and when he did, his uplifted arm exposed the .357 slung across his chest. The hick picked up his coat and left the bar.

Paul was left standing next to Susan. Though the

music had stopped, she was still swaying. It occurred to him that she hung out here late at night after he'd gone home, because she seemed like a regular. She was skinny, but her face was bloated from drinking or, more likely, because Paul had seen this kind of bloat before, from strange living habits. From sleeping most of the day. From having nothing to do for long stretches of time. Boredom bloat. She wore little sandals, her toes painted pink, and shivered.

Paul put his hands on her shoulders and stilled her movement. "How'd you get here?" he asked.

She grinned.

"You sick or something?"

She wrapped her arms around him, smelling musky and sour, like she hadn't showered in at least a week, and put her ice cold lips to his neck.

The sensation was both erotic and repulsive.

He gave her his coat, told Danny to keep his mouth shut, and drove her home.

NINE
Another Fall

Susan's apartment was on the south side of town near the trailer park. She lived on the second floor of an old wooden house. Graffiti was spray-painted on her sidewalk and front stoop. It said things like: *Susan Marley sucks cock. A witch lives here. Best lay in town. She is always hungry; she is never satisfied.*

Such abuse of the local loon bolstered Paul's theory that the majority of Bedford's population was the product of inbreeding. He stepped over the graffiti and helped Susan through the screen door and up the stairs to her apartment. The door was unlocked, so he pushed it open and searched for a light while she stood behind him, swaying like at the bar to music that came from her head.

He had not been here for over a year. Even then, it had been only to drop by, to make sure that all was well and to play that game that all people who once knew each other play. No hard feelings? You don't bear any grudges that might entail stalking my wife or mailing dead rats through the U.S. Postal Service? Nod your head if you mean "yes" and shake it if you mean "no." Fantastic! See you next year. Merry Christmas, Happy New Year, have a good Easter, and don't blow anything up on the Fourth of July.

When he flicked the switch to the single bulb hanging from the ceiling, he saw that the room was very different from when he'd last visited. The first thing he noticed was the soup.

There were fifty or so cans of Campbell's Tomato Soup on the green shag carpet, atop the kitchen table, and on the side of her bed. Some were inverted. Inside a few were spoons that had congealed to whatever black residue was left inside the can.

With one look, Paul created the scene. Overwhelmed by too many options at the Shaws Supermarket and with fifty dollars or so in hand, Susan had gone the staple food option. Tomato soup, she must have decided, would cover all her nutritional requirements. She had probably been good at first. She had probably heated it up on the stove. But after a while she'd said, what the hell, it's only heat, and spooned it right out of the can. After all the spoons had been used up—this might have taken as long as a week since she probably ate only a can a day—she had decided, why do dishes? Why not just guzzle that slop up like a V8? And then, at some point, maybe over the last couple of days, she had run out of soup. She had decided to go to the bar and see if she could find someone willing to pay for a meal. But perhaps he was giving her too much credit. Perhaps there had been no forethought at all.

Along the walls were six large mirrors, each hanging at different levels, none straight. They were the cheap, Kmart, faux-cherrywood variety, and they were fixed to their places by thick layers of duct tape. Inside them, he saw an infinite number of drunk Paul Martins with their left hands rubbing their foreheads. As he entered the room, they came at him all at once.

"Shit weeps," he pronounced.

Susan had stopped swaying, and was now eyeing him. The blue in her irises got big, and then small, and a shiver ran down his spine. Was it possible for eyes to do that?

He noticed that her hands and feet were dotted with pinprick-sized red spots: frostbite. "Come on," he said. He pushed the dirty clothes and soup cans from the bed. Like a somnambulist, she let him arrange her body so that her arms were at her sides and her head on top of the pile of clothes he had made for her as a pillow.

"Get some sleep," he whispered. He thought about it for a second, then gave in to the impulse and kissed her on the forehead. Soon her breath rose and fell as steadily as a metronome.

In the quiet of the apartment, he went about looking for a kettle to warm some water for when she woke. But there was no kettle, only stacks of dirty dishes in the sink and little roaches that scampered near the drain. It was a mess too big to bother with. Better to throw everything away. Better to nuke it with some of those flammable chemicals stored at the mill. The room was so filthy that his skin literally itched.

He picked up her phone. Surprisingly, along with the crumbs lodged in the receiver, there was a dial tone. He ordered a pizza for her and a six-pack for himself. Then he left to see her landlord, in search of a kettle.

When he opened her door, he saw Rossoff standing at the bottom of the stairs. Rossoff lived on the ground floor, and their apartments were connected by this back entrance though he was never supposed to use it. He was a vet with a bum knee who smoked his days away, giving himself emphysema. From the top of the stairs, Paul could hear the whistle of his wet lungs.

"What are you doing here?" Paul asked.

Rossoff grinned. At six feet tall and about half as wide, he was the living proof of what happened to sumo wrestlers when they got too fat. "Just checking. Never know who's coming and going with her. Like to keep safe." He wore a full beard, much of which was tangled, all the way down to the open collar of his frayed polo shirt.

"You keep safe from inside your own door from now on," Paul told him.

Rossoff nodded and smiled. Paul had seen this smile before. It was the smile some of his students used: *Sure, I'll do my homework, just as soon as you explain to all of us why you got soused for your own protest.* A good deal can be conveyed within a shit-eating grin.

"I think she's sick up there, got a case of hypothermia. You got a kettle I can use? I want to make some tea or something."

Rossoff took a deep breath and that breath fought against him, churning. "She likes you, I can tell. Maybe she's in love," he coughed out.

"What?"

"Feel like something's on its way. Can't stop thinking about her. Bitch gets inside your head. Knows what you don't want to see. Does the mill burn in your dreams, too?"

Paul stopped for a second, and wondered if he was hearing this right. Hadn't Brutton and his wife dreamed the same thing? Surely this was only a coincidence. She was just a girl. A girl with wide eyes. A girl who knew things. But still, just a girl. "A kettle," Paul said. "They have handles. You boil water in them."

Rossoff shrugged. "She owes me four hundred, last two months."

"That's nice. You got a kettle?"

"I don't got nothing."

"I see your education did not place its emphasis on grammar."

Rossoff's mouth turned down in a look of contempt. "I need my money."

They looked at each other for a while. "Fine," Paul gave in. "You got a pen?" Rossoff produced a greasy Bic from his jean pocket and Paul took it while avoiding touching the man's hand. He opened his wallet, where he kept a few extra checks, and wrote one out for two hundred. Rossoff grabbed it and the pen as soon as Paul scrawled his signature.

"Can I get that kettle now?" Paul asked.

"I told you, I don't got one," Rossoff said. He then winked at Paul, opened the door to his adjoining apartment, and left. A smell wafted through the hall as Rossoff shut his door. A smell of staleness, squalor, and human sweat. It was worse than the smell in Susan's apartment and it made Paul think that there was something rotten at the core of this house. It rose and filled every room.

"Thanks, you've been a big help," Paul called out while lightly kicking the door. "That's what society's all about, helping crazy people not die from hypothermia."

With two hundred less dollars in his checking account and no kettle for his troubles, Paul started back up the stairs. He was winded when he reached the second floor, and he realized that, in addition to being miserably out of shape, he was also nearing sobriety. His head was beginning to pound. The unwelcome

Jiminy Cricket in his head asked one question before he silenced it. *What rational person drinks this much and still calls himself rational?*

As he neared her door, he heard a buzzing sound. He stopped, leaned against the wall in the hallway, and listened. All he heard was buzzing, like a thousand voices speaking all at once. He waited, but the voices did not go away. His heart was beating fast, and he realized that for the first time in a long time, he was frightened. He snorted to himself; a grown man frightened of an eighty-pound anorexic who played her television too loud. The booze was making him soft in the head.

He opened her door, and the buzzing stopped. There was actually a shushing sound and it quieted. Out of the corner of his eye, he was sure that he saw movement coming from the mirrors. He was sure he saw a crowd of people. Angry people.

For a moment he understood, and he was too frightened to move. The rain. The dreams all the people in this town seemed to share. The corpse of the paper mill whose sulfuric air, on certain days, he could still smell. The way Susan Marley's irises danced. These things added up. This place was haunted. Susan was haunted. This entire town was haunted, and the only person in this room that wanted saving was himself. If he had been sober, he would have run. But he stood for a few seconds too long, and his moment of clarity passed. In its place returned numbness, the cloudy filter of booze through which he viewed and lived his life.

Paul blinked, and the faces in the mirror were gone. His normal reflection replied to him. He winked at it. Waved at it. It waved right back. He decided he was just too damn drunk.

Just then the bell rang, and he remembered the pizza. Better yet, the beer.

He opened the door a crack. The drenched kid holding the box turned out to be a student in his class. "Hi, Mr. Martin." The kid smiled from pimpled ear to ear.

"Hello, Craig. Long night with this rain, huh?"

The kid tried to peek behind the door, and Paul moved so that he was leaning against its opening.

"How's everything," he asked the boy, handing him a seven-dollar tip on a thirteen-dollar order.

"Good." Craig bobbed his head, trying to get a glimpse past Paul's shoulder.

"Okay. Good night, then." Paul shut the door in the kid's face.

When he turned around, Susan was standing right behind him. He jumped. "Jesus. Don't creep up on people like that," he said.

She grinned, looking less tragic than when he'd seen her in the bar, and more menacing. He remembered the buzzing sound, and the shelf in his stomach dropped a few inches.

"Come on," he said, guiding her to the table. He pressed down on her shoulders so that she sat. Then he placed a slice of pizza in her hand, holding it up for her so that she would not plop it down into the cigarette ashes.

"Eat your pizza," he told her.

She lifted the slice up to eye level and inspected it. He took it from her and fed her a bite. Red sauce slathered the corners of her mouth and cheeks like she'd just earned her wings. She took the slice and began to feed herself.

He looked for a napkin. None present. No paper towels. Toilet paper though, about five sheets left. He thought it might be rude to finish it all and left a square hanging off the brown roll until he remembered that social etiquette was not a pressing factor. He ripped off the last sheet, crinkled it together with the rest, returned to the main room, and handed them to her. "Use this," he said.

She straightened the ball and laid it across her lap. "On your face, Susan."

She held the paper in her hand, considered it, then patted it daintily over her lips.

"Crap," he said. He opened a beer and looked out the window at the long pipe of the mill. Susan stood and brushed her lips against his neck. She smelled of cigarettes and, oddly, paper mill smoke. It came from deep within her lungs. The skin on her upper arms was drawn taut over her bones. She smiled at him because she thought he liked what he saw.

He touched her stomach, her ribs. Unlike his wife, she moved with his touch. He wanted to kiss her. Feel a warm, responsive body, next to his own. Instead, he literally shook himself, stepped back, and kicked over an empty can of soup in the process. The spoon inside it rattled as it hit the green shag carpet. "What the hell happened to you?" he asked. He knew this was a stupid question. He could have asked her this yesterday. He could have asked her this a year ago. But he'd never seen her this deranged until now.

"What's with the mirrors? You really lost it now? You gone over the edge here?"

She grinned and lit a cigarette. It occurred to him that she was having a grand old time. Whooping it up. Watching him squirm was fun for her.

He wished he'd let the hick deal with her problems. Let the hick pay the mute's rent, see how much he liked it. "How long you gonna go without talking? Mimes don't make much money, you know. Or do you only talk when you're alone? I'm a little lost here on the artistic statement."

She blew a smoke ring.

"What should I do here, Susan? Should I call your mom? Should I call the men with the butterfly nets? I can't let you starve to death." She didn't answer. Just like Cathy. A massive brick wall. Maybe a beer would add some levity, lighten the mood. Yes, a beer was in order.

After his third, he started to feel better. But not enough. "You got anything else to drink?" he asked.

She pointed at a cabinet in the kitchen. Inside was the bottle of Jack Daniel's he had left there a year before. He opened it and took a slug, knowing that tomorrow he would be too hung over for work, knowing that he would lose his job, knowing that he didn't even want a drink. He was drunk enough. But it would calm him down. Yes, another drink, and he'd feel much better.

After he sipped what amounted to about two highballs, the room didn't look so bad. Just messy. And the mirrors, they were an artistic statement. She was commenting on the degradation of working-class life. She wanted to be a ballerina. Whatever. Who the hell cared.

He was no longer imagining what her life was like, waking up here every morning. How she probably got up and then realized that she had no plans for the day. But she'd get dressed, just like everyone else. She might forget the little things, like shoes and a coat, but she'd get dressed and go on with the rituals of living. She'd go to the store and buy a few packs of cigarettes, maybe wander around town. And then she'd get tired and go back to bed unless she brought some hick back with her because there was nothing left. Nothing to do. Nothing but four walls, six mirrors, and a can opener. Nothing. Back to this cell.

He wasn't even thinking about how this room was what the inside of his wife's mind had looked like for years. Cluttered with crap and closed within itself. (Was it Bedford that did this? Had Bedford done this to all of them?) Or how shitty it must be to have nobody to take care of you when you get sick. How incredibly shitty it is to be set adrift at eighteen with no place to go. What an exquisitely rare and unforgivable thing had been done to her. A thing that could never be fixed, no matter how bad he felt right now. Well, maybe he was thinking about these things. Maybe just a little bit. He took another swig.

"Shit," he said. He buried his head in his hands. Nope. No better. Not feeling much better right now, thanks. She got up and pulled her dress over her head. It dropped to the floor, and he saw her naked body. She was so thin he caught his breath. Impossibly sharp bones jutted out against pale skin. The sight of her made him understand why he'd lost his faith in God.

She touched his cheek very gently. She caressed him. It was a painful kind of touch. It reminded him of the first time he had been with her. That feeling of being swallowed. The pleasure of your own downfall, knowing that it would be hard to fall any further. She was just a kid even now. Twenty-three years old.

She curled herself around him and he could feel her warmth, the beat of her pulse. She bent down and unbuckled his belt. He was horrified to discover that he was hard. In one of the mirrors, he could see the two of them. A lanky man with bloated cheeks and a naked woman who no longer looked like a woman. Maybe he did this to end that image. To change the story. To curl it into something of beauty. To affirm that he was still a man. Maybe he was just drunk. He kissed her cold lips. She returned that kiss. He did not like himself for thinking this but he knew it was true. It did not matter what they did. If what he was doing was wrong, it did not matter. He imagined that most of the men she brought here had thought the same thing.

He carried her to the bed. She was as light as dry bones. He fumbled with the buttons on his shirt, and she took his hands away and moved them to the outsides of her thighs. It was a pantomime, he knew, of wanting him so badly that she could not wait for him to undress. It was just as false as his desire for her. Had they ever meant this for real?

He pushed down his pants and leaned over her, shoes still on, and she pulled him down. There was a mirror over her head. Though he knew he would not like what he would see, he couldn't help but look at it. He did not see his own reflection. He saw Susan's face. It was gaunt. Black wires weaved their way down her neck, and blood trickled along the side of her face, and he knew that if he made love to this woman, something very bad would happen.

He blinked and the image was gone. He saw only his own drunken face staring back at him. She pulled on him, placing him inside her in a way that made him feel disconnected from his own body. Violated, in some indefinable way. What they did after that could not have been characterized as making love. There was too little touching. She felt . . . cold. She felt dead.

He didn't think that he would come. He did not even try. He found himself wishing, even during the act, that it would be over. That it could be taken back. He pulled back but she stopped him. She stroked him. He waited. He held her thin arms, felt the bones of her legs, and it excited him, the frailty of her. He came looking into her wild eyes.

When he finished, not even out of breath, he zipped his pants and stood. "I'm sorry," he said. "I have to go. I'll be back. I just have to go right now."

She didn't answer. Her head was bent, and he couldn't see her face. Crying probably, over what he had done to her. He fought the urge to leave. He wanted to leave very badly. It was a rush of adrenaline. It was what every instinct tells you to do when your life is in danger. A trait only the higher species possesses: not exactly fight or flight, just guilt.

She raised her head and when she did, she was smiling. It was a happy smile. He had never seen her happy. It terrified him, and he knew, suddenly, that he'd been tricked. She stood and walked toward the door. He grabbed her torso as gently as he could and pulled her back, "You need to put some clothes on," he whispered.

She sank her pearly whites into his arm. He howled and let her go. She left the apartment. Cradling his arm, he followed her. Thinking, because he could not help it, because he was a monumental shit, that Rossoff would see her and they would know. All of Bedford would know the dirty things Paul Martin did to sick women behind closed doors. She faced him, stark naked, at the top of the stairs. Her heels teetered over the edge and she smiled. Her face was flushed.

He heard the same buzzing sound he'd heard before, only now it seemed to be coming from Susan. Only now he thought he could hear his own voice in the din, too. What the hell was happening? Too drunk. Way too drunk.

Behind her, he saw a housefly. It buzzed around Susan as if attracted to her scent, then flew back over the steps that rose fifteen feet, way up in the air, and then it descended. He no longer heard it buzz. It went out the door or into Rossoff's apartment. Or maybe its wing broke and it fell to its death. It was the fly that made Paul remember that though right now was very close to a dream, though, by rights, it should not have been happening, it was real. It was that fly that made him understand.

Susan lifted her hand. She waved. He tried to grab her arm. She jumped back, stepping into nothing but air. She tumbled down. It happened almost in slow motion. Smiling, she fell backward. When she first came into contact with the stairs, she hit the underside of her head, the swell of cranium where the spinal cord ends and the cerebral cortex begins. Then she tumbled, limbs splayed, until she hit the landing.

He ran down after her and checked her neck for a pulse but none was present. When he tried to lift her, her head rolled parallel to her shoulder. It reminded him of that ghost story about the girl with the black ribbon around her neck. Her husband unties it while she is sleeping and her head rolls off.

He walked back up the stairs. At first, he could not find the phone. He couldn't remember where it was. And then he couldn't remember whom to call. He started to dial his own number before he realized what a bad idea that was. And then he was going to call the hospital because maybe it wasn't so bad, maybe she wasn't really dead and they could fuse some things and put her together like Humpty Dumpty, except all the king's horses and all the king's men couldn't put Humpty back together again, and she really was dead. Humpty dead.

He replaced the phone on its receiver. He took a deep breath. That didn't help. He looked at his shoes. They needed polish. Humpty needed polish. No, Humpty needed the police. He thought he was going to vomit. He sat down on the bed she had been lying on only a few minutes before, closed his eyes, and opened them again. He could not stop shaking. He noticed the way the room was kept: crap all over the floor, a layer of cigarette ash coating all the surfaces, the bottle of whiskey he should not have been drinking, and he knew he should have seen this coming.

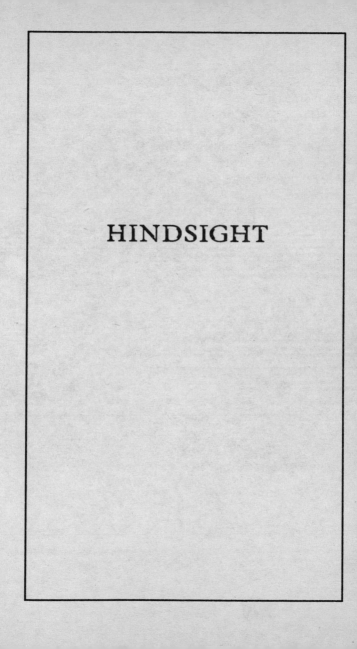

HINDSIGHT

Thursday was a big day in Bedford.

Most had dreamed of senseless things that they could not remember in the morning. There were dark woods and smoldering paper mills and lost, pretty girls turned ugly.

That afternoon, so many little hands reached out the windows of the Bedford School to feel the rain that an observer might have thought that the building was about to set sail. At three o'clock, the younger ones climbed onto their buses, taking their seats in one of eight rows. Some of the younger children pressed their ears to the windows and let the motion of the bus tickle their skin. Some laughed and talked. Others watched the rain. Some were teased. Some did the teasing. Matthew O'Brian and his best friend huddled together, pondering whether Washington, D.C., was a city or a state.

The drops of rain were thick and cold. Arthritic fingers and toes, healed bones, and old war injuries ached throughout the town. School would be canceled in a few days. Stores would shut down. Basements would flood.

Ed O'Brian's conference call ended on an unhappy

note, and he arrived home to receive a message on his answering machine from his daughter, Georgia. He proceeded to cook dinner for her, his cranky girl, because she would be tired. He then retired to his study and began composing the speech he would deliver to his staff. "Dear friends . . ." it read. If his wife were alive, she would know what to say. She would tell him to write about all the years of invaluable service, the loyalty, the sadness they would all feel as this era of their lives, this town, these United States, came to a close. She was dramatic like that. Ed crumpled the paper into a ball, lit a cigar, and started a hand of solitaire. There would be no speech. Tomorrow he would start the phone tree and tell them, *Looks like our luck's run out.*

At eight-twenty, Danny Willow returned home from Montie's Bar. He found his wife crying in the dark. She said she couldn't find a picture of the dog to show people. How could they not have a picture of Benji? It was his fault, she'd bought him that nice digital camera and he'd lost it. And look, he'd been drinking, too. She'd sent him to find Benji and instead he got drunk. No help at all. Danny took his wife's wrinkled hand and kissed it.

Also at eight-twenty, Mary Marley rang up Colette Dubois' Crest toothpaste and pork rinds, flipped the "Open" sign on her register to "Closed," and took a break. Though she had never been intuitive about her children, she knew in some hidden place that the anxiety in her stomach had something to do with one of her own. She tore the heel from a loaf of day-old Italian bread and called home. She told Liz to be very careful tonight. *Please don't go out into the rain. Do you want to talk about anything?* she asked. *I was in a terrible mood at dinner but if you want to talk, please let me know. I can come home anytime.* Nope, Liz told her, I'm just fine. Mary hung up and went back to work, chewing away at the bile in her throat. In her mind's eye she saw a little girl in pigtails. "Mother, may I?" the little girl asked.

In Corpus Christi, Georgia read last month's *People Magazine* about celebrity adoptive mothers at her son's bedside and felt grateful that this long day was almost over.

Paul Martin thought about a broken egg that shatters into so many pieces that it can only be fixed in hindsight.

At exactly eight-twenty, Susan Marley fell down a flight of stairs. People all over Bedford stopped what they were doing and listened to a soft buzzing that droned for a few short seconds, and then was gone. Some trusted their instincts and left Bedford right then, but most did not.

PART TWO

THE BODY

TEN

Excruciatingly Tight
Acid-Washed Jeans

At eight-thirty Thursday evening, Liz Marley fidgeted with her turtleneck. Pulled it this way and that. Inspected the marks with her Cover Girl blush compact. Thumbs in the front, three long fingers on each side of her neck. She shut her compact and hid her head under her pillow. Oh, this had to be a joke. She sat back up and looked at the marks again. She tried not to cry. She hitched her breath again and again. This wasn't happening: the thing in the woods, the dream, her neck, all just a coincidence. A flight of fancy. If her mother was to be believed, the initial stages of madness.

You. It should have been you.

A tear rolled down her cheek, and she knew she was on the verge of a full-on crying jag. This would not do. Bobby could *not* see her like this. He'd think she was nuts or something. He'd decide to scratch dating Susan Marley's sister off his list of charities.

She knew how to make something bad go away. She'd done it enough, having shared a house with her father and Susan. It took a careful balance. She had to count a lot of things. She had to get very quiet, so quiet that she couldn't hear anything going on around her. And she had to think happy thoughts. She could not think about Sylvia Plath's sad poems, or the weirdos looking out their windows at her. Or even how strange it was that every year, it rained for seven days. And she definitely didn't think about the handprints on her throat, or the thing that took a swipe at her leg, no way. Because if she didn't think about these things, like magic they became less real.

She didn't even think about the good times. The way she and Susan used to play dress-up, vamping around their room in strategically placed towels. Or how they'd hold hands when they were frightened. She didn't think about how odd Susan got over the years. How she started talking to herself, silently moving her lips when she thought no one was looking. Or the increasingly vivid nightmares everyone in this town had, in which Susan was always the starring character.

No, the part of Liz that went to school and ran errands and smiled even when she didn't feel like smiling was not thinking about any of this. It was the other girl, the angry girl who cried for no good reason and raged with such a fury that she sometimes bit her own skin, who was thinking about these things. Deep inside, she was connecting dots, solving a mystery whose answer was just beyond her grasp. Deep inside, she was spinning and spinning, the very model of hysteria.

Liz knew what to do. She thought about the one thing that was good in her life, or close to it. She thought about Bobby.

Bobby Fullbright was what people generally referred to as a tool. A power tool. He was the first son of the only doctor in town and he had a nice car and a nice house and people hung around him because of it. They ate the Twinkies and fresh donuts his mother kept in the snack drawer, and he was always the designated driver on weekends, carting all his friends around in the back of his souped-up Explorer, thinking that they liked him for it. Never mind those things they called him, those names like pygmy and ass wipe. Those were terms of endearment.

Before they started dating, she and Bobby rarely spoke. Liz hardly ever spoke to anyone. But she ran into Bobby at the Corpus Christi Library during her junior year of high school. He was short. Cute, but short. And he walked with this swagger like he was trying to make up for it. They had both been trying to find books for a research paper on Shirley Jackson's "The Lottery," and said curt hellos before going in their separate directions. She'd watched him swagger and pose, leaning up against any and all things handy. He accidentally knocked over a stack of New Age self-help, and then made a hasty retreat to the other side of the room. After the librarian April Willow told him to please pick those books up, she knew he didn't make messes in his own house, he'd better not do it here, he returned them to their places and sat at a desk behind her, watching.

After a little while of staring at her like she was some kind of carnie freak, he got up and joined her. She knew why he did it. He wanted to prove that he was one of the few souls possessed with an enlightened view concerning social strata. Yes, he could prove that he was the kind of guy who would hire an untouchable in India. He would sit next to Liz Marley when his friends weren't around.

She bent her head over an analysis of the incidence

of cannibalism in small New England towns, and tried to make it look like she was really busy.

He sat backward in his chair and nudged her, sticking a book under her nose. It was Albert Camus' *The Stranger*. "You ever read this?" he asked. His voice was unnaturally deep.

"No," she answered.

"You're smart enough. You'd like it." He puffed out his chest, and his voice, somehow, got even lower. "I'm an existentialist." He said this in that way that meant he knew from smart. He might hang out with the dumb kids, but he had a deep need for a kindred spirit. And for now, until she proved herself otherwise, he had decided that Liz would understand.

"Actually, I only have a forty-five IQ," she told him. "No one ever thought I'd be able to dress myself. I've only been doing it this last year or so."

He frowned, like he might walk away. *Great*, she thought, *a guy tries to talk to me and I tell him I'm retarded. That's just great. No wonder I have no friends. Great.* And then, after a second or two, Bobby got the joke. He laughed.

Then he pulled his chair closer, and told her his theories. He talked about how the middle class appropriated rebellious art forms and made them their own. How dominant ideology represented the status quo and those who struggled against it might win out for a little while, but in the end they always failed. *Saturday Night Fever* had once been about a bunch of poor Italian Catholics with no way out until some lame-ass Bee Gees fans turned it into a pop-culture disco anthem. He talked about how the only people who wanted subsidies to keep the mill open were the ones who didn't think anyone in Bedford could rise above where they came from. He talked while waving his hands around like a madman. He talked so spastically that the veins in his neck bulged, and she'd wanted to giggle. He talked a lot.

At first she felt stupid because she didn't know what ideology meant and she had never heard of *Saturday Night Fever,* and then she realized that this was what people did. Friends. They talked about things that mattered to them; they wasted time. She was sorry she'd missed out on this. And finally, as the hour passed, she'd just felt sorry for him. She imagined him saying these things to Steve McCormack and she understood that they didn't make fun of him because he was short. They made fun of him because he was Bobby.

"Time to go home, children," Mrs. Willow finally told them as she started turning out the lights in the stacks. Bobby moaned. "Chil-dren," he mocked in an imitation of Mrs. Willow's prissy voice, and it seemed all wrong coming out of his mouth. It seemed like he thought he was supposed to be mean, but he couldn't pull it off. A very endearing tool.

He gave her a ride home that night, and when he dropped her off he asked her out for the next night, a Friday. "Yes!" she told him, so nervous and excited that she shut the door and fled for her house without saying good night.

In English class the next day, he did not talk to her. He draped his arm over the back of Steve McCormack's desk and asked things like, What are you doing this weekend, huh? Huh? He pretended Liz was not there, even though she was sitting right in front of him.

Under ordinary circumstances, she would never have called him that night. She wasn't much of a talker. Didn't even know how to wave with conviction. She told herself that she called because she was angry at the way he had treated her in school. She planned to tell him that he had risen to her expectations: He was, indeed, a power tool. But mostly, it was the idea of staying at home that made her call. The week-long rain had started falling that evening, and the thought of being trapped inside the house with no reason to leave, no one to leave with, had made her wonder if perhaps she had been offered a way out and who cared whether the emissary was Charlie Manson or Bobby Fullbright, she'd better take it.

She didn't bother saying hello when he picked up the phone. Didn't even ask if this was Bobby she was speaking to. "Are we still going out tonight?" she asked.

He sighed and she knew this had been a mistake. She should have told him she didn't like him anyway. And even though he used lots of big words, he was still a tool. Did he know everybody thought he was a tool? "Uhhhhh, is eight o'clock okay? I could pick you up then," he said.

He arrived at exactly eight. Her mother kept her waiting at the top of the stairs, saying: This is how sophisticated people behave, they interview the suitor while the daughter gets ready. Since your father's not here anymore, I'll have to do it myself. At the door Mary asked questions like, "Are you getting financial aid for college, or are your parents spending some of their doctor money on tuition?"

When Liz finally came down the stairs (she decided that if she waited for her mother to retrieve her, he might run back to his car, leaving a Bobby-shaped hole in the door), Bobby took her in with his eyes. For a moment she saw what he saw; Susan Marley's ugly sister wearing excruciatingly tight, secondhand store acid-washed Jordache jeans that made her ass look like two quarreling dogs, and a lot of black eyeliner she didn't know how to apply.

They got into his car. Before he started the ignition, he looked at her. He had dark brown hair and soft skin like someone very young. He was the kind of guy you brought home to Mom and Dad if you happened to have a dad. The kind of guy who took pity on wallflowers but would never sink so low as to date one of them. She knew what he was going to say: *Let's go to a movie in Corpus Christi.* He'd put their coats on the chair between them, saying he liked the legroom. After it was over, he'd drop her off and tell her, *Let's keep this to ourselves.* She didn't care so much about going out with him, she wanted to explain: It would be nice just to have a friend. She didn't say anything. And then, somehow, her eyes got watery. Just a little. Enough to notice.

He broke the silence. "Your mom always meet your friends at the door?"

"I wouldn't know."

He took a deep breath. "Since they stopped running night shifts at the paper mill some kids have been going there. We found a way in, and as long as we're quiet, nobody cares. It's dry and we can drink, so it's cool. Some of my friends'll be there. You know them, right?"

"Yeah."

"You up for it?"

She thought she had been very wrong. He was not your textbook nice guy. He was the kind of guy TV mothers warned their children about. His friends would not be there. It would be just the two of them. Alone. In an abandoned building. "Okay," she told him.

They drove east, past Main Street and the river,

farther still, to the mill. He pulled over to the side of the road. They got out of the car and she jumped onto the snowy ground. "It's just over here," he called above the rain. From above, she could see a small plume of smoke coming out from the pipe of the paper mill. She followed him down the path and through the side door whose lock had been pried open.

To her surprise, his friends were there: Louise Andrias, Owen Read, Steve McCormack, and a few of the older kids who had graduated or were about to graduate from Bedford High. They were warming their hands around the fire they'd built from dried wood inside the mill's empty vat, and drinking from cans of Milwaukee's Best. Rusted old machines were stored in a corner, and some of the windows along the private offices were broken. There was no night watchman, and no one so far had come looking to see why smoke was blowing out the mill's pipe. From the look on Bobby's face, she could tell he thought all of this was great fun.

A yellow Sony radio played "Fairytale of New York." Louise danced around the room with her arms outstretched; the physical embodiment of what looked to Liz like joy. These were the people she had lived with all her life. The normal people, though to her, they seemed on the periphery, someplace not quite fully visible. For a fleeting instant, she hated every one of them.

There was a chemical smell to the burning. She guessed there were remnants of sulfur in the vat. She'd learned in chemistry class that when sulfur burns, particularly hydrogen sulfide, it becomes toxic. It mixes with air and irritates the lungs as acid rain, or mixes with heat and water and becomes explosive. And here were the cool kids of Bedford, hanging out in an abandoned mill smoking pot and breathing the stuff. It became clear to her right then, in a way she'd never before recognized, that she was poor.

She followed Bobby as he walked toward them. The song ended and Louise stopped dancing. Bobby slowed and they stayed in the shadows like Peeping Toms, feeling the mood of the group. This couldn't be easy for Bobby, taking her here.

Louise looked up at the ceiling. "We could blow it up, you know. All these old chemicals. Pour them out, throw in a match, and the whole thing will go."

"You're such a pyro." Owen laughed.

Bobby stepped forward and smiled. "Hey," he said. "Brought somebody."

They turned to Liz in unison.

In that moment, Liz let her imagination run away with her. She didn't usually let it out to play, but somehow it had escaped. It was climbing trees, it was doing penny drops, it was extending itself to its limit. Human sacrifice, it was thinking. Bobby had brought her here as part of his initiation to the cool people's club. He could join, so long as he slit her throat with a serrated beer can and threw her into the fiery vat. Brought some *body*.

Louise wore loose blue Levi's and a hooded jacket. Her wool gloves were cut off at the fingers so that she could hold her Camel Lights unencumbered. The instant she saw Liz, the air changed. It became thick. "Hey, Liz," Louise said with a gravelly voice and a smile too wide to be real.

"Hi," Liz said.

Bobby spread his L. L. Bean fleece down on the dusty floor and sat, motioning for Liz to share it with him like a picnic blanket. She did. Steve McCormack spat brown chew into an empty can of Milwaukee's Best.

"She screws for money, right?" Steve asked. A few weeks ago she'd seen Steve spray painting the side of Susan's apartment. In red letters he'd written, "Susan Marley sucks cock." Maybe that was the kind of thing popular people thought was funny. Maybe Steve McCormack was a jerk.

"She's a witch." Louise giggled, and Liz guessed she was high, even though she'd never seen someone get high before, never smelled pot before, never even smoked a cigarette or filched her mom's cheap wine. Louise gestured at the paper mill where they were sitting. "Susan takes me here when I sleep. We go to the basement. People died down here, you know. Lots of them." Then Louise was laughing convulsively, until she was red-faced and crying.

"What are you talking about?" Bobby called over the sound of Louise's laughter.

"Susan Marley, she screws for money," Owen Read jumped in. "Right Liz?"

"Or a free pack of smokes, I hear," Steve said.

Liz looked at them in the dark mill: Louise, Owen, and Steve. The light flickered under the fire. Their eyes were empty, without intelligence. Feral. Their irises got big, and then small. They bore a resemblance, for just a moment, to Susan.

"Shut up." Bobby laughed, in that same kind of tone that he had used when mocking April Willow. The tool voice. Like it was all a joke. "Where can I get a beer?"

"None left for a Marley," Louise answered, still giggling ferociously. Her hand was raised protectively over the full six-pack by her side. Bobby shuffled uncomfortably.

Liz turned to Bobby. "I feel kind of sick."

Bobby nodded. "I'll take you home."

She was already on her feet and walking out the door. She got to his car before him and leaned up against it, trying not to cry. She should have known this would happen. She should never have called him. It was probably all a trick, and even Bobby was in on it. She was the grand prize in a dogfight. Right now, all of them were laughing at the ugliest girl in school.

Bobby came up behind her and opened the door. They drove without speaking. "I'm sorry," he whispered as he pulled in front of her house.

To her surprise, he called the next day and asked if she'd like to go for a drive. Against her better judgment, she said yes. They took the highway north, crossing that very same bridge, and drove for miles. The rain stopped falling when they reached Penobscot County, and they rolled down their windows. "It doesn't rain in other places the way it does in Bedford," he told her.

"Yeah."

"You ever think Bedford is haunted?"

She shrugged. "By what?"

"I don't know. By itself, maybe. By the things that happen here."

Liz nodded. "Maybe people haunt it, too."

He looked at her for a while. "Like who?"

She shrugged, though it was clear to both of them that she was speaking of Susan.

"Yeah. I guess they can," he said. Then he nodded at the road. "Sometimes I wish I could just keep driving."

"Yeah," she said. "Let's run away together. We'll survive by our wits."

He laughed. Then he said, much to her surprise. "You're really pretty."

She looked down at her feet and wondered whether he was mocking her.

"Your smile, I mean. I like it."

She laughed nervously and tried not to smile. "Thanks."

"It's funny. You sit across from me in math. You're always spacing out. People say things to you. They say not nice things, mean things, and it's like you don't even hear them. Sometimes I see you smile to yourself, and it's like, I want to know someone who can smile like that, even when nobody else is happy."

This probably should have made her happy. It did, in fact, make her happy. But it also hurt somehow, in a good way, like she wanted to cry. That someone had bothered to watch her. That someone had bothered to think she was worth something. He held out his hand and she took it, and that made her want to cry, too.

"You know, I had no idea those guys would be like that."

"Like what?"

"At the bridge. I wouldn't have done that to you," he said, his voice one octave deeper than his normal speech, like he was trying very hard to do the right thing.

She nodded.

"They like you. I'm sure they do."

"No, Bobby. They don't."

Ahead, they saw a sign for Canada; sixteen miles to go. They had been driving for three hours. "We should go back," she said. Getting caught out of Bedford when it's raining is a bad idea. You never know when the bridge is going to go out. You never know if you'll be able to get back in.

They sighed simultaneously as he turned around at

the next exit and headed south toward Bedford. "They're not always nice to me, either," he said, and it occurred to her that she might not be the only person looking for a way out.

The summer after they started dating, they had sex for the first time in the back of his car. She hadn't expected it to hurt. She was sore when they were finished and she didn't bother to pretend she liked it. She thought maybe he was sticking it in wrong. Sex could not possibly be that unpleasant. They were dazed when they drove home that night, neither talking very much. They had each hoped that it would be perfect, and somehow, it wasn't.

But they tried again. And again. And again, until one day, she liked it. A month after that, she really liked it. A month after that she told Bobby that next to roller coasters, sex was her favorite thing in the whole world.

They called each other every night. Sometimes he told her he could smell her on his sheets. He said that it made him happy to go to bed because he could smell her with him. Almost every afternoon when he was done with basketball practice, they went to the Dugout (Liz always had a Diet Coke, he had a root beer and a double order of cheese fries that she picked at), and they sat and talked or didn't bother to talk at all. When the other kids came around, sometimes saying hello to Bobby, never saying a word to Liz, they pretended that they were in a world all their own. A world they had created where only they lived.

In the fall Bobby would enroll at Bowdoin, and if she kept her grades up in chemistry, UMO was giving her a free ride her freshman year. Sometimes they invented silly names for the children they'd one day have.

Bobby liked Dylan with the middle name Thomas. Liz liked Perciville Sweetwater, so the kid would have a sense of humor. But she knew the plans they made were pretend. Every once in a while, she would remind herself of that. She would look in the mirror in the morning and tell herself: This won't last. Don't depend on this. But for now, she was happy to take it while she could.

ELEVEN
When Bogart Was King

Bobby Fullbright loved cigarettes. He especially liked Lucky Strikes. That's what they used to smoke back in the old days when movies were good and Humphrey Bogart was king. He only smoked occasionally (even if all that stunt-your-growth crap was just Big Brother hype, he didn't plan on staying five-foot-four forever), but he carried a stale, half-smoked pack in his front jacket pocket wherever he went. After he and Liz had sex in the back of his car, he'd always take them out, tap on the pack until just one fell loose, and bite on it like a toughie. "Come with me, my warm little potato, and I will show you the world," he'd tell her in a perverted Frenchman's accent while she giggled.

Tonight he had the idea that he would not be smoking any postcoital Luckys. No one visited Susan Marley, not even her family. No one wanted to. He didn't want to. The girl was a total freak.

He still wasn't sure if Liz was pulling his leg about tonight. He'd almost asked her why she'd decided on tonight of all nights—the first night of rain—for some family reunion, but then he remembered that it was the fifth anniversary of her father's death and he'd sort of understood. They were family, after all. Not a bit alike, but they were family.

He'd called her a little while ago to let her know he was going to be late because he had to put his twin brothers to bed. "Do you mind?" he'd asked her.

"No, it's fine," she'd told him, but he could tell from the distant tone in her voice that nothing was fine. He'd realized, in fact, that she'd been especially spacey all day, and if she wanted to visit her whack-job sister tonight, something had to be very wrong.

And so, he tried to hurry the evening along.

"Okay, what story?" he asked the twins, both of whom were squirming above their Spider-Man sheets. He was thirteen when they'd been born, and thought of himself as more of a close uncle to them than a brother.

"A scary story!" Alex said. The more outgoing of the twins, he jumped to his feet and bounced on the bed. "Tell a scary story, like last time."

"No. No scary stories. I hate scary stories!" Michael bellowed from the other bed.

Bobby waited for them to settle down. He would not tell a scary story because, while Alex loved them, Michael would not be able to sleep, and would eventually climb into their parents' bed. Bobby's father had recently ordered him not to tell stories about bloody roses or men with hooks for hands anymore, and it left him with the disturbing yet incontrovertible evidence that his parents led an active sex life.

"A scary story," Alex said while looking at Michael with a perverse smile on his face. "Bobby, tell a scary story."

"No, a book. You both have to agree on a book. Just

one book, no more than that. I'm going out with Liz tonight."

"I hate Liz," Alex said.

He'd just started using the word "hate," and threw it around like a preposition. "Well I think you smell," Bobby said.

Alex howled. "I do not! I don't! She's bad and I hate her. She goes to the graveyard at night. She digs up the people."

This is what his brothers had learned in kindergarten; the alphabet, blocks, and how to hate the Marley family, because no one seemed to care that Liz was not Susan.

Bobby glared. "Sorry," Alex said. He might have started his lecture about how nice people don't listen to losers, but he looked at his watch and saw that it was almost nine o'clock. He thought again about Liz's voice, and how its coldness had reminded him of their first date, if that's what you'd call it, at the paper mill. How she'd sat straight as a corpse on the drive home, trying to pretend that it had never happened at all. Of course he'd called her the next day; he couldn't let it end that way. And then he called her the day after that. And the day after that. And then, almost without his knowing, they were going out.

Bobby directed his words at Michael because he knew that Michael would be an easier convert. "I have to go out tonight. Aren't you guys my friends? Don't you want me to have fun? I thought you were my friends."

Michael looked torn, like he was deciding between his favorite stuffed animal and his left arm. "Friends want each other to have fun, don't they?" Bobby asked.

"Yes," Michael answered.

"We'll pick a book," Alex agreed.

They picked a book. It was *The Three Billy Goats Gruff*. Bobby pretended to be the oldest goat, stomping across the room and neighing while reading the story. He made a quick exit afterward, before they could convince him to read it again. This was their logic: one book, read twice.

In the hall, he passed his sisters, both of whom were primping in front of the bathroom mirror. They were in the seventh and eighth grades and considered themselves paragons of fashion. Margaret had dark hair and pale, powdered skin. She wore black nail polish that was always chipped, and her corduroys hung loosely off her hips.

Bobby leaned into the bathroom doorway. "Hey kids." He smiled.

"Kids," Margaret scoffed. Katie grinned from ear to ear.

"Painfully Deep Goth Chick," Bobby said, raising his chin at Margaret.

Margaret slammed the door in his face. "Shut up, shortie," she yelled and he laughed.

He stopped in his parents' room next. He found them sitting at their desk. His mother was punching numbers into a computer. She was wearing her favorite velour leisure suit, the one she always wore around the house like she thought she was a middle-aged J-Lo. It was light blue and had elastic at her plump waist, her wrists, and her ankles.

His father turned. He still had on his white jacket from the hospital. He sometimes wore it and his stethoscope around the house like he was trying to prove he was employed. "Mom's trying to teach me how to use Quickbooks." His father pointed at the computer.

"My mom, or yours?"

"My son the smart ass."

"Unlike you, Adam," his mother said, not looking up from the screen. "Now look, it's easy. See, just pull down adjusted total under tools with the mouse and it all comes up."

"Now you're talkin'," his father said, the sentiment laden with sarcasm.

"I'm going out with Liz for a while," Bobby told them.

"Okay, be careful," his mom said.

"He took sex ed," his father added.

"Adam!" his mother shrieked, and then the two of them started that bantering that made Bobby feel like he was invisible and he closed the door behind him.

Though they'd made it clear from the start that they didn't like Liz (his father said she was too fragile, and his mother said she dominated his time, but Bobby knew that, really, they just didn't like her connection to Susan Marley), they never asked him where he was going or when he'd be back. They knew he wouldn't wind up in some hospital getting his stomach pumped like Owen Read, and no way he was stupid enough to smoke meth like the kids on the south side of town who'd started a lab. He wasn't into anything heavier than pot, especially now that he dated Liz, who thought a half can of beer was life on the wild side. Only once, at fourteen, had he ever staggered into the house and puked his guts out. But he'd also cleaned it up, and risen at the crack of dawn to make breakfast for the girls while his parents had fed the twins their bottles. He was the oldest, and responsibility was part of the job. But still, this trust they gave him sometimes made him feel like one of those dorks who stacks books at the Corpus Christi Library to make a few extra quarters.

Bobby walked outside and into the rain. The cold air made his teeth chatter, and to stay warm, he jogged to the Explorer his parents had given him for his eighteenth birthday. Feeling wild (what the hell, basketball season was over—not that he ever got off the bench), he lit a cigarette and popped in some old school Nirvana. As he pulled out of the driveway, he looked at his house. Through the windows he could see his sisters and his parents, the soft glow of the twins' nightlight. He thought about how nice it was that he owned all the people inside it, that they belonged to him. And then he thought about how much better it would be once he got out of here.

TWELVE
The Body

"Hey," Bobby said when Liz Marley climbed inside his car. He was parked in the driveway of her house. He gave her a wet, sloppy, silly kiss, and peach fuzz tickled her upper lip.

She wrinkled her nose. "You smell like smoke."

"Yup."

"I thought that was just for after sex. Do you have a blow-up doll in your backseat?" He looked shocked at such a suggestion and she laughed. "Sorry."

"That's not funny," he said. "It's demented."

"What about a cadaver? Do you have a cadaver in your trunk?" she asked, still giggling, unable to stop. It occurred to her that perhaps she was not as calm as she'd hoped. She was still a little frayed around the edges. A card short of a full deck. A screw or two loose. Gray matter gone black.

"What's the matter with you?" Bobby asked, morally indignant, because Bobby was not a person who could juxtapose "corpses" and "sex" in the same sentence. He was not even a person who said "fuck" to describe sex. Never.

Liz kept giggling.

"Hey," she heard him saying, "hey," in a soothing voice like he thought she was crying. It made her laugh louder. She brayed. Silly Bobby. Silly Bobby thought he was so tough. Silly Bobby loved Elliott Smith and whenever he heard "Needle in the Hay" he'd get all singer-serious and hum along like he could totally identify with some heroin addict from Oregon who stabbed himself to death. Silly Bobby with his perfect family. Easy for people to be tough when they've never had anything to fight.

"Liz!" he said.

She stopped laughing. He put his hand on her back and patted, hard, like he thought she was choking on something and he wanted to get it out. "I'm okay," she said.

"Whoa," he muttered, pulling her close. She felt his warmth, right down to the center of him. Bobby was always warm, even the tips of his fingers and toes. Like all the years his mother had given him hot chocolate on cold days had protected him from chills for the rest of his life.

"What's the matter?" he asked. She didn't answer. She saw through the gutter window of her house that the light in the basement was still on. She imagined that her mother had not actually gone to work. She was hiding in the basement and would soon emerge, a newspaper draped over her head to preserve her coif, to say hi. *Hi, Bobby,* she would say. *Is Liz telling tales again? Such an imagination. Always inventing. You know, when she was little, she told me she saw a monster in the basement but it was only her father. Always telling fibs, my chubby girl.*

"It's like I don't even know how to be," she said.

"What do you mean?" he asked.

I mean that I'm not sure I can trust myself. I mean that I think I might be crazy. I think those kids you don't hang out with anymore were right. There is something wrong with me. "Oh, I don't know."

"Oh." He edged toward her, and she could see that he was thinking about giving her a hug. Instead, he edged back again. Yes, he was cute. But he would never know from looking at her what she was thinking. He would never be able to take her in his arms and tell her that everything was going to be okay.

"Do you want to tell me about it?" he asked.

"Wouldn't do any good."

"How was the cemetery? I heard you went there after school. Margaret saw you. Why didn't you tell me? I would have gone with you."

"It was fine."

"It's the anniversary of your father's death, isn't it?"

"Yeah. Five years. My mom'll probably lock herself in her room and throw a party."

Bobby chortled. "Is that why you want to see Susan?"

She shook her head.

"Are you going to tell me why you dragged me out here tonight?"

"Because she's my sister and I should visit her. I just want to stop by and see if she needs anything." In fact, the last time she had visited Susan's apartment had been over a year before. She'd ridden her three-speed there after school. When Susan came to the door, she'd looked Liz up and down, opened the door farther, and let Liz see that she had company. A weird-looking fat man whose breath had sounded like drowning.

"You were serious when you said you wanted to visit her?" he asked.

"Yeah."

"I thought you might be kidding."

"Yeah, well, it's hard to tell."

"It *is* hard to tell," he said with his jaw clenched, and she could see that he had decided to be annoyed with her. When people are uncomfortable, they get mad at you. Liz had seen this before. Yes, he would probably break up with her now. She could see it coming.

He pulled out of the driveway and turned right on Chestnut Street. "Susan's is the other way," she said.

"Really?" he asked, still driving. He clenched his jaw so tightly she thought he might dislocate it.

"Do you want to turn around?"

He didn't answer, kept driving.

The snow had melted by about a foot, and every time the Explorer made a turn, she could hear the sound of sloshing water. There were a few workmen clearing out the gutters on Nudd Street. They did that every year though it never seemed to help. The roads always flooded.

"Well?" she asked.

They were at the top of the hill now, near the woods where they sometimes turned off the headlights and made love. She squinted and looked out the window, thinking that perhaps Susan was out there. Susan was waiting for her, in the dark.

He stopped the car and pulled the keys from the ignition.

"What are you doing?" she asked.

Bobby leaned back. His jaw unclenched. He did not seem angry, but sad. "Remember the first time we came here? I told you I'd done it before with Andrea Jorgenson but I lied. You knew, didn't you?"

"Yeah, I knew." No, she thought, he would not leave her. He was Bobby, the guy who had defended her under the bridge. The guy who called every night, and even though she never told him about the fights she had with her mother, he would sometimes ask, when she was feeling very low and talking softly about nothing, "How are you holding up?"

She touched his outstretched arm and he flinched. "Don't treat me like that," he said.

"Like what?"

"Like the enemy. Like your mother," he told her.

"I don't."

"You do. Like you hate me."

"That's stupid. I don't. And I don't hate my mother."

He winced. "I'm not stupid. I know you're different, that things are weird. I mean, you tried to tell me that Susan was a photographer for *House and Garden* magazine and that's why she's always wandering around, she's trying to see in people's houses. She doesn't talk, Liz! I mean, she doesn't even talk and you try to pretend she's normal. Like I don't know about her. Everybody knows there's something wrong with her. Even my mom has nightmares about her! You tell me these lies and I guess you're trying to make a joke but sometimes I think you want me to believe it." Then he turned to her, yelling now, as if this last part was what really galled him, this last part had sent him over the edge, "And when I asked you what was wrong at school today you told me it was the Mormons. You were talking about the stupid Mormons, Liz! Why were you talking about the Mormons?"

"The Mormons?" she asked. She couldn't help it. She knew how angry he'd get. She giggled.

He narrowed his eyes. "I'm sorry," she said, still giggling. "I really am. But you just went totally nuclear. It's like you were possessed."

"I'm serious," he growled. And once again, because his behavior was so out of character, it kept her laughing.

"Come on, Bobby." She lowered her voice in an attempt at seriousness. "I'm not laughing *at* you, I'm laughing *with* you."

He did not look happy. Not exactly mad, closer to embarrassed. She stopped laughing. She wasn't being very nice. Probably she was being a little mean. The kind of mean that other kids had been to him not too long ago. The way you treat a tool.

"Hey," she said. "You okay? I didn't mean to make fun of you. Really. I'm just upset."

He smiled a strained smile like he was trying to prove his feelings weren't hurt. "That's all right. You weren't laughing at me, you were laughing with me."

"Really, Bobby. I'm sorry."

"Fine."

She shimmied across the seat and into the crook of his arm. After a while, he cupped her shoulder. "Something happened last night. And then maybe today, too. I guess I'm upset."

"Tell me," he said.

For a moment, but only a moment, she was annoyed. Because there was an implicit agreement here. A give and a take with which she was not sure she wanted to be involved. And then it was gone. This was Bobby, after all. She told him everything: her dream, the blood in the snow, the thing that had chased her in the woods, trying to talk to her mother about it tonight, and then finally, she showed him her throat. She thought this would the hardest part—like he'd see it, and know that something really was wrong with her. But it turned out to be a relief. He was someone who cared, and wanted to believe her. Still, she didn't tell him about what Susan had said: *You. It should have been you.* That was between her and her dream.

Very gently, he traced the edges of her neck with the tips of his fingers. It made her feel safe in a way she had not expected. When he did stuff like this, it was clear to her that one day he'd be a doctor.

"It's crazy, right?"

"Which part—does this hurt?"

"No. It faded a lot since this morning, but I think you can still make out the hands. All of it's crazy. Every part. Or maybe I'm crazy."

"Could you have done this to yourself in your sleep?" He let go and looked at her.

"I guess. In a way, I hope so."

"Yeah. But you think she did it. She got inside your dream." She couldn't see his expression in the dark, just his shining eyes.

Liz nodded. "I've dreamed about her before. But lately the dreams are more vivid. Last night felt so real. And then today—there was definitely something in the woods with me. Maybe it was something left over from the dream, or some kind of wild animal, or maybe it was Susan. I don't know. But something chased me . . ."

Bobby sat back, and she wasn't sure whether he was

just considering everything she was saying, or deciding whether he should start fitting her for a straitjacket. She decided, for once, to be optimistic.

"When we were kids we used to play memory, you know, with a deck of cards all turned down? She could go through the whole deck without losing a turn. She'd go from card to card all in a row and find its match . . . Anyway, she's getting stronger. Next time I dream about her, I'm afraid my nightmare will follow me into the real world. Or worse, I won't wake up at all."

He squinted his eyes. "So why do you want to see her?"

Liz looked out the window. The rain pounded against the roof of the truck like someone wanted to be let in. "I need to know." Then she sighed. "I wish she didn't hate me. We used to get along. When we were kids. I loved her, I think . . . I still do."

Bobby spoke softly. "She's sick, Liz. Whatever else is happening, she's sick. You didn't do anything wrong."

"I guess. Do you ever dream about her?"

"Yeah. They've been getting worse for me, too."

She hadn't expected him to say this. This was Bobby, after all. The boy whose family played Monopoly together on Sunday nights. "I didn't know you dreamed about her."

"I thought it would upset you."

"It does, actually. I think it makes me mad at her. What do you dream?"

"I can't really remember," he said. "All I remember is her, you know?"

She touched her throat with her fingers. "Bobby, something's gone wrong since the mill closed. Can you feel it?"

He nodded. "Yeah. I can."

"I'm scared."

She felt his arm around her. "Me, too."

"Then you believe me?"

"Yeah, I do. It might not be exactly what you think, but I believe you."

She closed her eyes and tried to make the lump in her throat go away. They listened to the rain patter against the windshield. "I wish we didn't live in Bedford."

He nudged her. "Wait till college. Everything's better in college. You only have to come home for Christmas and you can eat pizza three times a day."

The lump in her throat burst and came out as a giggle, quickly followed by a snort.

"Gross," he said.

"Um. At least I don't eat the old whoopee pies I find in my glove compartment, Bobby Fullbright."

He smiled. They both laughed a little, and felt some of the pressure of the day release.

"Do you still like me?" she asked.

"I love you." This was the first time he had ever told her this, and it made her feel so good that for a moment everything was right with the world.

"I love you, too, Bobby."

Before heading to Susan's, they made love in the back of his car, and he had his second Lucky of the night while whispering sweet nothings in a Frenchman's accent.

The south side of town where Susan lived stank of the mill. The wind had carried it there for almost one hundred years, and it had gotten into the dirt, the trees, the water, and the wood of the houses. If you lived there, Liz imagined, you could probably scrape the sulfur out of your pores.

They got out of the car. The house was old and dilapidated. A shutter flapped in the wind, and there was graffiti along the sidewalk that in the dark she could not make out. She rang the front bell. Bobby wrestled in vain with the umbrella, but it turned inside out and they both got wet. "It's okay," he told her when he saw that she was so frightened she was shaking.

She nodded and twisted the knob. The door opened. They stepped into a small vestibule at the foot of a narrow, wooden staircase. The place stank like rotten eggs. In the dark she could make out a figure, maybe a person, sitting on the floor. "Suze?" she asked. No answer. Bobby flicked a switch that lit up the stairway. Liz gasped. Bobby pulled her back outside and into the rain.

When they came into the house again, they saw the same thing. A naked woman, her back pressed up against the foot of the stairs. Blood. Eyes open, but unseeing.

Liz looked down. Her feet were inside a puddle of blood. She jumped back, and her shoes left wet, circular tracks on the floor. "Oh," she said. She tried to wipe the blood from her Keds by scraping them against the walls and stairs, but instead she smeared everything she touched with red. "Oh!" She moved quickly, her body jerking, and then covered her face with her hands. "Get it off! Get it off!"

Something grabbed her.

Who grabbed her? It was the thing in the woods! It was her Father! It was Susan!

She screamed. Someone was speaking but she couldn't make out the words. Bobby. His mouth was moving. He was trying to tell her something. He repeated himself a few times. "I found a pulse on her thigh," he was saying. "She's alive."

She pushed away from him, opened the screen door, leaned outside, and vomited steamed broccoli and eight postdinner Keebler E. L. Fudge cookies onto a melting snowdrift. He held her shoulders. "We have to call for an ambulance," he said. "Do you know CPR? She's not breathing."

Liz didn't answer.

He shook her. "Do you know CPR?" She didn't answer. "I'm going to call upstairs," he said, leaping over the body and up the steps.

Liz looked at her sister. Blood trickled down the side of her face. It was exactly how Susan had looked in her dream. The room was very bright suddenly, and she heard the low buzzing of a fly. Her hand hovered near Susan's cheek. She wanted to touch her. But then, no, she couldn't. No, she didn't want to. Because even though Susan's eyes were blank and unblinking, even though the floor was red, she could feel Susan right now. She could feel Susan watching her.

She took a deep breath and stepped over the body and up the stairs. "Let's go," she said to Bobby, whose wide eyes were focused on the squalor of Susan's apartment. There was a pizza box and some cans of Budweiser atop a small kitchen table. An unmade bed, sunken at the middle. There were about six mirrors, and Liz could see an infinite number of herself inside them. There was something else in those mirrors. Something she'd see if she looked closely enough. There were faces in those mirrors.

She pulled on his hand, and led him to the door. "Please, let's get out of here."

Once out of the apartment, Bobby recovered. He raced down the stairs, calling out to her, "I've never done this before, but when I called nine-one-one the guy said I should try." Then he put his mouth over Susan's and breathed. Susan's chest rose and fell. Up and down. Up and down. On the floor, a stain of blood grew larger.

She inched in closer to Bobby, and when she did her shoes squeaked. Blood. Sticky blood. The room skidded to the left, and then to the right. Sparks filled the air, and then there was darkness.

Liz Marley fainted.

THIRTEEN
Wraith (Paul's Flight)

The car was parked by the side of the road, its hazards flashing. Like a man so unaccustomed to crying that when he does so the result is an awkward fusillade of misdirected emotion, Paul hadn't communicated with his subconscious for so long that it was angry with him, and his first dream in a decade was horrific.

In the dream he was a different man. A sober man. The very model of a model citizen. A man who wore a shirt and tie to the corner store. A man who tucked his kids into bed at night. The dream went back in time, to the day of the protest, only this time he didn't go to Montie's. This time he showed up. He brought a megaphone and gave the speech he'd written instead of setting fire to it the night before. He'd lamented the crimes Clott had committed against the people of Bedford; low wages and polluted water. Busted unions and generations of men with broken backs. Then the people of Bedford had followed him. Together they'd marched to the mill. This time Georgia O'Brian had smiled at him with pride, and he'd known right then that there was more of his life to be lived.

But as he walked the sky became dark. Suddenly he was alone. Even Georgia was gone. The street was empty, and rain began to fall. He looked toward the mill, and there was Susan. She beckoned him. She was dressed like a hooker; leather miniskirt and tank top on a cold winter day. Against his will, his body announced pleasure at the sight of her. There was a buzzing sound, too. Like bees, only intelligent, somehow. Human, somehow.

The worst part came when she grinned at him. Her lips spread across her face. Wide. Wider still. So wide it must have hurt, and he wanted to tell her to stop. And then her lips split open. A deluge of blood ran down her chin like foam from a rabid dog, and still, she smiled. Her split lips made a hole that revealed her small, white teeth. Behind her the mill started to burn. Smoke poured into the sky. She tipped a bottle of scotch in his direction, and he licked his lips. Suddenly he really needed a drink.

She walked toward him. Her head had been shaved bald. Her skin hung loose off her bones, and black blood trickled from the orifices of her body: her nose, her ears, her eyes. She opened her mouth to speak, and black slime came oozing out. "I'll come for you, Paul. When I'm dead," she gurgled.

The buzzing got louder, and it was the sound of screams.

Out of self-preservation, he woke himself up. When he opened his eyes, he did not remember his dream, nor did he realize that because of the act he'd committed with her, Susan had found a way inside him, just as she'd found a way inside the rest of Bedford.

* * *

There was a divider in the road that separated north and south. In the middle of it were pine trees whose branches were pushed parallel to the ground by the wind. The car was parked halfway over the right-hand lane and halfway up a curb that led to some woods. He laid his head back.

After he left Susan's, he had taken a drive. And then he'd decided to go to Canada where it probably wasn't raining and then, somehow, a truck had almost pushed him off the road and he'd remembered that he couldn't see anything—the short, white, painted lines—because he didn't have his windshield wipers turned on. He'd pulled over and now he was here.

She was fine. He had not gone to her apartment and none of this had happened. He'd been too drunk to find his way home and wound up passed out on the interstate. The whole thing was a dream and it seemed real because he was so drunk and dreams are always close to real when you drink. He would go home and fix himself a drink, and later he'd stop by her tidy apartment where right now she was sitting down to a big steak dinner with spinach and mashed potatoes on the side. He'd tell her how sorry he was for not having checked up on her more often and he'd bring her some flowers because she loved lilacs and oh, Jesus, she was dead. The woman whose blood, the other blood, he'd tasted on his tongue was dead.

He should have called the police. Any moron knows that. That's what you're supposed to do. Someone dies, you call the police. You don't leave them alone to collect flies because then they think it wasn't an accident. They blame you even if you try to explain that you got scared like some half-wit set loose from the asylum in Waterville and oh, buddy, you're losin' it.

He took a deep breath and rolled down his window for some air. It was cold on his face and he could feel his skin tighten. He closed his eyes and there she was in his mind, soaking the floor in blood. Funny that people still bleed when they're dead.

He heard honking. The Buick tipped back and forth over the curb and he remembered where he was. He looked behind him on the road and saw a pair of head-lights in the dark. High up, maybe a truck. It shifted left and passed him with a long and thunderous whine of its horn.

He opened the glove compartment and pulled out a map of Maine. Ten o'clock. He imagined what other people were doing tonight. Georgia on a date with some shit kicker who spit-shined his vinyl shoes; his wife scrubbing the grout off the bathroom tiles; Thursday night happy hour, throngs of yuppies in suits and ties in some rich commuter city, bitching about the nine-to-five grind. He located where Canada would be, the blank nothing anywhere north of Maine, with his finger.

He wished, not for the first time, that he was a different man.

He pulled onto the highway, turned around at the next exit, and returned to Bedford.

FOURTEEN
Dead Soldiers

Bang! Bang! Paul heard from the window of his car. For a moment, he thought it was Susan, breaking her way inside.

No, please, no.

"I almost couldn't find your car in this rain," Danny said as he opened the door and sat down. Paul looked around the empty lot behind Main Street where only one other car, Danny's Jimmy, was parked, and wondered if Danny said stupid things just to break the silence. He sat facing forward, his white-knuckled hands wrapped around the steering wheel, breathing slowly, one breath at a time.

"So what's the big secret?" Danny asked. His rubber raincoat squeaked along the leather of the car. "I told April there was a brawl over at Montie's. I feel like I'm playing cops and robbers here."

"You are a cop," Paul said.

"True." Danny looked closer, examining Paul's face. "What is it?"

Paul didn't answer.

"What's the matter with you?"

"Center's not holding, gyre's widening."

"Lord," Danny muttered. He unsnapped his yellow raincoat. "You didn't get pulled over for DWI, did you?"

"No, Danny," Paul moaned, "Do you think I'd call you to out to the Kmart parking lot for a DWI?"

"I've heard of stupider things. You get into a fight with Cathy?"

"Danny . . ." Paul looked down at his hands.

"Out with it," Danny said. "It can't be that bad."

Paul shook his head. "It's bad. There was an accident and Susan got hurt. She died."

Danny sucked out his breath. "Oh, no. Susan Marley?"

"Yeah. She fell."

"Where'd she fall?"

"I checked for a pulse. But she's dead and I'm drunk."

"You drove after the bar? I thought you were just walking her home."

"I'm telling you somebody's dead and you want to arrest me for a DWI?" Danny lifted his hands in surrender, and Paul continued. "She looked sick. I thought it was the cold. But her place, you should see it. It's not a place anyone should be living in."

"What's the matter with it?"

Paul's lips contorted into a sneer. "She was alone for too long. She wasn't acting like a person anymore."

"Oh, Paul. That poor girl never acted like a person."

"Would you shut up, Danny? She bit me, for Christ's sake, like she was rabid." Paul's eyes began to tear, and he did not look at Danny until he gained control of himself.

Danny turned on the overhead light and examined Paul's bite. Punctures shaped like child-sized teeth had broken his skin. The half-moon wound was swollen and red. Danny blew out his breath in a low whistle. "Did you call the hospital?"

"No. She fell down the stairs and I was going to call somebody but she was dead and then, I don't know . . . She waved at me when she fell."

"Like hello? She waved hello at you?"

Paul's face turned red. "Like good-bye, you ass, like good-bye. She waved good-bye and she jumped."

He gritted his teeth. "Oh. So then you came here, called me?"

"I took a drive."

"You fled the scene."

Paul's whole body sagged. "Shit," he said. He banged his head against the steering wheel hard enough to rock the dashboard. Once. Twice. The third time, he remained slumped against the wheel. It occurred to Danny that his wife might have been right all along. There was something wrong with Paul. He was not just a big talker. He was not just a drunk. When pushed, when his life was going badly enough, he would get violent, and that violence would be unleashed on whoever was unlucky enough to be standing in his way. If you had told Danny this a year ago, or even this afternoon, he would never have believed it.

"I really screwed things up, Danny," Paul said.

Danny sat straight. "I've got one question for you: She fell down the stairs, right?"

"Right."

"And the fall killed her."

"Right."

"Did you push her?"

"No," Paul whispered, still with that violence underneath the curl of his lips.

"You didn't tap her, maybe knock her off balance? No accident?"

"No. I swear to God," Paul whispered, and Danny knew it was true. He also knew that he didn't care. Because there was a line, and maybe it had been crossed tonight, maybe a long time ago, but it had been crossed. After this night Danny would no longer call Paul Martin his friend.

"Then don't say that again. Don't ever say that again. You start telling people it was your fault she fell, and even if you don't go to jail, it could last for years."

"Shit."

"Ride with me in my car. You can't drive. And don't talk to anybody but me when we get to the department or somebody'll want to give you a Breathalyzer."

Paul's brows knitted. He looked like he might argue, but reconsidered. He pulled his keys from the ignition.

"I'll call it in and then you and I'll drive over to the police station. You can make a statement and we'll put some alcohol or something on that bite."

"Iodine," Paul corrected.

"Whatever, Paul. I don't give a horse's ass."

When they arrived at the police station, one of Danny's deputies informed them that Susan Marley was alive and had been taken to the Mid-Maine Medical Center in Corpus Christi an hour earlier. Danny presided over Paul's tape-recorded recollection of events in the interrogation room. "If she dies and the autopsy checks out, there won't be an inquiry so don't say anything about your little drive," Danny told him while they sat in a small, dingy room with folding metal chairs that Paul imagined, aside from himself, only drug dealers and wife beaters had ever graced with their weight. "If she lives, you'd better be telling the truth."

Danny quelled Paul's fears of being caught fleeing the scene of an accident, and gave rise to new and more subtle ones when he turned off the recorder and said, "You're not popular around here so it's tricky, but everybody expected this to happen to her. It's no surprise. If it had been someone other than Marley, you'd have real trouble on your hands."

Later, as Danny pulled up in front of Paul's house, he said, "Don't go to the hospital, I'll go down and explain everything, they're not gonna want to see you. I'll have a couple of my deputies drop off your car, leave your keys in the mailbox. I'll tell 'em you were too upset to drive."

"Thanks, Danny. But I don't want you to lie. They'll understand if you tell them what happened," Paul heard himself say.

Danny nodded toward the door for Paul to get out. "Who's gonna understand, Paul? I don't even understand." Then he peeled away.

Paul walked on tiptoe through the front door. Poured himself a glass of water. Danny's words kept running through his head. The whole time they were at the station, he'd been looking at Paul like he was the dumbest man on earth. "If I'd known I wouldn't have left. I thought she was dead," Paul had said.

"Or maybe you were pickled and you left a little girl," Danny had answered under his breath on their way out.

In the den he could see his son James watching

television. Lights flickered against James's face. Paul suddenly felt angry that the kid was not in bed while, upstairs, Cathy was probably sleeping the peaceful sleep of the terminally stupid.

He went into his library, the liquor cabinet. Nothing there, absolutely nothing but a bottle of tonic. Cathy had been screwing around with his stash again. He went to the kitchen, looked in the garbage. There they were. Absolut, Bombay, even the red wine. Poor dead soldiers who'd never even gotten to see battle. One had a broken neck. Susan had a broken neck.

"James," he called a few times until his son walked into the kitchen. Paul put his arm around his son's bony frame. James bristled. He pointed at Paul's gauze-covered arm. Brown paint stained its edges.

"What happened?" James asked.

Paul considered what the best explanation might be. There was no best explanation. "You'll hear about it tomorrow," he said.

James nodded. His hands were curled into balls underneath the heels of his blue flannel shirt. "What'd you do tonight?" Paul asked.

"Nothing."

"You should be in bed."

James shrugged.

"Well, shouldn't you?"

"I don't know."

Paul pointed at the garbage. "Your mother get a little crazy?" he asked with a smile. Maybe he could turn this around, make it a joke, something they could share. Turn that day upside down.

James didn't answer.

"Yeah, she's crazy, all right."

"No, she's not," James whispered.

"She awake?"

James pursed his lips like he was protecting her, and it made Paul want to slap him. Something rose in his stomach, a slow-burning bile, and Paul felt himself shake. James stepped back. "James," Paul said, but there was nothing else to say because the boy had read his thoughts, and while he had never raised a hand to either son in his life, it was out there, the threat, and could not be drawn back.

"Go to bed," Paul said.

James fled the room. A few seconds later, a door slammed. Hard.

Paul looked in the direction of James's room for a few seconds and considered following him, but he didn't. The condition he was in, there wasn't much chance of making things better, and a hell of a good chance of making them worse. So instead, he felt his way through the dark house. He lay down on the couch in front of the television and thought maybe he'd just sleep here tonight. Not see Cathy, sleep next to her, smell her, on the same night he'd watched a woman bleed inside her head.

He closed his eyes and things swerved, crossed, jiggled. He ran to the bathroom and threw up. Again he thought: *This is your life, a grown man gagging as quietly as you know how so your son doesn't hear you steer a toilet.*

When he got out, Cathy was waiting for him. She was wearing a frayed terry-cloth robe. She crossed her arms around her waist in a hug.

"He can hear you," she said. She looked like she was going to cry. When she cried, it was a soft crying, and you only knew it if you looked at her closely and saw her tears.

He wanted to tell her everything would be all right and he'd take care of her and sorry, so sorry, little Cathy. But he didn't do that because you're well now, right little Cath? You're fit as a fiddle and now it's somebody else's turn. You're not the one waiting for a phone call from Danny about whether a girl died tonight. But you're standing there because you want me to say: *I'm glad you tossed out my booze. I love you so much I don't need it.* "Who can hear me, Cath? That's only if you believe in a higher being," he told her, flinching as he said it because this was Cathy, and being cruel to her was about as admirable as kicking a puppy.

He expected her to cry. Fully expected it the same way he knew when she wasn't taking her lithium and claimed the Prozac worked just fine on its own; she didn't want any drug giving her hyperthyroidism. That wasn't hard to notice because she'd cry about her messy hair when she woke up in the morning.

He expected her to cry right now because he always knew what she was going to do before she did it. She didn't cry. She leaned against the opening of the doorway, saw the toilet that reeked of bile and booze, and then looked back at him.

He crossed his arms.

"One of these days he's going to hate you and you won't be able to take it back." Not at all what he had expected. The sentiment itself was not original, but the delivery, baby, the delivery. He thought about telling her that if it weren't for him, she'd be in a loony bin chasing down piles of pills with water-filled Dixie Cups, but he could smell his own vomit. He wondered if he was sober right now, whether her words would sting more than they already did. "Which day, Cathy?"

"Andrew's with you but James won't be and I don't know how much longer I'll be with you, either."

"You what?" he spit at her. "Who do you think you are?"

Now she started to cry. The tears came down, one at either end of her calm, pale face. "We'll talk about this later," she told him, enunciating every syllable like his brain had gone too soft to comprehend English.

"Talk about it now."

She sighed. "I don't know what to say."

He took a deep breath, had a quick retort, but bit it back. She looked so frail. She always looked so frail. He could never say a goddamn thing to her because she always looked like she might break.

"I was worried about you today. I don't know why. I was afraid something might have happened. Did anything happen?"

This concern took him by surprise, and all he could do was shake his head.

"I had this feeling you might be hurt. Are you hurt? Is there some way I can help?"

Again, he shook his head. She'd never asked such a question, and he was vaguely suspicious, like maybe next she'd announce that for the last three months she'd been serving high tea to little green men. This was the woman, after all, who'd pretended she had pneumonia the night before his protest, just so she could worm out of standing by his side.

"I feel like something's coming. Maybe it's just the rain, I don't know. I had this terrible dream about Susan Marley."

Paul shook his head. "What are you talking about?" His lip curled into a look of contempt. For a moment he forgot what had happened to Susan, or even that he'd dreamed for the first time in decades, too. He forgot everything except his pride, and he knew that shaming his wife was the only way he had left of holding on to it.

Cathy shrugged. "Forget it. Anyway, James is out of school in a few months."

"So?" Paul asked.

"After the rain, I thought I'd take him to Saratoga Springs to see his relatives. I can travel now. I can do things."

"I see. And when will you come back, dear?"

"When things are better."

"Tough love?"

"Is it love?" she whispered. She waited for him to answer and when he did not, she turned and went back upstairs.

FIFTEEN
Down a Rabbit Hole

By the time the EMTs arrived at Susan's apartment, Liz had fainted. She woke up speeding sixty-five miles an hour in a gurney next to Susan's naked body. When they got to the hospital, she'd recovered. She watched as a pair of orderlies in pink scrubs pushed Susan down the hall and out of sight.

Bobby, who had followed the ambulance in his car, rushed into the emergency room soon afterward. Taking her quite by surprise he hugged her hard, then kissed her cheeks and the bridge of her nose and finally her lips. "You're okay," he said. "I was scared you weren't okay."

To keep from crying she started talking. "I guess I should call my mother now," she said. "I told her I wasn't going to see Susan. There's blood on my shoes. It was so good you gave that CPR—you're so good at that stuff. You're so smart," she babbled. Then she saw the troubled look on his face and tried to slow down. "I'm okay. Don't worry. Really." She came close to crying again. "Do you think someone did this to her? How could someone do this?"

Bobby led her to the visiting room chairs. "Take a deep breath," he said. She did. "Another one," he instructed. She did. "Okay, now give me your hands." She put her hands in his. "Squeeze," he said, "No, not like that, really squeeze as hard as you can. Harder." She squeezed until the muscles in her fingers cramped. "Better?" he asked.

"Better," she said.

"I'll call your mother," he told her.

Within a half hour, Mary Marley came storming through the waiting room doors, her Shaws grocery store apron still wrapped around her waist. Liz sat back and closed her eyes while Bobby did the talking. Distantly, she heard him say, "Yeah, we went over to her apartment. No, we've never been there before, at least I haven't. . . . It was lucky we found her though, so I guess you should be glad we went."

A half hour after that Sheriff Danny Willow arrived. Holding his hat in his hand, he stood before them in the waiting room and spoke softly like he was in church. He told them that Paul Martin had witnessed Susan's fall. He hadn't thought to use her phone and had called the police from a pay phone instead. They'd just missed each other. Then he held up his hands in a show of frustration as if to say: That's the way these things always happen. It's absurd, but there's never anything you can do. There's a lot of spilled milk in the world. Mary nodded in agreement. Yes, lots of spilled milk. All kinds of spilled milk.

"How is she doing?" he asked.

"Oh, we don't know. She's a sly boots. Can't believe a thing she does," Mary answered.

"She's got internal bleeding and brain damage. She's

going to die," Liz said. Though she did not turn to look at him, she felt Bobby's hand reach for her own, and they clasped fingers.

"I'm sorry," Mr. Willow said.

Mary took a deep breath. "Accidents happen," she said.

Liz let out a quick, nervous giggle that sounded less like laughter and more like a noisy facial tic. "Right Mom," she said.

Before he left, Sheriff Willow smiled warmly at Liz. He was a small, round man with thick arms and callused hands. Seeing him made her wonder what her own father might have looked like if he'd ever lived beyond forty. It made her miss him, as she always missed him when she wanted someone to hold her tight. "You let me know if you think of anything you and your mom might need, okay?" Danny asked.

"Yes," Liz said, "I'll let you know. Thank you for coming all the way down here."

The three of them sat together after that, none speaking. Bobby sat to her left, her mother to her right. Like at an airport; each with one arm on a seat rest, waiting for their flight to be called. Or maybe they were following Susan down a rabbit hole.

Now she stood and stretched her legs. The fluorescent overhead lights buzzed in low tones like mental static. The waiting room was mostly empty. The chairs were orange vinyl, each linked to another in six rows. There was an old woman twisting a wrinkled handkerchief between her fingers, sitting alone. A nurse at a desk. A junkie lying across three chairs, probably waiting for a friend who had overdosed. She paced the room. She asked the nurse, whose name tag read "Arlene," if there was any news. None. She gazed at the remnants of her family; Bobby, her mother, the space between them, meant for herself. Her mother looked no different from any other day, any other time. A stranger would not be able to detect that anything was amiss in their lives if not for the apron strung across Mary's waist. But then, something had always been amiss in their lives. Only now another little piece of it was out in the open.

She thought of praying like when she was little, kneeling next to her sister at the foot of her bed, her father leading them in the Our Father. The Hail Mary had always seemed too close to blasphemy, the Glory Be too short, and "Now I lay me down to sleep" like asking to die. So it had been the Our Father. She started to say the words, then stopped. "Good luck, sis," she said out loud, because that was how she felt.

Just then, Bobby joined her. His eyes were bloodshot and she suddenly wondered what time it was, how long they had been there, if it was morning yet and he was tired. She looked at her watch, eleven; they'd been here only a little over an hour.

"Can I talk to you?" he asked.

"Sure."

"Not here, away from your mom." He pulled her into the corridor outside the main waiting room. Nurses and attendants walked by all in white.

"What is it, Bobby?" she asked in what she hoped was a warning voice. *Please don't fall apart. I don't think I could deal with that. Not from you.*

"What do you think she was trying to tell you in your dream?"

Liz shrugged. "I don't know."

"I just don't get it," Bobby said. "It doesn't make

any sense. If Mr. Martin was there, then why didn't he call the hospital instead of the police and why isn't he here now?"

"What are you talking about?"

He rubbed his eyes, spoke in a whisper. "What if somebody did something to her? She was naked, you know."

"Bobby. I don't want to talk about that. I don't want you to talk about that." She wondered then whether her father was really dead, if he had done this to Susan and Bobby had somehow guessed.

"I'm sorry, that was really uncool. I should never have said that. I don't know why I said that." He squeezed her hands, and she knew he thought she should be crying. She tried to encourage tears for his benefit but they would not come.

Her mother found them in the corridor. Mary's feet were wet. She had left the store without her boots or coat. She shivered, and Liz thought about finding her a blanket, someone should do that. Someone should do a lot of things.

"What were you doing there, anyway? I told you not to go there, didn't I?" Mary asked. Liz did not respond, and when Bobby opened his mouth to explain, Mary waved her hand. "It doesn't matter now." She opened her black vinyl purse and took out a wrinkled five-dollar bill, appraised it, then added another five and placed it in Bobby's hand. "Why don't you two go get something to eat. I'll come get you if something happens."

At the cafeteria, Liz concentrated on the buzzing of the fluorescent lights. She tried to decipher a pattern. All the electricity in this building was connected to a single generator that was separate from the storm, the town, the mill; linked to every light, every vending machine, every respirator. She listened for her sister's voice underneath that buzzing.

SIXTEEN
The End of the World,
and Nobody Knew but Him

It was a little before midnight by the time Bobby and Liz got to the cafeteria. There were about fifteen people eating at various tables. A group of six, mostly orderlies in light blue uniforms, drank coffee near the register where a small woman sat behind a counter, reading Eudora Welty's *Golden Apples* in paperback. The walls were painted blue. Bobby had read someplace that blue was supposed to have a calming effect. Like people were these lemmings, and if you shined the right light into their faces, they'd feel exactly how you wanted them to feel.

He'd kept thinking that Susan would breathe. Her breath, it had been so strange. Like cigarettes and paper mill. Every time he'd exhaled into her lungs and her chest rose, he felt like he'd been giving life, watching a miracle. When the ambulance came and the EMTs lifted her from either end, they tried not to move her too much, but her head rolled parallel to her shoulder anyway. It was then that he understood he had been breathing into a corpse waiting to happen. Even now, he could taste her smoky breath on his lips.

He'd called home and told his dad what happened. He knew he shouldn't have said it, but no one was in hearing distance, and he told about how he'd administered CPR. His dad had whistled like: *Pretty cool, Bobby, I'm proud of you. You've got that doctor blood in your veins.* Worst of all, he was proud of himself.

His father had offered to come, and Bobby now regretted saying that it seemed like a family thing, maybe later; he didn't know if he should be here himself. But neither Mary nor Liz was acting the way they should. He wanted to give Mary his jacket, or find her a blanket, or tell her to stick her hair under a hand dryer in the bathroom. He wanted to tell her to please talk to her daughter, because Liz didn't look so good right now. She looked about an inch away from hysteria. *Please take care of your daughter, Mrs. Marley, because I don't know how just yet.*

If his father were here, he would have said all these things with the confidence and ease dictated by the gray hairs on his head. His father would have asked Mr. Willow what the hell had really happened, and it would have sounded fine coming from his father, it would have been perfectly reasonable. No one would have said, *And who do you think you are, asking that? Who do you think you are, asking anything?*

He looked across the table at Liz. Her eyes were kind of wild, and every time somebody at the other table laughed she practically jumped out of her skin. If she didn't calm down soon she'd wind up fainting all over again. That would be bad. Really bad. When she fainted at Susan's apartment, he'd tried to wake her up, but her body had been like dead weight. He'd started crying, and when the ambulance came and she still didn't open her eyes, it was worse than he ever could have guessed. He'd felt like the end of the world had happened, and nobody except him would really understand.

Bobby cleared his throat and Liz startled, as if just then remembering where she was. "I could call my dad and ask him to come down."

"Why?"

"He works here. He already called somebody at the ER and told them you were a friend of the family. It might be good to have him around," Bobby said.

"What would he do, Bobby?" she asked. Her voice had this high pitch to it like she was about to yell at him.

"Forget it."

"There's nothing wrong with my mother, she can handle this just fine."

"I know that."

"You think you need to call your dad because we're too fucked up to handle this by ourselves."

"No. That's not what I was saying at all."

"Fine," she told him. "You know, everybody's gonna be talking about Susan at school tomorrow and it's not like they have a right to talk."

And it all fit together. Of course she'd say that. That was exactly the kind of thing she would be thinking about. She enjoyed having secrets, tragedies that belonged only to her. Like she thought she was a better person for having suffered. Every time he complained about having a bad day or some shit like that she could say, *Yeah, but you don't know. My dad died. My sister's a fruitcake. You don't know, Bobby. Only people like me can be mature.*

What would good old dad tell her? He'd shrug like he had no idea what she was talking about, give her a hug, take her away from this place, and pop a sleeping pill down her throat.

"I know how you feel," he told her, because he was not his dad.

"No you don't. I know you try but you can't get it, you can't ever get it. That's the problem. You're Wonder Bread, boy wonder."

He reminded himself where he was, that she was tired, that she meant none of what she was saying before he answered. "That's not true."

"You know it is."

"Are you trying to say I think I'm great? Is that it?"

"No," she told him.

"Or you think I'd spend time with somebody I didn't like? You really think that? Why else would I be with you if I didn't like you? There's no good reason."

A look of surprise crossed her face and the thought that passed through his mind before he pushed it away was: *I'm Bobby Fullbright and I could be with anybody in the high school that I want as long as they're under five foot five, so don't look so surprised.* And then he was sorry. Because thinking bad things about somebody who's just seen their sister's broken neck is pretty bad. Thinking bad things about your girlfriend is even worse.

"No good reason?" she asked.

"I didn't mean that."

"Yes, you did."

"I'm sorry," he said.

"Why, it's how you feel, isn't it?"

"No, it's not."

He put his hand over hers. She had soft, pale skin

that didn't burn in the summertime. Short, white fingers. He could leave her after this, after high school. She would be one less string tying him to this town. But for whatever reason, he liked that string.

She stood. "Your mom would have gotten us if something happened," he told her.

"I know. I need to go to the bathroom. I need to go for a while. I'm sorry, Bobby, I'm glad you're here, but I have to go for a while."

"Okay," he said. And then he thought, *You know how to act; it's Liz. You know how to make her feel better. You don't need Dad.* He got up and kissed her. When his lips touched hers, she jumped back and ran out of the room like this was the fourth grade, and she'd just been the victim of a particularly cruel joke.

SEVENTEEN
Collision

It was close to midnight. Georgia O'Brian had been at the hospital for several hours. She sat at the side of her son's bed and watched his slumbering face. Her father had been right. She was turning into one of *those* mothers. The kind that can't leave their kid alone for more than five seconds. The kind that have nothing better to do than act like smothers. It was time to go home.

Before she left, she took one last look at him. He was nothing like her. She had a brief understanding of the man he would become if all went well and he didn't fall off any roofs or decide to drink some of that polluted water in the Messalonski River. He would be small and dark with bookish glasses, and he would leave this town. He would leave this dead mill town, and be something better than where he came from. She hoped that, at least.

On her way out of the hospital, Georgia swerved to avoid colliding with Liz Marley. Georgia recognized her, kept walking, then turned around and caught up with her. She tapped the younger woman's shoulder.

"Liz Marley, I used to babysit for you," she said. "Hi, how are you?"

Liz was a pale, pretty girl with a natural flush to her cheeks. Georgia remembered having seen Liz at the Chop Mop a year or so before and finding her frumpy. She smiled that this was no longer the case.

Liz uttered a sound of surprise. "Oh. I didn't know, I thought I was alone, uh . . ."

"Georgia, remember? I used to babysit for you."

"Oh, I know. I should have known. I'm just all shook up, I guess. I'm sorry, Georgia. How are you?" Liz asked. Then she looked down at the waxed floor and traced the cracks with the tips of her Keds.

"How are you?" Georgia replied.

"Good."

"Are you visiting someone?"

"Oh, my sister," Liz said.

"Susan?"

"She's fine. I mean, no, she's not fine." Liz cradled the back of her skull with the palm of her hand in a sympathetic gesture. "She hit her head."

Georgia looked down at Liz's feet, and realized that the red dust on her sneakers was Susan Marley's blood. "What happened?"

"I knew she wouldn't like it if I brought Bobby with me but I was afraid to go alone. He's nice. He doesn't need this." Then Liz looked up into Georgia's face. "She hates me. She hates everyone."

A chill ran down Georgia's spine as she remembered her dream, and more importantly, the way she'd grinned at Matthew before his fall. *Was it possible that Susan had caused it?* "Tell me what happened," Georgia said.

"Bobby and I found her and he called the hospital. I

think it was the hospital. My mom didn't even say thank you." Liz looked at Georgia, waiting for her to make a judgment on this statement, but Georgia only nodded.

"Susan wasn't popular in high school. Neither am I. I don't know why Bobby likes me. My mom says she'll find us when it gets really bad but I'm not even where I'm supposed to be. I'm supposed to be at the cafeteria with Bobby. He tried to kiss me but he gave Susan CPR. I could taste her on him." Liz looked again at Georgia for affirmation, and whatever she saw on Georgia's face made her squint. "My sister's hurt and I'm talking about Bobby. I'm talking like an idiot."

"You're just shook up."

"I can't stop thinking about her. I always think about her," Liz said. Then her eyes watered. "Sometimes I think she's not really a person. Like she can't die. She's different from everyone else. But the thing is, I want her to die."

Georgia blanched, not because Liz had just confessed that she wished her sister harm, but because she realized that she felt the same way.

Liz smiled a bitter smile. "You must think I'm out of my mind. I'm sorry. Forget it. How are you, anyway? I haven't seen you in a long time."

Georgia reddened from the memory of the last time she had babysat for Liz and her sister. She had not thought about it for years. "It has been a long time. I always meant to see you after that. I wanted to tell you I did what I could."

Liz seemed not to understand. She gave Georgia a quizzical look. And then she sucked in a quick breath, as if she had been physically struck. "I'm sure you did."

Georgia shifted uncomfortably. "What happened to your sister?" she asked.

"You saw. Your mom told everyone in town. Danny Willow even came to our house."

Georgia coughed. She looked at the ceiling. "I mean, that she's in the hospital."

"They're saying it was an accident. Bobby thinks it might have been murder but I know it wasn't my dad. He's dead, too."

"I don't understand what you're saying, Liz."

This silenced Liz for a while. Then she said, "Maybe I'm crazy, just like her."

"No," Georgia told her without conviction.

Liz considered, and then she shrugged, as if she didn't care what Georgia thought, and for this small act Georgia liked her. "Would you give me a hug?" she asked. Georgia opened her arms, and Liz squeezed her so hard that she knocked the breath out of Georgia's chest. Soon, she began to cry.

Sitting there with Liz in her arms, Georgia wished she had found the bathroom before this had happened, and wondered why an almost grown woman she no longer knew was crying on her breast, or why she had decided to turn around and reacquaint herself with this girl in the first place. Over Liz's shoulder, she could see people in the cafeteria eating dinner, the late shift. Meat loaf, soup, their hands curled around large cups of coffee. She wondered what it would be like to work at a hospital. Like another world where nothing counts but what is happening right then. Your whole life in a big building with colored tape and white uniforms and the smell of Top Job cleanser. She could feel the softness of Liz in her arms. She wondered if the staff was looking; if these things happened all the time. If they no longer cared very much, just something they watched, enacted before them every day.

After a while, Liz sat up. "Sorry."

"Don't be sorry. It's okay."

Liz blushed. "Thank you. You're nice."

"Glad to help. Do you want me to leave you alone?"

"I'd kind of like it if you stayed," she said.

"Okay." Georgia wiped Liz's hair from her face. "How did it happen, anyway?"

Liz recounted the events of the evening. When she finished, Georgia asked, "Where is he, then?"

"Who?"

"Paul."

Liz did not understand.

"Mr. Martin, your teacher," Georgia said.

"I don't know. Mr. Willow, the cop, police officer, said he was gonna see him later."

"If she's about to die, shouldn't someone call him?"

Liz looked at her with recognition and it made Georgia's cheeks redden. A small town. A very small town. "I'd feel weird calling a teacher. And I don't think my mom would like it."

"I can call him if you want, just to let him know what's happening. He should be here," she said. "He should be told what's going on."

"I guess you're right. But later, maybe? Could we just sit here for a while?"

"Yes," Georgia said, "we can."

EIGHTEEN
Phone Call

The most unsettling thing about Georgia's visit to the hospital was not Susan Marley's unhappy circumstances, or crying Liz, or the memory of her old babysitting days, but the fact that she remembered Paul's phone number. She had not used it often. Only at night, when his wife had been sleeping. Once Andrew, the angry son, picked up the phone. She hung up. And then, before a relationship had ever really formed, they broke up.

At Olsen's Diner, she'd asked him how, exactly, he planned on leaving a sick wife and two young children. He told her he didn't know, but he'd figure it out. *Just say the word, Georgia. That's all you have to do and I'll worry about the rest.* He'd said this impatiently, as if she had been Thomas fingering Christ's wounds.

It would have been nice if the three of them could have lived happily ever after and all that, but it wasn't worth the time thinking about, really. Because she knew he would never leave his wife. It had sounded like a good idea at the time, but when he went home to the woman who couldn't get out of bed without his help, he'd change his mind.

In the waiting room, only feet away from the Marley family, she dialed his number from memory. It was as simple as remembering her old locker combination from high school: letting her fingers move without thought.

"Paul?" she asked as soon as he picked up the phone.

"Georgia," he said without having to be told. He whispered this, and she knew that the rest of his family was sleeping. She heard movement, a bump of some sort, a muted curse, and imagined him carrying the cordless phone into the bathroom on the ground floor of his house, and then sitting on a fuzzy pink toilet seat.

"To what do I owe the pleasure?" he asked, breathing heavily.

"I'm at the hospital."

"What happened?"

"Matthew took a spill."

"Do you need me to come down there?"

"No. He's sleeping. It's Susan Marley. I don't know if Danny Willow told you and I thought you should know. She's not going to make it through the night."

There was a long silence. She heard tap water running. "How'd I get to be such a fuckup, Georgia?" he whispered. "When did that happen?"

Her throat tightened, and immediately she wanted him to explain himself. She wanted to ask him why he was not at the hospital, if he was trying to be considerate of the family, or why he'd been sniffing around Susan Marley in the first place. What happened to you, Paul? she wanted to ask. But she chose not to open that particular can of worms. With Paul, it was so easy to get sucked in. So easy to see the world the way he saw it if she let him talk. He used to rant about the mill for hours unless she stopped him, always asking: Didn't she care? Why didn't she care? As if he thought that pointing out the bad things in life was the same as fixing them.

"You're drunk," she said.

"Always."

"Your liver's gonna explode, you know."

"Really? I never went to college and took biology."

"Neither did I. Liz Marley said she wouldn't mind if you came down here. They know it was an accident."

"Danny told me not to go. They'd get upset."

"Oh. Liz, her sister, said they wouldn't. She's about to die."

He waited a while before answering, and she knew he could feel her disappointment. "Do you think I should come?"

"You should do what you want."

"I want to say I'm sorry."

"Good. I'm leaving soon, but good luck or something like that."

"You're not staying at the hospital?"

"No."

"It'd be nice if you stayed."

"Can't Cathy come with you?"

He didn't answer.

"I guess not."

"You don't have to wait for me. I know that's asking a lot," he said, but the statement hung in the air like a question.

No, she wanted to say. I can't do that. I dropped you a long time ago. My father just got fired. I have almost no gas in my car and it's raining so hard in Bedford that I don't even know if I'm going to make it across the bridge back home if I wait any longer. The Marleys don't have fond memories of me. You must be kidding to think I'd do that for you. No.

She told him yes, she'd wait for him at the cafeteria. It surprised her as much as the fact that she remembered his phone number.

NINETEEN
Everything That Rises Must Converge

The clock in the cafeteria ticks. Its second hand wavers for a moment, as if it will go backward.

Paul waits at the hospital with Georgia. He is not sure why he has chosen to come. He will have to see Susan again. If she dies, whether they know it or not, he believes he will carry a good deal of the blame. Things not to think about now, another item to add to a very long list.

Georgia hands him a cup of coffee, and the steam rises and curls under his nose like cigarette smoke. He wishes he was drinking something other than coffee.

She pats his back out in the open because it does not mean anything anymore, at least to her. He thinks this is nice, I wish I could take you home, Georgia. I wish you hadn't been such a prig when I knew you or things would have been different. But you still live with your dad, darling, you'll never get away from Daddy, and no matter how many times you tell yourself it's because you want your son to have a grandfather, you know you're just afraid.

The woman behind the counter stares at Georgia. He has forgotten the eccentricity of her appearance, the way eyes always follow her lips, hair, and stature across a room. She carries herself as if she does not know that she is any different.

He tells her thanks, again, and she nods. This is what he likes about her: She does not talk when there is nothing to say.

"How's Matthew?" he asks.

"He'll live."

"Can I see him?" he asks, he doesn't know why; he doesn't want her son to see him in this condition. Maybe to test the limits of this kindness she is showing him.

"He's sleeping," she says. What she really means is, even if he wasn't sleeping, you couldn't see him. The kid you offered to adopt as your own. You'll never see him.

She does not mention the times he has called and hung up. Or the times he has visited her house, watching. He thinks that if there had been one person, a single, sane person in his life, he would not be here right now. He wishes he had married a woman other than Cathy. He wishes he loved Cathy. Well no, let's not get dramatic. He wishes he didn't live in this town where life is dark and cuts to the center of him and that he was not shaking either because he needs another drink or because he needs to vomit. Again.

He waits.

Georgia rises, tells Liz that Paul has arrived. They will be waiting for word in the cafeteria. Liz mutters something, agrees to find them if Susan's condition changes. When Georgia returns, Paul smiles and she knows he is glad to see her, that he has missed her. She has missed him, too. She does not like to admit that.

She stays with him because he is alone. She thinks he deserves to be alone. She cannot let him wait by himself.

He smells to her like an alcoholic. She has not been this close to him for a very long time. This is the change in him: He is resigned. He thinks it is Cathy who has done this to him, but it is not Cathy. Paul does not understand that life isn't always fun. He thinks that when he leaves a room, everyone else gets up and has a party, dances the Charleston. He thinks that Cathy has prevented him from this life. He thinks that he could have been more. He doesn't understand that if that were the case, he would already be more.

She waits.

Liz paces in slow, elliptical figure eights. She would like to make love right now, on the hospital floor. She doesn't know why. She thinks it might hurt, the hardness, her head slamming against it. She thinks she might like it.

She waits now.

Bobby imagines the sound of the rain against the windows in his bedroom. The hospital is cold, open. He thinks about going outside, smoking a Lucky; he'd have an excuse to be somewhere other than here. Oddly, the one thought he can't get out of his head is that he should finally face the truth: He will never be tall.

He waits.

Mary does not think at all. She can hardly feel. The daughter she loved died long ago. She wants to be home, watching television. She wants a glass of wine. She wants to cut her vision apart, make the world all black, run a knife through it and pull back the reality. She wants to hold Liz, pacing Liz, and by touching her be reassured. But Liz will shake her off, and so she continues reading the same magazine article she has been clutching since she arrived at the hospital because she can't get any farther than, "Parsley is the much neglected garnish in American cuisine."

She waits.

They all wait.

In Bedford the mill is quiet. Rain falls and makes hollow splashes. There is no thunder. Only black. There is no sound. Snow melts, feet of it, and drifts along the banks of the river. Things buried during the long winter surface and float in the water. There are mittens, bottles of beer, pipes, shoes, their laces swerving like worms, dead animals, all clogging the gutters or falling inside, into the depths.

Houses are dark. Shades are drawn for the night while water rises and circles the town. People have prepared, readying their flashlights, fortifying their cellars. The banks will soon flood. The valley will not drain. The road to I–95 will be impenetrable. This will be the worst rain in Bedford's history.

It is three A.M. on Friday when they stand over her bed, all of them. They think time has stopped, that it is past and present, mixing. If there were sound, it would travel in a curve, a loop, a circle.

Georgia does not want to be here. Paul has begged. He needs to see Susan again. He cannot do it alone. She touches Paul's shoulder to tell him that she is going to wait outside. He puts his arm around her and she is frozen where she stands, unwilling to hear her own voice in this silence.

Liz and Bobby stand together. Bobby sees Paul's action and mimics it. Liz shudders. Bobby holds her tighter. Mary stands far off, in the back.

Susan's eyes roll. She has returned to consciousness. She fixes on a point. On Georgia and Paul. Paul looks down at his feet. He moves backward, and Georgia follows. Susan's eyes drift. She sees Liz and Bobby. Liz takes a step toward her sister, but Bobby, his hands clamped tightly, anxiously, does not let her go. Susan's eyes drift again. She looks in Mary's direction and Mary shuffles out of view.

Their dreams return to them; a stain of blood in white snow, a little girl in Mary Janes, a hooker proffering a bottle of scotch, a mill in flames, a woman giving birth to things that have no business in this world. Susan smiles, and they know that she has sent these visions to them.

"Soon," she whispers. Her soft voice is so resonant that it carries through the buzzing fluorescent lights, and the beeping machines, and the walls of the room. This is the first and last word she had spoken in five years. Her eyes do not close when she dies. They do not roll back. They remain open, while in the corner, a heart monitor makes one long beep.

For a long time no one takes a breath. Something is coming now. They can feel it.

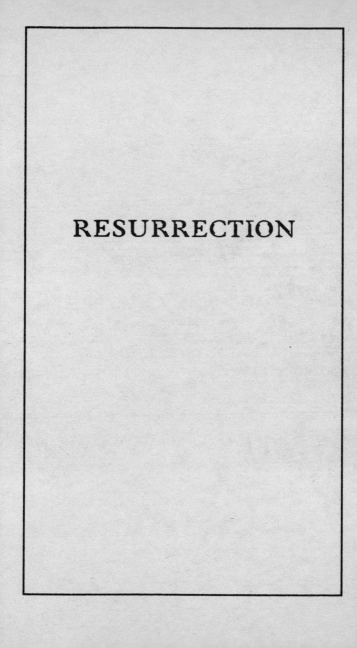

RESURRECTION

The next few days passed quickly.

Early Friday morning, Georgia and Paul were the first to leave. When they left the hospital, Georgia knew what she was about to do. She knew how this would look. What people would say. She did it anyway. She kissed him on the cheek, took his hand. Told him to get into his car and follow her home.

At her house, she raised her finger to her lips to show him to be quiet. His hands were shaking so she made some coffee, liberally spiking both cups with brandy. They sat next to each other at the kitchen table that was spotted with Chips Ahoy! cookie crumbs.

"More brandy?" she asked in jest.

"Yeah," he said, "as a matter of fact, I'd love some more brandy."

He drained half his mug in one gulp and she filled it to the top with more of her father's cherry brandy. "Swill," he said after sipping it.

"You're all charm."

"Sorry, no indication of my feelings for you," he

said, sipping, not looking at her, his words so dry and bitter that they could not have been sarcastic.

"What are you going to do?"

"Move to Spain. Watch the bullfights. Drink absinthe. Want to come?" She had a blank look on her face. "Hemingway, Georgia."

"That's nice."

He raised his hands in defeat. "I'm going to go home and sleep this off, unless there happens to be a police car waiting at my house, in which case I'm going to jail for fleeing the scene of an accident. Really, it all depends." He gave her a wry smile. Not a slur. Every word spoken with slow concentration. She wondered how much he would have to drink in order for it to affect his mind. His body, she could safely say, had already been affected.

"I don't mean to sound like such an asshole," he told her.

She shrugged. "I used to babysit for Susan. I had a run-in with her parents. There were things going on there."

He didn't answer.

"Something feels very wrong about all this. It's like I'm waiting for the other shoe to drop."

"Has anything ever been right in this town?"

She shrugged again. "Were you with her long?"

"No. Just for a little while after you." He said this as if there was a cause-and-effect relationship in there somewhere.

"But you gave her money," Georgia said.

"For rent sometimes. She didn't have anywhere to go." He cradled his head in his hands.

"Do you think she needed to be hospitalized?"

"My fault, too, right?"

"Well, I don't think it's as easy as all that. She might have been crazy or mean or, well, I don't know what, but I never heard about anyone except you treating her decent."

He pushed his empty cup away. She made a motion toward it. "No, I'm all set, don't you think?" he asked.

"Yeah." Her eyes watered and she rubbed them. There usually comes a time when you see someone that you once cared for, and realize that you do not care any longer. When that happens, it is easy to show affection. It is easy to talk. It is easy to give a kiss on the cheek or a happy wave hello. Though that time should have come long ago, she still didn't feel it. He noticed the water in her eyes, seemed to draw something from it, inspecting her, and then pretended not to notice.

"You're a beautiful woman, Georgia," he said.

"No, I'm not."

He smiled as if this admission only made her more attractive. "How's Matt?"

"Fine."

"And how are you doing, Georgia?"

"I've been better."

"Yeah."

"My father got fired yesterday," she told him.

"Figures."

"I thought you'd have more to say."

He shook his head. "I don't."

Before he got up to leave, he leaned over to kiss her on the cheek. She tilted her head a little, and their lips touched. He left without speaking. It was not until several hours after he was gone that she admitted to herself that she still loved him.

Saturday morning Mary confirmed funeral arrangements. It would be a quick ceremony. Susan was not insured. She called the bank and the funeral parlor. The wake was scheduled for Sunday, the burial Monday. Then she called the *Corpus Christi Sentinel,* let them know the times. They would print a notice in the weekend edition. When the reporter asked for more details she'd answered, "Ask Paul Martin. He knows her better than I ever did."

The autopsy results showed no skin underneath Susan's fingernails, no bruises on her face from a violent struggle, no cancer in her womb that would have killed her anyway. Accidental death, the coroner had declared it. Misadventure.

Mary had been given the next seven days off from work. She did not know what she would do with herself during that week because she could hear Susan around every corner on this bleak and rainy day, within the walls of her memory.

She was tired, but could not bring herself to climb the stairs to her bedroom. Instead she poured herself a glass of wine and sat on the couch. Too early to answer phones, listen to people say how sorry they were.

But the phone did ring. She did not want to answer it. The machine would click on. The phone kept ringing. She picked it up. Said hello. No one answered. The connection was bad, all static. She did not know why she said this, could not explain to anyone, except that once, this had happened before. Once, someone had called, then hung up, and only later had she guessed who it had been. "Susan?" she asked. There was a buzzing on the line. "Susan, come home," she said because it was something she always should have said. The person on the other end hung up.

Only the Fullbright and Willow families paid their

respects at Susan's wake Sunday evening. The rain was falling hard, and after picking up supplies to collect the rain that seeped through their ceilings, most people stayed indoors. Because of the autopsy and the position of the injury, the casket was closed. Nevertheless, Susan's body was fitted into a high-necked blue dress that Mary had supplied. The night was a quiet one, interrupted only by the sound of the rain.

The funeral the following Monday was even less attended. Danny Willow was called out to a traffic accident at the old train tracks on Mayflower Street, so only the Fullbrights made the trek to the top of the hill. The shallow grave was only four feet deep. The mattock the gravediggers used to loosen the earth had cracked against a six-inch-thick sheet of ice in the middle of the job. Almost all the snow had melted on the hill. The sewers in the valley were clogged, and the water-logged old railroad tracks mired several small cars. The sound of hydroplaning could be heard all over town. At the cemetery, Liz Marley listened to Father Allesando talk about ashes and dust and the great hereafter, while she held Bobby's hand.

When Liz and her mother got home Monday night from burying Susan, they sat at the kitchen table. Two people lived in the house, when once there had been four. There were worlds of things they could have said to each other. Worlds of regrets, and desires, and emotions like love that had somehow persevered. In the corner of Liz's eye was a clump of yellow sleep, and Mary reached over and wiped it away. Liz did not flinch or raise her hand defensively, as Mary might have expected. Instead she sat perfectly still. Stiff.

On Tuesday evening, Susan Marley opened her eyes. She was trapped inside something very dark and underground like the basement she had lived in long ago. It was so small that she could hardly move her arms. She heard a rapid patter, like knocking, and when she forced her way through the lid above her, a deluge of wet, grainy matter surrounded her. Mud. It filled up the box and she swam, not needing to hold her breath, not breathing, until she reached the top.

When she was out, she stood atop Iroquois Hill, among gravestones, one of them her own. Her feet sank down into wet dirt. She felt something on her neck, her thighs, and the insides of her elbows. It was like blood only not blood. Darker, no pulse. She touched her breasts with her fingers, and they were as cold as the rain.

She could see the town down there, all of it. There were lights glowing in the valley below and she could see each person in each house or apartment or trailer. Some made love, some slept. Some drank black coffee before leaving for night shifts at the hospital or the toll plaza on I–95 or else they stayed awake because they were afraid of what they might find waiting for them in their dreams.

She descended from the hill and traveled home. If it had been a clear night, someone might have seen her muddy silhouette striding into town. Jerome Donally, who was pilfering Oh Henry! bars at the Puff-N-Stop, or Amity Jorgenson, who was sitting outside her sister's trailer and wondering if this relentless rain would ever end, or anyone else that night might have seen her slumped shoulders and the way her eyes shone, like a cat's in the dark. But they only felt her in their hearts or their bowels or their stomachs. They only knew she was coming.

It happened on the sixth night of rain. Georgia was

giving Chuck Brann a trim. He liked it to be cut dry so that there wasn't any extra cost and he always asked for Georgia, because she smelled like sweet musk. Georgia felt it like a knife running inside her, coming up from the bottom and twisting between her legs. She dropped the razor to the floor, where it buzzed in little circles on the tile like a cockroach.

Paul was shaving with a dry razor and hand mirror in the quiet of his study. He felt her presence inside him. He almost called out her name. He knew it was she, no question. He did not look into the mirror in front of him, for fear of seeing her face. So he ran out into the rain, leaving her behind.

Bobby didn't know. But he felt uneasy. He went into his yard and tried to let the rain wash this feeling from him, but it didn't. Back in the house he found Margaret sitting in the dark kitchen. "Hey, dollface," he whispered. "I think I'm scared of the rain," she told him. The skin by her lips was very chapped and her eyes were sunken deep. He gave her the kind of warm, comforting hug that only a big brother can give.

Mary was sipping her wine, eyes closed. She could hear voices in the house, memories. There were good ones, but she did not remember those. She knocked the glass over, and thick, sugary wine spilled onto the table. It made her cry. Stupid to make her cry. Just sponge it up. She let it drip onto the floor, the sound in rhythm with the fall of the rain. And when it happened, she felt nothing. She was so inside her own cold grief that it was as if she had understood all along how things would be.

Liz was waiting to cry. She was looking through the old photo album, trying to make herself feel. Susan in her Sunday dress, Susan with the big black bruises,

Susan with the meanness swallowed down and digested so it was all over her body like embalming fluid. And when it happened, Liz felt it worse than anyone else. It crept inside her slowly like a bitter cold, working its way though her extremities and to her center. A voice inside her said: "You," and then it was gone. And she told herself it had never happened. That the voice was a form of grief. That it was not saying that it should have been Liz, it should always have been Liz.

Other people felt shivers or just a sadness so fleeting that they did not remember it in the morning. They slept fitfully that night, saying nothing.

PART THREE

THEY COME BACK

TWENTY
The Place Where Gravity Bends

She walked down Iroquois Hill and into the valley. In the hallway of her old apartment, bloody footprints formed the pattern of a widening spiral. Rossoff's door was shut tight, and a blue eye peeped through the keyhole at her. A man's breath churned, and she could smell his fear. She slowly dragged her hand down the side of the door so that she could feel his warmth through the wood, the way his heart beat faster. His nose began to bleed, and he backed away. She started up the stairs.

The people in this town were like strange and varied songs, and she knew each tune by heart. When they were lost or sad, they thought of her. Though they did not know it, in their hours of desperation, it was her name they called. In her apartment, her bare feet sank into the green shag carpet. Her blue dress brushed against the tops of her bruised shins. In a line from her neck down to the V between her legs were black plastic stitches, and she walked slowly to keep from tearing her lifeless skin.

She stepped through the cigarette ashes that speckled

the air, and looked at the paper mill out her window. It was silent for now, but would not remain that way. Then she turned. In the mirrors, she did not see her own reflection. Instead she saw the familiar and foreign faces of this town. Dark things. Lost things. Buried things. Ugly things. They watched her, trapped inside the glass. They banged hard, clamoring to be let out. She felt them banging from inside the mirrors; she felt them banging from inside her own body.

The things in the mirrors encroached. Their motley songs howled all at once, vying to be heard, and the sound was a discordant buzzing. It was the sound of madness, but she was accustomed to that.

They pushed at each other: a furry black spider with pale blue eyes; a woman holding the half-smoked Parliament that had been extinguished on her teenage son's soft flesh; a dapper William Prentice wearing a three-piece suit. He smiled a crocodile smile, while his hands clasped behind his back dripped blood. There were thousands of them. She lifted her hands and smashed the first mirror. Slivers of glass shattered in a circle around her fists. Her fingers bled black blood. She smashed the next mirror. And the next. And the next. And the next. And the last.

Out from the broken mirrors came a procession of things, all half formed. River creatures whose livers were riddled with holes. They moved in weaving circles. Men with burnt skin and black lungs who'd once worked at the mill. An infant wrapped in a plastic Hefty bag. It was too young to breathe and yet, somehow, it squalled. A yipping dog named Benji that had been mowed down by Douglas Boucher's snowplow a week before. A six-year-old girl whose pigtails were tied with yarn. "Mother, may I?" the little girl asked. Ted Marley five years dead. He held a spade in his hand, and remembered the stars in the sky. An army of them crawled out of the apartment and down the steps. As the dawn broke early Wednesday morning, they slithered quietly, unseen, to the places where they belonged.

TWENTY-ONE
Mold

You've gotta do it.

There was a smell coming from the basement. These long days of rain had made everything wet and musty, and Mary Marley listened to drops plink in rapid succession against the metal drainpipe outside her kitchen window. It was around noon on Wednesday, the sixth straight day of rain, and the room was dark. The chair Mary was sitting on was speckled with clumpy white dust, and she mistook it for moist paint chips, some leak she wasn't aware of, until she remembered the baking.

She had baked a great deal over these last few days. Her manager at Shaws had not charged her for groceries this week. A bereavement gift, like a mourning rate at the airport. Every parent who has a daughter die should get exactly thirty dollars and seventy-six cents worth of flour, imitation vanilla extract, butter, chocolate chips, and Crisco for free. That makes everything better.

This morning, Bobby Fullbright knocked on her back door and asked if he could take Liz to school. She told him that Liz was sleeping; he should go ahead without her. She probably wouldn't want to face the world for another week or so. He asked if he could visit with her anyway. Against her better judgment (boys should never call on young ladies in their bedrooms unchaperoned), she told him yes, mostly because she did not have the energy to say no. She had not slept well since Susan's death and her thoughts were increasingly difficult to string together. They were names disjointed from their faces that fluttered like the thin wings of moths in a somnambulist's dream.

Ten minutes after Bobby arrived, he and Liz were walking arm-in-arm down the stairs together. Mary felt a tinge of envy when they left, although she could not locate which child her envy was focused on.

Soon after they were gone, she noticed the smell. At first it was just a kind of moldiness like the underside of a mushroom, and then it was thicker, like rotting. It came from the basement, and while she knew she should check on it, she saw no need to hurry. Nothing could be done until the rain ended. So she opened some windows and the drapes puffed outward. The wind circled the house in gasps. It reminded her of the way Susan used to play ghost when she was six, hiding inside the drapes, whispering *ooh, ooh,* at Mary, making the baby giggle. And then she thought about the way they used to bake cookies together. How Susan refused to lick the beaters or the bowl, would have none of the batter, only the first cookie that came out of the oven. Neat little thing.

To escape the smell, Mary went to Shaws and bought groceries. As she drove, all she could hear was the swishing of water under her tires and the voices of things that had happened a long time ago. The river underneath the bridge had swelled almost as high as the street. Workmen dressed in green plastic slickers from Corpus Christi had already been recruited to jetty the side of the river with bags of sand, Lord knows why. They'd never be able to keep the river from flooding or mobile homes from sinking into the mud.

On her drive Mary spotted several cars with chains secured to their tires for traction. Packed to the brim, they sped through the valley and across the bridge to the highway. At Shaws she heard that Theo Adams, the manager of the People's Heritage Bank, along with his wife, Lois, had fled for Waterville without advising anyone of their departure. The bank, along with the Chop Mop Shop and most other stores in town, was closed. Some people, Mary guessed, had gone on vacation or else found jobs in other towns. But still, it was a strange time to leave, and with such haste. Most of the families on her block; the Murdocks, the Kellys, the Gustavsons, and the Brennans, were gone.

Before going home, Mary stopped by the high school and parked her car twenty feet south of the lot. She sometimes did this when she was nervous or tired, an involuntary act. Years ago, when both her girls had been in school, she had gone there with plans to take the children and never come home. But these days, there was no design to her visits, just the shadow of what she had once intended still looming close. She sometimes pretended that she was a young woman again with that same choice ahead of her. She sometimes pretended, while watching that school, that both girls, their fates not yet determined, were inside. She did not imagine taking them away from Bedford. Instead she imagined that moment, sitting in the car, trapped in time, with the choice and its repercussions still ahead of her.

She had watched the building today, thinking about how one daughter, let's be honest now, her favorite daughter for no good reason except that the sound of her laughter had been the only thing that had made living in that house tolerable, was warm and safe. One daughter, her favorite daughter, in whom she had intentionally bred no love for Bedford nor loyalty to family, would survive. One child was sitting at a desk, and the other was buried in a pine box less than a mile away.

Then Mary went home, unloaded her car, and baked. Now she sat, overlooking the mess she had created in the kitchen. Flour and sugar speckled the floor and her jeans. Cookies, some of them almost raw, were stuck to the counters, spotting grease into paper towels or through cooling racks. Waffles were stacked and Ziplocked in the freezer. On the table was a three-layer chocolate rum cake, Lord knows why, a death-day cake maybe.

The phone rang. It had been ringing all morning. She didn't answer it. Probably that gossipy nitwit April Willow wanting to bring over a vegan casserole or tofu or some other useless thing. She let it ring. It felt good to let it ring.

Mary poured herself a glass of Gallo Zinfandel. The clock read two-thirty. The smells of baking did not obliterate the other smell, as she had intended. It was rotten like spoiled eggs and she lifted a dish towel over her nose to filter the stench. She did not want to go down there now, see that old stuff, the clothes, how Susan had lived during those last few years; amid the sound of the boiler, able to hear the footsteps of everyone else in the house.

You've gotta do it, there's nobody else. You can't

ask any of your buddies from Corpus Christi. They'd get their pretty Ferragamo pumps all wet. You've gotta do it. She had been thinking this all morning.

She took another swig of Zinfandel, and headed for the basement.

As she climbed down, the smell grew stronger. It reminded her of meat that has gone rancid in a broken freezer. When she got to the bottom of the basement steps, she found herself breathing through the collar of her turtleneck. She'd been down here only a few days ago, so how could anything smell this bad this fast?

Leaks in the foundation had left about an inch of water across the brown-tiled floor. Along the ceiling was a mass of pipes coated in so many layers of plaster insulation that it bunched in places like elaborate papier-mâché. As she walked into Susan's bedroom, the stench overwhelmed her and her eyes teared up. Could mold make this smell? A sick animal? She moaned aloud: a skunk. It had to be a skunk that got scared and sprayed the whole damn place before it died.

When she looked around Susan's old room, what she saw made her stand very still. The room was bright, lit by a black and blue striped ceramic lamp on the old dresser. The bed was made, eyelet sheets folded under the quilt she had packed away in the crawl space five years before. She closed her eyes. Opened them again. But the quilt, the lamp, Susan's old sweaters folded on top of the bed, did not go away.

Liz. It had to be Liz, using this place for herself and Bobby. But no, Mary had been here Friday, and there had been only the dusty bed frame, the old mattress. "Who's here?" she called. "My husband's upstairs and I called the police."

No answer. She considered doing just that. But whoever had been down here seemed to be gone. She'd call, and Danny Willow would think she was some kind of jittery wreck having hallucinations after her daughter's death. Or worse, he'd come inside the house and see the kitchen, the baking. No, she couldn't call anyone. And maybe this was the way she had left things, maybe she really was imagining.

"My husband's got a gun," she called.

Just then, the closet door opened and a monster stepped out of it. A lifeless thing, gaunt and pale. A thing so terrible that Mary's heart stopped and she cursed God. It wore the dress Mary had given it, high collared and refined. But the buttons had all been torn, so that Mary could see black stitching knots along its throat and down its chest. Its skin was sewn together in a sloppy but functional manner, the way you might thread stuffed veal before placing it in the oven.

Mary leaned against a wall, but there wasn't a wall to lean against. She stumbled backward and fell into the dirty water. It surrounded her thighs and splashed against her face. The monster watched her. The monstrous thing; she knew its face.

This wasn't happening, Mary decided. She was dreaming. She was back home in Corpus Christi, still the apple of her tyrannical father's eye. Or maybe she and her girls were driving the old Buick with all the windows rolled down, heading across the bridge and out of town. This life she'd lived the last fifteen years, it was the path not taken. It was the nightmare from which she would soon wake.

The boiler kicked, and the water churned. The monster approached, and something inside Mary died. She heard, or maybe just imagined, a snapping sound. She heard her sanity break, like a record needle that skips, and is returned to the wrong groove: All was well. All was fine. All was lovely. Where's the wine?

Mary closed her eyes. Opened them. Looked down at her hands, at the ceiling. When she looked back at the closet, the monster was gone. Mary smiled widely. "My lovely," she said.

In place of the monster stood a little girl of about six years of age. She wore pigtails tied with thick blue yarn, and a blue dress bordered with white lace. A darling girl.

"Where am I?" the little girl asked. Her voice was flat and without inflection. Cold.

Mary smiled. All was well. All was fine. All was lovely. A box made out of pine.

"Sweetie," Mary said. The little girl's eyes were cornflower blue. The boiler roared, and shallow whirlpools rushed across the floor. Mary crawled through the icy water. She leaned in close to the girl. So close that she could smell the child's sour breath, feel the moisture of it collect on her cheek. "Don't you look pretty, my Little Miss Muffett," she said.

The girl cocked her head, and Mary was reminded of a young Susan who had held her one-year-old sister in her arms. She hopped up onto the edge of the bed and sat. Her legs were too short to reach the ground, and her wet shoes dripped water.

"I've got no place to go," the little girl said. She smiled at Mary, and her teeth were spotted with specks of red.

"I'm so sorry," Mary said, and began to cry. She tried to stop. She'd never cried over Ted's death, or even at the funeral this week. But that was fine and well.

That was right and good. This was just a dream, and she was not really in hell.

The girl kicked her legs against the side of the mattress. The whirlpools on the ground churned faster, slapping against Mary's thighs. Making her numb. "My mother abandoned me," the little girl said.

"Maybe she didn't know any better. Thought what her husband said was law."

"I've got no place to go," the girl said.

"This can be your home," Mary said, because it didn't matter that this girl stank like something foul. It didn't matter that she wasn't eager to please, as her own Susan had once been. It didn't matter that her clothes were muddy and her skin was washed out and gray, or that every sane part of Mary was telling her to run right now because this child was a gift. She had to be.

The girl smiled. "No place like home, Mom. Home sweet home. I'm hanging my hat. Home again, home again, jiggety-jig."

"I'm glad, Susan," Mary said, and she couldn't remember. Had Susan died? Was this little girl Susan?

"Are you really glad?"

"So glad," she said. "We can set up your room and I'll clean it for you and I baked you a cake, Susan."

"This room here, in the basement?" Susan asked. Her feet rocked so hard now that her whole body was swinging.

"Wherever you want."

The little girl's smile spread wider. So wide that her lower lip split open, and black blood trickled down her chin. "Show me how glad you are."

Mary's panic returned, and this time she could not marshal it. She blinked, and saw for an instant that this thing was not a little girl at all. It was a woman.

Her blond hair was gone—there was only the pale white of scalp and the black of sutures. A terrible thing. A godless thing. A familiar thing. She blinked again, and the little girl returned. The happy, sweet, beautiful little girl.

"Show me," the child commanded. She beckoned Mary to the bed with a pudgy little arm. Her aspect shifted, at once a child, and then a tiny woman, and then both. Mary looked around the room, expecting to see blood or plague or the end of the world, or a man, her husband, but there was nothing.

Mary followed her daughter to the bed. She hugged the girl. Sweet Susan. Lovely Susan. The stench of paper mill and rotting meat was so strong she gagged, and Mary realized, too late, that this was no gift and it was no dream. The house began to moan, then, and through the air and the walls and the deep blue holes of this little girl's eyes, Mary could hear the sound of laughter.

TWENTY-TWO
Acid Test

In homeroom at the Bedford School Wednesday morning, Liz Marley expected a few raised eyebrows, a nod or two of sympathy, and perhaps a mention of Susan's name. But although more than half the class was absent, it was another day as usual and no one said a word to her. Instead, they watched the rain. After the pledge, some of the kids stuck their hands out the windows and opened their mouths wide as if to breathe it. Andrea Jorgenson hurriedly wrote out the homework she had not done the night before, and Owen Read threatened to spit on her in a light-hearted, flirty kind of way, but sucked it back into his mouth instead. "You're gross," she told him. "You're easy," he told her, and she hid her head behind her notebook.

In math class they talked about derivatives. Liz scribbled out her notes, and tried, repeatedly, and failed, to solve for y. In English class they talked about *The Great Gatsby*. Dori Morrison said that talking about the moral implications of running a woman over in a car on the way to East Egg starts to become irrelevant when you're dealing with amoral people to begin with. "I know he's supposed to be some romantic American dream and all that, but isn't it really egotistical to buy a house and throw parties just so some chick will notice you?"

In gym they played dodgeball. As usual, no one tried to peg her with a Nerf. In the locker room she changed back into her corduroys, realized that those thick, velvet ribbings made her look like a cow, and began to wonder if she had lost her mind. Perhaps the reason no one had mentioned Susan today was because she had never died. She was still alive, wandering through Main Street or else sitting in her apartment, chain smoking and acting professionally weird.

After she finished changing, Andrea Jorgenson approached her. Andrea lived with her aunt and mother in the Halcyon-Soma Tent and Trailer Park on the south side of town. She also wore thigh-high FM boots, that stands for Fresh Meat, and all the graffiti on the bathroom walls said she was a slut.

She touched Liz's shoulder. "Are you okay?" she asked, tucking her thin auburn hair back behind freckled ears.

"I don't think so," Liz said. "My sister died. Did you know that?"

Andrea shuffled on her high-heeled boots. Around them was the surreal white noise of chatter; lockers being shut, makeup being applied in front of mirrors, and bodies being appraised by friends: *No, you don't look fat.*

Andrea lowered her voice. "Yeah. It's not right."

"What isn't right?"

"I feel her. Can you feel her? It's like she's inside me. Is there a word?" Andrea furrowed her brow. "Possessed. That's the word."

Liz's mouth felt like dust.

Andrea looked like she wanted to say more, but instead she left the locker room. The other girls were now watching Liz. Carrie Dubois and Laura Henrich, Louise Andrias and Jaine Hodkin. All of them. There was something about their eyes that was empty. Lifeless. They reminded her of Susan. Liz closed her locker. When she turned around again, the girls had gone.

Because of the intensity of the rain, school was letting out early. Fourth period chemistry would be Liz's last class of the day. She sat at her lab station in the back of the room and tried to listen as her favorite teacher, Ms. Althea Gonya, who had platinum blond hair that was black at the roots, recited the lesson.

The fluorescent lights above buzzed, and the rain pounded against the windows. A half mile away was the cemetery, whose black gates she could see from her seat. She doodled in her notebook, squiggly lines and figure eights.

Ten minutes later, she was at work on her experiment. She was supposed to find the saturation point of a stable solution when a solid is added. The theory was that while most heated solutions suspended and dissolved a certain amount of solid material, once they reached a certain point, their saturation point, they can hold and dissolve nothing more. At this point, all the suspended solid in the solution falls to the bottom of the beaker. It was a universal truth that held not just for chemistry but for life: There is only so much crap that anybody can take.

She filled her beaker with solution and readied her solid suspension. The lit Bunsen burner glowed like a prayer candle at church. When she lifted the beaker, it slipped through her fingers and bounced against her hip before shattering on the floor. Hydrochloric acid stained her blue sweatshirt. Fragments of glass scurried across the freshly waxed floor like the legs of a crab. Fearing that the acid would burn her skin, Steve McCormack, who'd once informed Liz that her sister fucked for money, filled a liter-sized beaker full of water. She might have told him that the HCl was diluted for a reason, and that the only thing it might eat through was a chewable aspirin, but there wasn't time. Steve poured the water all over her lap. It soaked her pants and ran down her legs.

The classroom went silent. They were all looking at her. Just like the night at the mill. Just like the faces she'd seen inside the mirrors of her sister's apartment. Just like the girls in the locker room today. Faces.

Looks like you wet your pants. The thought was almost funny. She covered her mouth and started to laugh, not hard laughing, just giggles. *Looks like you're a joke. Now nobody's gonna like you.* Almost funny, not as funny. She laughed harder. *You fat, stupid cunt. Now they'll never stop talking and they'll tell Bobby you're an idiot. They'll tell Bobby and he'll finally leave you because he'll figure out the truth. He'll wake up and see you for what you are. A fake. A loser. A waste. A nothing.* These thoughts raced through her mind. They were not her own. Close, but not hers. She laughed harder. *Looks like you wet your pants. They think you wet your pants.* She looked down at her wet corduroys, and now she could not remember: Had she wet her pants? No, she couldn't have; she'd feel warm. *You got so upset you wet your pants and now they all know you're fucked up. They know everything. They see how you wet your pants.* Whose voice was that?

You worthless piece of shit, it should have been you.

Susan. The voice belonged to Susan. She was not dreaming. It was daytime. And Susan was in her head. Holy crap. Susan was inside her head. Liz was laughing so hard now it sounded like crying.

Ms. Gonya made her way to the back of the room. Instead of smiling she looked at Liz with a vacant stare. She reached out and lifted Liz's chin. Long, hot-pink painted fingernails grazed her neck. Liz jerked away, for an instant thinking: *This woman is going to slice my throat right open.* "Elizabeth?" Ms. Gonya asked.

"Looks like I wet my pants," she said, and then she started to cry.

After her episode, it was agreed that Liz should go to the teachers' lounge, where the school psychologist would call her mother to take her home. But her mother could not be reached over the phone, and so it was Bobby who stopped by the lounge, carrying her backpack along with his own.

They left the lounge together, and as they walked, the bell rang and the halls filled with people going home early because of the rain. She could hear echoes: laughter, shouting, and underneath that, a buzzing. An electrical whine. The sound was familiar—this buzzing. It was the same sound she'd heard in her dream the night before Susan died, and she thought that it came from the people in the halls. It belonged to them, was underneath their laughter and polite conversation. Things started to come together for her then, and she began to understand what was happening.

As she walked, she rubbed her hand against Bobby's. He picked it up and squeezed. "I love you," she whispered, because it was one of the only truths she could believe in right now: wood made a particular sound when you knocked on it unless it was on fire; things fell down instead of up unless you were in space; bloody sisters did not visit you in cemeteries unless they were Susan Marley; and she loved Bobby Fullbright no matter what.

When they walked outside the front doors to the school where her mother had parked only two hours before, every student and teacher stopped what they were doing. Mr. Brutton dropped his briefcase onto the wet pavement, and did not bother to pick it up. The seniors in the parking lot stopped running toward their cars, and the ones who were driving slammed on their brakes. The buses did not move forward, and the kids standing under the awning did not climb aboard. "Let's go to the mill tonight," Liz heard Louise Andrias tell Owen Read and Steve McCormack amid the general murmur of conversation. "In my dream—" and then the words died on Louise's tongue. All the words died.

It went completely quiet, except for the sound of the falling rain and the buzzing, still that buzzing. No cars moved. Only faces, watching them. Every person at the Bedford High School, watching them. Familiar faces. Angry faces. She remembered the faces in the mirrors at Susan's apartment, and from out her window the night Susan died, and from the locker room this afternoon, and from chemistry class twenty minutes ago. Faces. They looked like Susan. Every one of them.

Bobby squeezed her hand tighter. "What the hell?" he whispered.

She yanked him forward, and together they ran to his car. As they drove away, she looked out the window and saw that slowly, people were starting to move again. Like a trance that had been lifted, they trembled, and then opened car doors and drove off, or picked up their briefcases, or perhaps they even resumed their conversations. "In my dream," she could almost hear Louise Andrias say, "Susan Marley came back."

Liz knew what was happening. Just like tapping her ruby slippers three times, she'd known the answer all along. She fought the urge to scream.

TWENTY-THREE
The Road to Kitty Dukakis
Is Paved with Good Intentions

A round four o'clock on Wednesday, Paul woke up in his study with the kind of headache that feels like internal bleeding. Pound, throb, pound. Each time his heart beat, he could feel it like a drum smashed open inside his temples. The DTs. Yes, here they were, the real thing. Not the kind where you wonder if you're having them. You know you're having them. Just about right: forty-eight hours since he'd had a drink. Just like clockwork, this perfect machine of his.

The house was dry as a bone, and he had not had so much as a shot since he'd polished off his emergencies-only stash of scotch two nights before. Tempting as dropping by the liquor store may have been, he'd decided he'd rather eat paint thinner than answer pointed questions from the locals about Susan.

There had been some changes in the Martin household over the last few days. On Friday Brutton had called to tell him that if he showed up on school grounds, he'd be physically removed by police escort.

On Sunday Cathy told him she was leaving. "Write when you get work, dear," he'd told her, because he really had thought she was kidding. What kind of person leaves a man when his luck is the worst it's ever been? But then he woke from his nap on the couch, and found two Post-it notes taped together on the refrigerator that read:

> *Dear Paul,*
>
> *Gone to April's with James.*
> *Take care,*
>
> *Cathy*
>
> *PS—The AA hotline is open twenty-four hours (207) 774–3034*

Tammy Wynette she was not. And how had Cathy explained this to his son as she took him away from the only home he'd ever known? What had she said to him? Best not to think about that now. Best to add that to the ever-growing list.

He spent the next few days drying out, which sounded like a lot more fun than it actually was. And now here he was, a soon-to-be-divorced alcoholic with a dead ex-mistress, standing in an empty kitchen on a rainy afternoon in Bedford, Maine. Who would have guessed? Certainly not him. This occasion called for a beer.

He opened the refrigerator. No, not the moldy blue cheese. Not the greasy clam chowder. Nothing in the crisper. Nope. He searched the cabinets. His head was really pounding. The thing he'd considered a headache a few hours ago, compared to this, was a too tight hat. He tossed things out. Oatmeal, bottles of condiments, canned chicken soup; they fell to the floor. Nothing there. And then he remembered: the cooking sherry.

There it was. Behind the Heinz 57. Usually by this time, he would have had a nip. A sip. Not to get drunk, just to stay neutral. But never cooking sherry. Never had he gone the way of Kitty Dukakis. This was an all-time low.

He turned the bottle over in his hand. *Tide you over,* a voice whispered in his ear. *You'll feel so much better once you have a little nip.*

"Christ," he said out loud because he knew that hearing his voice would make him feel better. "Jesus Christ." He looked at the bottle. Almost funny. Truly funny. Funny because you can see cherry red stains running down the white label of a dusty old bottle. Funny because you're smart enough to know exactly the kind of failure you are but not tough enough to figure a way out. Pathetic funny.

He dropped the bottle to the floor. It didn't shatter. It rolled. He gave it a kick. It just kept rolling and no matter how hard he kicked, he just couldn't make it break.

It was wet out. Not just the rain, but the air. And dark. He could hear water rushing like a river on the ground. He absentmindedly rubbed the place on his arm where Susan had bitten him. It itched with healing and he could feel the hardness of scab underneath his bandages. After the incident with the impenetrable sherry, he'd had to get out of the house. He took the car. As he drove down the hill, more and more water filled the streets. The car swerved, hydroplaned. He pulled over a few blocks from his house and walked to town.

It was still daytime, probably around three o'clock, but it felt much later. The black clouds overhead were full and threatening. Lightning lit up the sky every few minutes and was closely followed by the crackle of thunder. Each time this happened, his path to town was illuminated for a few seconds, maybe less, by a yellow, electrical light that, were his hair dry, would have made it stand on end.

Kansas, Nebraska, Iowa, Utah. Those were the names of some of the license plates mounted on the wall behind the bar. He read all thirty-seven of them, trying to focus, as he wiped down his wet clothes with the brown paper towels he'd acquired from the sawdust-covered men's room.

The television was tuned to the local news. The main story was the flooding in Bedford. There were interviews with people from the town, saying in that slow, man-of-the-people way they had of saying everything: These things happen. We'll make out all right. There were also a few inside-the-house disaster sequences that showed flooded basements. Cameras panned in on cardboard boxes and stored furniture floating across water-corroded floors.

As an end piece, the anchor reported that the Clott Paper Mill had recently closed, and the future of the town was in question. A clip showed a small caravan of cars heading south on I–95. Strapped to their trunks were bike racks or extra boxes, and it looked like many were abandoning the place. Would people stay in Bedford, the anchor intoned, or with a population that had been dwindling over the last fifty years, would future maps mark the area as deserted woodland?

Paul muttered something about inbreds, morons, and looked back at the license plates. Only he, Montie, and some old-timers were in the bar right now. There was The Duke as in John Wayne, so named because he grew increasingly silent as he drank, and that guy, Cancer Dan, who had this growth on his nose like he'd been out in the sun all his life but had never heard of the word "cancer." He was the greenskeeper at the Corpus Christi Country Club. Last was Sean, whose low-slung jeans revealed the hairy fissure of his ass. They were playing cards. Each had his own bottle of something, what they'd brought with them and didn't want to have to pay extra for, and a beer, which they sipped, just in order to stay in the bar.

Paul's worst fear was being liked by these assholes.

"You smell her?" Montie asked. "I can smell her on my skin. Like she's inside me."

Paul cocked his head. He wanted a drink right now. He wanted a drink really bad. No time for barroom philosophy emceed by a man with an intelligence quotient of sixty. "What are you talking about?"

"Nothing. What can I get you?" Montie asked.

Paul felt incredibly grateful. He paused, trying not to look desperate. No one likes an obvious drunk. "Coffee," he said. He did not know why he said that. He tried to change his order, but saw the way Montie's eyes widened in surprise, and his pride wouldn't let him take it back. Yes, his first drink would be coffee. His second, a triple scotch.

Montie poured him some coffee and sat on a stool next to him. He wore his usual uniform; a white T-shirt full of holes underneath an apron with the map of the London Underground printed on it. His fingernails were bitten jagged and low. Still, there was dried blood and dirt underneath them, like he'd been digging his own grave. And gin. No matter how drunk Paul ever got, he could always smell that gin coming off Montie's pores. The fact that the humidity inside the bar was high enough to make the wood under Paul's hands slick and soft to the touch did not make that smell any better.

"Why do you collect all these license plates?" Paul asked.

Montie looked up as if seeing them for the first time. "Oh, them? They were here when I bought the bar."

"When was that?"

"Eighty-eight."

"Oh. I thought you collected them."

Montie laughed. His stomach folded on itself so that Brixton and Central London were one. "Why the hell would I do that? Just a lot a crap."

Eighteen minutes later Paul sipped his black coffee and winced. His stomach cramped and gurgled, but still, he sipped his coffee. This was the plan. This was what he would do. Because he didn't want people thinking that after his family left him, after Susan died, that he went out and got drunk. Went straight for the bar. He didn't want to think that himself. No, he would wait until six o'clock. Exactly twenty-three minutes from when he'd arrived. Functional alcoholics start at five. He would start at six. Five minutes left. Like counting down until the end of class.

At three minutes before zero hour, Montie made him a sandwich; two pieces of bread slopped together with mayonnaise and pickled egg. The bar was mostly empty;

Cancer Dan, The Duke, and Sean now departed for whatever dry-rot shelters they called home. He pictured them hiding in their moldy dens, waiting for this maddening rain to end as the people of this town did every year, as they would do every year, forever. He pushed his sandwich away. "I'm not that sick," he said.

At two minutes before zero hour, Danny entered the bar. It was the first time they'd seen each other since he'd driven home from the police station Thursday night. The sight of Danny gave Paul a flicker of déjà vu. What he remembered most was the toilet paper Susan had used as a napkin. The slathering of pizza sauce on her lips. Then it was gone. Same thing, he thought, like nothing happened, like a girl didn't die. Same old shit. Less than a minute left. The second hand on Paul's watch wavered as if it might go backward. He resolved to give up counting seconds. It was impossible to count that slowly.

Danny stood. Paul motioned for him to sit. He didn't. Well, maybe not same old shit. Montie lingered behind the bar, watching them as usual. "Cathy was at my house," Danny said.

"She does that."

"She shouldn't have gone out with this rain. I don't know how she did it, but she got across the bridge. Probably in Saratoga Springs by now."

Paul ordered his drink. Montie nodded and got it for him, then stood over the two of them, waiting no doubt for their jeers to devolve into violence. Paul sipped his drink. Slow sip. Then a big gulp. He drained the glass and felt that familiar, welcome, wonderful burn. A few drops rolled down his chin and he lifted them up with his finger and tasted them.

Danny curled his lip in disgust, and Paul turned to him. "What am I supposed to say?"

"You know what really pisses me off—"

Paul knew just from the look on Danny's face what he was about to say. There are things you know, without being told. Things you already feel. "—No, and I don't care," he said, cutting Danny off. Then he ordered another drink. Montie gave it to him. He took a sip. It was the cheap stuff that tasted like Tide detergent though Paul had asked for a neat Johnnie Walker Black.

"Everybody does these things for you," Danny said.

"What exactly do they do?"

Danny gave Paul a knowing look. "Well, nobody's comin' around asking you about fleeing the scene of an accident, are they?"

"You're kidding." Once, a week ago, he could have pushed Danny around. Once, a long time ago, he would never have been in this situation to begin with. He would have had better things to do than loiter in this bar with a stomach full of worry and a gaggle of half-wits by his side. The worry that persisted whether he drank nothing or a quart of whiskey. He looked down and noticed that he was fingering the place Susan had bitten. Through the bandages, there was blood. He must have been picking at it for a long time without even knowing it. "She won't go away. I don't think it's my fault, but she won't go away," he said.

"She's worried about you."

Paul picked up the trail of the conversation. "Is that what she told you?"

"Yeah, and a few other things." Danny again looked like he was about to continue, to go on and on about the few other things. *Great, Danny, wait till my life is so shitty I can't even stand and then attack. Great, Danny, I know just the kind of guy you are.*

"So ring her bell and have a 'Crucify Paul Martin' party. You leave James out of it, though." He had meant this last part to come out soft, threatening, rational. Instead it was nasal and loud, like a cartoon version of himself.

"You know what pisses me off, Paul? You know what really pisses me off?"

"What, Danny, what really pisses you off? Tell me," Paul yelled. He lost his balance, grabbed the bar, and pulled himself back onto the stool.

Danny sighed.

"Well, fuck you, too, Danny," Paul said, but it sounded like, "WAFUYOOTOO," some distant, aboriginal language.

Danny stood for a while longer, in what Paul considered a kind of gloating. Paul managed to stand. He took a swing, right hand up under Danny's chin. Sucker punch. Danny reeled backward, seemed almost to gain his footing, but then his knees buckled and he hit the floor. Montie came out from around the bar and knelt next to him. "Get out of my bar," Montie said, while Danny croaked indecipherable sounds from his bruised windpipe.

P aul left before his clothes had a chance to dry. He stood outside the bar for a while, waiting for Danny to appear, maybe finish this thing they had started. But Danny did not come. Hiding, probably, and telling Montie that because he and Paul were friends, he did not want to have to go outside and arrest him.

He felt like a human sponge. His wet clothes chafed at every place they touched his body. And the shaking, still the shaking not in the least diminished by four ounces of eighty proof. Could a man die from withdrawal?

He decided to walk, he did not know where, passing houses and the trailer park, until he stood in front of her house. He went around to the side entrance. Inside, he saw the place where she had fallen six nights before. There was no yellow police line, no marker. Just a stain, a little more brown than the rest of the wood, at the foot of the stairs. He tried to think of something to leave for her. Reached into his pockets and found his wallet. It held eight dollars, an American Express card, a library card, his driver's license with the photo taken seven years ago (back when he'd carried a few extra pounds and his smile had been a little more easy, a little less self-mocking), and a People's Heritage bank card. He took off the iodine- and blood-stained gauze from his arm and dropped it on the floor, hoping that if she was watching from somewhere above, below, wherever, she would accept this gesture in the manner in which it was intended.

Rossoff poked his fleshy head out of the entrance to his apartment. Paul felt an instant unease. Rossoff's door was open only a crack, but beyond, Paul could smell the man's house. It smelled of secrets. People who count their money every night and do not say personal things over the phone because they think someone might be listening. People who change their clothing in the dark. People who hoard food in their refrigerators until it rots. People who do not take out their garbage. People who wait until their babies are sick before they change their diapers. It had that kind of smell. Nothing specific. Just a mold.

"Don't come around here," Rossoff said. He was so

fat that he could hardly fit through the door, and in his beard were little pieces of white cotton.

"I won't," Paul said.

Rossoff smiled. As he opened the door just a little wider so that they spoke face to face, the cotton things squirmed. A speck fell out of his gray beard and onto the collar of his black shirt. It continued to squirm. The blood drained from Paul's face, and bile rose in his throat. Crabs. Pubic crabs.

" 'Cause I wouldn't want to have to call the police," Rossoff told him.

It dawned on Paul just then. Maybe he had known it before, just never believed it. She never locked her door. She never paid her rent. This man, Susan.

"Because none of us needs that," Rossoff said. "None of us needs the police. Like to hear about all your pissing around here Thursday night. Pissing in dirty pots." And then, he winked. A quick, skilled wink.

This man, Susan. At first Paul walked, but after a few steps he was running. Rossoff yelled after him but, thankfully, he did not hear.

Around eight that Wednesday night, when he normally would have been eating pot roast with his wife and son while doing his best impression of a guy having his first drink of the evening, his feet were bloody. The muscles in his stomach clenched again and again in dry, painful heaves. Don's Liquor Bonanza was closed. He'd been tempted to break in, but he wasn't in such great shape. He probably wouldn't have escaped before Danny pulled up in a squad car, lights flashing, ready to arrest him. Not a tempting prospect. He could have knocked on someone's door and asked for something. It wasn't like his reputation was something that needed to be upheld. He could have asked some friendly Bedford neighbor, maybe the parent of some student at his place of former employ: *Sorry to disturb you, after I leave, please go on about your business and forget that I was ever here, pay no attention to my appearance, but could you spare a drop? Anything will do.* Or he could have gone back to Montie's and done some groveling. But he did none of these things. He took a stroll, thoughts of white insects and runaway wives not even entering his head. He took a walk and let things empty out, and he kept walking until his mind was an absence of memory, his physical body in such agony that all else was wiped clean.

That was his state as he sat on the bench next to Susan Marley. She looked like hell. Worse than him, even. She was wearing a blue dress with white trim. Her head had been shaved bald, and she struggled to hold it erect. Black autopsy sutures weaved their way down her throat and beneath her dress. It might have been a tasteless joke: Devil in a Blue Dress. In might have been a DT hallucination. This might even have been happening. Sadly, he didn't care.

He first saw her at Don's Liquor Bonanza. He had taken a seat on the edge of a gutter. Kicked out some leaves with his wilted wing tips so that it drained a little better and then just sat there, recognizing this point as the lowest of his life. He knew what Cathy might do right now, were she in his place. Only he had kept her from doing it. But he did not think those very dark thoughts. They were not in him, not just yet.

He saw her shadow. It moved in jerks like someone carrying something very heavy. She walked on the outer soles of her feet. He lowered his head and let himself believe that what he saw was just a dream. And then, on the ground, he saw her feet. They were bare and bloody. Her fatty pads hung loose like flaps, and underneath them he was sure he could see the ivory of her bones.

He could not help but follow. She waved to him and he got up from the gutter. They did not walk together. He kept a distance, yards behind. She limped farther south. In the dark and wet, he only saw her silhouette. She had a tiny body, like a child's. And this is how he kept from thinking about what was actually happening: It was not simply the pain of withdrawal that made his mind a blank. He never saw her face.

She led him to the river. The tide had risen above the two-foot railing. She waded to the center of the bridge and stood between Bedford and the outside world. There was lightning, and he kept his eyes squinted so that he would not see her clearly when it came. But he did see.

She pointed at the water. There were whirlpools, crests of white. A bucket floated. He followed its path with his eyes. It rushed under the bridge, heading toward the lake thirty miles south. He imagined that it would wash up on a bank there, covered in rust. Really, this was what he wanted. This was what he had been looking for since he moved to Bedford. A way out.

His life flashed before him. Grandmother and her cigarettes. Chess. Meeting Cathy. Telling her the night before the wedding that he loved her, he really did love her, so no matter what happened everything would work out. Seeing, smelling, the Clott Paper Mill before they even got off I–95's Bedford exit. Its shadow had blanketed Main Street like something out of a nineteenth-century novel, and he'd thought: People still live like this? And then he'd thought: Yes, of course they do.

He remembered Susan Marley. Even in high school, her eyes had been wild. And Georgia, who'd first cut his hair ten years ago. She'd shown him pictures of her son, "Smart as a whip!" she'd told him. And then she'd spun him on her swivel chair once, twice, three times, laughing: "Everybody likes a ride, right?" Was it so surprising that he got his hair cut every other week that summer?

He thought of his children most. What would they think of him if he died in this river? Andrew, he could not say. It had been so long since the boy had been his boy. And James, well, James. He might make it through. Paul pictured him all grown up. Years from now he might be sitting in a bar, offhandedly telling a second or third date about his dad. *Yeah,* he would say, *you might know my dad. He's not the guy who writes books and appears on* Journal Report. *He's not the guy who helped my mom through a hard time. My dad was a drunk. Every town has a few. He killed himself.*

Paul turned from Susan and the river then. Left without fear or in haste. Knowing this would not be the end just as he knew he was not ready to do what she wanted. Not yet.

She followed him. Things in the town seemed to change, maybe just his perception of them. Maybe just his sickness. But there was an echo as she walked behind him. He could hear it above the rain. An echo of water splashing, one foot a quick splatter of water, the second a slow gulp, and on and on.

Had he not been so sick, had the shaking in his body, even his hands, subsided for just a second and allowed him a shred of mental coherence, he would have seen the people who looked out their windows when he passed. He would have noticed how some of them stood on their porches, not bothering with coats, some in flannel pajamas and robes, some in yellowed undershirts and boxers. They watched, not him, but something behind him. He would have understood that they saw Susan Marley.

When he reached the park and took a seat on the bench, he was not surprised when Susan joined him. The bones in her spine made popping sounds as she bent to sit. Rigor mortis, he thought, without being able to connect this thought to the present action. Like her relationship with Rossoff, too awful a thought to place.

He did not look at her. He watched the way the see-saws bounced up and down with no ostensible cause of momentum. Watched the swings rock. They pumped themselves. He could hear this as well, the rusty creakings. As if inside an enormous haunted house that had no limits, he could hear it above the rain.

When it was time, when he was ready, when he knew he could handle it, he saw her face. It was a massacre of skin; premature wrinkles caused by decay, funeral parlor makeup in red and brown splotches, and stitches. He believed then what he had not allowed himself to believe before. "Oh, God," he said. In a moment of clarity that chilled him so deeply he could feel it in his bones, he wondered: Where had she gone, and what had she brought back with her?

Before he had the chance to run, she placed her hand on the back of his head and squeezed. At first he felt only the dampness of his fingers. It was the coldest touch of his life. And then she squeezed harder and there was pain. She squeezed harder still, and a flood of emotions filled his consciousness. The sound was like a loud fluorescent light, a discordant buzzing. He heard the stories of the town. He heard April Willow praying for her dog. He pictured Liz Marley climbing a fence in a cemetery and landing in another world. He saw Susan prowling the woods. He heard Bobby Full-bright trying to make a fist. He saw inside Louise Andrias, and the color was black. Cruelty so pervading that everything she'd ever touched was marked by it. He heard Georgia O'Brian fantasizing about a merchant marine who looked a good deal like himself. He saw Cathy's uncertainty like a thick suspension cable that over the years had gotten thinner and thinner until this week it became a piece of twine that broke. He felt himself going insane. "Stop," he shouted. "Please stop."

Susan squeezed harder, and the voices stopped. He looked in her eyes, and he saw his own reflection. He saw himself through Susan's eyes. In her left eye was a man to whom she was grateful. In her right eye was a man who had betrayed her. These men stood side by side. One man was bigger, but then a drinking man's devils are always stronger than the angels of his nature.

He waited, quite sure now that he was going to die. She squeezed harder, and the three bones of his inner ears (he really could feel them) rattled. He waited. He was so tired. He was so sick of upholding the fiction that there was a better man inside him that was trapped beneath a bottle when really there was nothing. Really, he was a loser. A coward who, let's be honest, some-times exaggerated his own drunkenness so that to himself, his wife, the people who believed in him, he would in some way be less accountable. He was so tired of fighting when never once had he witnessed grace.

Susan kept squeezing, and he saw that she meant to crush his skull.

TWENTY-FOUR
High Tide

The three of them stood at the edge of the river. Louise Andrias, Owen Read, and Steve McCormack. Voices prodded them, like scalpels carving new gullies in their minds. They listened. They watched the water. They were not conflicted. They had known all along what they would do.

Louise Andrias wasn't a nice girl, not at all. There was something inside her that didn't feel, like poking needles through nerveless skin. She smiled the right way, and she dressed the right way, but she sometimes forgot that the people around her were people at all. She forget that they breathed, or that when they were alone they had their own thoughts that she would never know. Once, she squeezed a calico kitten too tightly and it stopped moving. So she squeezed the second kitten, just to see if it would happen again. She wasn't sorry that they died, but in order to keep her allowance, she made very sure to cry about it to her mother.

Nobody had ever hurt her growing up. Nobody had lifted an angry hand, or locked her in a closet. She was just born without a conscience, the way some people are born with extra toes.

Louise liked Owen and Steven pretty well. They were nice to her, which was important. Owen didn't like girls, not *that* way. He'd never said so, but he'd never needed to say it. He didn't look at girls' asses, didn't get hard-ons when they watched porn on late-night HBO. Didn't ever have crushes or ask girls out. He flirted with them all the time, told them they were pretty, teased them, pretended to be hot for them, but mostly Louise could tell he was just mad at them. Mad because he knew he was supposed to like them, but he didn't.

Once, she led Owen by the hand into the basement of the mill. Cajoled him into a dry-lipped kiss. Unbuttoned his jeans and rolled them down his legs so that he looked all vulnerable and frightened, like a kitten. She'd smiled at him, thinking: He can't run very far, not with his pants down around his ankles. Then she took him in her hands. This wasn't her first time, and she knew what she was doing. He tried for her. She saw him try. Saw him close his eyes, furrow his brow. Try. Try. Try. After a while, he came. Then he held her and started to cry, and she knew he'd convinced himself that he loved her.

After that she and Steven McCormack shared a sleeping bag in the mill a couple of times. When they made the sounds of sex, Owen would wander the dark basement, all moony and depressed. The boys never fought with each other; she made sure to play the one off the other in just the right way. That's how she managed to keep them by her side. Three points that would never form a triangle.

At the river now, Louise Andrias pulled the hood of her jacket over her head. To her left was Owen, to her right, Steven. The water rushed the banks, and rain fell. The buzzing spoke to them. They heard it like a song they knew by heart. Like intelligent déjà vu. It had always existed, would always exist. Louise bent down and touched the water. It rushed so fast it slapped her hand, and its coldness cramped her fingers into a claw.

Once, she'd imagined her future. Glimpsed it from far away. A nurse in a pretty white uniform, living in a small apartment she'd furnished with her own money. A wicker table just because she liked wicker. The boys nearby, so she could see them every day. But she was no fool. With a job after graduation waiting tables at the Weathervane in Corpus Christi that she'd been lucky to get, she knew what was to come. Sure, she knew the world didn't owe her anything. And yet, sometimes, she was sure it did.

She'd always liked Susan Marley. Her eyes like corpses stacked in a pile. A few months ago she'd sent Owen over to knock on her back door and pay the man who lived on the ground floor fifty bucks. Sit with her. Watch her. Fuck her. Just a test, really. She hadn't expected Owen to do it. But he did. *Like death,* he'd explained after he left the apartment and found Louise smoking a cigarette on Susan Marley's front lawn. His khakis hadn't even been zipped yet, which had made Louise laugh, and he'd told her, *Like waking the dead.*

Things changed after that for all of them. They changed after that, in a bad way. Louise liked it. She slept with Owen one more time, and Steve, too. When they looked at each other after that, sometimes they saw Susan Marley. She populated their dreams. Her smell was on their skin. She infected them. When they went to the mill to drink their beer and light fires after that, they started to hear voices. Murmurs of men long dead. They pressed their ears to the wet floors until they became haunted, too.

They'd talked about their plan last night, and then again this afternoon outside the school. They'd decided to meet here at the river. Give themselves one last chance to turn back. A last chance to say no. But no one backed out. The water rushed fast, and they knew they'd never make it out of Bedford. The current was too strong, and the bridge was out. No place to go. They came to a decision then. The three of them. They did not need to speak aloud; they did not need to.

They would go to the mill tonight. They would do what the voices asked. What they'd planned, for months, to do. A final prank on this shithole town. A mill of fire, just like in their dreams.

TWENTY-FIVE
Grape Juice and Children's Toys

"That angel was so stupid. Like this one guy really made a difference because of a savings and loan that probably invested in some nineteen-forties version of Enron."

"Bobby?" she asked. They were sitting Indian-style underneath the pool table in his basement.

"Call me Peppe."

They had been talking about their senior trip to Portland, the prom, whether marriage was a defunct social convention or the saving grace in an otherwise selfish existence, which third-world nations had nuclear weapons, and whether a preemptive war was justifiable. Well, Bobby had talked, filling space until the lump in her throat diminished, and she was no longer ready to burst into tears. "Right," she had said. "Yes," she had said.

He had just been about to launch into his favorite speech, about the fallacy of Frank Capra's American dream in a town called Bedford Falls, when she worked up the courage to tell him what was on her mind. In her mind, for that matter. And her dreams (*dreams?*), and the air, and the raised hairs on the back of her neck.

"Peppe?"

"*Oui?*"

"What do you think happened in the parking lot at school today?"

Bobby let out a deep breath, and she understood that he'd been waiting for her to calm down before talking about it. She touched his hand, thanking him silently for that. For being someone who cared enough to put on an act. "It was messed up the way they stared," he said.

"What do you think was going on?"

He shivered. "I don't know. People in Bedford are weird. I don't know why my parents stayed here. Except for you sometimes I wish they hadn't."

She swallowed deeply, and looked down at the carpet. There were no buckets collecting leaks down here. No brown worms curled into balls. Just thick, white carpeting stained with grape juice, and children's toys spread out over the floor, waiting to be picked up for more play. "They know something. That's why they stared."

He nodded. She saw that he was near tears. Sometimes they pretended that she was the sensitive one, but that wasn't really true. It was always Bobby who felt things first. It was Bobby who had a sense of how things in an orderly society should work, and became enraged when that contract was broken. She, on the other hand, had never held such high expectations. "Did anyone say they were sorry to you today? They let you spill that shit on yourself and watched you cry and no one even came over and said they were sorry. It's because of her, too.

They all talk about her like she wasn't a person. Even my family does that."

"You care. You were nice to me." He bowed his head as if to show her that he hadn't been fishing for a compliment, and she kissed his cheek.

They were silent for a little while, and she closed her eyes. From above she could hear his siblings tearing across bare wooden floors in stocking feet, and his mother setting out snacks. Cookies, probably. The perfectly shaped, store-bought kind, along with glasses of milk, or juice for Margaret, the strict vegetarian. Until she met Bobby, she hadn't known that some mothers sat with their children after school, and asked them about their days.

"I hate Bedford," she said.

He nodded. "Yeah. Me, too. Remember how I used to hang out with those guys? Louise and Owen and Steve? We'd go to the mill and drink beer. Sometimes when we put the kindling in the vat and set it on fire, these fumes would come out. And it was like everybody was waiting, even hoping, that something bad would happen. They wanted to get sick. Especially Louise. Nobody ever talked about getting out, or doing stuff, or taking a road trip to Portland, or even visiting a museum or something—not like I'd want to go to a museum, but you know what I mean. It was like living in slow motion, and most of the time I wanted to be home instead so I wouldn't have to deal with it, but you get sick of being home. I do, at least. They made fun of me, too, did you know that? They made fun of me," he said, blushing, because it was the first time he'd openly admitted this to her. "They made fun of me for talking about books all the time, and for doing my homework, like normal people don't do their homework so they can get into a good college. You'll see, they won't even get into a bogus school like UMO," he said, forgetting that if she got lucky, that's where she'd be headed in September. "And the thing is, anybody whose parents might care, anybody like me moved away a long time ago. The people who stayed here don't care."

"I care, Bobby." He seemed to take little solace in this, and so she added, "You'll get out of here. You'll get out and you'll see other places."

"I know. I can't wait."

She stiffened, but said nothing.

"People treat you so badly, and it's all because of something made up. Like they heard Susan was some kind of monster for so long they believed it."

She shrugged. "Bobby? There's something I want to tell you, but I don't know how to say it."

"What? You can tell me anything."

She looked at her pale hands that were practically pruned from all this rain, and at the carpet, thick and full, and at her faded Keds. There was a butterfly in her stomach the size of a basketball. "I'd know if she was gone. I'd feel something, but I don't."

Bobby pulled away from her so that he could look her in the eyes. "She's dead, Liz. You buried her."

"Yes. She's dead."

He held her shoulders, squeezing through her T-shirt with his small hands. "It's not your fault."

Her throat constricted. How would he know what was her fault? How could anyone say for sure? "Have you dreamed about her since she died?" she asked.

He averted his eyes. "No," he said, and she had the strangest feeling that he was lying. Why would he lie?

"Oh. Remember how we talked about my dream, that she could hurt me inside it?"

Bobby inched a little farther away from her on the floor. Probably he didn't even notice he was doing it, but she did. "Yeah."

She rubbed her neck, where the bruises were now healed. "Well, I think I was right. Except it wasn't exactly how I figured."

Bobby's eyes were wide, and she knew she was supposed to laugh now. She was supposed to say: *I'm so silly, Bobby! Why do you put up with me? I get the strangest ideas sometimes! I'm a regular Lucille Ball!* She didn't laugh. "In a way, she really was a witch. She was born different. She could see things that other people couldn't, and because of that she went crazy. Somehow, by seeing those things, she made them more real, and when they got more real, she got even crazier, and they fed off each other. If she'd been born someplace else, or people had been nicer to her, she might have been okay. It wasn't just my dad and the stuff he did to her that made her screwed up. It was the way she was born, and this town, and the mill, and all the thoughts that she couldn't control . . ."

Bobby shook his head. "What bad things are you talking about?"

"Think about it. If you're inside a haunted house and it's colder than it should be, then that's a physical property, isn't it? It really is cold—atoms really are moving more slowly. So maybe if Susan saw what was making the place cold, some old echo of what had once happened, like a murder, or just an angry person who once lived there, that made it more real. The place got even colder when Susan was in it. And then, that made

Susan worse, too. What if Bedford is like one giant haunted house that Susan brought to life?"

"You believe this?" Bobby asked.

She looked at the underside of the pool table instead of at him. Yes, she realized, she did believe it. She was sure of it. A part of her, the part that had lived with Susan for twelve years, had known all along. She wasn't as frightened as she had expected. Instead she was numb. "In my dream in the cemetery I heard this buzzing, these terrible emotions. I think that's what Susan heard her whole life. And as time went on, the buzzing got louder, because all that bad stuff was becoming more and more real. There was good stuff, too, I guess, but it got forgotten. Susan didn't listen for it. When we were at her apartment, I saw these faces in her mirrors. They were kind of messed up, you know? Warped. But also familiar. I thought I was going crazy."

"Umm," Bobby said. She tried not to look at him, afraid that if she did, her numbness would crack wide open, and she'd burst into tears.

"At school today I heard the buzzing again, kind of like voices. And I saw some of those same faces as in the mirrors, only they belonged to the people watching us in the parking lot. Louise Andrias and Mr. Brutton and Steve McCormack . . . It was like they were the same people, but also different. Darker."

"I'm not following," Bobby said, but she got the feeling he did follow. Some part of him may have guessed, only he didn't want to believe. She could understand that. She didn't want to believe it, either.

"I'm saying that over time, the things that haunt Bedford became a part of Susan. That's why she could be in our nightmares, because our nightmares were buried inside her. That's why I saw those faces in the mirrors; because she *was* those faces. That's why I heard those voices when she visited my dream, or whatever it was that happened. Because those voices, that buzzing, the dark part of Bedford, Susan carried them inside her. And the reason she could hurt me in my dream was because those things were getting stronger. They were starting to become real, like the thing that chased me in the woods. And now that she died, they're not inside her anymore."

Bobby let out a long breath. "Where are they?"

"Have you noticed how many people left town this week?"

He raised an eyebrow. "Liz, this is too much."

"I think some people guessed what was going to happen and they left town." Now Liz was beginning to feel it. Her throat was tight, like a balloon was inflating inside it, and she fought the urge to curl herself into a fetal position and turn into an hysterical pile of Liz Marley. "She's my sister. Don't you think, of all people, that I'd know why she's different? When she talked to herself, it was crazy, sure, but it also made sense. She was talking to ghosts in the room—things that had already happened, or were about to happen. She knew when my dad was pissed about something, and she knew about the people who'd lived in the house before us, even though we'd never met them. When she was mad at me, I always dreamed about her. It was always some fucked-up nightmare, you know? Like a dog would bite me, or we'd be sitting in a tree and she'd shove me out of it. In the morning I'd tell myself that it was just a dream, but it was more than that. It was her way of getting back at me. I wish I could forget. I wish I could pretend this wasn't happening, but I have to tell you about it. I don't know what else to do. I grew up with her, Bobby. I *know* she did something. And people wouldn't have been watching me in the locker room, or in the parking lot today, if they didn't know, too. Are you sure you didn't dream about her? Maybe you dreamed something so bad that you can only remember little bits of it?" Her voice was starting to break.

Bobby's face went completely red. "I did not dream, Liz."

She ran her fingers through the thick carpet. "I'm frightened, Bobby. I think, well, I think I can feel her inside me." He didn't answer, so she tugged on his shoelace, but he'd made double knots so she couldn't pull it free. "You think there's something wrong with me, don't you?"

"No," he told her, "There's nothing wrong with you. Not like you think."

"What do you mean?"

"What did your dad do to her?"

"I don't remember," she said, but of course she did remember. It was one of the many things that boiled in her mind, bubbling to its surface on occasions she least expected, like when she was eating dinner with her mother, or taking a drive with Bobby, or in the middle of chemistry class while all the normal people thought their normal, happy thoughts.

"Try. You must remember something."

She looked down, playing with her socks, pulling at the cotton ribbing and snapping it back into place. Then forced the hem of her T-shirt over her knees. He could probably guess. Everyone in this town, for that matter, could probably guess.

It should have been you. Why wasn't it you?

"I can't remember."

"What is the bad stuff? You keep talking about bad stuff that's like alive or something because of Susan. What bad stuff?"

She looked down at her feet. "Just bad things."

He took a deep breath. "I heard somebody hit her. I heard that Georgia O'Brian used to babysit for you, and she called the police. That's what I heard."

She balled her hands into fists. "I don't know anything about that."

He leveled his eyes at her, and they both knew she was lying. "I heard how she paid her rent. Owen Read said his brother went to her, but she was too freaky so he left. Maybe she learned that someplace, what she did for a living, if you want to call that living."

Liz put her hands over her ears. She was very near to crying. A tickle in the back of her mouth. A lump in her throat. A storm in her stomach. "Shut up, Bobby."

"I heard you used to ride your bike by her house. I followed you once, when we first started dating. I got the feeling that even though you never talked about her, you couldn't let her go. Like maybe you want to think she's alive because you can't let her go."

"Shut up!" she screamed.

She heard footsteps overhead, and Bobby's mother, perhaps in the midst of eavesdropping, dropped a dish.

Bobby waited a second or two and then asked in a hushed tone, "Why can't you talk to me?"

"I'm trying to talk to you," she whispered, conscious now of her voice, of his family, of her wrongness in this clean basement.

Bobby took her fists and forcibly uncurled them. She

saw that she'd squeezed them so hard that the skin on her palms was spotted with blood. "Oh," she said, trying to pull her hands away while he held them tight.

"God," he said.

"It's nothing, really Bobby."

He lifted her hands to her face so she could see where her skin was broken in four half-moon patterns on each palm. "Look what you did to yourself."

"I didn't do anything. It was an accident."

"You did. You do it to yourself. You do everything to yourself."

"It doesn't hurt, they're not deep."

"Did it ever occur to you that you gave those marks around your neck to yourself?"

She was so stunned that at first she didn't answer. "I can't believe you think that."

"What does hurt?" he asked, only his voice was not kind. Only he was so furious that his nostrils flared, and the veins on his neck bulged.

"What?"

"What does hurt you, I'd like to know. What can't you forget?"

"I don't know what you're talking about."

"You said your dad did things to her. You said you can't forget. You're afraid the town knows things. You were thirteen years old when she ran away. What do you blame yourself for?"

She tried to ball her hands into fists again, but he held her still.

"I'm tired of this," he said.

"What?"

"Everything with you is pretend. It's like it's all a test you want me to pass. Like I'm supposed to guess everything because you can't bring yourself to say it."

"Bobby, I'm telling you everything!"

He was on the verge of tears. "Do you see what you did to your hand? I can't believe you did that."

"It's skin, Bobby. I'll grow more."

He shuddered. "You treat me like the enemy, but you need me, so once in a while you throw me a bone."

"Would you just listen to me?"

He glared at her. "You fill your head with all this bullshit. You get mad at me for the stupidest things, like that time I forgot to call you when I said I would and I know it's because something else is bothering you, but the scary thing is, Liz, *you* don't know. Your sister's dead and you'd rather think about her ghost than mourn her. Do you know how psycho you sound? You sound like one of those homeless people that think cell phones are part of the alien conspiracy, do you know that?"

"You're not listening to me," she said, "You're only hearing what you want to hear."

"That makes two of us, Liz. And I've got to be honest, I'm sick of it. I know it's not a great time to talk about this, but I can't remember the last time we had a normal day. I can't remember the last time we just went on a drive or something, and had fun. I don't mean you're not supposed to be sad. You should be sad. But you're all closed up, and you won't open."

"But what if I'm right about all this, Bobby?"

"Even if you are, I feel like I could be anyone to you."

"That's not true."

"How would you know? You don't have anyone else."

Her stomach dropped, and she had to think for a few seconds before his meaning became clear. "Do you want to break up with me?"

He shrugged, and she knew the answer was yes. Maybe he'd change his mind, maybe they'd work this out, but for now the answer was yes. For the second time today, she started crying. He did not comfort her. She hid her face until the tears were gone, and they sat without speaking for a long time.

"I'm sorry," he said, but it felt like an obligatory apology.

"Me, too."

He moved closer to her, so close they shared each other's heat. She lowered her eyes and tried to decide what to do next. She did the most important thing. The thing that counted. She kissed him. It took him a while, but he kissed her back. They made quiet love.

When they were done, he did not speak in a Frenchman's accent or kiss the top of her head. Instead, he pulled on his jeans. "My mom might come down," he explained. She realized that during the entire act, he'd never once looked her in the eye.

She hurriedly pulled on her blue T-shirt and her high-waisted Hanes Her Ways. "Are you mad?" she asked.

"No. I'm not mad. But dinner'll be ready soon, you know?"

"No, I don't."

"I mean, dinner'll be ready. And your mom probably wants you home."

Liz saw where this was going. She felt like she was in a car, skidding over ice. That last instant before the crash, when everything is still. "Do you want me to leave?"

"It's just that I have all this homework and stuff."

"Oh," Liz said.

"It's not like I don't like seeing you every day and everything, but sometimes I get tired."

"Tired of me?" she asked.

"No. But I could use a break, you know? We could take a break for a while, and when we're feeling better, we could see each other again."

"You want to break up with me? We just had sex and you want to break up with me?"

He shrugged. "All this stuff is happening with your sister, and college, and us. It's not making sense for me anymore. I keep feeling like you want me to be all these things and I can't."

"What do you mean? I don't want anything from you," she said.

"I don't know. I just can't . . ." he said, and she saw he'd made up his mind. Sometime while they had talked, or worse, while they'd made love, he'd made up his mind that it was over.

Should she have expected less? The dutiful son? Boy wonder? Yes, she thought. She might have reminded herself a thousand times that this wasn't forever, that she didn't deserve him, that he'd smarten up one day and meet someone better, but in the end, she had trusted him. She had thought that this boy she loved would never leave her. She had thought, deep down, that it really was forever.

"Do you mean it, Bobby?"

He nodded. "Yeah, for now."

Nothing scared her anymore. Not Susan, not the thing in the woods, not the people in this town. Nothing mattered, because she wished, quite suddenly, that she was dead.

TWENTY-SIX
The Atom Bomb Is Your Fault, Too

At six o'clock that Wednesday evening, Bobby pulled his car in front of Liz's house. Though the trip was only two miles, the slow drive through hard rain took twenty excruciating minutes. The town was quiet, and almost no cars were on the road. The flooding was so severe in the valley where Liz lived that Bobby could not pull into the driveway but instead parked in the middle of the street.

The earth had shifted with the flooding, and much of the sidewalk and street were broken into chunks of asphalt and cement. Trees had fallen. There was a buzzing in the air, still that buzzing, only louder. She could feel Susan's presence in this town. In the air, in the rain, inside her own skin. It felt like drowning.

In the driveway Liz saw her mother's car, but the house was dark. "She's probably sleeping, that's why she didn't answer the phone," Bobby said. "I'll wait. Flash the lights in your bedroom if she's home."

Liz looked at Bobby for a very long time. She didn't cry. She didn't plead with him. She just turned and met his eyes. He said nothing, and she felt herself unravel.

She walked slowly to the back door.

When she flicked the switch for the overhead light in the kitchen, she saw the mess; a plethora of baked goods. Cookies and brownies sat above grease-stained paper towels or within humid Ziploc bags that were stacked on the counter. None looked edible. A dough-like ginger snap stuck to her hand, and she scraped it into the garbage. The floor crunched like sand under her feet, and when she bent down she realized that she was walking on a layer of sugar.

She was not truly terrified until she saw the chocolate cake. Susan's favorite, chocolate cake. She let out something between a giggle and a moan. Poison, she thought. Chocolate death, it's poisoned. Her mother was hoping she'd come home and eat it.

"Mom?" she called out, "You home?" She climbed the stairs, two at a time, and reached her mother's bedroom. The bed was unmade and on the floor was a sweater covered in white dust. The dust dissolved in her wet hands. Flour.

Back in the kitchen, she checked the answering machine. There were two messages from the school guidance counselor, saying that Liz had had "an episode" and would Mary please call back? Two more from Bobby's mother, Alexandra Fullbright, saying, "Uh, Mary? Your daughter's in my basement. I thought you should know." Liz picked up the phone and dialed information, asking to be connected to the Shaws Supermarket.

Before the connection went through, she hung up. A light shone through the crack in the closed basement door. It was more yellow than white, like jaundice. She opened it and called her mother's name. The boiler kicked, and she jumped. Then she started down the stairs.

There were at least three inches of water on the basement floor. It seeped though her Keds and was cold enough to curl her toes. "Mom?" she asked. She hoped that her mother wasn't down here. She hoped this place was empty. But she knew better. Something was down here; she could feel it.

The water swished under her feet, building momentum like a weak current that pulled her deeper into Susan's old bedroom. Someone (her mother?) had made the bed. White eyelet sheets were folded over a warm down quilt. Out of the corner of her eye she saw something small, perhaps a child, race across the room. It happened so quickly that her mind didn't fully register its presence.

She started when she saw movement on Susan's bed. Something rocked back and forth. A shadow from the car headlights shining through the window? A thin cotton shirt on a hanger?

It looked up at her, and its hair was matted to its cheeks. Its face was white. Not pale, but white. Even its lips and the lashes of its eyes were scabby and white. She was frozen for a moment. The thing kept rocking. The only part that wasn't white was its blue eyes.

The thing, it was mad.

The thing, it was her mother.

Flecks of white dust shined as they fell to the wet floor. Liz looked closer at her mother's pale, lumpy face, and saw that she was wearing a mask of flour.

"Susan," Mary murmured. "Let's eat your cake."

"It's Liz. I'm Liz."

The flour had hardened to the wrinkles on Mary's skin. She looked like an ancient old crone. A clump of the stuff fell like wet snow to her lap. She dumbly inspected it, as if unable to determine what it was, or why it now stuck to her fingers.

"The other daughter. I'm the other daughter," Liz whispered.

Mary cocked her head.

"Bobby's outside. He might try to come in."

"Is she here?"

"No. He's outside."

"Susan's outside?"

"Mom. She died? She's dead?"

Mary smiled drunkenly. "Oh, it's you, Liz. I didn't know."

"It's me."

Mary looked at her daughter and recognition set in. At first it was a subtle change. Her eyes focused on Liz's hair and soft cheeks. And then she startled. Her eyes lingered on the closet door where a piece of yarn bobbed in the current, and a child's raincoat dangled from a hook. "Oh, no," she said.

"Mom?"

Mary's eyes darted from one corner of the room to the next, searching. Frantic. But there wasn't anything down here with them, was there? Then Mary closed her eyes. Then she took a few deep breaths. Then she went into another kind of sleep. When she woke, she was changed.

"Oh." She laughed nervously. "Oh." She looked down at her wet clothing, and began wiping the flour from her jeans and face. She continued pawing herself, mortified, until it was mostly gone, and she'd left the features of her face red and swollen. "When did you get here?" she asked. "I was just cleaning down here and I fell asleep." She smiled guiltily. "I had a little wine."

"Did you?"

Mary shrugged. "Would you like to help me finish cleaning?"

"Was someone here?"

"You're here," Mary said. "We've been waiting for you."

A drop of warm urine slid down the back of Liz's leg, but she hardly noticed it. "We?"

"Did I say we?"

Liz took a deep breath. She felt the air closing in around her, wet. She wondered if she could drown, just breathing it. "I'm scared, Mom," she said.

Mary seemed genuinely surprised. "Why are you scared?"

"It's a mess."

"I know. That's why I'm cleaning it." Mary walked over to the dresser and began to pack Susan's clothes inside it. There were old dresses, hand-me-downs that Liz had once worn, T-shirts that had never made it to Goodwill, baby clothes, and a white sweater that Mary held close and sniffed before placing in the bottom drawer.

Mary was wearing a bulky, white turtleneck, and on it Liz saw something that made her freeze. She put her hand to her mouth, and then in her mouth. She bit down on her fingers all at once. Through the white cotton, Liz could see the outline of her mother's nipples. Above that were the faint impressions of small, wet teeth. Like something had bitten her. Something from a dream maybe, that had become real. Something, she realized, that was hiding in this basement, right now. Liz cried out at this sight, and then let it go. She watched it go. It was too horrible to know.

"I love you, Mom," Liz said. The words came out before she thought about them, or knew whether they were true.

Mary's smile faded. "You what?" she asked, looking around the room now, her eyes skittering from the leaks in the ceiling to the water on the floor, to the clothing, to the open closet door.

"Nothing. Forget it."

Mary crossed her hands around her waist. Uncrossed them. Looked down at the floor, and then, finally, knelt in front of Liz so that the joints in her knees popped. "You should go."

Liz pressed her cheek into the crook of her mother's neck. "Mom?" she said through muffled tears, "He never loved me."

"What?" Mary asked, her voice soft and crooning. "Who wouldn't love you?"

"Bobby. It's my fault."

"No. No, baby. You didn't do anything."

"I wish I was dead. I wish it was me instead."

Mary lifted Liz's chin. "Maybe you can stay with Bobby tonight. I'm not feeling myself. I don't think it's good for you."

"Go?"

"Until the rain is over."

"I can't leave you."

Mary shook her head. "It's best."

"But it's not right here, Mom. Nothing about it is right."

Mary let go. "You can stay at the shelter in the church if you're not getting along with Bobby."

"It's never been right. We just pretend. Like we

pretend we can't feel her. You sleep in that room where Dad used to sleep. And I sleep where she used to sleep. Like it's only half of us now. Like they're still here, only we pretend they're not. We pretend it was always just the two of us but there were four, Mom. There were four."

"That's enough." Mary closed the bottom drawer of the dresser. All the clothes were now packed away, just as they had been before Susan left home.

"I think I'm sick. Maybe I should get Bobby to call his dad and have him come over."

"You're not sick. No one's sick. I had too much to drink. I made a mess upstairs. I'm going to clean it. Don't call anyone," Mary said.

Liz looked down at the water where a piece of blue yarn floated. It bobbed up and down. She could smell something rotten down here. Something dead. Along the swell of her mother's left breast, she thought she saw a speck of blood. She hoped, very much, that she was going mad. "I have to tell Bobby."

"You don't have to do anything."

"You put her clothes away."

"So what?"

"Mom?" Liz pleaded.

"I'm tired of this conversation."

"But—"

"It's not for strangers, Elizabeth. I won't have you dragging strangers into my house."

Liz closed and then opened her eyes. The room seemed to blink. The water got warmer. The tide circles became still. Just her house, after all. Just a house made of wood and cement. Just a woman in front of her, her mother. Just the rain that fell every year. Just some excessive baking, and a dead sister whose rotting corpse she could smell right now. That's all. Don't worry. Nothing you can do about it, anyway.

"I'll tell him to go home without me, that you're here."

"Don't you tell him anything," Mary said.

When she went back up the stairs, she found Bobby waiting for her in the kitchen. She hoped that he would put his arms around her and tell her he loved her, he'd protect her, but he did not.

She gestured at the cookies, the cake, and said, "She's drunk. I guess she went Martha Stewart OCD."

"Oh, man," he said. She noticed that he was looking at the cake. It reminded her of that night at Susan's apartment. The way his eyes had gotten wide at the sight of her filthy apartment, only this time he seemed to be getting used to it. "I heard you talking to her down there. I didn't mean to. I just came in to see if I could help. But I heard her," he said.

"It's not her fault. She doesn't feel well."

Bobby picked up a mostly raw cookie and pointed it at her. "Yeah, it's your fault, right? Everything's your fault. The atom bomb is your fault, too." The cookie stuck to his hand when he tried to put it back down. He fought with it for a second or two, but it clung to his skin like putty. The absurdity of this moment, the room, what he was saying, overcame her.

"No, that was Einstein. You told me all about him when you were worrying about where the Russians were selling their nukes because God forbid someone blow up Bedford," she said.

"This isn't funny," he said.

Oh, but you are, Bobby. You are, she thought. *Don't you know what's happening? Can you really be this naïve?* She went to him and as she walked, sugar crunched under her feet. When she reached him, he backed away.

"We should call my dad," he said.

"No."

"Why not?"

"You'd better go. Dinner'll be ready soon, right? I'd hate for you to miss dinner."

He crossed around himself, and she wondered if he could feel it. The air. If he could smell her, too. His eyes lingered on the cake. "This is bad," he said.

"It's not anything. Forget it. You dumped me, re-member?"

He glared at her until she lowered her eyes. "You almost like it."

"What?" she asked.

"It's not special. It doesn't make you special."

"Shut up."

He ran his fingers through his hair, started to say something, stopped himself. He looked at the cake again. "It's true. You think bad things are your prop-erty. You think they only happen to you."

"Isn't that why you like me?" she asked.

He didn't answer. She stepped closer. Close enough that the loneliness of the house seemed just a little less palpable. "Remember when you said you loved me?"

He didn't say: *Yes, and I still do.* He didn't say: *Of course I do.* He nodded slowly, like he wished he'd never said it at all.

"Oh," she said. With that he became Bobby Full-bright, the power tool once again. The boy she hardly knew who drove an Explorer and bragged about his father's job. Taken back. It had all been taken back. This past year. Gone.

"You should go," she said.

"You sure?" he asked. It was one of those questions for which the answer is irrelevant.

"Yeah."

He leaned in to kiss her, but then drew back and nodded instead. He left. From the front window, she watched the truck drive away. She imagined that it was warm inside that car.

TWENTY-SEVEN
Evacuation

Power went out at around eight P.M. in Bedford, and Danny Willow stayed at the police department to answer the phones. He received two complaints about Susan Marley. The first was placed by little Andrea Jorgenson. "I saw her in the park," Andrea said. "I thought you should know. Please don't tell my mom I called. She says I shouldn't talk about it. But I like Liz. I always did." The second call was anonymous, but Danny recognized Montie Henrich's voice. "That crazy dead bitch followed Paul Martin to the park," Montie shouted into the phone, like he thought maybe Danny had gone deaf since Paul had slugged him in the throat. There were other calls, too. A rabid dog was spotted drooling its way down Main Street, Susan Marley's apartment had been trashed, and someone had even seen Ted Marley tilling the flooded soil in the garden behind his old house.

Danny was pretty sure this was the result of mass hysteria and booze. But he sent Roger Tillotson over to the cemetery to check on Susan's grave anyway. People had certain ideas about that girl. A few of the local loons might have taken a can of spray paint to marker or worse, dug her up. Roger radioed in to say that while there was no graffiti, Susan Marley's body was missing. The rain had shifted the levels of the ground, unearthing several of the coffins in her row. "You think there's some sick fuck running around?" Roger asked. "Maybe," Danny answered. "But we've got bigger worries right now, Roger. The state troopers are working on a jackknifed petroleum truck on I–95, and Central Maine Power won't be able to get through with this flood. There's nobody around but us."

Twenty-eight of the seventy-nine people who lived in the Halcyon-Soma Tent and Trailer Park had once worked for Clott. Some had retired quietly, others learned about their severance packages over the phone tree just this week. There were the black sheep of the area, who did not pick up after their dogs, or who drank during the day. There were the dreamers, like Kate Sanders, who got dressed up every Sunday and then sat on her stoop, waiting like Persephone for a kind or not so kind stranger to carry her away. There were families who broke bread together on picnic benches during the summer, and children who played tag at night by the headlights of the trailers. Most often, they played the waiting game. They waited for jobs to open up, they waited for résumés to be considered, they waited for their shifts at empty restaurants to end, they waited for morning to come, and then for night, and then for another day. As with every place, there was happiness and sadness, though not always in equal measure.

At seven o'clock Wednesday night Danny Willow came to them with blushing cheeks and a bruise on his throat that made his words sound like whispers. He knocked on each door, taking off his hat and refusing to come any farther, refusing to intrude any more than necessary. He said that he did not know how much longer the land would hold, how much longer before their homes sank, how much longer before a mud slide came and took them all away. It had already flooded much of the valley. It had already uprooted the cemetery.

Thomas Schultz watched as Danny approached. Thomas had lived in Bedford for forty-six years, and though he still looked like a man in his prime, he felt old inside. It was the winters in this town, and the way the cold took root inside him and made everything still. It was the cans of Rheingold that he drank in the evenings with his friends, when always he felt there was something better for him someplace else. It was this contented life he lived (populated by the comfort of people he knew, and his two Siberian huskies Jack and Pete), and this town he understood, in which he was not at all content. But he was too old for regret, and too smart to tell himself that the fates had conspired against him.

He'd never wanted to be an artist, like the man who lived in the trailer next door and wrote poetry at night. He'd never had a true love or even a calling. But long shifts at the mill had given him enough time for fishing on the weekends and hunting in the fall. He hadn't bothered to send out résumés or move to another town after the mill closed. There might be jobs yet here, or at the hospital in Corpus Christi. And he was in no hurry. Things moved slowly in Bedford, where there were no decisions really to make, because you did not know yourself what caused the burning in your stomach, or how to make it go away.

Thomas watched Danny knock on each door, mentally preparing himself for each person, making sure to remember every name, always taking off his hat. Just like a nervous bride. Would they please come to the church? Please? Danny asked them. He promised that there would be no looting; they could take whatever possessions they wanted and would be driven to Our Lady of Sorrow where they could wait this thing out. The church had its own generator, and there was power enough for heat and light. It was safer there, he promised. If it had been anyone but Willow, they would have shut their doors on him. No one but Willow had enough humility for the job.

Danny came to Thomas's trailer last. He had instructed his deputies to wait outside the entrance of the park so that they did not intrude any more than was necessary: strangers on a land that was a kingdom of its own. Danny smiled uncertainly. He held his hat in his hand. "They're not sure. I think if you go, it'll be easier to get the rest," he said.

Thomas shrugged.

"Maybe you can help me with Kate. She's drunk," Danny continued. And Thomas understood that if he did not help, that at some point they all might be forced to leave. That their trailers really might topple in the mud. Still, Thomas hesitated.

"Please," Danny said.

"Yeah, I'll help." Thomas packed some things. Then he joined Danny and the two of them talked Kate into coming. "Here," Thomas said, showing her the bottle of Smirnoff vodka he'd taken from his freezer, "I brought this for you. A present. Danny'll let you take it to the church, won't you, Danny?"

"Sure," Danny said. "I could use some myself."

They helped Kate onto the bus. The others followed. They sat quietly, with their bags of belongings in their laps, and not one person complained about the heaters that were broken, or mentioned the trinkets or wool socks or photo albums they had left behind.

When they got to the church, they were not surprised when their thoughts turned to Susan Marley, and things long dead came to life. They knew intuitively what the lucky cannot fathom: Sometimes things don't work out.

TWENTY-EIGHT
Invisible City

With a few very notable exceptions, not a soul was outdoors in Bedford by eight o'clock on Wednesday night. No one walked the streets, or tried to rescue trash cans rolling in the wind. They did not open shops on Main Street, or call friends, or admonish their children that although school was closed, there were still chores to be done and math lessons to be completed. Many had left Bedford. They'd gone on vacations to Florida, or on job-hunting expeditions, or fishing the coast for flounder, or they'd left for good, packing cars to the brim with loose items and speeding out of town. They told themselves they left because the timing was right, and because they needed a break from the long and bitter winter that had rendered them numb. But most of them had left for another reason. They were consumed by an inexplicable fright.

Bedford became something less than solid after Susan Marley broke her mirrors. The town filled with cold water and winter threatened like an impolite guest to stay forever. The earth flexed its muscles, tearing concrete and asphalt to bits. Trees fell into houses and slashed power lines so that by eight P.M., everything was dark. The river gushed like a swollen artery. Houses moaned.

The same fear that compelled some to leave held others captive in their homes. They waited for the rain to end. They waited for light to return. No use repairing basements, roads, the cemetery, the sidewalk on Main Street that had been uprooted. They waited for what they thought they deserved, and when Susan Marley came walking down their streets, and shadows in their rooms became flesh, they were not disappointed.

TWENTY-NINE
The Pact

T he three of them. They could see through Susan
Marley's eyes. They saw a park at night, they saw
the place where they were going, they saw a fire, they
saw themselves buried underground.

Louise let the boys take the lead, because it let them
feel in charge. Owen to her left, Steve to her right. They
walked through the knee-deep rain, and past the uprooted pieces of sidewalk and lawns that now floated.
They walked past ghosts; an old woman still angry at
her parents for acts committed and imagined. She was
all wrinkles and gray skin, and she banged on her father's front door, even though the man was long dead.
They walked past a rabid dog whose mouth foamed,
and a crippled tree stained by old blood. They walked
past William Prentice, who tried to hide the blood on
his hands with fine white gloves, but the gloves turned
red. They saw a woman in the park who walked in jerking motions, and they knew it was Susan Marley. Louise
probably should have been frightened, but she wasn't.
She liked it. So the boys looked back at her and she
smiled, they pretended not to be frightened, too.

At the mill the voices were strongest. A thousand voices, all saying one thing. The mill told them what to do. What they had always known, on some level, they were meant to do. The boys hesitated, and she walked to the entrance. Mud had slid into the valley and jammed the door, and she tried to force it open with her hands. Then the boys followed, taking turns. They rammed their shoulders against the heavy wood. Owen's arm made a popping sound, but Louise did not wince. Steven was next, and then Owen again. They switched turns until the door flew open, and they went inside.

Water sought its lowest level. It ran down the steps and into the basement where dead ghosts screamed. Wet rats climbed atop tables. Old lockers opened and closed. On pieces of masking tape adhered to each metal door were names like O'Brian and McMullen and Willow. In some were sweaters and safety goggles that had never been claimed.

Voices filled the place. Old voices, new ones, too. Shadows of men who'd founded Bedford lined the sides of the room. They were trapped here, like all the dead. From the basement were even more voices. And below that, far underground, were even more. They shouted in a language (Indian?) she'd never heard, but still, she understood. "Burn it," they said.

Against the vat were three industrial-sized canisters of the stuff. Sulfuric waste products. Owen and Steve were already opening them. The control box for the auxiliary generator was along the wall. She knew this. She'd been here before. In her dreams, Susan Marley showed her everything. In her dreams, she and Susan were the same. She opened the box, pulled two levers up, pressed the buttons below them, and the panel lit up red.

The lights went on. The conveyor belt began to turn.

A flame ignited underneath the vat. The boys climbed the ladder and emptied the canisters into the wide hole. For a moment, there was nothing. But then something popped, and black smoke poured out from the vat. It funneled through the pipe of the mill, and into the atmosphere of Bedford. At first it was a little furl, and then a tuft wafting in the wind, and then like ink in water, in stained the air black.

The room filled with smoke, and Owen and Steve started coughing. They climbed down the ladder and tried to pull her with them outdoors. The voices in the room began to scream as if in pain. As if they were alive, watching the mill consume them.

Owen and Steve grabbed hold of her arms. Their plan was to run to the top of Iroquois Hill. To watch as the smoke circled Bedford. Then they'd clear a path through the woods and keep going until dawn. Maybe make it out. Maybe not.

She saw her future ahead of her. A clear vision. Even if this night had not happened, things would never be the same as they were in this moment. In five years she'd be a veteran waitress slowly losing her looks. There was no better time for her than now. "I'm staying," she said. She'd planned this, too.

"What?" Steve shouted.

She smiled as pitifully as she knew how. Her lower lip quivered. "Please . . ." she said, "Don't make me stay by myself."

"Louise," Owen begged, "it was a mistake. Something made us do it. Please let's go." The smoke was so thick that everything looked blurry. It burned her nose and ears.

Louise shook her head. "I can't. I'm scared."

"Shut up and let's go, Weese," Steven said. He yanked

her arm and she slapped him. He froze. Then he narrowed his eyes at her and ran. He did not look back.

Owen kept coughing. "You'll stay, won't you, Owen?" she asked. There was water in his eyes, and she was delighted to see that it was not from the fumes.

She saw he understood what this meant, that he would die for her. She saw that he liked the idea of this, of loving someone so much you could not bear to live without them. "Okay," he said.

Soon, the air became so thick that they could not see, and so they held hands as they stumbled into the locker room and finally sank to the floor. In every corner she saw a face, someone who'd once worked here, or laid the concrete for the building, or cut the trees, or been murdered for the land. They all sounded the same now. All one voice, shouting, screaming.

She'd thought that it would be quick. A tuft of smoke like the hand of God wrapping its fingers around Bedford and putting it to rest. An explosion. But instead the stuff crept into the air, withering it like nylon on fire. Instead, this hurt.

They sat together with their feet pointed out from the wall. They held hands. He rested his head in the crevice of her neck. "I know what you are," he whispered. He was coughing, and so was she. His nose bled. She watched with interest as the hairs on his head and knuckles slowly withered into ash.

"You're worse than *her*. You're a monster inside," he whispered.

A fit of coughing overcame her, and she covered her mouth with her hand. When she took it away she saw that her palm was full of black phlegm. Strange to think she was dying. She had expected someone to save her by now.

His body went into a spasm, kicking and jerking. He squeezed her hand so hard it cracked. Something smelled, and the legs of his trousers turned brown. In his last act, he took his hand away from her. Then he was still. His face was frozen forever into narrowed eyes and a furrowed brow. A look of hate. She tried to push herself away from the wall and toward the open door, but her legs were like noodles. She'd lost the energy to cough. Around her, the room was screaming.

She knew now why she had done this. It wasn't just her dreams, or Susan Marley, or Bedford, or even wanting to have the boys in a way that no one else could. It was wanting, just once, to feel. Her life emptied out of her body, and still, she felt nothing, even as she realized, too late, that this was not what she'd wanted, after all.

THIRTY

Five Cent Redemption
at the Barricades of Heaven

He saw his two selves in her eyes, a cripple and a man standing tall.

Ever hear the one about the priest and the rabbi in heaven? he thought. *The guy with the duck on his head at the psychiatrist's office? Two brunettes and a blond upside down? The drunk in the bar?*

Do it, he thought. *Do it now.*

They sat on a bench in the park at ten o'clock on the last night of rain, Paul Martin and Susan Marley. Her hands squeezed against his ears, and the pain was sharp, like bursting metal.

Please, he thought with what faculties he was still able to form thoughts: *End this.*

A seesaw bounced up and down. A swinging fence turned round and round. Susan's hands eased their pressure very slowly. For a few seconds after she let go, the pain remained sharp. His ears rattled. Adrenaline coursed through his veins. He prepared for his end, and his life seemed to him a very short and finite story that he could hold in his hands. A fragile thing that he would rather crush than inspect. But eventually the pain remitted, and he understood that he would not die just yet.

When he stood, he saw Susan leaving the park. Her wet dress clung to her body, and her bare feet were now just mangled bones and tendons. She limped through the gate.

She was both crying and smiling, and now that she'd touched him, he knew why. It was the same reason she had not killed him just now. Rossoff had been right. She loved him, and she also hated him. The horrific things that were happening on this last night of rain were both what she wanted, and what she did not want. So she cried and she smiled, and it was not clear to him which demon inside her was stronger. He and Susan were not so very different.

He looked up at the sky. The rain fell hard but he didn't feel it. His clothes were wet but he didn't shiver. From the direction of the mill, he smelled burning sulfur.

He left the park and entered flooded Main Street. A golden retriever came paddling past him. It treaded water so that its head bobbled in fits below the surface. Except the dog wasn't exactly golden. It was covered in soot and he only knew its true color because he recognized the dog. Benji lumbered against the current. Paul grabbed its collar to help it reach dry land, but it growled and snapped its jaws at his fingers. Paul let go and it continued paddling on down the street. Except it hadn't really been Benji, had it? Did Benji bite?

At some point, power had gone out so that the streets were black. Even houses were black. Things moved in the darkness, they slithered. In the distance he saw a giant red spider spin a web around Chuck Brann's house.

If Chuck tried to leave, he'd get stuck to one of the sticky ropes like a fly. Ghosts walked the streets, their feet high above the water. They were a century old, or else pitifully young. They took no note of Paul, their intention only to return to the places they belonged. Down the street, the paper mill spouted black smoke that burned his eyes.

He considered running, as he had done so many times before. He would break into Don's Liquor and steal a few bottles of scotch. He would swim across the river to the highway. He would hide in some small corner of this town and wait for morning. He would slit his wrists so the worry inside him would finally be quiet.

Instead, he started with the house nearest to him. It was a Cape Cod with blue shutters. Paul banged on the door, and Allie Brutton peeped out from behind a curtain. Paul kept knocking until his knuckles were swollen. Finally, his former boss Kevin Brutton opened the door. He was breathing through a monogrammed handkerchief that he held over his mouth and nose. A stench of rotting meat wafted out into the night, and Paul almost gagged. "You've gotta help me," Paul said. "We need to evacuate the town."

"Go to hell," Kevin answered, and slammed the door in his face.

Paul ran to the house across the street. The door was so cold that when he knocked on it, his fingers burned. Peering out from the second-floor window, he saw Jaine Hodkin and her boyfriend, Craig Pittsfield, watching him. They stood in the candlelight of what looked like a hallway, shivering. He could see their cold breath. Paul threw a rock at the window they were standing behind and broke the glass. "Get out of there!" he yelled, but they retreated farther into the house.

He knocked on another door that belonged to the Andriases. "Don't you know what's happening?" he yelled. Inside the door, he heard scuffling, and then retreating. All down the rows of houses he saw faces, and when he approached, those faces hid. Familiar faces. Warped faces. They looked more and more like the faces he'd seen in Susan's mirrors. Actually, they looked a lot like Susan.

Up ahead was the mill. Susan stood in front of it with her arms wide. Her chin was lifted into the air. Lightning tore the sky, and everything was illuminated. The mill, the smoke, a once beautiful woman. She was smiling and crying all at once. It was an awesome sight.

Engines roared. Tufts of smoke billowed up from the pipe of the mill, followed by more smoke, followed by thick, black, viscous stuff that filled the sky, and the rain, and the ground, and his lungs. He suddenly understood what he was smelling, and went pale. It was worse than he'd imagined. A lot worse. Sulfuric waste products. Someone—now he could see it in his mind, Louise Andrias and her idiot cronies, had opened canisters of the stuff and cooked them. Combined with a little free-floating carbon, or better yet, heat, sulfur is a dangerous thing. You can breathe the concentrated fumes of hydrogen sulfide for maybe thirty seconds before you drop dead. And if you have some way of dispersing the stuff, say the pipe of a paper mill or a little rain that people might swallow, well then, what you have on your hands is an environmental disaster worse than Love Canal. The haunted town was the least of their problems. If enough of this sulfur got out, by the time the state troopers got here tomorrow, they'd pull off I–95 and into a graveyard.

"No," Paul whispered.

Susan turned to him. Her face was calm. "Yes," she said. In her voice he could hear every emotion, from regret to pity to joy to fury. The smoke poured into the sky until there was only blackness. No clouds. No stars. No moon.

He ran into the mill. The few light bulbs supplied with electricity from the emergency generator did little to combat the smoke. He could hear the pumping of an eighty-year-old machine. A saw moved across an empty conveyor belt. A vat boiled. Gas heaters fanned the room.

Phantom men worked the assembly line. They sliced and lifted the logs. They pressed the paper with a hot iron. All around him were phantoms of this town. They wore three-piece suits and torn work shirts, shit-stained boots and top hats. There were thousands of them. There wasn't enough room for all of them, so they stood inside each other. Their faces were a combination of features. Young and old. Man and woman. Ugly and beautiful. Down below, he could hear something else. The men who'd been murdered by the mill's founder, William Prentice. Their bodies had salted the earth, so that nothing good would ever grow. They made a single sound, all of them. It was a scream that did not stop. The longer he stood in the mill, the louder it got. And their eyes were Susan Marley blue.

He thought about turning around. Running. But he understood better than most that there was no place to run. And so he passed the threshold, and entered the paper mill.

He searched in the dark for an emergency brake. It would not stop the chemical reaction, but at least it might contain it to a small part of the valley. He moved through the dark, through the phantoms, like a blind man, feeling the hot machines that burned his hands. Smoke kept coming. It was noxious stuff, and already he was dizzy. His face, his hands, and the exposed parts of his neck itched. He knew he should get out. He should run right now, before he lost his chance.

But then he found a box against the wall. There were two levers up, three down. He made a guess and pulled another lever down. It eased without resistance and the conveyor belt stopped turning. "Yes!" he shouted, except his voice was a gurgle. He pulled the handle on the second lever. It broke apart in his hands so that all that remained was about a half-inch of splinters. He reached his fingers into the fragmented wood but couldn't force it down. The heater under the vat continued to boil its contents, and the mill continued to spout noxious smoke. He bent over and vomited. The taste was alarmingly salty. Alarmingly like blood.

Minutes passed. Five. Six. Seven. The voices screamed. The voices, he knew, wanted the place to burn. They surrounded him, these ghosts. He walked through them. He dug again at the broken handle until his fingernails tore away. Then he bent over and took a deep breath, forgetting that there was no air to breathe. He vomited again, and this time he was sure it was blood. He could feel his lungs bubbling. It wasn't phlegm. It was the skin in his lungs turning to liquid.

He ran to the vat and tried with his bare hands to suffuse the heater underneath it. The white-hot pain made him realize what a truly stupid idea that was. He searched blindly along the vat, looking for an emergency stop button, but his hands were so badly burned, they had lost their feeling. Still, he searched the rim and the walls and the floor. He found nothing.

Soon enough, his breath gave out. Soon enough, he could no longer walk, and his lungs felt like fire. "Please," he called. "Susan, stop this." Only his voice was gone, and he was drowning in his own blood.

Susan entered the mill. She walked unevenly on a broken ankle, and her head lolled above her neck. The only thing about her that was animated was her eyes.

He laughed an empty laugh that this was how it would end for him. He would die in the paper mill he'd spent years trying to save. The irony was not lost on him. Then he sobered. This was how it would end. One thousand people tonight would meet their maker.

He thought of Cathy, and was proud of her that she had found a way out. And then he thought of Georgia, who had not. He remembered his sons, and wished most of all that he could live another day, to tell them that he loved them. But at least, yes, at least he was not running. And maybe that was good enough. Maybe for once, he could let go. In a way, he'd found a kind of grace.

The last thing he saw was Susan standing over him. She touched his cheek, only this time, it did not hurt. He whispered her name. The sound of his voice carried throughout the town so that for a moment every person in Bedford heard his prayer, and then just as suddenly, he was silent.

THIRTY-ONE
Thief

It was after midnight, and April Willow was close to hysteria. It was not having to sleep in the basement of this church with dirty trailer people (they all carried scabies—she knew it!) because she hadn't wanted to be separated from Danny during the storm, or the open confessional doors upstairs made her feel like she was supposed to step inside one of them and recite the Act of Contrition, nor was it even this rain that leaked through the windows and into the air so that the skin on her face glistened with small beads of water. It was Benji. She knew the dog was probably dead by now. Run over and buried by some neighbor who hadn't wanted to encounter her wrath. Her poor dog. She imagined him wandering through town, sick and cold and missing his mother.

No one down here sleeping. They listened to the rain. It lulled them. It made sounds that rain should never make, like the din of internal voices from a dream. When had that happened? When had the voices started? She wasn't sure. But they felt familiar, like déjà vu, and it was not clear to her whether she should be comforted or terrified.

Retarded Bernard McMullen was wrapped in his mother's hulking arms. Amity Jorgenson and her daughter, Andrea, pressed their hands against the gutter windows, as if trying to commune with the thick drops that fell. Over the last half hour, the rain had gotten darker, and its strange chemical smell made her nose itch. Thomas Schultz sat between his two Siberian huskies. Some were on cots, others stood. All were still. All were quiet.

This is what it feels like, she thought, *when someone walks on your grave.*

She put her hand on Danny's stomach. It was big and soft, and at night when they were alone she sometimes encircled his entire girth with her arms, to let him know that she could. "What's out there, Danny?"

"Listen," he told her. "Just listen."

She closed her eyes and heard the voices. The chatter, like a thousand different radio stations competing against each other at once.

This is what it feels like when someone knocks on your door, she thought.

"Is Benji out there?" she asked.

"Hush, April. Hush," Danny said, and then, ashamed, he turned away from her. She saw that he was crying. She saw that many of them were crying.

This is what it feels like when a thief carries your heart.

Her footsteps made echoes inside the church basement. No one noticed. Not even Danny. They were too busy listening to the rain. She went upstairs into the church. She entered the confessional, and closed the door behind her so that she sat in a small box that smelled of hot metal and electricity. She slid back the screen. "Forgive me, Father, for I have sinned," she said, crossing herself, "It's been six weeks since my last confession." There was no answer from the other side. She fingered the prayer book, and read aloud the Act of Contrition mounted against the wall. Downstairs, she knew, they were waiting for her. Downstairs, maybe they could even hear what she said. Maybe it carried with the rain.

"Forgive me, God," she said. "I'm sorry I never confessed it. I'm sorry, I never wanted to tell another human being. Dear God, forgive me. Please give me back my Benji."

She waited for a long time, but the walls did not crumble around her. The screen on the other side did not open, and she did not see the face of her wrathful God.

This is what it feels like when you steal from yourself.

The door to the church was open. It wasn't usually. But tonight, in case people found a need to come or else go outside and smoke, Danny and Father Allesando had agreed to keep it open. She thought that maybe Benji was out there. Maybe he was hunched miserably on the front step, and all she had to do was look and if she didn't, she'd see him in purgatory or worse, limbo, because they don't allow pets in heaven, and he'd say he'd been waiting for her. Why hadn't she looked for him? Why had she left him all alone?

April peeked outside. Rossoff was having a cigarette. He had come here because he said his own house was flooded. But that wasn't true. He didn't like being alone in that squalid place after Susan Marley had died. It smelled, and no matter how much Pine-Sol he poured over the floors, that smell didn't go away. She haunted him in his waking hours, not her ghost, it didn't even need to be her ghost, just her memory, that was enough. She lingered in his bed. She laughed at him with angry eyes. She bled from the places he'd once struck her. Last night the faucets in his house had all run red.

Poor man, he would die soon. She wondered how she knew that, that he would die, that he was afraid of his own home, but she was sure of it. There were little cancer worms crawling all over him like lice. He turned and tipped his hat to her. She tried to smile but couldn't. He was an ugly man. A pimp.

She heard heavy breathing. It was not Rossoff. "Who's that?" she called into the night. "Who is that?"

She saw her dog swimming up to the steps of the church. Her Benji. Oh, her baby had come home. God had answered her prayers. She could see his eyes shining. She'd know his eyes anywhere. But his coat, it was so dirty it was black. Something about him had gone sour. Poor baby. He carried something in his mouth. He came closer. It was a garbage bag, something inside a plastic Hefty bag. The bag was covered in black, too, as if it had been dug up.

This is what it feels like when they dig up your body.

April gasped. Her fingers ticked in the air like the movement of a spider's legs. All ten of them spasmed in quick, disjointed movements. Benji plopped the bag in front of her and then retreated a little, as if offering her a gift.

"Looks like he brought your baby," Rossoff said. The worms crawled out of his mouth and down his beard. "I know you missed it. A girl, right?"

"Yes," April said. "A girl. She never cried."

"Really?" Rossoff asked.

"Just once," April answered.

Rossoff flicked his cigarette into the darkness and went inside. April looked down at the still bag. She squeezed her hands into fists to stop their movement. "Benji!" she called. "Benji, come here." But he got down on his hind legs. He growled at her, waiting for her to accept his gift. She called him again. He growled louder and went back on his hind legs, like he was about to attack.

She took a step back. Then another. Something in the bag moved. It wriggled, and she told herself it was the wind. She took another step back. Through the threshold. She shut the heavy door. Had to kick the plastic bag just a little bit so the door would close tight. Felt her foot come in contact with something soft. Too soft. Hardly even formed. She could hear Benji whining as she shut him out. He'll drown, she thought. He'll wait out here for me to come back and the water will rise. He'll get tired of treading. He'll drown. She heard him whine behind the closed door. It was an awful kind of wailing. But was that Benji, crying?

This is what it feels like when you don't know who you are. The things I could have taught you, little girl, you do not want to know.

Back in the basement, everyone in the shelter turned to her, breaking their reverie with the rain. Some stood, some turned away from the windows. Their eyes went through her. She hid her face.

This is what it feels like to remember.

Danny extended his hand. Did they disapprove? Did they loathe her? April Willow the hypocrite. April Willow the shrew. She put her hand over her baby's mouth.

But no, she could hear them in this rain. Their voices carried. They did not disapprove. They welcomed her.

"Danny?" she cried.

He wrapped her in his arms, and together they joined the others as the rain seeped through the gutter windows, and their breath turned black.

THIRTY-TWO
Inside the Mirrors
(the Other Side of the Fence)

They were growling again. He didn't like the sound.

Thomas Schultz was circling the periphery of the churchyard with his dogs. Was this hallowed ground out here? Blessed by priests? Sanctified? He chortled to himself. The same cranes that had dropped the cornerstone for the church had built the paper mill. Like the rest of Bedford, this place had been blessed by no one. Godforsaken, as a matter of fact. How else to explain this night?

Jack and Pete were restless. Lumbering beasts, his boys. They'd started foaming at the mouth over the scraps of leftover donuts being served in the rectory, and he hadn't liked the way they'd growled at little Andrea Jorgenson, so he'd taken them out here to run their fears ragged. Right now they were speeding around the church grounds, lap after lap. Soon, they'd be so tired they didn't care about the strange sounds of the night. This buzzing. Or the smell of this rain, like old socks set on fire. What was that? Couldn't be good. Sometimes he wished he was a dog.

The sounds of the night lulled him. He watched the dogs chase their tails, around and around. Dumb dogs. Good dogs. He'd grown up around animals, and he understood them. They were honest creatures. Loyal. But when they were cornered, they tended to attack. A frightened animal is the most dangerous kind.

As a kid, he'd found his black Labrador Curlie chewing on a bone in the kitchen. It was from bad meat he'd helped his mother put in the trash, and he'd grabbed Curlie's mouth to take it away. Curlie bit down hard, and Thomas had screamed loud enough to wake the dead. Wearing pink curlers, his mother had come sauntering into the kitchen like every day was another problem she was perfectly capable of fixing. She'd kicked the dog in the gut until it let go of Thomas's mangled hand. A tragic-comedy in one act, "Frick and Frack meet Frankenstein," the story was named when retold over the years. Thomas's tendon never fully healed, and even now he couldn't make a fist all the way. The dog never forgave his mother, and always kept its distance after that. And his mother, playing along, told people that her foot was never the same: *Just doesn't kick as good anymore.*

Anyway, once he let go of Thomas's hand, Curlie was cowed. He abandoned the bone and followed Thomas across the room, all the while whining over all the blood Thomas was dripping onto the floor. Probably didn't even remember that he'd been the cause of the harm. Dogs were like that. Simple. That's why Thomas liked them better than people. Their motives were easy to read.

Jack and Pete made another lap. They moved with

grace through the rain and dark. Their eyes shone. Jack took the lead. He was the more nervous of the two. He barked when Thomas was gone too long, and he had a habit of catching birds and laying their husks across the threshold of the Gulfstream Conquest. Pete was the older one. His eyes were going, so mostly he sat by the stove.

They came charging toward him, and suddenly Thomas was afraid. Their eyes shone bright and other-worldly, as if they knew the wrongs he'd done. These perfect beasts. *They are godforsaken, too,* he thought. But then they slowed, panting and out of breath. They took their places on either side of Thomas and he pet them to let them know that by tiring themselves out they'd done good.

Through the gutter windows, he could see people sitting on cots in the rectory basement. They sat still as corpses, listening. There were sounds in the dark. Voices. There were so many that it was hard to understand what they said. Hard to cobble together his own thoughts, like sand that keeps sliding downhill because it has no foundation.

The dogs were growling again. He didn't like the sound.

—Funny, the thought belonged to him, but he didn't remember thinking it. Like a prescient's denied confession, it lingered.

To assure himself of their innocence, he patted their heads. They quieted, and he realized they'd been growling. Some nights when he was down, he found himself wondering why he had such a hard time letting a woman stay with him for more than a month, when there had been a fair number now that would have suited his needs. He knew he lacked something. Some vital thing that made him need another person. Even Georgia O'Brian, when he thought about it, would have been a solid choice. That night she called, he still could not explain why he'd pretended not to know her. He guessed the boy might be his son. Strange to think. His life could have been very different.

On nights when he was down about these things he did not know how to fix, the dogs kept him going. They nosed their way to the edge of his bed and licked his feet.

Through the church window, he saw the people of Bedford. Their eyes were blue. Blue?

He thought about the things holding him to this town and knew there was nothing. He could go now. Tonight. Make his way to the top of the hill and through the woods. He'd been an Eagle Scout once upon a time. Moss on the north side: It wasn't rocket science. Should he get the woman and the boy? Claim them as his own and leave this place? Right now? The idea excited him. Thrilled him. Yes. Leave right now. What was holding him here? And then the idea burst inside him. He was older than his years, and the woman by now wouldn't want him. Leave now, what would be the point?

"What do you think, boys?" he asked the dogs. They looked up at him, warily, as if they didn't recognize the sound of his voice. He knew then that they were hearing the sounds of the night, too. They were hearing the same things he was. But the buzzing was confusing them, and they were afraid. His mind played a trick on him, maybe, and he thought their hazel eyes had turned blue. Blue?

"Yeah. I think we'll go. An adventure. You'd like that." He rubbed Pete's thick coat. The dog bristled.

He headed toward the hill, and the dogs followed. One on either side of him. Up north was town, and then the cemetery, and behind that the woods. His jeans were soaked. He shivered. This wasn't so bad. He could do this. Didn't mean he was going anyplace. Just walking.

They were growling again. He didn't like the sound.

Pete began to growl again. These dogs weren't as good as Curlie. Inbred, he guessed. That happened sometimes. It had taken him longer to housetrain them. Longer for them to learn to offer a paw or endure the attentions of a rough-handed toddler. Still, they were good company.

He walked, and he began to notice the night. Things crept. Shadows. But he'd known that. A part of him had known all along. Even before she'd been born, he'd expected a girl like Susan Marley to come. Chuck Brann was stuck inside a spider's web. The more he struggled, the more he got stuck. White fabric like a bride's gown enveloped him.

Thomas stopped. What the hell?

The Hodkin house was covered in ice. The street was flooded. The paper mill spouted smoke.

What the hell?

He picked up his pace. He'd spoken to Georgia O'Brian only that one night, but he knew where she lived. If he found her, he'd know what to do. It didn't matter if she knew him, or even liked him. It he found her he'd have someone to protect.

He broke into a jog, and the dogs became alarmed. They barked. Siberian huskies are big dogs. They don't need to bark, and when they do they mean business. The sound spooked Thomas and he started running.

Something tugged on his jacket. He kept going, and then, suddenly, he was on the ground. Jack was on top of him, pinning his shoulders so he couldn't move. Drool dripped from the dog's jowls. Its blue irises moved in waves, in and out. The dogs did not recognize him. They looked at him like he was a predator after their food.

He knew animals. He knew these animals. In just one night, they'd gone feral. It had happened right before his eyes. Yesterday they'd been licking his toes and now they were wild. He knew what was going to happen now. A frightened animal is a dangerous animal. He knew what they were going to do. The voices told him so.

Pete bent forward. His jaws opened up to a black cavern that smelled like meat. Thomas tried to speak, "Calm down, bo—" he started to say, but the sound of his voice sent the dog into a rage. Pete gnashed his teeth and ripped out Thomas's throat.

It hurt only for a moment, and then the adrenaline of a dying man filled his bloodstream, and he felt nothing. He watched with horror as the blood bubbled out from his windpipe, and the dogs began to feed.

They growled as they ate, and he didn't like the sound.

Back inside the church, Andrea Jorgenson sat on a cot next to her mother. She'd *told* Liz something was wrong today, and even called Danny Willow, but no one had listened. They didn't think a girl like her, a slut with high-heeled boots who lived with her mother in a trailer, was worth listening to. But she could feel something inside her. Something bad. She could feel Susan Marley inside her, and she wanted to get her out.

She started for the rectory bathroom. She'd taken something from the RV, kept it hidden inside her coat. Shiny and new. Its edges certain and perfectly defined. At night it called to her like a lover. In school she thought about it. The things she could do when she got home. The things no one would guess. When she was alone.

The insides of her thighs were a testament to her hurt. Things she never said. Things pushed down so deep she had to cut herself to remember them. She locked the stall in the bathroom and sat. Took out the shears. So big. But this was a big hurt. A big night.

Do it, a voice told her. *You know you want to.*

Was it her voice, or Susan's? She couldn't tell. Andrea's eyes tonight had turned from brown to blue.

This would cut Susan out of her like a dark mole or a tumor of the breast. She knew how to do this. Unlike sex, she'd done it before. She pulled down her jeans. So tight that the zipper had imprinted itself on her skin. She wasn't a slut. It was Bobby Fullbright who had started that rumor, and told everyone at school they'd had sex in the Kmart parking lot. Not that she cared. That wasn't why she liked sharp things. She liked them because they were dependable. Solid. If you pushed your skin against them, you knew what would happen.

In the grand scheme of life, this meant nothing. A little cut in a world where people got sick, aged, and died. She would grow out of this. A stage, like any other. These cuts were nothing, and so was she. Insignificant little scabs. When she was afraid she could pretend to hide inside them.

She drew the shears in a line from the seam of her thigh to the underside of her knee. Longer than any cut she'd ever drawn before, but this was a special night. A tiny dribble of blood. Hardly enough, if she applied a little toilet paper, to soak through her jeans. So she went over the line once more, pressing deeper. Just a little. A little deeper. And on the other leg, too.

Only once had she really hurt herself. One time, the blood had not stopped for half an hour. Too close to an artery. The whole thing had terrified her, and she'd promised never to do it again. But one day she'd been alone at home, the safety pin had looked especially shiny, the old fears had faded like healed scabs, and she had started all over again.

Now she was bleeding, just like that time once before. It ran down her legs, all over the white-tiled floor. She looked at her thighs and caught her breath. Gaping wounds. So big. Her open skin like sails flapping in a sea of blood. They'd all know. Everyone in the church would know.

But they knew even now, didn't they? Even now, they guessed. They could hear. They could hear everything. Then why didn't they come to stop her? She was nothing, that's why.

Do it. You know you want to.

She started to cry, and tried to mop the blood with toilet paper. It made the paper flower like red roses, and then disintegrate. Nothing. She tried to put down the shears, but they were stuck to her fingers.

Do it. You know you want to.

But did she? Maybe. Maybe she did.

As she watched, the scissors came to life. They were hot in her hands, metal coalescing around her fingers. Their grips held her firm. The blades became sharper. So sharp they sparkled like diamonds. So pretty.

Was this happening?

Of course it is.

She sobbed. The shears were melted to her fingers and she could not let go. Against (against?) her will they sliced. Her arms, her pretty face, her stomach, her crotch. Open wounds. Red. Arteries. Cut the long way, so that they would not heal. She couldn't get out of the bathroom. She couldn't stand. And then she was dizzy. And then she felt and heard the crack of her skull as it hit the floor. And then everything went red.

*H*e *hated the smell of burning. The very thought turned his stomach.*

Steve McCormack panted, his lungs sore and out of breath. He'd made it home from the mill. Why Louise had wanted to stay, he had no idea. But he'd been wanting to get away from Louise for a long time. It was only tonight that he'd realized why: She was out of her fucking gourd.

And the fire, what was that all about? He hated fire. Hated the smell of burning. It was the worst thing in the world.

At his house, he started to pack a bag. Then he hollered for his brat of a little brother. "Joseph! Get your ass in here!" he screamed. The smoke would be thick soon. There wasn't much time. They'd go to the woods. He hadn't planned to take Joe with him, but now that he was in the house, he knew he would. Dad was off fishing for the week on the coast, and he'd been left in charge. The kid could whine like a little bitch, but he was family, which counted for a hell of a lot more that Louise Andrias's easy cunt.

"Hey, shithead, shake a leg!" he yelled. He grabbed his bag and started down the hall. Where was that kid? Not in the room they shared, or the kitchen, or even the attic he was so terrified by ("I heard *rats* up there, Steve, *rats*!" he'd babbled last week like a little scuffling overhead was a sign of the apocalypse).

Finally, he opened his dad's bedroom door. Sitting on the easy chair like she'd never left was his dead mother. "Steve," she cackled, "I've been waiting."

Steve started to cry right then and there. Full-on sobs.

"Come here, Steve," she said. She puffed on a Parliament Light. Trailer trash smokes. But that was what she came from. God, he hated her.

"Joseph?" he shouted for his brother, but he knew now that the kid was hiding. That was the problem; between the two of them, his little brother had always been the survivor. Joey had come through life with Mom without a single scratch.

"Steve, show me your hands. I know they're dirty because you're a dirty boy," his mother said.

Steve took a step into the room. Dark hair. Dark skin. Part Indian, his mom. Him, too. She held up her cigarette. Bitch. The things she'd done when no one else had been around to tell. The things people do, because they can. He was crying now. He couldn't stop.

The air was thick with smoke. He couldn't stand the smell. Her fingers were talons wrapped around his wrist. He tried to pull away but she was strong. Stronger than she'd ever been in life.

They'd said it was the tumor that had made her mean, but he'd never been convinced. They said the thing had eaten up her gray matter, the part of her personality that had made her a person. But he'd always thought that the cancer had been an excuse. He'd always wondered if all women were like his mother, once you scratched below the surface.

"You cried too much when you were a baby. I always wanted to cover your mouth. They put me on medicine. Said I was depressed. But that's not true, Stevie. I wasn't depressed. I just wished you'd come out with the coat hanger. Now show me your hand."

Steve made a fist. This time he wouldn't let her hurt him. This time she wouldn't get the best of him. Since he buried her he'd imagined a thousand times the way he should have pushed her down the stairs. Those brittle bones, they would have broken like clay.

She took a drag off her Parliament and its tip crackled. That sound. That terrible sound of burning stopped his heart. When she was well, she'd been okay. When she was well, he'd adored her.

"Give me your hand, boy," she whispered.

"No," he cried like a little baby. Like a fag. He couldn't stop.

She squeezed his hand. Her fingers were long and hairy. An animal's fingers. Her feet were hooves. This was what she was like on the inside. This was what she'd hidden from everyone but him. She lit her cigarette and smiled.

Oh, please. Not again. You died, you bitch. You died.

He tried to pull away, but he couldn't. She squeezed, and the bones in his hand popped. He fell to his knees. Her face was hairy with stubble now. Drool ran down the sides of her mouth. Then came the cigarette. Its cherry was the brightest thing in the room. It hissed when she pressed it against his skin. That sound, that terrible sound.

She pressed again and again, lighting and extinguishing all along the back of his hand and up his wrist. She wasn't a woman anymore. Maybe she never had been. Her legs were like a goat's, and up above her face was hairy. She smelled like the paper mill. He screamed when he saw what was coming, but he didn't get away. The cherry burned through his closed eyelid. It crackled. The pain was so bad he fainted. When he woke, he felt thick jelly running down his cheek. When he realized what had happened, he fainted again before she started on the other eye.

The smell of burning, he'd never been able to stomach it.

Inside the paper mill, Susan Marley stepped over Paul Martin's body. She walked out the door, and into Bedford. She did not look at the fat spider with hairy legs that was twice her size. It laid its eggs inside the nourishment of Chuck Brann's corpse. She did not look at the ghost of the newly dead young woman with stooped shoulders who rang the Andriases' front bell. The Andriases turned their locks, and the girl walked through the door.

As she walked these things parted for her. They made an aisle down Main Street. She waded through the rain that fell, and the smoke, and the darkness of the night. The skin on her body was loose now, sliding off her bones. She walked, because there was one final place she wanted to visit before this night was over. A familiar place. The place where the girl she'd once been had lived. She was going home.

THIRTY-THREE
The Third Billy Goat

No matter how hard you try, she'll never get any better.

A branch banged against the window, and his thoughts left him. Where was he right now? What was this place? Oh, right, he was in his room. Sitting at his desk, looking out the window into noisy blackness. His limbs felt heavy, as if his blood had turned to lead, and every breath he took was an effort.

What was this on his face?

Oh, right, he'd been crying again. Why was he crying? There wasn't anything wrong, was there? No, nothing was wrong. He always cried. He cried when he was happy, he cried when other people cried, he cried like a pussy. He shouldn't be crying now like some kid. There was something he was supposed to be doing, wasn't there? Something important? Something to do with his family? No, not his family. Something to do with the girl. What was her name? Liz. That's right, they'd broken up today.

Bobby frowned. Break up? Why would they break up? He looked out the window, into the darkness. It moved like fog taking form. Just the night, he told himself. *This is what it looks like at night, only I've never noticed it before; it looks like faces at my window.*

His stomach growled, and he realized he was hungry. When was dinner? Funny, it was two in the morning, and his mother hadn't yet served dinner. Where was Liz? They'd broken up, that's right, they'd broken up today.

He shifted in his chair. His arm had gone dead.

Pins and needles, needles and pins. It's the bitch in the blue dress who always grins.

The branch of an oak tree banged against the side of the house and it lulled him. How long had he been sitting in this chair? What about the girl? He'd been in her house and it had smelled rotten like mill air. No, not like the mill—like death. And he'd wanted to tell her to come back with him. He remembered now. In that house he'd started to believe. Her sister was alive, and had somehow woken up the dark part of Bedford.

Why had he left her there?

The branch of a tree knocked at his window. He blinked, and his thoughts were gone. Like a dog chasing its tail, he'd been asking the same questions all night, tears running down his cheeks, but they led nowhere, like wind. Like being stuck in the same moment over and over again.

Why was he sitting in his room while the rest of his family was sitting in the kitchen, listening? Listening to what?

When he got back from dropping Liz off tonight, his family had been waiting. His dad had come home early from work with day-old gray stubble on his face. "Give me a hand, will you, Bobby?" he'd asked. The two of them had gone from room to room, checking for leaks and locking windows. They'd shoved dishrags under doors so that nothing would get through the cracks, and made sure the roof was not leaking. When they reached the study, his father had pointed at the bookcase filled with medical texts and leather-bound classics by Dickens and Shakespeare. "You take that end." His father pointed, and the two of them had heaved the entire thing into the hallway and propped it against the front door. "In case someone tries to get in," his father explained.

"Who would try to get in?" Bobby asked.

His father looked him dead in the eyes in a way that had made him feel as if he'd failed on some very basic level to understand the fundamentals of adult life.

Then the family took their seats at the formal dining room table: Alexandra, Adam, the twins, Katie, Margaret, and Bobby. They sat like that for a long time, no one speaking. Power went out, and Adam placed a lit candle at the center of the table. Shadows flitted against the walls. They blanketed his family's faces so that it looked like they wore ever-changing masks.

"Shhh," Alexandra said when Michael started crying. "Shhh, it's just rain."

But no one cooked dinner, and no one got up, not even to pee. No one laughed or teased. The scene was familiar, like something lived before. Margaret squeezed his fingers tight. Across the table the twins shared a chair, and held each other close. They wore matching SpongeBob SquarePants pajamas. His father slumped down in his seat, and for the first time he saw that the old man really was getting old.

"I wish Liz was here," he thought, only his mind made a sound that carried through the air.

"You never should have brought her into this house.

It's her fault. It's all her fault," his mother hissed, pulling Katie close and looking around the table at her children like an angry wolf. Only she didn't say a word.

"Let him alone," his father answered in a tired sort of way. "You can't blame some girl." But again, no lips moved.

Bobby stood. Margaret squinted to keep from crying. His father wore only a pair of red polka dot boxers, and his round belly flopped over the elastic waistband. Something smelled, and Bobby realized that Michael had taken a crap in his pants and no one had bothered to clean it up. The bottom of his pajamas sagged.

His family turned to him in unison. In his mind he could hear all of them speaking. *Stay,* they said. *Sit with us. Watch the rain. You belong to us.* But was that them speaking, or was it Susan Marley looking out through their dead eyes?

"I don't belong here. I have to go," he whispered.

It took all the energy he had to climb the stairs and sit in his chair. In his room he thought about the girl. What was her name? Liz. He picked up the phone to call her, but couldn't remember what to say. Couldn't remember who she was. Only that she was important. Only that he had failed her. How had he failed her?

He sat like that for several hours, and now he wondered: *Am I dreaming?*

A tree branch banged against his window, and his thoughts circled. A voice, it might have been his own (hidden deep down someplace where this night could not touch it) told him: *Put away your toys. You can't hide in that room forever. They belong in this house, you don't.*

But he did not leave. He sat in his chair, his limbs

like lead. He was safe here, in this house at the top of the hill. His family knew better than the rest. They locked their doors.

From whom? What was happening to him?

It was two-thirty in the morning. By now the twins should be in bed. Long ago he should have heard pots banging, and been called for dinner. Someone should have knocked on his door and said, "Hey, Bobby, what are you doing in there?" But they were still sitting at the table, weren't they? All this time, hours, they'd been sitting there, quiet as mice. Sure, everyone else was supposed to act weird, sure, everyone else was in trouble, but not him, not his family. His family was safe, watching from a distance. His house was on solid ground.

But this year was different, wasn't it? This year was worse. Because she'd been right, hadn't she? She'd been right. Bedford was haunted. Bedford never forgets. It's in the air and the dirt and the rain and this year someone had set it loose. Susan Marley had unleashed it, and he could feel it crawling inside him, making him dead.

Who had been right?

He tried to make a fist but couldn't. He knew the answer to this question. The girl. Liz. She needed him. More to the point, he needed her.

He could picture her in his mind. Long, shaggy hair that got tangled when they made love. Always looked on the verge of tears except when she was laughing. Not so pretty. He'd always thought she was pretty, but maybe that was because she was the first (only) girl he'd ever had sex with. Not so pretty after all.

What was happening in her house?

She'll die in there. She wants to die, that's why he broke up with her. Not because she wouldn't tell him things, not because she had problems. Because it hurt so much to know that no matter how hard he tried, she'd never get any better.

The branch knocked against his window, and his thoughts left him. They fled like shadows in light. The lead in his limbs felt heavier, and his whole body went numb. How long had he been sitting here?

He'd been crying again. He was always crying. He hated that he was the type of kid who cried. The type of kid who got quivery lip at the slightest teasing about his height in the schoolyard. The type of guy who even now practically browned his pants (*Pants? The twins?*) when someone raised their voice at him.

Just then, he heard a knock at his door. "Yeah?" he called, only his voice was very low. Only, had he spoken at all?

Margaret joined him at the window. She pulled on the fabric of her Project Greenpeace T-shirt, stretching it from inside out with hands balled into fists so that little knobs of fabric jutted out over her flat belly. She sat very quietly. She always sat quietly. She, like Liz, had a fear of breaking the things she sat upon with her weight. "I hate the rain," she said. The statement lingered in the air and he thought he could touch it.

"I do, too," he told her.

"It's not going to end this year," she said. Then she nodded her head in the direction of the rest of the family. "They're pretending we're safe but they know we're not."

"It'll end," he said. "It always does."

She looked out the window and pointed at a thick cloud blowing from the direction of the mill. It was most dense near the valley, but its tendrils reached up the hill and toward the river, and even into the woods. "It's getting closer."

"Stop it, Margaret."

"It's a sickness she brought back. It makes us forget who we are."

"Margaret—"

"We'll die in this, all of us. And then we'll never get out. We'll be stuck here forever, just like all the other ghosts."

In a quick and terrifying moment he was tempted to strike her. But just as quickly the moment was gone. Margaret rubbed her hollowed-out eyes, and he knew that she had not slept for some time. He felt a swell of affection for his sister, the odd duck of the family who never seemed to measure up in looks or smarts or charm. The one who stood on the outside. And yet he loved her no less than the rest. "Why aren't you with Mom and Dad?" he asked.

"Did you dream about her?" Margaret asked him.

"Yes." It was the thing he had not been able to tell Liz. The thing he wanted to forget. He'd dreamed that he and Liz got married. He transferred to UMO to be with her, and they lived in a cheap apartment that she decorated to look like a home. In his dream he came home one day, and instead of Liz sitting at the kitchen table, he found Susan. She smiled at him, her lips stretching so taut that they ripped apart and blood splattered all over the floor. Only she didn't care. Only she liked it. "Hi, Bobby," Susan gurgled. In the dream her voice was just like Liz's, and he realized that they were the same girl after all.

"I've had the same dream every night since Susan Marley died," Bobby said.

"Me, too," Margaret said. "I dream the valley burns to ashes. In my dreams, we burn, too."

The branch knocked on his window, and his thoughts

circled. Where was Liz right now? Why had he left her all alone? Not alone. "What's happening?"

Margaret pointed out the window and into the darkness. "She brought back the dead."

Bobby got up from his chair and opened the window. The rain rushed in, along with the voices, a din of voices, like madness the color black. Like the things he'd been hearing in his head all these hours, the things that had made him forget, for a little while, the name of the girl he loved, only louder. Only worse. Only shouts and moans and laughter all at once. He heard April Willow crying. He heard Paul Martin laughing a death laugh an hour ago, he heard his mother screaming inside her head right now. How could you possibly remember yourself if you listened to this? How could you possibly remember who you were? No, not even this house was safe. Nothing was safe. His nose itching, his eyes burning, he shut the window, picked up the phone, and called Liz.

THIRTY-FOUR
I Heard a Fly Buzz

It was one o'clock on Thursday morning. Liz heard humming, like dissonant music from far away. A collective sound, like a thousand voices. The buzzing made her think of a fly: *There was a little girl who swallowed a fly. I don't know why she swallowed that fly. I guess she'll die.*

She was curled up underneath her bed right now, a flashlight in her hand, shaking so hard that the arc of the light was unsteady and her teeth chattered. She held her other hand over her mouth to muffle the sound of her breath.

The walls were painted pink, like the clean inside of a lung, and right now they were breathing. With every drop of rain that fell and churned in the bucket near her bed and every groan coming from the floors, the walls moved. They expanded and constricted as if she were inside the stomach of an animal.

She had to pee, and so she let go of her mouth and held her crotch. Her shaking became jerking, silent sobs. Still, she did not let go of the flashlight.

A part of her was under the bed right now. Another

part hovered in the corner, urging her not to give up. Another part giggled hysterically: *Oh, waiter, there's a fly in my head!*

After Bobby left she'd said good night to her mother. The power went out and she'd stood at the foot of the basement steps but had been unable to bring herself to go down those stairs. *Good night, Mom,* she'd called into the darkness below. *Sleep tight, Mom. Don't let the bedbugs bite, Mom.* And her mother, after some time, called back. *Yes, Liz. Go to sleep, Liz. It will all be better in the morning.*

For a second or two, she had puzzled before walking away. A slight narrowing of her eyes. Had she spoken, just then? Had her mother answered her? Yes, they had spoken, but not with words. In their thoughts, carried through this rotten house like a secret whispered by an old man. And then her frown was gone. Yes, it was all fine. Not to worry, fret not. It would all be better in the morning, right? And if not, who cared? How much worse could things get if she didn't wake up tomorrow?

She found a flashlight, and took it to the room she and her sister had shared more than a decade before. Plink, plink, plink went the sound of the water dripping down from the ceiling and into the tin bucket near her bed. She climbed under her soft quilt but did not close her eyes. There might, just might, be things that hid in the dark. They slithered, moving slowly, until you fell asleep.

She kept watch in her room for a very long time. So long that she forgot what she was watching for. At some point, she could not remember when, she started to hear snippets of conversations, soft chattering from the walls. A game of hide and seek, a game of quicksand, jumping from bed to dresser to bed without ever touching the floor. Two sisters sitting before a mirror. The elder smearing two lines of red lipstick across the glass, the younger adding black circles of mascara in a figure eight above. Each taking turns looking into the mirror, and becoming this conjured woman trapped inside a vanity.

She held a pillow against her side like an old stuffed animal or a missing boyfriend. *(Bobby. How could he? How could he pretend to care and then leave her like this?)* She covered her ears. She burrowed beneath her blankets. She decided that if she was quiet maybe all of this would go away. If she was very quiet. The same as smearing lambs' blood on her door; God's murdering angel would pass her by.

She circled the flashlight, looking behind her, in front, above, under the bed. Shadows moved. Forms took shape and then collapsed like ice turned to water.

This haunted place, she thought, *you carry it with you.*

She tried to think happy thoughts. It reminded her of a time, years before, when she had done the same thing in this very room. She had closed her eyes and thought of nice things like swimming in the summertime and her mother reading bedtime stories and she and Susan playing parts from movies after covering their faces with baby powder because Susan had said: *That's how they did it in the old movies, they had to be very pale,* and helping her father plant beans in the garden, be sure to leave the little plastic label so people know what you've buried, just like a headstone, and yes, she remembered this like yesterday, like it was happening right now, hiding in her in room and trying to conjure happy thoughts while unspeakable things took place in this very house. She remembered quite well.

When the walls started to move, puffing in and out like damp skin, she crawled under her bed. Drool trickled along her chin and she held her crotch. Her thoughts fell downward, like letting out every last bit of your breath and sinking into deep water.

You know why they all stare at you? You know why they hate you? Because his love came from blood.

Hadn't her life always been like this? Hadn't the last year with Bobby, when things seemed nice and wonderful with the possibility of a future, really been the nightmare? The tease that could never happen? Yes, this was her life. Right now. This was what she deserved.

You. It should have been you.

She let go of her crotch and pee trickled down her legs. She urinated all over the floor. The shameful warmth made her blush and her sobs became audible.

Oh, no. Please no. Please let this stop now, she prayed, to whom she was no longer sure: *I'll do anything.*

Just then, a sound startled her. Shrill and violent, like broken china. It sounded again. And again. And again. She thought she might scream. And then she saw the phone, ringing. It was the phone. She picked it up without speaking into it, and listened for a voice.

"Hello?" she heard on the other line. "Hello? Mrs. Marley? It's Bobby, Bobby Fullbright."

"Bobby?"

"Liz, it's you! I shouldn't have left. I was being stupid. Are you okay?"

"Bobby?"

"Are you okay? You sound funny. You sound really far away."

She took the phone away from her ear, and looked at it, trying to decide whether to hang up. She heard him speaking, asking her to please come back, please talk to him, don't be mad. She put the phone back to her ear. "It's bad, Bobby. It's worse than I said."

"What's happening? Are you crying?"

"No. I'm not crying. It's bad, Bobby. It doesn't go away. You can try, but it never goes away."

"I'm coming over, Liz. I don't know how I'll get there, I can't drive in this rain, but I'm coming over."

"You should stay home. It's not safe here."

"Is it Susan?"

Liz shone the flashlight against a wall, and instead of shadows, there were two very real little girls dressed in blue denim overalls, giggling. They laughed at her with hands over their mouths, or were they laughing at something behind her? Was it her father they were laughing at? "Yes. No. He did it to her. I watched, once."

She turned around, fully expecting her father to be standing over her, but instead there were just more shadows. When she looked back, the girls were gone.

"He raped her?"

"I guess that's what it's called," she said. "I think she murdered him, though. So maybe they're even. Now she's just after us."

There was a droning in her ear. Persistent, and annoying. *Shoo*, she wanted to say. But the droning continued, and she recognized the sounds as one word, repeated over and over again. "Liz," he was saying, "Liz," he was crying, "get out of there. "I'm going now, I'll start running. I'll meet you halfway. Whatever it is, get out of there."

She knew he was right. Still, she was not sure she could leave. If she wanted to leave. "I'm going now," he said. "Meet me."

"I'll try," she said, hanging up.

She might have stayed in the room, had she not shone her light from corner to corner, and seen, really seen, what she had not allowed herself to see before. The house was alive. The pink painted walls expanded and contracted in slow, deep breaths. The water, black water, dripped into the churning bucket. And what was that sound, that beating? The boiler in the basement going thump-thump, thump-thump. The heart, its beating heart. How could this be happening in her home, her room, how could anyone let this happen?

Just then, the back door opened. She heard shuffling footsteps. One foot was heavier than the other. Clip-clop. Clip-clop. It moved slowly, like something dead. Mary met the thing at the foot of the basement steps. "Baby? Is that you?" she called. The footsteps moved with intention toward Mary's voice. Clip-clop. Clip-clop. In her mind, Liz saw her sister's lumbering corpse winking at her.

Liz got up and ran.

She did not make it out of the house. While trying to reach the back door, she slipped on a sugar-laden floor. She sat there for a while, thinking that even if she didn't get out, Bobby would come, Bobby would save her, and then she heard movement coming from the basement. Two sets of footsteps. She stood again, and pushed with all her might against the back door, but it did not budge. Locked.

She did not have the presence of mind to think of keys, if keys existed, what keys were. She smashed out a window with her fist. She pulled her hand back against the shards without scraping her skin. Hadn't she always been the lucky one? When she looked at the opening she realized that she would never be able to climb out. How could she have been so stupid as to smash such a tiny window?

Two sets of footsteps started toward her.

She scrambled about the house but they were coming closer, no time, she would have to hide, make them think she was dead. But it was dark; was this her house? Where were the stairs? No, no place to hide. They would find her. She said a quick and pleading prayer: *Please, anyone dead, anyone at all, help me, get me out of this alive. Dad, if you're listening, I don't care what you have to do, what you have to do to her, but get me out of this alive.*

Susan's voice answered her in her mind. *Come,* she whispered, *Come here. There's nowhere else. You belong in this dark place. Do you think Bobby's coming? You know he's not coming. He doesn't love you. He never did.*

She tried the front door just as they got to the landing. It opened. She sobbed in relief. She stepped onto the front porch and the rain hit her. The sky was not just dark but black. It stank of chemical burnt rubber. Her nose itched. There was an emptiness out here, a loneliness worse than anything in this house. She hesitated. Which direction, which place was worse?

When she turned, she saw the two of them. The woman and her elder child. Susan beckoned with her eyes. Blue eyes. Her funeral dress was torn, exposing her anemic thighs. Her head was shaved bald, and her skin was beginning to separate from her bones. It bagged in places like an ill-fitted suit. There was no blood on her face. Instead there was black embalming fluid that oozed from her orifices and tricked down her legs like urine. *You wet your pants, too,* Liz thought hysterically, and Susan smiled, as if she heard.

Liz thought she felt herself split into two. Thought she saw the part of her she liked best, the happy part, run away, off into the rain, not bothering to stop at Bobby's, just away, to somewhere good. And she was left with the other part. The tired part. The frightened part. The angry part. She stood, indecisive, between the mouth of the house and the vast, cold night.

She entered the house only after her mother spoke. "My girl," Mary said, "come here." Liz took one step. Two. Three. Out of the rain, and into her mother's arms.

The three women sat at the kitchen table. Mary lit the birthday candle on the cake. The flame threw shadows against the breathing walls. Shadows that formed long, curled fingers, and bodies watching, like a crowd.

Don't be frightened, Liz thought, even while she cried. *Let go. It will be so much better once you forget who you are. It will be so much easier once you accept that nothing matters because you are nothing.* Susan lowered her hand over the cake and divided it in half. She handed one piece to Mary, and the other to Liz.

Mary chewed slowly, with no enjoyment. Liz watched. Chocolate frosting lined her lips. She ate mechanically, working on each bite until it was gone. Then both of them turned to Liz.

Liz lifted the slice to her mouth. In her hand the cake pulsed. Thump-thump. Thump-thump. Something warm dribbled between her fingers and onto the table. She looked up at her mother, and saw that Mary's mouth was caked, not in chocolate, but in the color black. Susan smiled. There was an emptiness on the left side of her chest, a grisly hole where her heart belonged. Liz whimpered. Thump-thump. Thump-thump. The sound was in rhythm with the boiler in the basement, with the ticking of the paper mill, with the soul of this house, with the soul of this town that someone had woken up.

Thump-thump. Thump-thump.

Liz felt her own heart beating in the same rhythm.

"Eat," Susan said. Her voice, oh, God, Liz had forgotten this, was indistinguishable from Liz's. They may never have looked alike, but they had always sounded exactly the same.

"Eat," Susan said again.

Liz looked down at the thing in her hands. It throbbed. She lifted it to her mouth. Thump-thump. Thump-thump. She put it between her teeth. She bit down, into meaty grease. She gagged. Thump-thump. Thump-thump. She took another bite. Another. Another. And it tasted so good. It tasted so goddamn good because with every bite, she devoured the part of herself she had worked so hard this last year to create.

PART FOUR

THE DEAD

THIRTY-FIVE
The Lady of the Woods
Summer 1990

It was her favorite place, out beyond the cemetery and into the deep pine and birch trees. Mushroom fungi grew there, spotted red and yellow. The soft ground was layered with leaves like the compost pile her father kept behind his shed. The sun did not filter through the sky, and all was dark. She wandered old paths, and kicked at used condom wrappers and beer cans: Pabst Blue Ribbon, Bud, Bud Light (for the girls, she imagined). After morning Froot Loops and armed with an apple or some berries for the road, she went there every day that summer of her seventh year.

Susan was a pretty girl. So pretty that people couldn't help but look at her. In town they stopped her on the street. They bent down and said, "What a pretty smile! Are you going to be a movie star when you grow up?" April Willow gave her as many SweeTarts as she wanted at the library during story hour. Dr. Conway had her blow on his stethoscope because he said little-girl breath made things shiny. At the grocery store where her mother worked, she sat on cashiers' laps while they petted her hair.

Her mother sewed light blue dresses for her. In the mornings before school she twirled and twirled until her hem reached the sky. "Little Miss Muffett," her mother said. "You live in your own world, my dear."

She did live in her own world. A world where if she flapped her arms fast enough, she could fly. If she drew a picture, it came to life. If she prayed to the Virgin Mary for a snow day, even in spring, it snowed. If she closed her eyes and fell asleep she might never wake up. And if she spun three times in front of a mirror and told Bloody Mary to go to hell, the bloody queen would appear behind the glass, captured.

But even she knew that these things would soon change. Her plump baby sister was already talking. She herself could now read, and even write. She kept a journal at school and in it she wrote: When I grow up I will have a dog. I will name him Sundance. We will live in a castle. I will have lots of babies. My castle will be so tall it touches heaven so that when people die I can visit them.

But things were changing. She could feel the change inside her, like a bubble about to burst. Things would be different soon. Her dreams told her so. Bad dreams. She would be different soon. And so she spent that summer in the woods, treading in Keds over moss-eaten earth, listening to buzzsaws that felled miles of trees, and savoring this premature end to her childhood. She crossed streams and tempted deer to eat berries from her hands. She lifted stones and inspected the multilegged insects that scurried from the light. She wrapped her arms around small trees, pretending they were phantom lovers. "Take me," she said, though she was not sure what that meant, only felt it in her body like a question without an answer.

Once, she saw a moose and hid behind a tree, watching the lumbering thing trample bushes while birds fled. Another time, she saw a boy and girl, old but not really old—not grown-up old—naked and tickling each other to tears. The last time she went to the woods she saw a tiny woman sitting on a rock. She had long blond hair, and a pretty blue dress. The woman waved a tree branch tied with string over the water, and like magic the water rippled.

"Come here, Susan Marley," the woman said. Her voice was like velvet. Thick and soft and monotone.

"Who are you? How do you know my name?" Susan asked.

The woman lifted her fishing rod from the stream. A minnow gleamed, its gills pumping helplessly, unable to breathe inside so much air. "Should I let it go?" she asked.

"Yes, let it go." Poor minnow, Susan thought. Trapped on a hook.

The woman tore the fish from the hook. It flopped between her fingers; flop, flop, flop! Then she put it in her mouth and swallowed. She smacked her lips while it wriggled down her throat. *Smack!* The wet sound gave Susan goose bumps. "You eat them, Susan. That's what you do with them, you eat them," the woman said.

Terrible. Not for little girls. Didn't this woman know that she was just a little girl? Susan took a step back. A twig snapped. Someone called her name. Who called her name?

Suddenly, the woman's face turned bloody. A nest of

black knots appeared in a line down her neck and below the high collar of her blue dress. "It's us, Susan.
The shit, the shinola. It's us," the woman said.

Susan ran that day, down the hill and through town
where April Willow lightheartedly asked, "Where's the
fire?" all the way to her house. Her mother sat feeding
the baby at the table, and Susan crawled on the brown
linoleum and hugged her woman-sized legs. "What's
the matter, Miss Muffett?" Mary asked.

But Susan could not tell her she'd been out in the
woods. She couldn't tell her she'd been anywhere but at
the park a block away. "I got scared," she said. "I saw
a raccoon at the park. I thought it might bite me."

Mary put down the baby's Minnie Mouse spoon
and looked at Susan. "A raccoon? Did its mouth have
white stuff, foam?"

Susan shook her head.

"Are you still scared?"

"Yes."

Mary lifted Susan onto her lap and held her close.
"Better?" she asked.

Susan closed her eyes. "Better."

The next day, the last day before she would start the
second grade, Susan went to the park instead of the
woods. There were no scary ladies in the park, just
kids who filled their buckets with sand. But the park
got boring. She was bad at the seesaw because she always forgot that if she got off at the bottom, someone
else fell. She hung upside down on the monkey bars for
at least five minutes, but all the blood rushed to her
face and she was afraid she might explode. Pop! Her
head would fall right off. And for how long could a
person swing? You never got anywhere. You never got
anywhere in the park, for that matter, because it was a

place with limits, when the woods went on forever.

She left the park and walked up the hill, waving at each person she saw. There was Mr. Willow, who was sad because he was lonely, so she smiled extra wide for him, and even did a curtsy. There were the Fullbrights walking their baby in the stroller, except she didn't like them very much; their heads were full of sand. She pretended they were vampires and covered her neck when they passed. And there was Cathy Prentice, who'd just moved back to town with her new husband.

"Hey you!" said the new husband. Paul. That was his name; people called him Paul. She knew him from someplace, but she couldn't remember where. "I've got your nose right here, you know that?" He put his thumb between his index and middle fingers. "You're a silly man," she said. "You're a cutie," he told her, walking away with his arm around Cathy's waist. *That's how people in love act,* she thought, *not like my mom and dad. Like them.* She watched their backs as they went down the hill, and his hand fell away. *Except they're soft in all the wrong places, and hard in the places where they should be soft. Like crabs with their bones on the outside.*

What did that mean? How can people be like crabs even when they look like people? Why was she seeing all these things when she usually had to look so hard? She had to scrunch her eyes real tight and concentrate concentrate concentrate just like the memory game with cards? Why were they coming to her now all at once?

She squeezed through the fence in the cemetery and entered the woods. On the rock she saw the woman. She was pretty again. Not scary. Susan tried to hide behind a hemlock bush, but the woman saw her.

Susan burst out from behind the bush and ran down

a path in the other direction. "Come back," the woman called. "I see inside you Susan Marley, and you're already dead. You're full of worms."

Susan ran until her legs felt like cooked macaroni. Then she slumped against a tree and cried for a long while. In her mind she saw the woman's face. It smiled at her. It beckoned. "Come to me," it whispered. "I want to tell you a secret."

She didn't come. She also didn't go home. Instead, she carved her name into the trunk of a tree with a broken piece of glass. She watched for deer and listened to the birds: a robin, a cardinal, a crow. But it was different now, not her woods. Everything was changed. She felt like a bubble had burst. Who called her name? Was someone playing a joke?

She went back to the river. She couldn't help it. There was something about the woman that was so familiar. "Why did you do that?" she asked.

The woman put down her fishing rod. At the end of the string was a giant hook. "Do what?"

"Why did you eat a fish? It'll swim in your stomach and make you sick."

The woman smiled. Red threads spun out from her blue irises and black blood trickled down her neck. Everything nice about her turned rotten. And then she was pale and pretty again. And then she was both things at once. She patted the rock, "Sit here, next to me."

"I don't like you." Susan shifted her weight between her legs as if she had to pee. Mom would be so mad if she knew that she was talking to a stranger in the woods. Mom would spank her silly. She wished Mom was here.

"But you want to sit next to me, don't you, Susan?

You want to ask me a question. I won't hurt you. I promise."

Susan peered inside the woman, and she knew this wasn't true. The woman did want to hurt her. The woman wanted to scratch her face until she wasn't pretty anymore. But there was something about the woman, an answer to a question that she couldn't remember. An answer she had to know because at night she couldn't sleep, worrying about it. At night she cried and she didn't know why.

"Come here, my dear. I don't bite," the woman said.

Susan looked up at her. *Yes, you do,* she thought, and the woman smiled, as if she heard. But still, there was a question burning inside her, and she needed to know the answer. She went over to the rock and raised her arms. The lady put her hands on Susan's waist and hoisted her up so that they sat side by side. Her touch wasn't cold or warm. It felt like nothing, like never being born.

"Tell me a story," the woman commanded.

Susan cocked her head. "A story? I heard about this man with hooks. Instead of hands he has hooks."

The woman cast her string into the water but it made no sound, only ripples. Then she smiled. Her blue eyes got big and then small. Solid, and then far away. She was two things at once. She was many things, but mostly, she was hungry. "Tell me a different story. You know the one I mean."

Susan twirled a lock of hair between her fingers. "At the sideshow circus in Bangor I saw a man who could put his legs over his shoulders. I'm too little to go in so I sneaked under the tent. You can't tell Dad. He doesn't know," Susan said.

"That's not the right story," the woman said. Susan looked down at the water and smiled at her reflection. Pretty girl! Then she saw the woman's reflection and she shivered. Two pretty girls. They looked just alike.

"I'll start, and you finish," the woman said. "Once upon a time there was a little girl, and she was very unlucky. She was born in a haunted place where nothing ever died."

"I don't like this story," Susan mumbled. "I only like pretend stories and cartoons."

The woman grinned, and her small teeth looked like knives. "It used to be a place like any other. It was founded, and people lived here, and mostly they were happy. There was a paper mill, and a river full of fish, and the soil was rich and fertile."

In Susan's mind, she saw Bedford. A pretty place. There were new houses clean and neat, and a train that cut through Main Street twice a day. Her great-grandpa poured the blacktop for the roads, and her great-great-grandpa chopped down the trees that made the hungry paper mill's first meal.

The woman continued. "But there are places in the world that are alive. They have minds and memories and wills."

"Like Bedford," Susan said.

The woman nodded. "Yes. Like Bedford. At first the place was pretty, and the people were happy. They were lured here by the man who built the mill. His name was William Prentice, and he promised them picket fences and healthy bodies and opportunity for their children. He promised them dignified old age and clean air to breathe. They erected a statue of him when he died, and even now a stone angel stands watch over his grave."

The woman stopped. She smiled at Susan. Such a warm smile. A hungry smile. The woman continued: "But William Prentice's words became salt in their wounds. The chemicals in the river began to kill the animals. The people got sick. If the work didn't break their backs, the dirty air did. It happened so slowly they didn't notice it at first. Their pay got lower so they worked harder. Their lungs and ears and eyes and the health of their children suffered, so at night they slept longer, and drank more beer to dull the pain. They didn't want to admit that a great man like William Prentice had lied. They didn't want to admit the things they'd done, the sacrifices they'd made to feed the ashes of their own greed."

Susan saw something in her mind. She saw William Prentice living in a mansion at the top of Iroquois Hill. He was a wealthy man in a three-piece suit. His face was clean-shaven and his fingernails were short and smooth. When he visited the mill he covered his mouth with a handkerchief to filter the fumes. He watched the people working there, who'd been maimed, whose eyes were tearing, who coughed black phlegm. He connected these things to the grown children of Bedford, who were shorter than their parents, and tended to get sick. He promised the people that he'd hire doctors, build better vents, and raise pay. Every time he made them, he intended to keep those promises. But then he'd leave the mill and walk into the bright sunshine, and he'd forget. So the people got sicker, and the fish started to float. And the frogs and turtles died. And only the strong survived.

The woman continued. "There were thirty-four men working the night shift the day the vents backed up. The doors were shut because it was winter. The fumes weren't yet cool off the pulp. An accident became a tragedy." The woman made a tsk-tsking sound, but Susan could tell she wasn't *really* upset. Really, she thought it was funny. "Half the men were dead before the foreman opened the doors. The rest died within the hour.

"He told himself a lot of stories. He came up with lots of reasons for what he did one hundred years ago. William Prentice ordered the bodies of those thirty-four men to be stacked in the basement of the mill. Then he set fire to the place, but not enough to raze the building; only enough to burn the bodies. That way nobody had to explain why the vents hadn't worked, or pay the widows more than their due. The bodies of those men were buried in the basement of the mill. They salted the earth of Bedford. Nothing good could ever grow again.

"William died, and his children took over. They squeezed Bedford dry, until the stores started to close, and the money left, and the factories shut down. And the people finally realized that the promises were lies. The Prentices moved away and never looked back, but the people of Bedford were left behind. Their rage at what had been done to them had no place to go but within. It got buried underground, and captured in rain, and it roiled inside queasy stomachs. It fed the souls of the dead."

"St—" Susan started to say: *Stop*. But the woman looked at her, and she fell silent. The woman's eyes danced. So wild, they drew her inside them. They made her forget her own name.

"The first sign that the place had soured was the rain that began to fall every year. After the rain came a thickness of the air, and a change in gravity. The place became so full of all that had been buried that it began to overflow. It slipped into nightmares, and the most basic instincts of everyone who lived here. Though they did not know it, it affected every action they took and every decision they made. Finally, the place became haunted. The flotsam of the dead, the lost, and the living began to speak. The place was forsaken by God."

"You're a liar," Susan whispered. But she knew it wasn't a lie. Sometimes, when she was sitting at her desk in school or else walking down Iroquois Hill, she would see the town in a certain light, and the place would look like it was on fire. The place would look so angry it was the color red, ready to burn itself into charred embers. Ready to collapse on itself like a hole as deep as this woman's eyes.

"And then do you know what happened?" the woman asked.

"No," Susan whispered.

"Watch." The woman smiled widely, too widely, and her lips split open. A drop of blood rolled down her chin and landed on the rock. Susan's eyes played a trick on her, maybe, and the drop grew larger. It covered the rock like paint. It splashed against the dirt, and the trees, and the sky so that suddenly everything was red as a sunset. Beautiful, even, in a terrible kind of way. But then the sky started to darken, and the blood turned from red to black. Then everything went black.

"You stop! I don't like this trick!" Susan shouted. The woman's eyes danced, wild blue against black, pulling Susan deeper and deeper. Susan listened for the voice the woman carried inside of her, and instead of just one or two voices, she heard thousands of them.

"Kill her!" one voice shouted, while another said, "I forgot how sweet she used to be. So sweet and pretty. Like a morsel I could eat," and another worried about the rain, and another was sad that Paul Martin was dead *(dead?)*, and another watched the stars on a clear night, and another laughed as black smoke curled its way through a house, and another imagined tying rocks to Susan's waist and throwing her into the river so that certain things *(what things?)* would never have the chance to take place.

"Stop!" Susan shouted. She kicked the woman hard even though she couldn't see her. She couldn't see anything. All black. All terrible. And in the darkness the woman laughed.

"Do you see?" the woman asked.

"Yes, I see," Susan answered. And she did see. She knew. She had always known, and now that she was getting older, she was beginning to understand.

The sunset lightened back to red and then orange and then yellow, until, finally, the sky was blue. The woman's eyes stopped dancing, and she loosened her grip. She was crying and laughing at once.

"Do you know what happened next, Susan?" the woman asked.

Susan didn't answer, even though she knew.

"It was inevitable that this sourness would seep inside the children conceived here. And so, one day, a little girl was born half dead like the town. She could hear and see the buried things. They crept inside her. They became a part of her. She carried them in her mind, her heart, her womb, like a woman pregnant with death itself."

Susan closed her eyes. She tried to wish herself away. She'd flap her wings and fly back home. She'd teleport herself like a unicorn to her mother's lap. "I'm just a little girl," Susan said.

"When it was time, the girl died, and in her death she gave birth to their rage."

"It's not true. It doesn't happen!" Susan shouted.

The woman's eyes danced once more, and now there wasn't any part of her that was pretty. Now black blood dripped all over the rocks, and the woman's skin began to slide off her bones. "It's true," the woman said. "It happens now. It happened then. It will happen. It always happened."

Susan was crying now, but too tired to heave her breath, too tired to blow her nose on the sleeve of her Wonder Woman T-shirt. "Why are you doing this to me?" Susan asked.

The woman grinned. "You came searching for me. I'm all you think about. You can't let me go. No one can let me go."

"You live in the woods?"

"We live here, Susan. We live everywhere."

Susan understood, and did not understand. She remembered a dream about a lady who lost her own reflection. She remembered people from town who crossed the street when she came near. She remembered a house where a boiler beat like a heart, and a town where a paper mill one day filled the sky with black smoke. She remembered her own gravestone; a small, neglected thing. She knew the woman was telling the truth. "Why was I born this way? Why is Bedford this way?" she asked.

The woman smiled. "It was a bargain the people of Bedford made with William Prentice. They traded their lives for his lies. Their bargain salted the earth, so that nothing good could ever grow. Nothing can die here, so long as his paper mill stands. And because of you, nothing will live here, either. Now ask your real question. The one you came here for."

Susan didn't ask. She knew the answer. She did not want to hear it.

The woman smiled a dead smile. "Shall I tell you the answer, Susan Marley?"

"Please don't."

"I am you," the woman said.

She awoke alone on the rock. There was a crick in her neck because she'd slept all funny, and it was dark. The bad lady was gone. Had there even been a bad lady? No, she was just a Little Miss Muffett. How scary! She hated scary dreams. What time was it? Mom was going to be so mad!

She started out of the woods, but something was wrong. Who was calling her name? She ran down the path and squeezed through the fence to the cemetery. Who called her name?

It was dark, and she couldn't find her way out of the rows of headstones.

"Susan! Come here right now!" a voice demanded. Where had it come from?

"Don't dawdle, little girl, it's going to rain soon," another voice answered.

"I feel so lonely, don't you feel lonely?" someone else asked. "It's so dark in here."

"Come here, pretty girl. I like pretty girls," another said.

And then they spoke all at once.

She started to run, and tripped on a stone. The big stone with the angel. The man below turned over and over. William Prentice. His hands were red, and he never slept. All down the row, they reached up from the ground. "Sleep," she cried. "Go back to sleep." But they pried at their coffins with their fingers. "Let us out," they said. *"Let us out!"*

She ran out of the cemetery and through the streets, to home. On her way, in each house she passed, she could hear the people inside: *With another woman, I'll bet!—It's my birthday tomorrow, and we're going to get hammered—She always sleeps with her back to me, like I've got bad breath or something—I hate school—Ever feel like you're watching your whole life, and you can see all the stupid things you do, but you just can't help it? I feel like my life belongs to someone else.*

Susan covered her ears with her hands. She sang, "I scream, you scream, we all scream for ice cream!" and who cared who saw her, who cared that she was talking to herself, but still, the voices would not stop.

When she got home, her mother nearly knocked the breath out of her with the force of her hug. "I was so worried, baby. We looked everywhere. I drove all over town. Oh, honey, what happened?"

It took Susan a moment to realize that her mother had spoken these words, rather than thinking them. "I was sleeping," she said. "And then I woke up."

"Sweetie," Mary said, hugging her tight. "Don't ever scare me like that again."

Her father put her baby sister, whom he was carrying, down on the floor. He came between Mary and Susan. She saw inside him then. Saw that he was weak. Saw that because of his weakness, the haunted things in this town had found a home inside him, even though he did not know it. Because of what he carried inside him, he wanted to hurt her. Her mother knew this, but could not believe it.

Susan saw the arc of her life; all the things that would happen, and the things that might happen, too. She saw that the woman had lied. She had told only bad things, because she understood only bad things. But even in Bedford there were good things, too. Mostly, Susan saw her own inexorable corruption like a hunger never satisfied, and it terrified her.

Her father looked her up and down. He turned her around, inspecting every inch of her. He was shaking, and in his eyes were tears. "Did anyone hurt you?" he asked.

"No," she said, crying. "No one touched me."

"Thank God," he whispered.

Her father pulled her close, and Mary joined him. They formed a circle around her. She cried in their arms. For a moment, just a moment, she felt safe. Fortified by the very people who would betray her, against the things to come.

But the voices did not stop. The voices never stopped.

THIRTY-SIX
Soil
1994

The week-long rain had recently ended. It seemed to get more reckless every year. Of course, there had been that one year in '79 that Ted Marley could remember. The pipe of the mill got flooded, and the town was closed off for three days. But now, as always, the rain was over. The snow was gone. And also, as always, the land seemed the richer for it.

It was a nice night. A little humid. The sulfur from the mill hung low in the atmosphere like a blanket between the earth and the stars. Ted Marley pushed his spade into the ground and dug into soft dirt. Some weeds were beginning to sprout. His spinach and tomatoes would be good this year. He knew this: how to make things grow. It was not in the naming of these things, their Latin roots, or the water or sun or places they were planted. It was an instinct that came from deep within. This year, his garden would bloom.

He was a small man with lean muscles that gave him a lanky appearance. He put down the spade and felt the earth with his hands. It smelled fresh and clean as it always did just after the rain. It smelled like the beginning of creation. He took his time, letting the soil fill his hands and fingernails, getting dirty.

Time passed. The stars shifted their place in the sky. He held out a flashlight and looked at the dirt. Had there been any money, he would have been a farmer. He would have worked in the field all day for something of his own. Corn, maybe. Corn so high that he would never be able to see where it was that he came from. Would never be able to see home. At night he would sleep with the animals. He would feed slop to the pigs and he would get down among them and sleep with them and he would never go back. He would be one of the animals. And he would watch his family from a distance far and very safely away.

There might have been a time, years ago, when he had thought he'd get out. He'd made plans, sitting on his uncle's porch and watching the stars, to go places. But then he met Mary, and she'd wanted to settle down. He traded his job slinging beers at Montie's Bar to peel bark off logs at the mill, and saved enough for a down payment on a house. He was not sure he'd ever loved Mary, but it had been relief to let go of all those dreams.

Now, he went into the house. Fixed himself a sandwich and watched the end of the ball game on the black and white Zenith. The Red Sox lost to Milwaukee. He tried to focus on these things but could not. He turned the volume down low and listened very hard. Listened.

He had a beer. And then another. A third. He was drinking for courage. He was drinking for absolution. He took the route he had taken so many times before that the air was rotten with history. He walked up the stairs and told himself that this time was different, this time he would go to sleep. He opened the door to his children's room, just to check. He was their father, after all. Elizabeth tossed. He would not touch her. He had never touched her. He looked at the other one. Susan. Eleven years old. He grimaced when he thought of this. Eleven years old. Little girl. She behaved much older than her years. But no, he would not touch her. He would never touch her again.

He caressed Elizabeth's shoulder. Sweet little thing. Quiet. Took after him in looks. Elizabeth did not wake. She turned in her sleep and he bent down and kissed her forehead. He ran his hand over the blanket tucked close, feeling the curve of her narrow hips.

It was easy being with her. She never tempted him. At work he would think of her. He would collect stories throughout the day to tell her that would make her laugh. He would never leave his family, as his own father had done. He would never leave Elizabeth to survive on her own. His hand moved farther down. He squeezed her thick little leg. His little girl. Perfect thing. Her breath hitched and he thought she might be awake. It made him angry that she was pretending to be sleeping. Afraid of her own father. He squeezed harder.

Susan stirred. She got up and unbuttoned the top of her flannel nightgown. He could see the flat plane of her chest that would one day become soft. She guided his hand away from Elizabeth.

Their fingers threaded. She was a strange girl. A cursed girl. A damned girl, just like him.

Susan guided him out of the room. They went down to the basement. There was a chill in the air. Though he had bailed out most of the water, there was still a half-inch film of it on the ground. The boiler hummed. Their faces were very close. He motioned for her to turn around so that she could not look at him. He could not really be a bad man. For her to keep these secrets, she had to love him very much.

She didn't move. The bottom of her long flannel night-gown spread out on the wet floor like a pink flower. In her eyes he saw a man growing older by the day. A man, thin and sickly, with too much of a taste for liquor. A man who bore no love for his past, or his future. He was this man.

He began to cry. "Oh, Susan," he said. He lifted her chin and saw that she was as unhappy as he. His quiet girl. His sad girl. He would comfort her. Her pain resolved into stillness. He kissed her on the lips. Tenderly. It always happened this way.

He pulled down her cotton panties so that they hung around her ankles. Then he turned her against the sawhorse and began. His shoes sloshed in the water. It made him sad, suddenly, that the rain had come and gone. That it had not washed either of them clean. Here it was, the ground not even dry, and he was inside her.

He never went too deep. He did not want to harm her. But this time, he did go deep. Had she thought that he was going to hurt Elizabeth? Had she really thought he would do that? He went deep. The water sloshed right along with him. It sprayed against the walls. It circled within itself in little tidal pools. The boiler kicked into motion and for a moment, he thought he heard the house itself rage against the thing he did.

When he was done, she turned and he saw that she had bled from below. She had also bled from her lower lip. Bitten into it to keep from crying or maybe just to keep from calling out. To keep from calling his name.

He wiped the tears from her eyes and kissed where they had fallen.

Before his wife came home and they dressed and he told Mary, as he always told Mary, that they had been working on the bookcase together that he had intended for the last six months to build, Susan told him not to touch Elizabeth; never to touch Elizabeth. "If you touch her, I won't tell. I'll kill you." She said this quietly and softly with the wet blood on her lips that made her look so lovely and she meant it. He knew she meant it.

The fury that she would betray him would come later. The biting fury because he knew he'd provided a better life for his family than he had gotten. But for now, it was fear he felt as he watched her hold her head erect, kiss her mother good night, and smile an angry smile at him with those knowing, ruined eyes. It was fear, because he wondered what he had created. He wondered if the soil had been sour to begin with, or if it was something he had done.

THIRTY-SEVEN
The Haunted Place
1994

She sneaked down the stairs one night. To the place they went when the mother wasn't home. Perhaps he and Susan whispered stories down there, or played games like Hungry Hippos or chess that six-year-olds are not allowed to play. Maybe they sanded the bookcase that her father was trying to build, or they mopped the floors as a surprise for Mom. It was a secret they shared though no one had ever told her so. It was the thing that made the air thick; made the house—its shutters and roof and swinging screen door—like an angry face. The thing she asked at night: Why not me? Does he love her more?

He didn't seem to like her more. She was weird. She knew things before you said them. She knew when Dad was in one of his moods and wanted to sit by himself in the big chair, and she knew when the lady at Olsen's Diner was going to try to pinch their cheeks, and she even knew that Liz had hidden her Skipper Barbie in the trunk of the Caprice Classic for safekeeping and then forgotten about it. Mom said Susan knew things because God had made her extra smart, but Liz thought it was because she was an alien, like from Canada.

It wasn't fair that they stayed up late after sending her to bed! It wasn't fair that they did fun things, secret things, while she had to lie in the dark and wait for sleep to come. What if she wasn't sleepy? But grown-ups could be scary, too. Maybe they did bad things. Maybe they were all aliens, casting spells on the human member of the family. She'd go down to the steps and find dead bodies, and they'd be drinking blood from skulls. It was possible.

Liz sneaked down the stairs and watched at the foot of the basement steps. A lit bulb in the ceiling made everything too bright. Near the half-built bookcase something moved. Her father's back was to her. He made sounds like an animal. She'd watched people make babies on *Melrose Place,* only they did it in a bed with sheets over their bodies. Her father's pants were around his knees and she saw his pale bottom. At another time, she might have giggled: Daddy's bottom!

Behind him, she could see Susan. Her eyes were wide open. She didn't say *Hello,* or *Go away,* or *You're in trouble: Dad said you had to go to sleep.* She didn't smile. She didn't laugh. She didn't see Liz, though she looked right at her.

Liz thought maybe she was dreaming, only it was too scary to be a dream. A grown-up thing. Maybe her real family was dead.

Susan blinked and a tear rolled down her cheek.

Oh, stop. Please stop. She doesn't like it, Liz wanted to say. But what if she did like it? What if this was what grown-ups did after they turned eleven years old? "Stop," Liz whispered, but her father didn't hear. There was dirty black water in the basement, and it churned in rhythm with her father's thrusts.

She thought maybe she was far away, and another girl stood in her place. A quiet girl made of tougher stuff than she. "Stop," Liz said again, only louder. "You're not allowed to do that." Still, her father did not hear.

Through her tears, Susan saw Liz and smiled. It was a bad smile, a dead smile. Her sister was dead inside. Yes, she understood now; that's why her sister knew so many things. That's why she seemed like an alien. That's why their parents were frightened of her. She was dead inside.

Liz ran back up the stairs and climbed into her bed. She tucked the blankets in close and closed her eyes. She counted slowly. One Mississippi. Two Mississippi. Three Mississippi . . . One hundred Mississippi. She chewed on her nails and bit her cuticles until they bled. In this house bad things happened. In this house no one was allowed to yell. In her mind she screamed.

THIRTY-EIGHT
The Things Grown-ups Do
1995

The girls were looking out their bedroom window. Liz was crying. She didn't remember why she was crying. She thought it might be about a dream she'd had the night before. Or maybe it was about something that happened. Something bad she saw in a basement. The rain had ended a week before, but the weather outside was still icy. She imagined opening the window and flying away.

Susan took her hand and squeezed it. Liz didn't say anything, or even look, because she didn't want Susan to stop.

Outside, a white Buick pulled up to their house and they both smiled. Georgia O'Brian got out of the car. "Pillows," Liz sniffled, and Susan answered, "Poker."

Georgia was the best babysitter in the world. When she came to the house, they could do whatever they wanted. They could slide down the stairs on their blankets, and they could skitter across the kitchen floor in socks. They could Rollerblade in the basement, and they could pile all the pillows in the house into one room, and make an impenetrable fort.

"Race you!" Susan said. She let go of Liz's hand and sprinted out of the room. Liz followed, but her shorter legs and rounder belly didn't make for much of a contest. They got to the back door just as Georgia came through it. "So big," Georgia explained. "You girls grow another inch every time I see you!" She lifted first Susan, and then Liz, and swung them each in a circle. Georgia was gi-normous. So big that when she walked, the floors rumbled. Bigger than most grown-ups. "What are we doing tonight?" she asked.

Susan grinned. Georgia was one of the few people that Susan ever let touch her. She hated most people, and when she saw them she covered her ears even if they weren't talking. She'd been tested for autism or autopsy—Liz forgot which—but the doctors said Susan wasn't retarded or mental. Just really weird. "Poker," Susan said. "In a fort for princesses," Liz added.

Georgia's expression grew somber. "Do you have any money?"

Liz shook her head and Susan giggled.

"No money at all?"

Liz dug into her pocket and produced a stick of Big Red gum. Georgia smirked. "Gum? Do I look like I was born yesterday? Gum doesn't count as money. Only peanuts!"

They found the peanuts and played four hands of seven-card stud before Mom and Dad came down the stairs dressed all nice in black shoes and starched collars. They waved good-bye, and Liz wanted to get up and hug them, but she knew Susan wouldn't like it, so she didn't. They weren't very nice to Susan, and Susan wasn't very nice to them, which Liz guessed was all part of being twelve years old.

As soon as Mom and Dad were gone, the three of them charged into the television room to watch *America's Funniest Home Videos*. When the show was over, Georgia told them to change into their pajamas. She said they could stay up as late as they wanted, but as soon as their parents came home they had to run to their room and pretend to be sleeping. This was one of the many reasons that Georgia was perfect.

In the bedroom they shared, Liz and Susan took off their shirts. Liz saw Susan's stomach. It was a sunset, dappled red and orange and black and blue. Liz had seen this before, for months she'd seen bruises like this before, but tonight, Georgia was babysitting. Tonight, she remembered the animal sounds her father had made. Can grown-ups do anything they want? They turn on you at any time even if they pretend to love you? She saw the sunset and she screamed.

She screamed loud and long, until the floors grumbled, and the house raged, and Georgia stood in the doorway. "Look," Liz said, "look what he did to her!"

Susan cowered in a corner. Georgia pulled her arms away from her stomach and looked at the sunset. "Help us," Liz told her. "You help us."

Liz thought Georgia would wave a magic wand and make the sunset go away. She thought Georgia would shout so loud the walls would crumble. Georgia was big, after all, so big she could blow the house down with just one breath. "Oh, shit," Georgia said.

"I fell," Susan said.

Georgia took them both into the bathroom and wiped down Susan's stomach with a towel. Bits of dried blood got wetted, and smeared, and then disappeared. Liz hoped maybe it would all go away.

"A boy in school," Susan said. "He doesn't like me. He hits me at recess."

Georgia sat down on the toilet seat and started to cry. Just a kid, Liz thought, a little kid. They were all little kids. Georgia took them both on her lap and held them.

The next day Officer Willow came to the door with a man in a wrinkled brown suit and he smelled like coffee. The man asked questions. He talked to them all together, and then alone. No, they all said. No. No. No.

He poked Susan's stomach, searching for broken ribs, but there weren't any. He didn't like the look in her eye, so he didn't talk to her for long. "I fell," she said. "I was playing on the front stoop and I fell."

When the man and Mr. Willow left, Mary called Georgia O'Brian to yell at her, but instead Rose O'Brian answered the phone. "I don't want Georgia babysitting for you anymore. I don't like your kind," Rose said, and her voice carried over the phone so that Liz and Susan could hear it ten feet away.

After that day Mary switched her schedule so that she didn't work nights or weekends. Susan moved down to the basement because she said she didn't want to share a room with a nosy little kid. The house continued to creak, only its groans were more insistent. At night Ted Marley stayed late at the bar or worked on his garden, and only after the girls were fast asleep did he come home.

THIRTY-NINE
Mouth Full of Sand
2001

Susan spent the next six years in the basement, amid the kicking boiler that sounded like the beat of a heart, and the wet rain that leaked through the gutter windows. When she thought she was alone she moved her lips, as if having conversations with people not there ("Creative! Special! Imaginative!" Mary told anyone who asked). Her voice deepened into a throaty alto, but she did not grow any taller than five feet. From a distance she looked like a child, and up close like something bound too tightly to grow.

Mary stayed up late at night during those six years. She sat in the kitchen with her ears pricked while her husband slept soundly, convinced that if she was not vigilant, an intruder would break into one of the rooms where her children slept. For this reason she locked all the doors and windows. For this reason she installed a deadbolt on the basement door, so that Susan could lock it from the inside. For this reason she had nightmares of men with strange faces peering into her daughters' bedrooms while she sat tied to a chair, her mouth full of sand.

She wasn't sure what had happened to her Little Miss Muffett. She'd always been different. Something to do with the girl's eyes that saw too much, and her skin that was too thin, and this town that was so dark. By the time she was ten, if Mary hugged Susan, she scowled. If she left her alone, Susan's eyes accused her of neglect. Other times Mary would sneak up on her daughter in a quiet moment, and for a short instant see another girl. A smiling girl. A beautiful girl. Most importantly, a kind girl.

Toward the end of Susan's stay at the Marley house, Mary began to have nightmares about terrible things. Monsters in closets, pricked fingers that never stopped bleeding, daughters sitting alone in small white rooms, their lips too red. From the way Ted tossed in his sleep, she knew he had them, too. He got thinner and thinner, and slept less and less. His diet became coffee and beer, and high blood pressure had made his artery walls paper thin. But even with sleeping pills, he didn't get any better. When Mary looked into Susan's eyes, she thought she saw the family nightmares hiding there. Living there.

For all these reasons, it was not easy to look at the girl. And so, after a while, she stopped looking. None of them looked, except for Liz, late at night, whom she could hear knocking on her sister's locked door.

A little before her eighteenth birthday, Susan left. She did not finish school. She did not pack a single bag. She did not leave a note. She did not say good-bye. She simply left. Her teacher found her a place to live as well as a job at the local pharmacy. Mary found this out, not from a phone call or a friend in town (she didn't have any) but from a knock on the door one March evening.

When Paul Martin entered her house he did not take off his hat or shake her hand. "I'm her teacher," he said, as if this explained everything. His coat, a fancy tweed number with a green cashmere scarf, had made her self-conscious.

She knew he was waiting for some explanation. As Mary looked at this handsome, well-dressed man so different from her own silent, angry husband (Why had she married him? Had she hated her own father so much?), she was tempted to tell him. Tempted to explain the parts that could be explained. But the moment passed. "She needs some things," he said.

Mary pointed at the basement stairs. "Her room's down there."

He came back with a bag full of clothes. He left, and she did not show him the door.

When Ted came home, she announced that Susan had left, but that she planned on retrieving her that very night. She would bring the girl home. She would sit her down. She would ask her what was wrong. She would ask her what could be done. "No," Ted had said.

"She's our daughter."

"I know that. I know she's our daughter. But there's a sickness inside her." He had looked very sad then, lost. Such a strange man. Silent, withdrawn. A solid man in so many ways. She'd never feared he would stay out all night carousing. In his own way (painting the house, gardening, sanding the floors), he adored her. In retrospect she would wonder if she had waited for Ted to come home because she'd wanted him to stop her.

She did not retrieve Susan. She did not call or visit her, though every week she intended to. She did not bring her the chocolate cakes she baked (every year announcing her birthday: Eighteen! Nineteen! Twenty! Twenty-one! Twenty-two! Twenty-three!). Even after Ted died, she did not deliver the groceries, or wool sweaters and pretty barrettes she bought. (These later went to Liz. Every time she saw her younger daughter wearing them she would think of the other daughter she had betrayed.) As time wore on, if she saw Susan in town, she crossed the street or ducked inside a store so that she would not have to see her face, and the accusation she was sure that it bore.

FORTY
Garden of Lost Souls
Present

She ran home that day with her hands over her ears. She moved down to the basement. She moved to the other side of town. She wandered the woods and the river and the streets of Bedford, but the voices did not stop. The voices never stopped.

The people in town who had once been kind began to glare at her, if they saw her at all. In Susan, Cathy Martin saw the specter of her illness, a gaunt decrepit thing. Ted Marley saw himself. Every time April Willow saw Susan, she thought of her own daughter, long gone. *(How old would she be? Twenty-six? Twenty-seven? Her eyes were blue, too.)* Georgia O'Brian added speed to her step, so that she would not have to smile an uneasy smile at her. *(I feel so sorry for her. But my God, the way she spends her time. She does anything she wants just because she's had a hard life. I wish I could fall apart, too.)* Bernard McMullen covered his eyes. Danny Willow sighed. Steve McCormack saw a horrible woman who used sickness as an excuse to cause harm, just like his mother. In Susan, Alexandra

Fullbright saw a Pied Piper luring her children away one by one. First would go Bobby, next Margaret, then Katie, and last the twins. Lured away by a Pied Piper into a world that made no sense. Bobby Fullbright intuitively saw his girlfriend's guilt, and despised its source though the name he gave it was pity. Liz Marley saw one moment in a flooded basement repeated so many times and in so many ways that it became a question and an answer, an act and its reason. There were others who liked to look at Susan. The men who visited, Rossoff, the women who peeped behind curtains, Louise Andrias in particular. They envied her darkness, and imagined themselves in her place.

The worst were the shadows cast by the dead. Some tried in vain to escape Bedford while others hovered, speaking insistently about all the things they should have remembered when their footsteps had carried an echo. They watched her from corners of rooms. They hurried through Main Street as if they had someplace to go. The older ones sat in their graves, practicing moving slowly. *(How long will it take to blink? A second? A year?)* The worst was her father, who walked behind her when she wandered through town, never approaching, never speaking. He didn't ask for her forgiveness. She didn't offer it.

She began to hear the sounds of Bedford; the rushing river like her own pulse, the pumping of the paper mill like her breath, the voices of the people who lived here like her own voice.

Time passed and she waited. The mill closed. The dead called to her more insistently, and the people of the town dreamed of her, or she dreamed of them—she was no longer sure which was which. The haunted things grew stronger, breaking through the fabric of the town, of her body, so that nightmares began to come to life. They visited Mary Marley during her waking hours, and chased Liz Marley behind a cemetery. They reached up from the basement of the paper mill, and showed Louise Andrias all that she wanted to know.

The haunted things called to her until there was only one story left to hear. They called to her until she could not stand to listen anymore. There was no Susan left. She looked into her mirrors and no longer saw her own reflection. Instead, she saw the faces of Bedford.

At last she found Paul Martin. She'd thought it had been to harm him, to force him into seeing what she had become. But when she saw him, she'd understood that she'd found him for another reason. She'd wanted him to stop her. Instead, the thing she had promised herself would never happen came to pass. She became the woman in the woods, the monster. She was the will of Bedford, and she set Bedford free.

By dawn smoke would fill the town, and the living would join the voices of the dead. In a few days, investigators would take samples of the sulfur-rich air and test the blood of the recently deceased. They would leave Bedford as quickly as they could, all the while wondering why, on such a nice spring day, they'd been unable to stop shivering, and what that barely audible buzzing sound that had filled them with dread had been. They would leave this place to Susan Marley, who would till a garden of lost souls.

PART FIVE

THE KEEPER

FORTY-ONE
It Should Have Been You

Around Liz Marley the house breathed, and the boiler beat like a heart. A giant, bright red fun-hop ball bounced down the second-floor hall, and in the den a television tuned to a twelve-year-old Red Sox game flicked on and off and on again. She could feel herself slipping away. Her voice, she did not remember it. Her mind, it did not exist here. Her name, it might as well belong to someone else.

It was three A.M. on Thursday morning. Just like old times, they sat at the kitchen table. To her right, Mary Marley openly wept. To her left, Susan pulled back her shoulders so that the hole in her chest where her heart had once been became prominent. The moment was so surreal that Liz was reminded of that board game Operation, which she had played as a child: a preposterous little man with a shiny red nose and missing anatomy. And then she wiped her mouth, and felt the black crust on her lips, and remembered why her stomach was so full. A cake. A heart. In her mouth. Down the hatch.

"Huh, huh," she said, trying to form words, trying to object in some way, and then she hitched, and sobbed, and finally cried out. Christ, was this really happening? Christ, are you out there?

"Why are you doing this?" Liz asked, only she did not speak. She didn't remember *how* to speak. Out the window, shadows crept like things being born. Smoke was thick. She thought about Bobby, his smell like sweet oil.

Susan nodded at the open basement door. At that moment the walls groaned, the house rocked, a little girl cried: *Stop, she doesn't like it,* and Liz forgot to breathe. "He's waiting, Lizzie," Susan said. "It should have been you. It always should have been you."

Mary became alert. "A man?" she asked. She started to stand, but then she saw the woman sitting next to her. She recognized her dead daughter, and began to weep.

Susan put her cold, oozing hand around Liz's wrist, and they locked eyes. Liz thought about a knife, a pair of scissors. She would stab Susan's ruined face. Sever her head from her body. But what difference would it make? How can you kill what is already dead? Liz blinked, and the battle she did not realize she was fighting against her sister was lost.

Susan flipped the round kitchen table that was between them and it went rolling. Pinned to the wall, Mary watched. She yanked Liz's wrist, and dragged her down the hall like a rag doll. Liz kicked against the floors and walls and Susan's legs. She screamed, and the sound echoed through the house, over and over, so that the house screamed back in bitter mockery. With the strength of all of Bedford, Susan threw her down the basement steps. She tumbled down, while up above, the door locked shut.

She sat dazed at the bottom of the stairs. No broken bones, only a few bruises. She waited as her eyes adjusted to the dark. She smelled something familiar down here. Irish Spring soap and paper mill sulfur. She could see the silhouette of something not far away. It was about Bobby's size, only she knew it wasn't Bobby.

As her eyes adjusted, she saw Ted Marley watching her.

FORTY-TWO
A Man in the House

There was a man in the house. Mary could feel him. All these years she'd watched for him; listening late at night, sniffing his clothes for a foreign scent (or a familiar one). There was a man in the house, she was sure of it. After her children's blood.

Mary kept her eyes closed. Maybe she was crying. She didn't know. Something was happening, but she couldn't remember what. She tried to wake up. Tried so hard. But the night had gone on for so long, and her heart had grown so cold.

Earlier tonight she had been sitting in the basement, talking to a little girl in pigtails and Mary Janes. They had told stories, and listened to the chattering walls. The girl hid in the closet when Liz came home, but she came back as soon as Liz was gone.

In the pocket of her blue dress, the little girl had carried a rubber ball. With her hand she'd bounced it against the wall, and with her mouth she'd sunk her teeth into Mary's flesh. But that was right and good. Better to bleed a little than a lot.

And then the back door had opened. Something

came down the basement steps. Worse than the little girl. Worse than anything in this world. A terrible thing with eyes so deep that Mary got lost inside them. Felt herself go mad inside them. The thing's steps in the churning water on the floor were slow and jerking. Slap-slap, slap-slap was the sound its feet had made.

Mary had looked at the creature; its blue eyes, its pale skin, its fingernails full of dirt, its funereal red rouge, and understood. Then she went far away. So far that her vision became two tiny specs, and her emotions as grounded as debris in outer space. What mattered? Did this matter? That? Her wet feet? The life she'd lived? Her courage, which had always walked too gently? Her daughter, who had died a ridiculous death at twenty-three? Or maybe just the itchy feeling on her scalp right now, that she dared not itch. That mattered, too.

The little girl in pigtails continued to bounce her ball. Thwack-thwack. The thing with leaden steps walked closer: slap-slap. The boiler kicked. The walls throbbed. Mary thought about the flooding this year, and the fact that Elizabeth always kept her socks long after she'd worn holes through their toes and heels, and whether hell is a place in which you are never allowed to forget the decisions you should have made.

Thwack. Slap. Thwack. Slap. The creature and the pigtailed innocent got closer and closer. Closer and closer. Thwack. Slap. Thwack. Slap. The child climbed down from Mary's lap, and went inside the monstrous thing. All the way inside, into a deep black hole, until the little girl was gone. The thing and the little girl became one thing.

After that, Mary went deep inside herself. So deep that she forgot her own name.

Together, they called Elizabeth for supper. And then there was a pulsing cake *(Let them eat cake!)*, and then stories Mary didn't like to remember, and voices so loud they hurt her ears. And then something else. Something that had happened before. A terrible thing, only this time, it was the other daughter.

And now here she was, sitting in a chair. Trying to wake up. Why? A man. A man in the house.

Mary startled suddenly. Next to her, the thing lifted the table it had overturned and sat down next to Mary. It pressed its bone white face into the crook of Mary's neck, and with its fingers began to tap against the wood. Tap. Tap. Only, the tapping was the sound of bone.

Where was she right now? In Corpus Christi, that's right, she was home with her mom and dad in Corpus Christi, swinging high on the tire swing attached to the crab apple tree. *(Don't eat the apples, they're full of poison! All mothers hate their daughters in their most secret place.)* Higher and higher she went. In the sky was a little girl's face. In the sky were twins who looked nothing alike. One girl fell to the ground, and the other flew away.

What was that smell? Why was the room so hazy? Was this smoke? Was there a fire? The thing smiled at Mary, and black blood ran down its chin.

Where was she right now? That's right, in the parking lot. Sitting in her car while her girls recited lessons at school. Black clouds filled the sky and in the distance there was thunder. She would pull up to the entrance, so the girls could climb in without getting wet. But a man stood at her window, knocking with callused knuckles.

Where was her daughter, the living daughter? Where

had she gone? *(In the basement, with the burglar. You let her go. What must you be made of to let this happen all over again?)* Mary saw two girls in her mind. One girl fell and the other flew away. Which was which?

Where was she right now? On her uncle's farm, feeding the rabbits he raised for 4H. *(Be quiet. She just had a litter and when they get frightened they eat their young. Where are your children, Mary Marley? You should have eaten them long ago.)*

The thing, a woman. Its lips were soft and black. It was smiling and crying at once.

"What are you?" Mary asked.

"Everything. Nothing," the woman said.

"What have you done?"

The woman looked out the window. From somewhere in the house a child moaned, and Mary thought: *Oh, Susan. I'm so sorry. How many times must I say it?*

Smoke thickened in the house. Black stuff, and it burned Mary's eyes. She tried to wake up. Tried so hard.

Again, a child moaned. Who was that? What was that sound? Oh, yes, now she knew. It was her living daughter crying out. It was her living daughter howling because there was a man in the house.

Mary sat up. Elizabeth? Her heart beat faster. A man in the house. The man from years ago. These men, they stole everything and called it love.

"What are you?" Mary asked.

"You know what I am," the woman answered, and God help her, she did know. A part of her had always known. Susan was different. This town was different. And all the phantoms and little girls and throbbing walls on this night were pieces of a monstrous hole, that over the years had found nourishment inside her daughter's unbounded rage.

Where was she right now? In her house in Bedford, sitting next to her elder daughter's corpse while down the basement steps her living daughter cried. Mary woke as if from a deep slumber with only one thought on her mind: her living daughter. Her second chance.

FORTY-THREE
The Troll Under the Bridge

Bobby Fullbright jogged down Iroquois Hill, toward Liz. The smoke was so thick, he had to breathe through the collar of his shirt. Halfway down the hill, he saw a man racing toward him. He was surprised to see that it was his friend Steve McCormack. "Steve! Hey, Steve!" Bobby shouted so that his voice would rise above the sounds of this night.

Steve stopped short. There was something wrong with his eyes. They were dark, and even by the light of Bobby's flashlight, they didn't shine. There were circular sores surrounded by black char on the exposed parts of his skin. Burns, Bobby realized with a wave of nausea. From cigarette butts.

Steve smiled a desolate smile. A hungry smile, and Bobby understood that his friend had gone insane. The sounds of the night whispered to Bobby, and he saw something in his mind. His old friends; Louise, Owen, and Steve inside the mill. Filling the air with poison.

Still smiling, Steven answered Bobby's question before he asked it. His lifted his chin, and Bobby saw that his entire face was burned. Her eyes weren't black, they'd been hollowed out. Fluid oozed from his open sockets, but he could still see. He was seeing through Susan Marley. Seeing through her eyes now.

"The mill? Louise's idea, but I helped. Thought it would make the dead stay dead. I didn't know we were dead already." Even his voice was flat like Susan's.

"You're crazy," Bobby said.

Steve's grin reached the empty sockets of his eyes, and Bobby could see Susan Marley in there. He could see her watching him. Bobby saw something else in his mind. He saw that Steve was headed for the most narrow part of the river. He was going to try to swim across, only he wouldn't make it. As soon as he was knee-deep, the current would wrest him from the shore. Rocks from the bank would tumble down and crush first his thighs, then his back. His body would bounce lightly just once on the river floor, and then it would be still.

"Wait," Bobby said, but then he knew that Steve wanted to drown. "Don't go there, Bobby," Steve shouted over his shoulder as he began to run toward the river. "You'll eat your heart out. You think they're different? They're sisters, Bobby. They're the same."

Bobby took a deep breath through the collar of his shirt, looked one last time at Steve, and ran in the opposite direction.

FORTY-FOUR
The Mill

Georgia O'Brian woke with a start. She tasted something funny on her tongue and her bedside lamp wouldn't light up. Stupid lamp needed a bulb. Then she remembered the rain, and that the power lines were down. She hopped out of bed. The cold floor jolted her awake, and she realized that something was wrong. Her eyes burned. Something thick in the air. Smoke! A fire! Her house was on fire!

In seconds she was at Matthew's bedside, rousing him from sleep. Together, they started into the hallway, where she found her father in his bathrobe and slippers. Disoriented, he asked, "What's all this racket?" She shook him awake. "A fire, Dad!" she said, and the three hurried down the narrow stairway and out the front door.

When they got outside, she saw that the rest of the neighborhood was outdoors as well. Among others, there were the Reads, the Gallos, the Bagleys, and the Duboises. They held pieces of wet cloths to their faces, breathing deeply or coughing. They leaned in doorways, they lay in the middle of the street, they held hands or ran in scattered directions like schoolhouse jacks.

"This ain't a fire," Ed O'Brian said.

She shook her head. The smoke started to make her fuzzy-headed, and her thoughts moved slowly. She noticed the rain. It fell hard. So hard it almost had a voice. "Do you smell that, Dad?" she asked.

"What?"

"It's sulfur, isn't it?"

Ed sucked out his breath, and his entire body sagged. "Goddamn."

"What?"

"The sulfur waste. Half a canister leaks, you're supposed to clear out for a mile radius and call the Maine State EPA. There's three of 'em over at the mill."

"Call the police, Dad."

"Trees knocked out the phone lines about an hour ago. You were sleeping."

At her side was Matthew. She could hear the rattle of his wet lungs.

"It's got to be the sulfur," Ed said. "We could try to get out of town through the woods but in the dark and with this rain there's not much time."

Georgia's stomach sank. "Somebody meant to do this, didn't they?"

Ed nodded. "I guess they did."

She looked east, and north, and then south. The town was closed off by the woods and river. No place to go but the mill. Plumes of smoke rolled down Main Street. The bandage slopped over Matthew's shaved head was long gone, and the stitches in his scalp were surrounded by angry red skin. The rest of his face was startlingly pale. She was so frightened for him that it felt like a physical pain. "Do you think we can stop it?"

Ed ripped the hem of his blue flannel robe with the pocket knife on his keychain. He gave one piece to Georgia and placed the other over Matthew's mouth. "We could try," he wheezed.

"Okay," she said. Then she lifted her arms high in the air. *"Hey!"* she shouted. Her voice was a siren above the rain. It rang clear and loud. *"Hey!"* she shouted again, and her neighbors all stopped to listen. "We think this stuff is coming from the mill! We're going to try to contain it!"

When she began walking, the rest of the neighborhood followed. Some came close while others trailed her at a distance. At each corner she passed, she was joined by more of them. People she'd known all her life, family friends, acquaintances, shut-ins. By the time she reached Our Lady of Sorrow where the people from the shelter had emptied out onto the front steps to get away from the smoke in the church, the crowd became at least three hundred. It was the protest that should have been. There were a few, she could hear them, who ran in the opposite direction. They tried to swim across the river, or find a way north through the woods. They cowered in their homes, even while thick smoke blackened their lungs. But most followed her.

As she walked, she heard each person's voice, each person's story. She heard Danny Willow trying to comfort his wife. She heard Steve McCormack take a last, gasping breath before the river carried him away. She felt Elizabeth Marley looking into the eyes of her long-dead father. She heard Kevin Brutton, who tonight had told his wife Allie that he loved her for the first time in their twenty-three-year marriage. She saw inside them all.

She didn't know why she was hearing all of this. She

didn't care. She only knew she had to get to the mill.

As she neared Main Street, Matthew's coughing tapered off. His face was red, as if from choking, and she saw that he was too weak to cough. She picked him up and carried him.

At Main Street they met with the families from Iroquois Hill: the Realmutos, the Fullbrights (who had broken from their reverie, pulled away the bookcase barricading their front door, and finally fled once the smoke filled their house), the Gonyas, the Murtaghs. Five blocks farther east, they reached the mill. She could not see it; she could only hear it. Pumping. Churning. Throbbing. Like a volcano, black smoke spouted from its pipe. It mixed with the rain and stung her tongue. It hovered in the atmosphere, so dense she could hardly see her feet on the ground.

The voices were loudest here. *I can't breathe,* one said. *Where are your children? You should have eaten them long ago. This is what it feels like, when you steal from yourself. There are pretty things, too, I wish I could remember them right now.* The voices became a thumping, a throbbing. They were one voice though they said different things. All one voice.

She looked behind her, and saw a crowd of frightened faces. All of Bedford. And then their eyes changed, and became the color blue. And then they were not people for one terrifying moment. They were Susan Marley.

She arrived at the mill's open door. "There's an emergency generator," Ed shouted over the rain. "It looks like a fuse box along the wall facing the offices. I'll go in." But his breathing was labored. His hand was clenched over his left side, and she knew that his heart was bothering him.

"No, I'll go," she said.

He started to object, but then nodded instead. She passed Matthew into his arms, took a deep breath, and ran inside.

The place was cold. So cold that it reminded her of the way her house had felt on the morning of her mother's death. Spiteful, and without hope. She wanted to cry, though doing so would have made her lose her breath. Grinding machines rumbled in her ears; steel and water and fire. She passed the rubber conveyor belt that wound through the old building. There were still bits of woodchips in its mouth. She passed the lamps that dried the pulp, and the office where her father had spent so much of his life. Though she did not breathe, she could feel black air burning the pink parts of her skin: her nose, her ears, her eyes, the soft parts of her hands and cheeks, and a fresh cut on her thigh from the corner of a steel shredder she'd bumped into.

On the far wall she found something that looked like a large fuse box, and hoped it was connected to the generator. One of its wooden stop handles was broken. She tried to pull it down anyway, but it would not be budged. She gave up, and started searching for an emergency stop button on the side of the vat that would stop the sulfur from cooking, but could not find one. The voices droned, so loud. So full of nothing. They droned, and she started to forget where she stood. She started to forget that her eyes burned, that everything burned. She tripped over something soft but substantial, and fell on top of it. The sound it made when she landed was a wet slap. It only took her a fraction of a second to recognize Paul's black hair, but it seemed like much longer. Then she was back on her feet, crying but trying not to cry. Trying to hold her breath even while the smog filled her lungs, and she wondered not at all idly whether he had been her last chance at happiness, and they'd both somehow managed to screw it up.

Shit comes from shit, Georgia Ellen O'Brian. You know he'll never amount to anything. You know you never wanted him, a voice that sounded just like Georgia's whispered in her ear. *Why don't you stop pretending you're someone you're not? Why don't you give up, the way you know you want to? Take a deep breath, Georgia. Take a very deep breath.*

Georgia slammed her fists against metal. She kicked the vat in slippered feet, breaking three toes so that they dangled awkwardly. "Stop!" she shouted, "Stop it. Stop!"

The mill filled with ghosts. People born two hundred years ago, people who'd died five minutes ago. They lined the walls. They watched with mad blue eyes. They worked the line, filling the vat, cooking the wood. And down below, the people who'd been buried in this place began to moan.

At first, Georgia couldn't distinguish them from the living. They all looked the same. But then she saw that some people had followed her inside. Danny Willow shot his pistol at the vat's engine and hot steam gushed out, burning his face while he screamed. Kevin Brutton wandered in circles like a wind-up doll. Amity Jorgenson sat down in the water and cried. April Willow ran laps around the room, searching underneath tables and inside lockers. *(For what? Oh, right, the thing she lost.)*

Georgia rushed outside and took a deep, wet breath. Matthew had fainted in her father's arms. Behind her, she heard another round of pistol fire, and knew without having to look that April Willow had grabbed her husband's gun and put it to her head.

For the first time in her memory, Georgia screamed.

FORTY-FIVE
Father

Though the power was out, she could still see the way the water moved in ripples, just like that time long ago. She could see the bookcase in the corner, half built, that had been chopped into splinters years before. There it was. The smell of fresh sawdust. She touched it and she could feel the smoothness of pine, freshly sanded. There it was. And loneliness. She could feel it.

Was this really her father, or a monster of Susan's creation? She looked across the basement floor, and knew that it was both things; a man and the shadow he had cast.

He stood in the darkness. A small man. She knew now that he was not an appealing man. Ugly little man. She outweighed him by ten pounds. His face was dark, his eyes drawn haggard. He held something in his hand. Picked at it with his fingers. It must be something awful. Something terrible, she knew. A knife. Something to kill her with. Or worse. A heart. His own rotten heart, picking at it, trying to make it whole. He stayed in the shadows and she knew he saw her. She knew he was watching her, picking at his heart. A scabby thing.

He started toward her. A little move, an inch or so. He picked at the thing in his hand. Yes, it must be his rotten heart. His sick and rotten heart. He placed it in the water where it bobbed up and down. She could not stop herself. She picked it up. Not his heart at all. A white rose. She held it in her hand. A gift for his girl.

He came at her and she knew what would happen. What always should have happened. Because he did not love her. That was the fairy tale. That was the joke. Oh yes, she knew what he would do. The thing she had escaped, not because he cared for her, but by luck. Dumb luck.

He extended his hand but did not touch her. He waited, and she hitched her breath. It came to her that this was supposed to be her decision. Her choice.

Tears filled her eyes, and she became present again. The different parts of her smashed together, the parts that wanted to die and the parts that wanted to live. They came together, the parts that remembered and the parts that forgot. The parts that loved and the parts that hated. All these things that could not be reconciled came together. They became one thing.

She let out what she thought would be a giggle. Laughter. So funny, eating a cake that beats like a heart. So funny, my father's a rapist who hated himself so much he willed his heart to stop beating. So funny, he came back to life, not to tell me the secret of existence, not to bother with something petty like telling me why, but to give me a flower. So funny, that big sisters, fathers, boyfriends who only pretend to love you, even strangers on the street carry these things inside them. So funny, that every one of them, deep down, is a monster. They're all so fuckin' funny I could laugh forever. This is the place I come from. This is ground zero. This is the reference point for every decision I have ever made, everything I will ever be. Oh, the joke's on me. Because I'm the only one who isn't in on it.

She did not giggle. She let out a sob.

He held out his hand. Her choice. What choice? She looked at him. She didn't want to know. She had to know. She had to know. She had to know.

She took his hand. He pulled her in. Put his mouth over her hair and kissed her. She closed her eyes. He squeezed her tight. He held her, and she remembered the other things she'd chosen to forget. She remembered her mother, who had once possessed a gentle beauty, and the safety she had felt at night, when she and Susan had shared a room. She remembered snow days, and the smell of warm Pop-Tarts at the breakfast table. She remembered that there were good things, too. She remembered that even when the worst happened, there was always hope.

"It's up to you, what you carry," he whispered as he let her go, and she began to sob.

Her father slowly left her, then. He became a shadow that faded into darkness that faded into nothing. All that was left was the smell of sawdust, and the old bookcase, and the churning water, and the inexplicably beautiful flower in the palm of her hand.

FORTY-SIX
Excitable Boy

Bobby Fullbright didn't reach the Marley house until almost five A.M. He stood before the threshold, and he could sense the house watching him. A pain radiated from his throat to his chest to his groin. His testicles retracted deep inside his pelvis, and he wondered briefly if they'd ever come back. But he had to find her. He had to tell her what he'd only realized for certain tonight. It wasn't convenience. It wasn't circumstance. He really loved her. He took a deep breath, and entered the house.

As his eyes adjusted to the dark, he stumbled down the hall and up the stairs to her bedroom. "Liz?" he called. *"Liz!"* he shouted. His voice reverberated through the house. It echoed. The first time it sounded like him. The second time it was deeper. The last time it whined her name. *"Liz!"* it jeered at him.

The smoke thickened with each passing second, and his mind moved slowly. Everything was dark. He started coughing and couldn't stop. His skin throbbed like he'd been standing too long near a hot fire. It came to him suddenly, as he dry-heaved on the green carpet that looked gray through the smoke. He could feel her right then. His thoughts descended down the stairs, into the basement, into the black hole. Into Susan. She was down, there, in the basement. Liz was down there, too. He could see her in his mind.

He got on his hands and knees like they'd told him to do in health class. Around him, he noticed how the walls breathed and the boiler beat. Alive, he thought. This whole town was alive. But pretty soon he didn't think about any of that, not even Liz. He just kept crawling for the sake of crawling, for the sake of instinct, for the sake of survival, until finally, he collapsed on the floor, right in front of the open basement door.

FORTY-SEVEN
Heart of Darkness

Like a polite guest, the smoke entered the Marley house through the front door first. It wiped its feet on the welcome mat and sneaked through the hallway. It coiled its black fingers around the kitchen table. It climbed the stairs and floated above the beds. It donned the cotton T-shirts and wool sweaters that its occupants had left on hangers, and smoldered them to rags. Finally, it married the rain that fell, and trickled through the basement windows just as Ted Marley gave his daughter a rose, Bobby Fullbright walked through the front door, and Mary got up from the kitchen table.

"Elizabeth Rebecca?" Mary shouted as she raced down the stairs. She reached out with blind hands. At first she only swiped at air, and she began to panic. But she grazed Liz's sweatshirt with her fingertips. Before she had the chance to pull her close, Liz rushed at her. She pressed her face into the crook of Mary's neck and began to cry in wracking sobs.

Mary did not try to stop her. She did not stiffen. She held her daughter. Liz cried harder, and for once Mary did not let go. She held Liz more tightly, and Liz let herself be held. She let herself forget, and remember, and love, and hate, and trust, because even on this night, the worst had not happened. Her father had not hurt her, and her mother had come to find her.

Mary took a breath and through the smoke was able to smell the scent of Irish Spring on her daughter's skin. She stiffened. "Where is he?" she asked in a flat, low voice that meant harm.

"Gone," Liz said.

She lifted Liz's chin, and through the smoke Liz could see the shine of her eyes. "What did he do to you?"

"He gave me a flower," Liz said.

Mary let out a sob of relief. Despite the heavy smoke in the air, Liz felt as if she had set down a great weight she did not know she'd been carrying. For the first time in a long time, the house was without secrets.

The smoke thickened, and both Mary and Liz started coughing. Together they headed out, but just then, someone came clopping down the steps. They stopped short, and Susan appeared before them.

Despite the darkness, Liz could see the way Susan's broken neck lolled this way and that. An inhuman thing. A human thing.

Susan grinned, and inside her blue eyes Liz thought she could see all of Bedford. Every gurgle of the river. Every deer in the woods. Every particle of smoke. Every melancholy winter night. There was no hope in there. No joy. No trust. No love. And yet, somewhere inside this thing, Liz could also see her sister. Susan Marley. A pretty girl. A smart girl. A girl who used to laugh.

Susan advanced, and Mary tried to stand between them, but Liz would not be budged. She thought she knew the way to end this. A little girl racing down a hill. A stain of blood in the snow. A sensitive girl, who felt what other people could not. "Where are you, Susan?" Liz coughed out.

Susan smiled. "Everywhere." Her voice sounded like Ted Marley. Like Liz. Like Mary. Like Susan. Like Paul Martin. Like Bobby Fullbright. Like Georgia O'Brian. Like Danny and April Willow. Like Andrea Jorgenson. Like Montie Henrich. Like Thomas Schultz. Like Louise Andrias. Like every person in this town.

Liz shook her head. "No. I can hear you someplace," she said, and then she stopped to cough while Mary held her by her shoulders to keep her from falling. "I can hear who you used to be."

Susan's smile became less certain. "That's why you came back here, isn't it? You could have waited in your apartment. You could have let the house get us, or the smoke, or these things you brought, but you wanted to see us. You just had to see us. What do you want, Susan?"

Susan's eyes flickered and her smile became a scowl. "Nothing," Susan said. "It's all nothing."

"He didn't hurt me, even though you thought he would," Liz continued.

Susan frowned, and Liz knew that Susan was surprised. She'd been unable to know or guess this. Unable to conceive of it.

Liz pressed forward. "Nothing is all bad." She looked around the smoke-filled room, where the boiler kicked and the walls breathed and the smoke had burned red welts into her pale skin. "Even in the worst places, nothing is all bad. You know that, or you used to know it. Even in this house, you had yourself. You had me."

She was coughing again, only this time, when she gasped for air, she found none. Her coughs became choking sounds, and then finally, she stopped coughing.

Without her noticing, somehow she and Mary were now down on their knees in the cold water.

Sparks flitted across Liz's field of vision, and her throat burned as if someone was strangling her. "What do you want?" Too weak to speak, Liz whispered this with her mind. "Tell me what you want."

Susan reached out her bony hand to Liz. "No," Mary said, but Liz did not hear. She did not hesitate. She took it. They were sisters, after all. Always, in the end, it came down to this.

When they touched, Liz felt a shock of electricity. Felt soft fingers prod her skin, inside her skin. Felt them ask permission, felt herself say yes. They opened her up, piece by piece. Through her skin, her blood, her bones. She remembered sleeping in bed next to her big sister, who had smelled like tea rose perfume. Sitting on her father's lap. Curling up under a blanket with her mother. Trying, and failing, to hock a loogie of phlegm through her fingers at the Nudd Street bus stop. Climbing trees. Playing quicksand with her big sister. A first kiss. A taunting for snarly hair and big hips. A family road trip that took ten extra hours because Dad couldn't read maps. Believing in everything, even when the evidence told her to doubt. Believing in nothing, because she dared not hope. A sister lost. A father's death. A mother drifting away. A first love. Living in this town, where all things bright began to look gray, and bad thoughts found a home inside Susan Marley.

As Liz remembered these things, Susan remembered them, too. She lived them. She became the younger sister, the woman on the other side of the fence. She saw a man in a basement who for once did the right thing. She saw a woman in a kitchen devour her own regret with one simple act. She saw all these things, and she envied them, and she wished that they belonged to her, and wondered why they did not, and at last made her peace with them, that the girl they belonged to shared her blood. The girl they belonged to loved her, and perhaps that was good enough.

Susan let go of Liz. Her blue eyes became still. She remembered the girl she had been long ago and the woman she had become. She saw the flower that Liz had dropped to the floor and wondered if it had been meant, not as a gift for Liz, but as an offering from a fallen man to his fallen daughter. She picked it up and tucked it inside the hole in her chest where her heart had once beat. Nourished somehow by what lay inside, its petals turned red and opened into full bloom.

She stood back and looked over the smoke-filled room. The smoke-filled town. The beating boiler. The ticking paper mill. The flooding roads that felt like blood through her veins. She did not want this. She wanted it. She had always meant to do this. She had never meant to do this.

Susan took a deep breath in. The sound was a high-pitched whistle, like wind against glass windows. The barometric pressure in the basement suddenly got very high, and Liz's ears popped. The smoke swirled in the shape of a small, black tornado. It circled the room, again and again, and still Susan kept breathing in. Her small chest puffed out to twice its size. The tornado smashed the bookcase into a thousand pieces on the floor, and spun the dresser and bed in the air, until it finally plunged inside Susan's nose and eyes and ears and mouth. She took another breath in, and all the smoke entered her, leaving the air bright and clear. She took another breath in, and Liz's own breath was lost.

It left her lungs, and entered Susan. Immediately, the welts on Liz's skin were gone, and her wet lungs were dry.

Liz looked over at Mary, who was no longer coughing or even out of breath. Susan smiled at them. Her grin was without cruelty. Still, her head lolled. Still, her bones jutted through her festering skin. It was so difficult to look at her.

Then Susan reached out her arms. For one long second, there was no one to receive her. Just Susan standing in the room with her arms wide and completely alone. But then Liz stood and embraced her sister. Mary followed. The three of them formed a circle. They held on tightly, trying in their awkward ways to express the inexpressible.

FORTY-EIGHT
The Keeper

At five o'clock Thursday morning, the smoke in the Marley house thinned, and Bobby woke up. He raced down the stairs and found the three women standing in a circle. At his approach the circle broke. Liz left from her mother and sister, and went to Bobby.

Susan turned from them and started up the stairs. She left the house and walked down the flooded and smoke-filled street. As she limped, one foot sliding along the water, the other thumping down through the mud, Liz, Bobby, and Mary followed from a distance.

At the mill, there was a crowd of people, all with blue eyes. The buzzing sounds of the night became one sound; an endless, soulless scream. As Susan approached, the crowd parted for her. She walked through them and toward the black pipe of the mill, as if marching down an aisle at a church.

She looked at every face, remembered every story. On the periphery of the crowd stood Bobby's family. They held the twins in their arms while their daughters stood by their sides. In front of the mill was Danny Willow, who was tending to his wife's body. He pushed down hard against the gaping wound that would not stop bleeding. Behind her, Montie Henrich pinned Kate Sanders to the ground to still her flailing arms. The recently dead were there too: Louise Andrias, Steve McCormack, Owen Read, Laura Henrich, Chuck Brann, and Thomas Schultz. And in the distance William Prentice was shrouded in shadows, a negligent father forsaken by his children.

Ragged and limping, Susan kept going. The smoke poured from the orifices of the mill like a bleeding wound. Its machinery made kicking sounds like the boiler of her house. Like a heart. Like the voices. Like the rain. It beat faster and faster. Faster and faster.

She got to the broken door of the mill, and then turned to look out over the crowd. She saw Lori Kalisz, Michelle Torrens, Artie Schupbach, and a handful of others, who would leave this town tomorrow if they lived, driving away as fast as they could. She saw the Fullbrights, who even now were thinking that they should have locked their doors, they should have lived farther up the hill, they should have built their house from steel instead of brick, as if such things could have made them safe. She saw Georgia O'Brian, whose only thoughts could be read on her face. *My son,* she was thinking, unable to go any further than that, shaking him, crying over him, listening to his chest for small breaths.

She saw Liz, who held her boyfriend's hand. They whispered words of consolation to each other, and Susan knew that together or alone, they would finish this thing better than they had started. She saw Mary, who smiled weakly at her. Mary was already beginning to forget. If she lived to see morning, she would tell herself that all of this had been a dream, and only remember the flicker of a moment in which her courage had overcome her fear. She saw her father's ghost standing far back behind the crowd. A shadowy figure, he nodded at her, and then turned away. There was one last person she looked at. She met his gaze. The worms wriggled through his beard, and into his mouth. They bored through his skin and the sockets of his eyes. Rossoff dropped to his knees and died.

She turned to the mill. Inside its doors, Paul Martin's ghost beckoned her. He stood taller, his stubble cleanshaven and his suit neatly pressed. She knew why she had been drawn to him years ago, why she had sought him out over and over again, why their fates had always seemed so inextricable. Because she had known that all things between them had added up to this moment, and that he would not let her go through this alone. He smiled at her; a kind, placid smile.

The crowd closed in around her. The mill kept beating, faster and faster. Faster and faster.

She hesitated even while they coughed, and two more fell down dead. One was Richard Miller, the other Jonathan Bagley. Jonathan's wife, Anna, knelt down and flicked his cheeks with rain as of to wake him from a pleasant dream.

Jerome Donally was the first to throw a rock at Susan. It missed, but then Bernard McMullen smashed a Heineken bottle against her face. It bounced off her chin and rolled downhill. They closed in around her. The crowd. Alexandra Fullbright ground Susan's shoulder joint out of its socket. Kevin Brutton yanked on her other arm until he came away with a sleeve of her skin. Faceless fingers poked through her stitches until her stomach opened, and her organs tumbled out. A spleen, a kidney, the gray tubing of her small intestine. They tore until she was only muscle and bone.

She collapsed to the ground, and the crowd stood over her. She saw their eyes, wild blue eyes, and knew that they had gone mad. They had become what she had been in life. She could read their thoughts. They did not want her to save them. They wanted to tear her apart.

Just then, she heard a loud pop, and the crowd pulled back. Danny Willow pointed his gun into the air and fired again, and they scattered. Still, the smoke kept coming. Three more fell. Sean O'Connor, Dan Hodkin, Amity Jorgenson.

Too weak to stand, she crawled toward the mill's open door. Georgia O'Brian hoisted her up by the waist and held her wretched body steady. With her mind Susan communicated what she had to do.

The two of them watched each other, and in Georgia's eyes, Susan saw her own reflection. She saw the things she had chosen not to know. She saw that while she had always told herself that none of the things she carried belonged to her, some of them did. She saw that a part of her had wanted all this to happen to Bedford, and had wanted it all along. She had fantasized of a black cloud that filled Main Street, and revenge for the life that this town had stolen from her. She had fantasized of a little sister in a basement, taking a punishment no one deserved. She saw that she hated every one of them, even the ones she loved. Especially the ones she loved.

Susan saw her true reflection in Georgia's eyes. A girl and a woman. Corruption and innocence. Cruelty and kindness.

The smoke kept coming. "Go," Georgia said. "It's not too late."

Still, Susan hesitated. In the distance, Matthew O'Brian took a final, rattling breath.

"Now," Georgia said sternly. "Do it."

Susan looked at the crowd one last time. She searched for a face and found it. Liz lifted her chin at Susan. Her favorite in the world was her sister.

Why not Liz? Why not anyone else? Why Bedford? There are no answers to some questions, no matter what you do. Susan walked inside the mill. Georgia shut the door behind her.

Inside, Paul Martin's ghost stood by her side. She took a deep breath and wind rushed the streets of Bedford. The black smoke receded, exiting houses in the direction it had come. It whirled back through chimneys and out of drapes. It carried the corpses of thirty-four men, and lost little girls, and dogs named Benji, and old hurts and grudges inside it. A tornado of shadows, of shapes, of buzzing noise, and of smoke whirled down Main Street. It spun past Don's Liquor, the Chop Mop Shop, People's Heritage Bank, Shaws, Kmart, Gifford's Ice Cream, and the park. It went down the mill's pipe. It shot through the vat, and inside Susan Marley. She swallowed it whole.

The smoke filled her pores, her skin, her bones. It whispered a thousand stories. It told her its worst secrets, her own worst secrets. It begged to be let out. She did not let it loose again. She knew then what she had become. Not a child running down a hill with a heart as white as snow. Not a woman made grotesque by her own corruption. She had become something different in this moment. She had become Bedford's keeper.

The mill kept ticking, faster and faster, until at last a pressurized pipe in the vat broke, and gas and flames ignited. She looked around the room that suddenly became bright, and she and Paul Martin watched it together like watching a sunrise. The fire licked her body, and touched the sulfur inside her, and then there was an explosion. The paper mill burned to the ground.

Outside, the crowd watched the blaze until the mill's embers grew cold. There was silence as the rain became a drizzle, and then a patter, and then nothing. All was silent.